Louie and BEAR
IN THE LAND OF ANYTHING GOES

BY
BRADY SMITH

Penguin Workshop

AUTHOR'S NOTE

This book is dedicated to my amazing wife, Tiffani. Thank you for your patience, encouragement, and unconditional love. Oh, and thanks for feeding Harper, Holt, and me. We'd constantly be eating cereal if it wasn't for you. I love you more than you know.

Also, a big ol' high five to my agent, Brandi at UTA, and a gigantic bear hug (pun intended) to my team at Penguin Workshop. Alex, Rob, Jamie, and Francesco, thanks for believing in Louie and Bear! They appreciate it immensely and think y'all are totally awesome! (Seriously, they just told me.)

ABOUT THE CREATOR

Brady Smith is an actor, artist, and author. He lives in Los Angeles with his wife, actress Tiffani Thiessen, their two kids, four dogs, six chickens, and one super-chatty parakeet.

You can see more of his art at www.bradysmith.com and lots of silliness on his Instagram account, @bradysmithhere.

PENGUIN WORKSHOP
An imprint of Penguin Random House LLC, New York

First published in the United States of America by Penguin Workshop, an imprint of Penguin Random House LLC, New York, 2021

This paperback edition published by Penguin Workshop, an imprint of Penguin Random House LLC, New York, 2023

Visit us online at penguinrandomhouse.com.

Library of Congress Control Number: 2021019901

Manufactured in China

ISBN 9780593659885   10 9 8 7 6 5 4 3 2 1 WKT

Colors by Meaghan E. Casey
Design and lettering by Jamie Alloy

CHAPTER 1

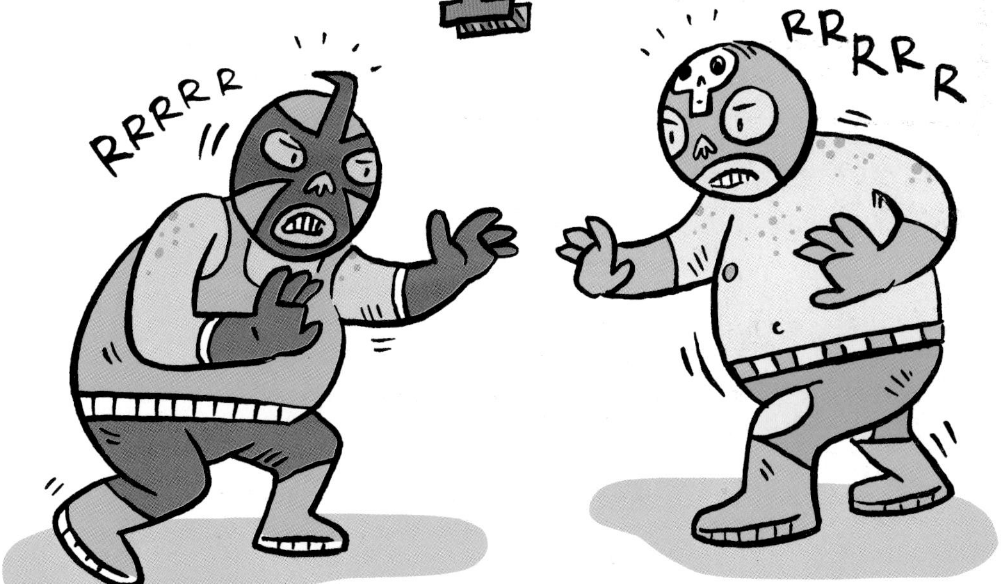
RRRRR
RRRRRR

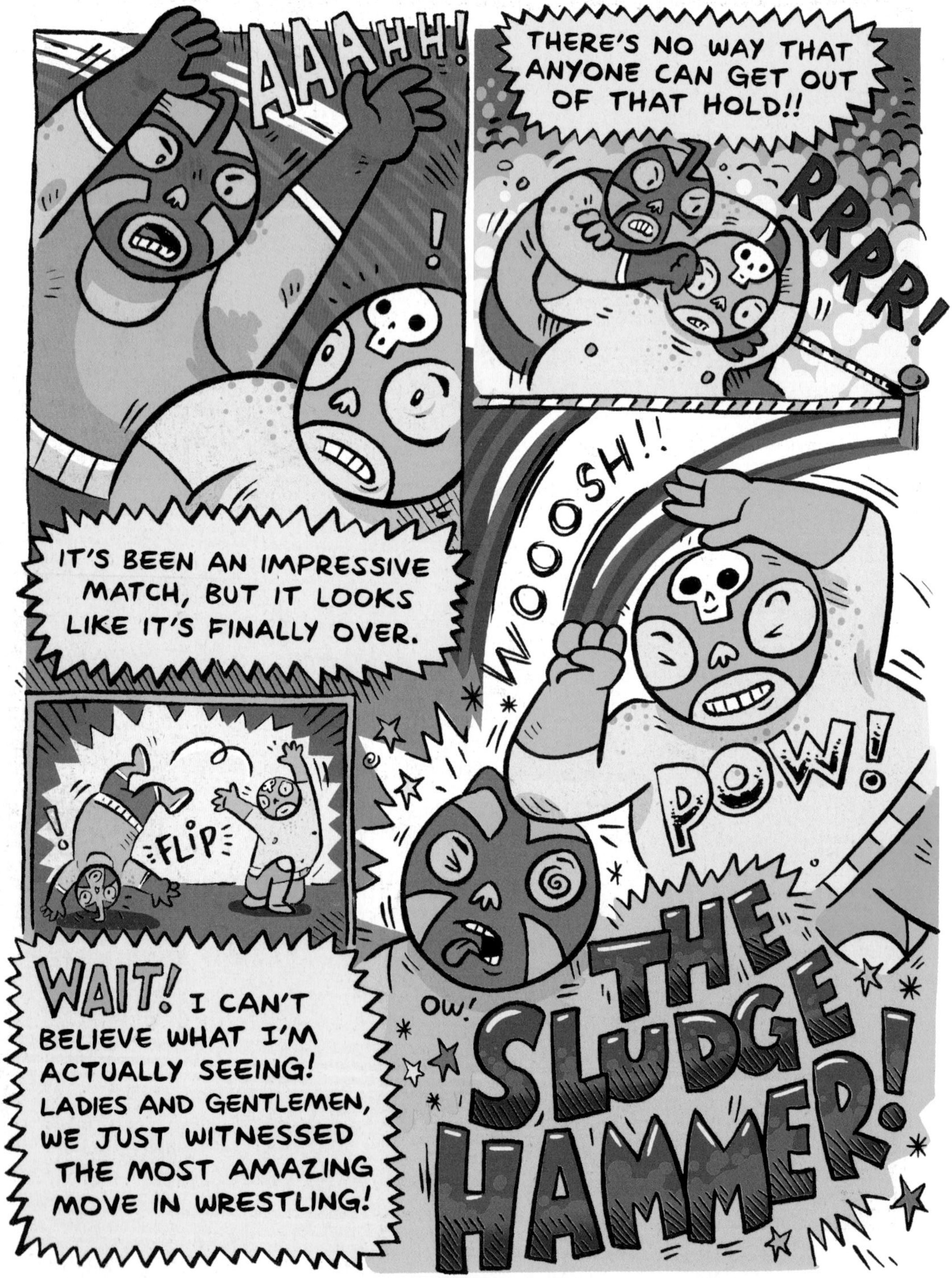
AAAHH!
!
THERE'S NO WAY THAT ANYONE CAN GET OUT OF THAT HOLD!!
RRRR!
IT'S BEEN AN IMPRESSIVE MATCH, BUT IT LOOKS LIKE IT'S FINALLY OVER.
WOOOSH!!
!
FLIP
POW!
WAIT! I CAN'T BELIEVE WHAT I'M ACTUALLY SEEING! LADIES AND GENTLEMEN, WE JUST WITNESSED THE MOST AMAZING MOVE IN WRESTLING!
OW!
THE SLUDGE HAMMER!

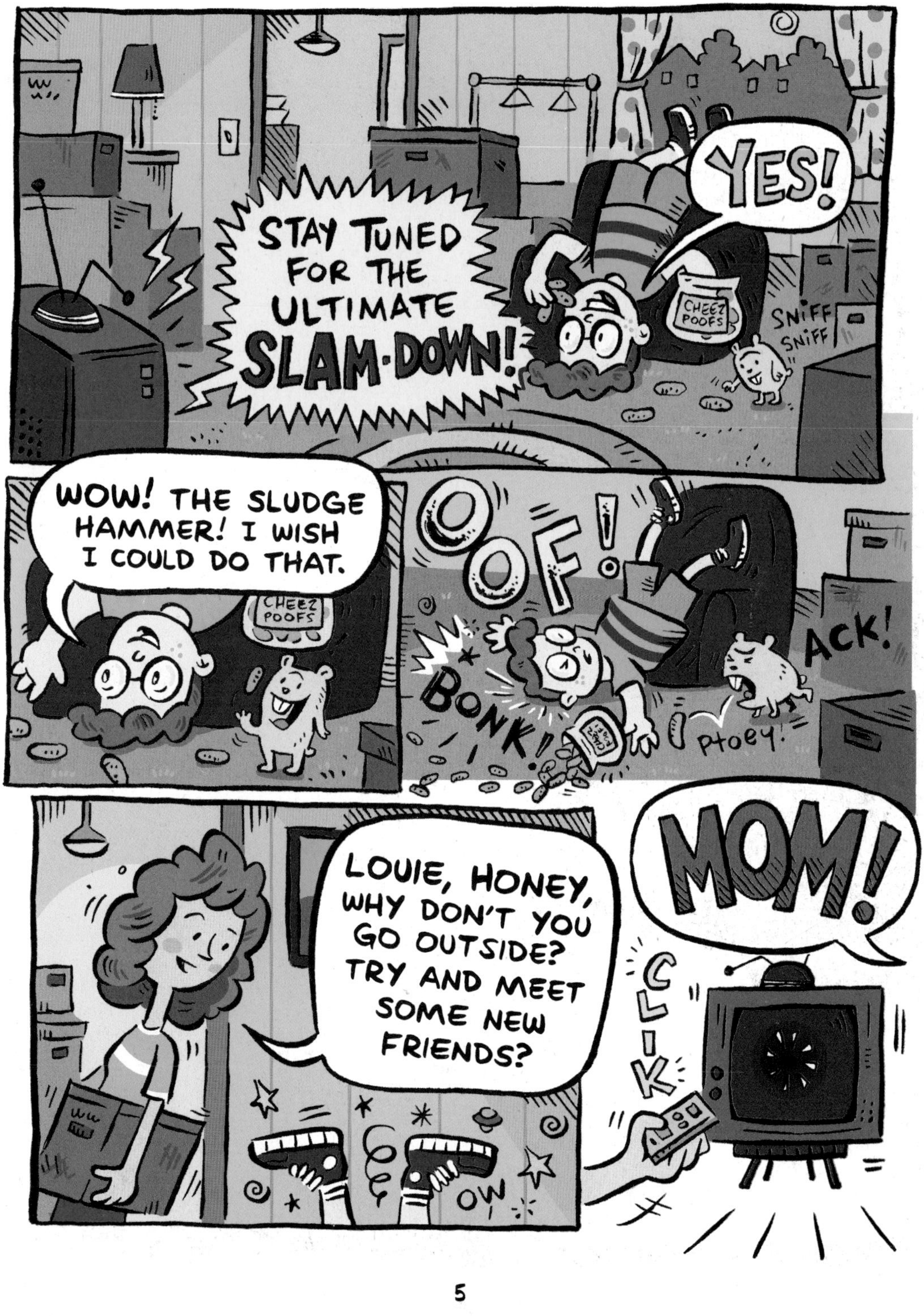
STAY TUNED FOR THE ULTIMATE SLAM-DOWN!
YES!
CHEEZ POOFS
SNIFF SNIFF
WOW! THE SLUDGE HAMMER! I WISH I COULD DO THAT.
CHEEZ POOFS
OOF!
BONK!
ACK!
Ptoey!
LOUIE, HONEY, WHY DON'T YOU GO OUTSIDE? TRY AND MEET SOME NEW FRIENDS?
OW
MOM!
CLIK

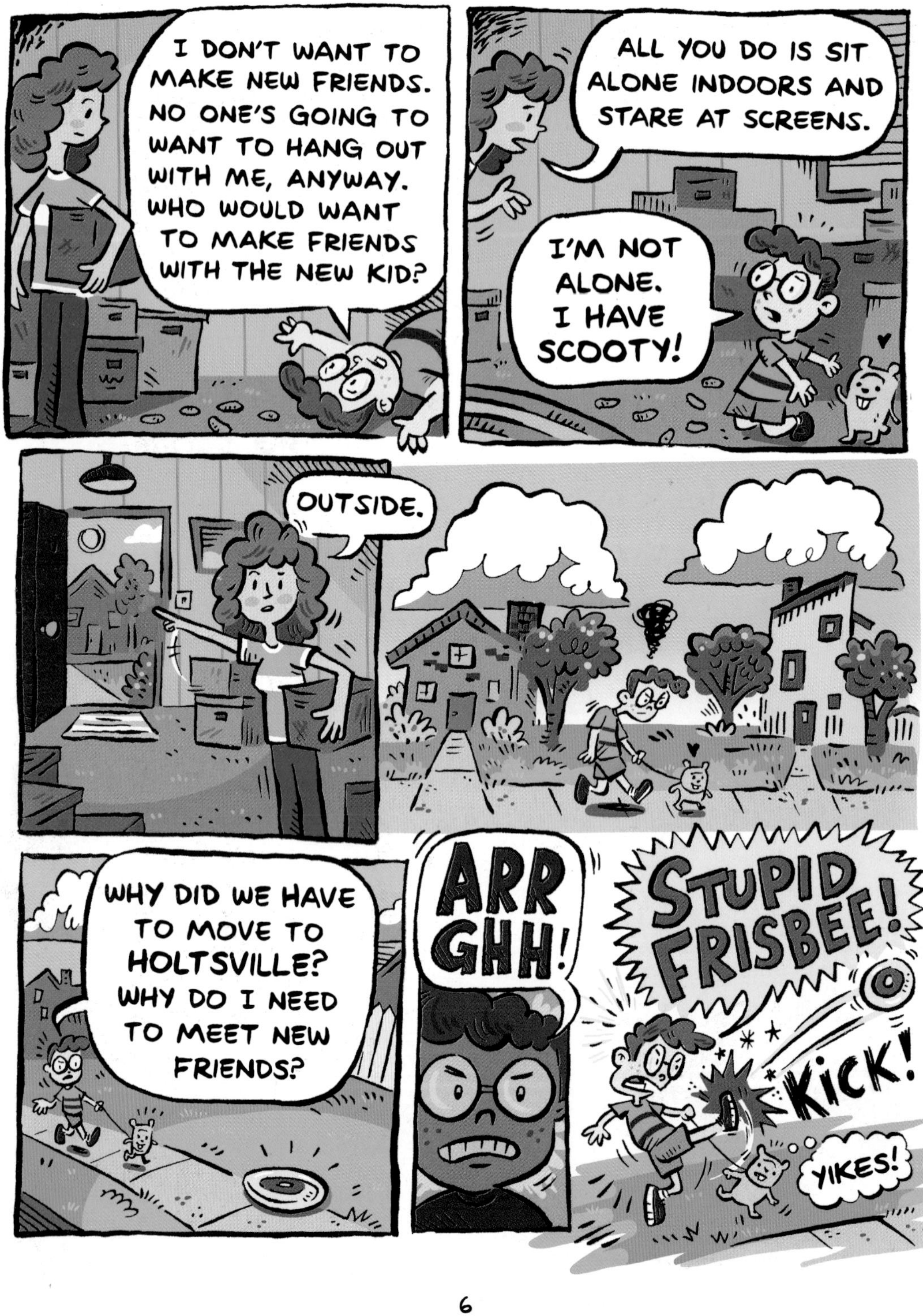
I DON'T WANT TO MAKE NEW FRIENDS. NO ONE'S GOING TO WANT TO HANG OUT WITH ME, ANYWAY. WHO WOULD WANT TO MAKE FRIENDS WITH THE NEW KID?
ALL YOU DO IS SIT ALONE INDOORS AND STARE AT SCREENS.
I'M NOT ALONE. I HAVE SCOOTY!
OUTSIDE.
WHY DID WE HAVE TO MOVE TO HOLTSVILLE? WHY DO I NEED TO MEET NEW FRIENDS?
ARR GHH!
STUPID FRISBEE!
KICK!
YIKES!

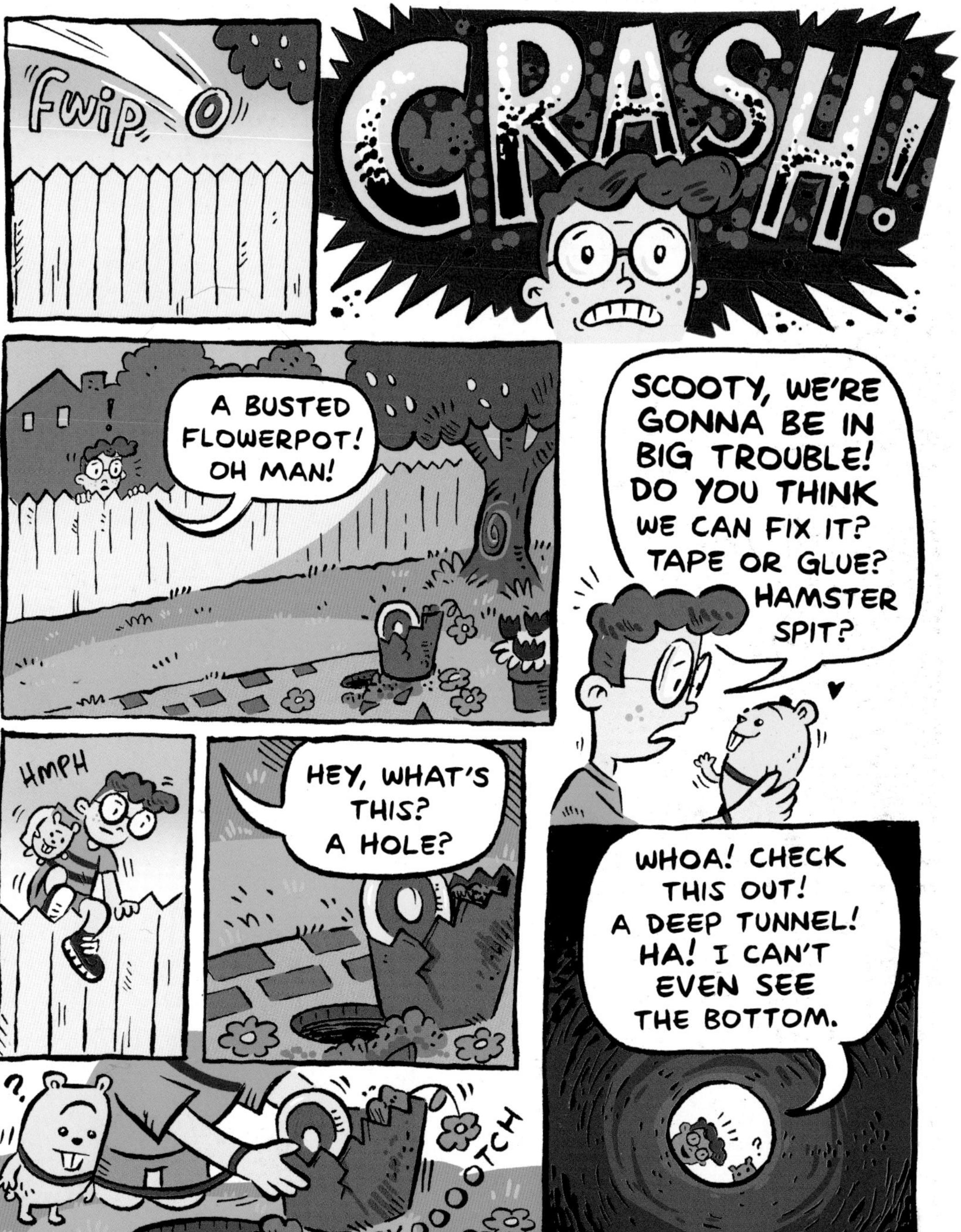

FWIP
CRASH!
A BUSTED FLOWERPOT! OH MAN!
SCOOTY, WE'RE GONNA BE IN BIG TROUBLE! DO YOU THINK WE CAN FIX IT? TAPE OR GLUE? HAMSTER SPIT?
HMPH
HEY, WHAT'S THIS? A HOLE?
WHOA! CHECK THIS OUT! A DEEP TUNNEL! HA! I CAN'T EVEN SEE THE BOTTOM.
SKOOOOTCH

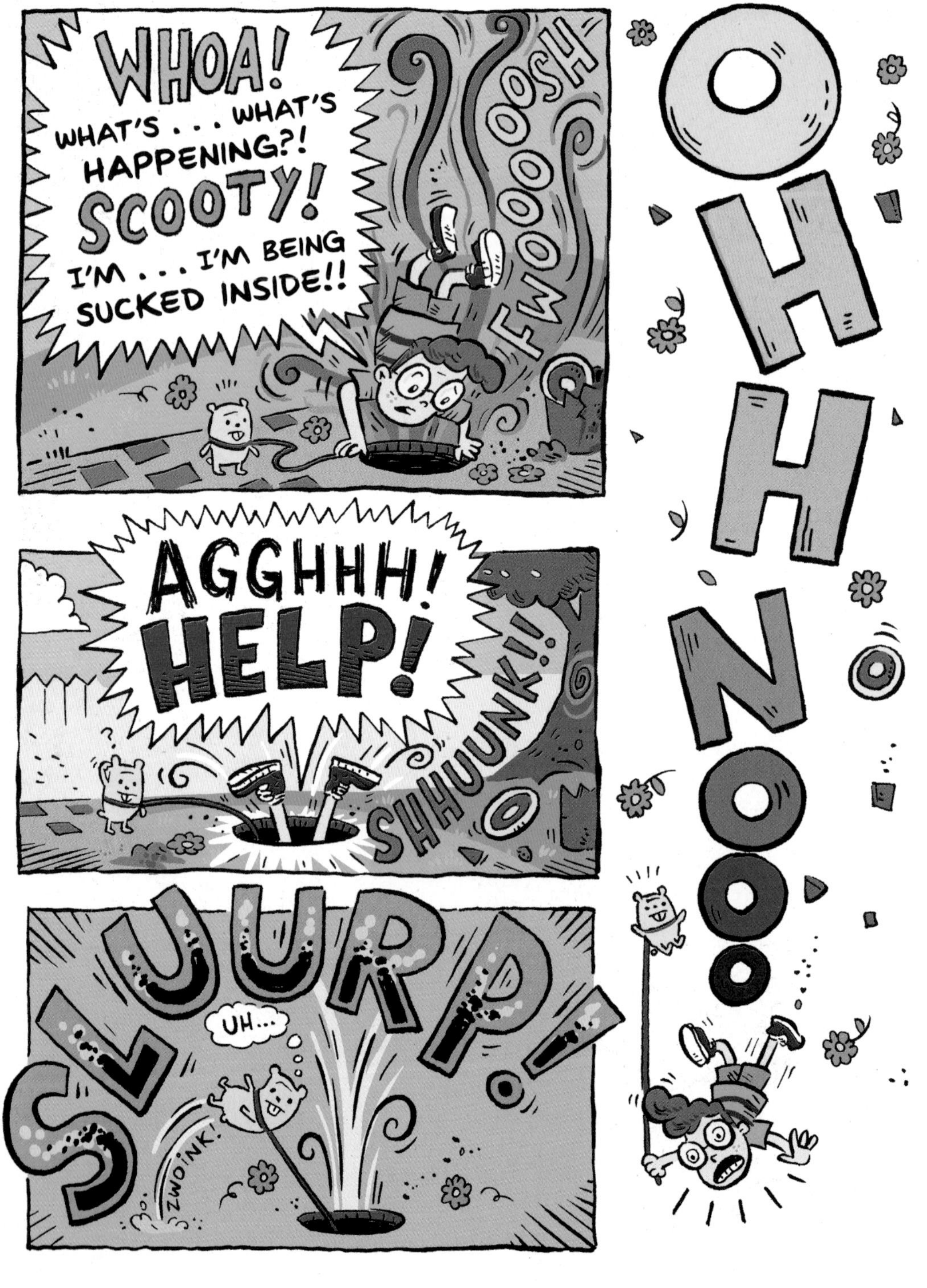
WHOA!
WHAT'S . . . WHAT'S HAPPENING?!
SCOOTY!
I'M . . . I'M BEING SUCKED INSIDE!!
FWOOOOOOSH
AGGHHH!
HELP!
SHHUUNK!!
SLUURP!
UH...
ZWOINK!
OHHHNOOOOO

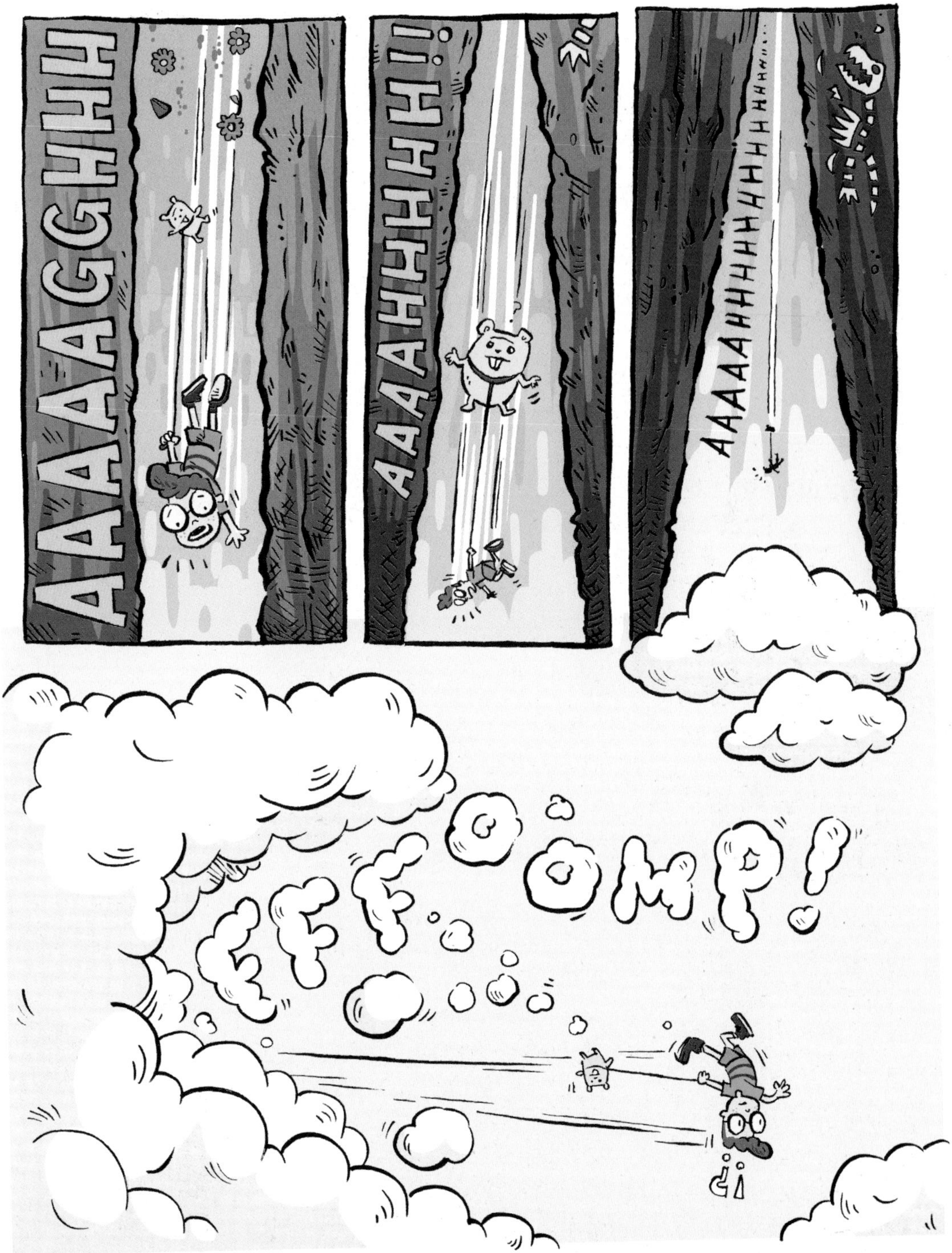
AAAAAGGHHH
AAAAHHHHHH!!
AAAAAHHHHHHHHHHHHHH...
EFFOOMP!
!?

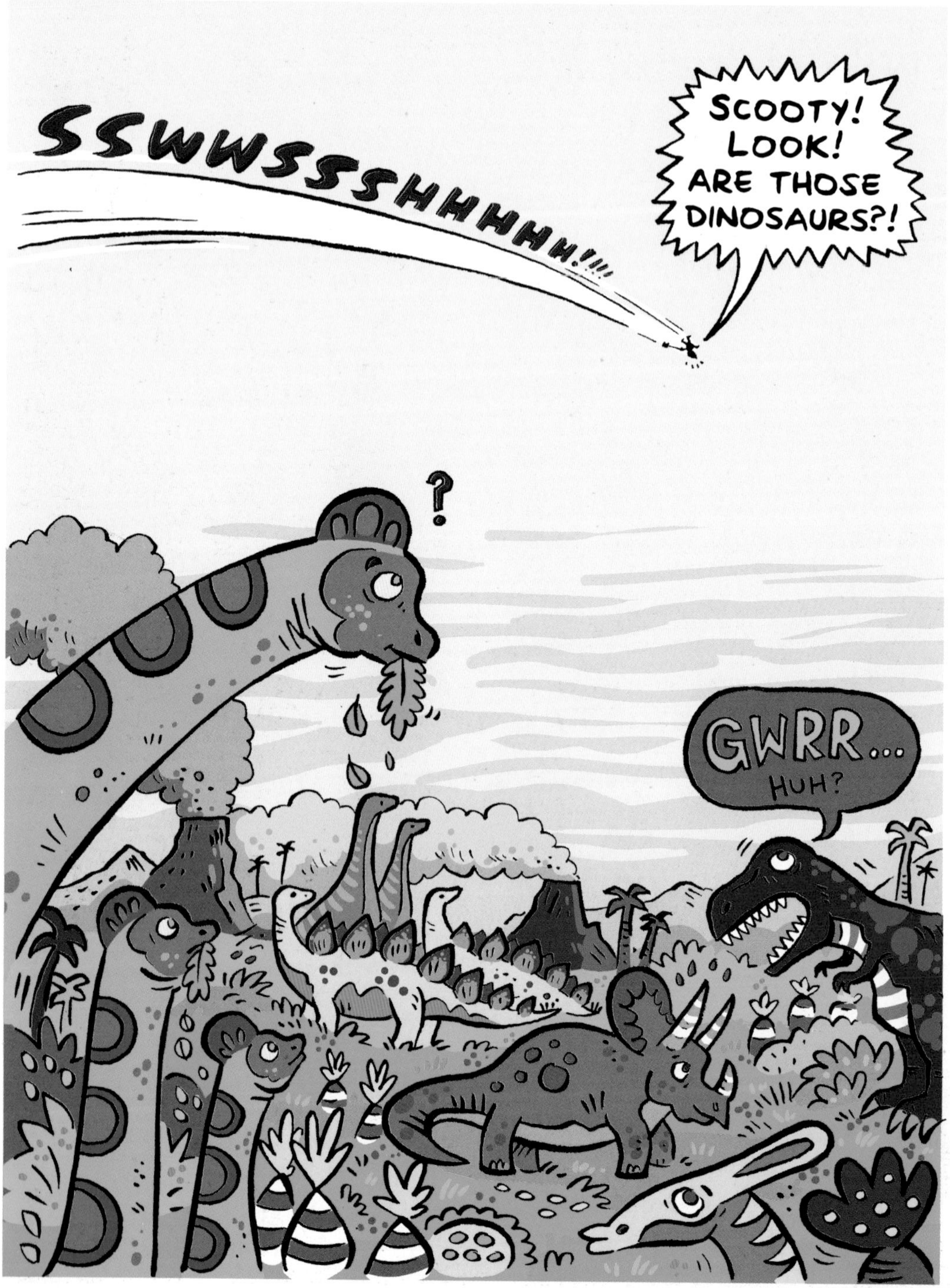
SSWWSSSSHHHHHH!!!!
SCOOTY! LOOK! ARE THOSE DINOSAURS?!
?
GWRR...
HUH?

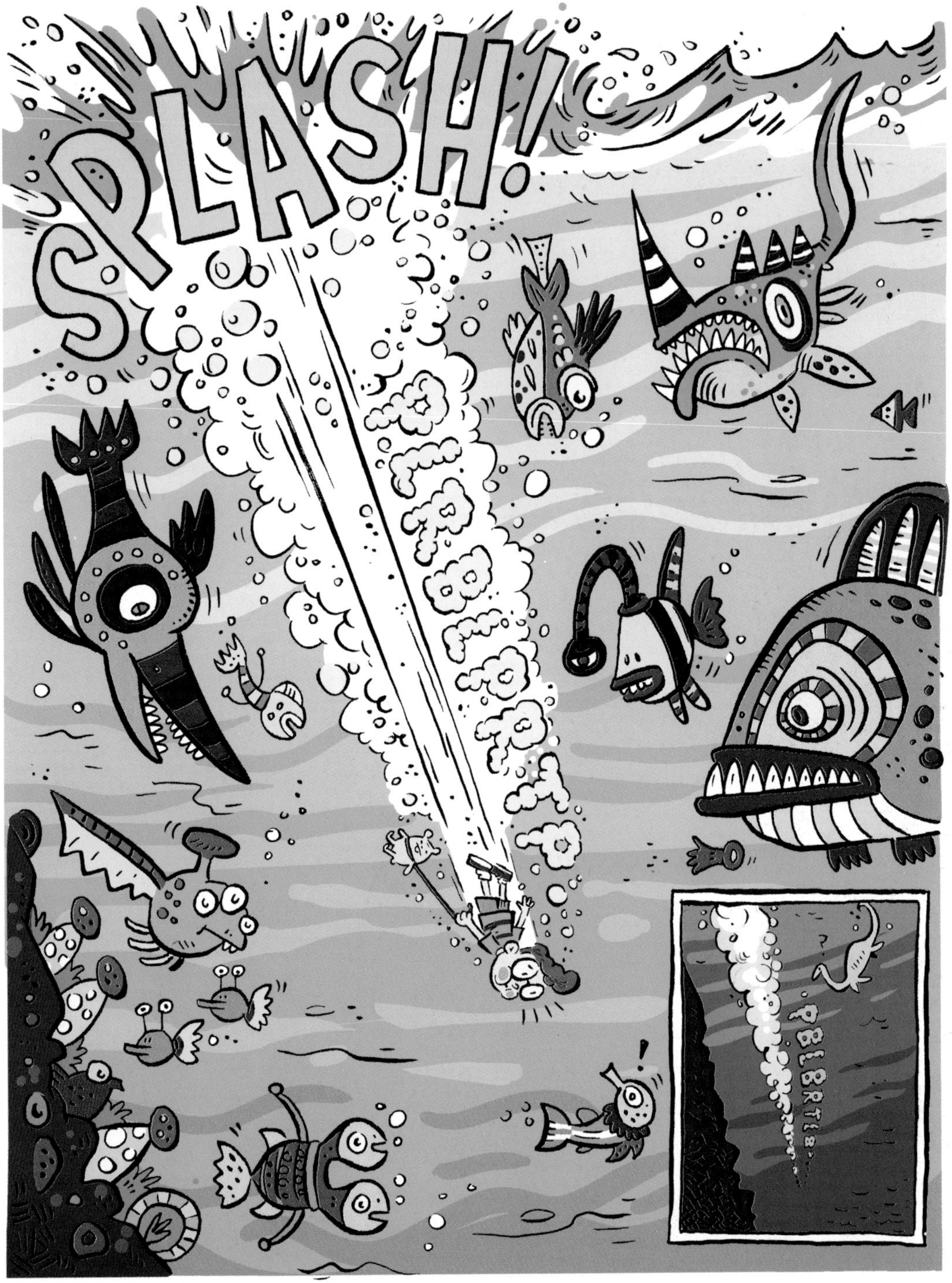
SPLASH!

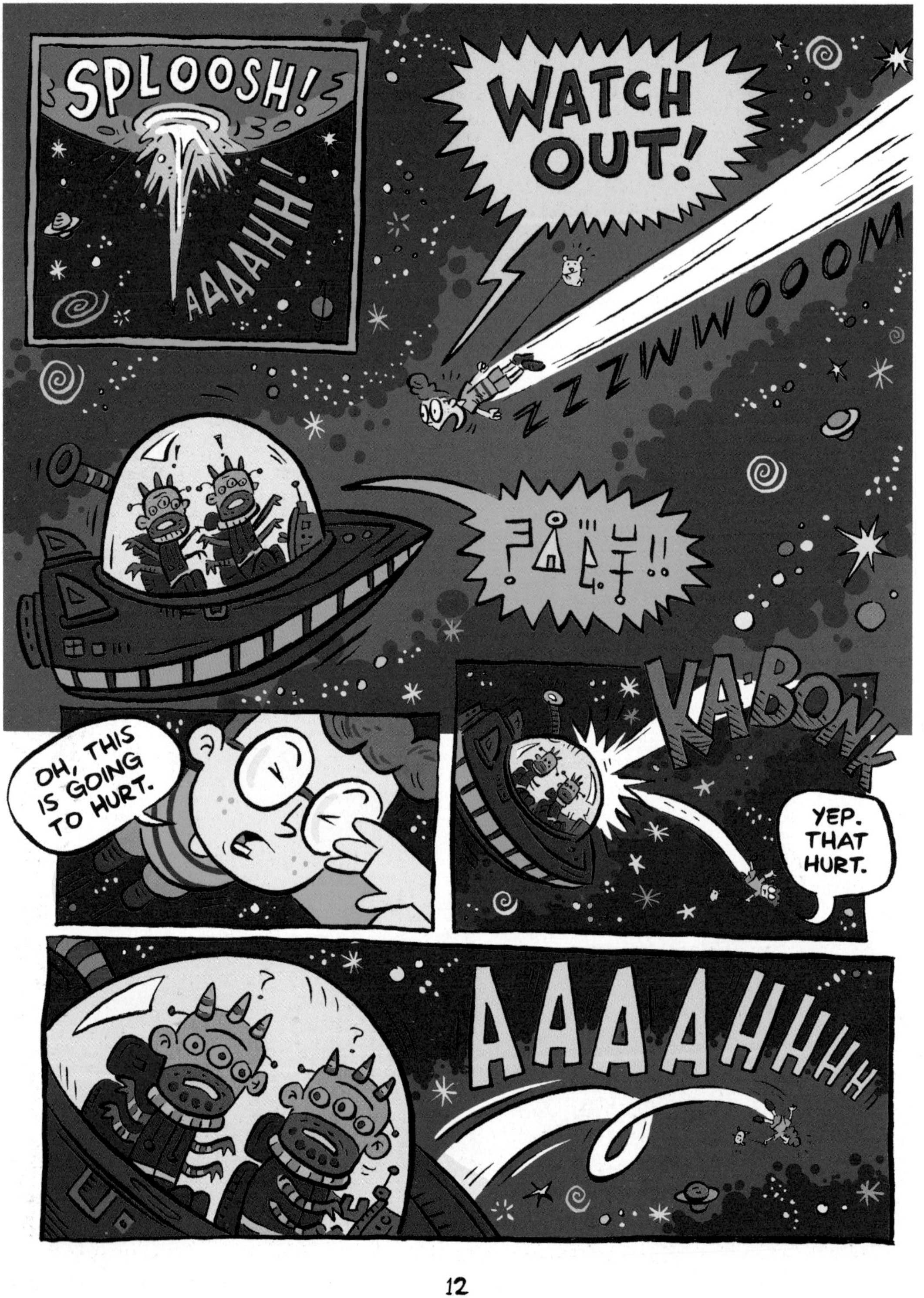
SPLOOSH!
AAAAHH!
WATCH OUT!
ZZZWWOOOM
OH, THIS IS GOING TO HURT.
KA-BONK
YEP. THAT HURT.
AAAAHHHH

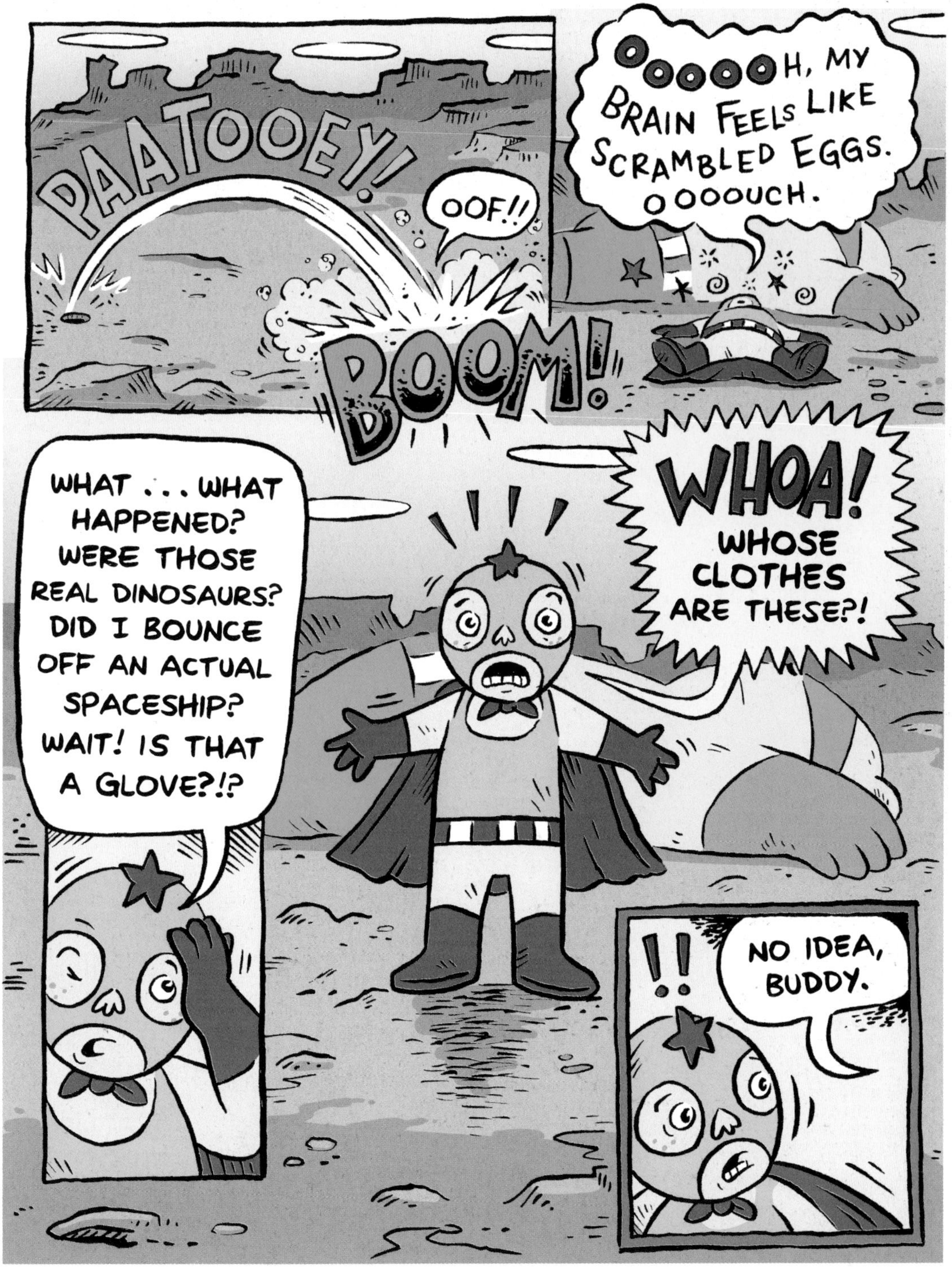
PAATOOEY!
OOF!!
BOOM!
OOOOOOH, MY BRAIN FEELS LIKE SCRAMBLED EGGS. OOOOUCH.
WHOA! WHOSE CLOTHES ARE THESE?!
WHAT . . . WHAT HAPPENED? WERE THOSE REAL DINOSAURS? DID I BOUNCE OFF AN ACTUAL SPACESHIP? WAIT! IS THAT A GLOVE?!?
!!
NO IDEA, BUDDY.

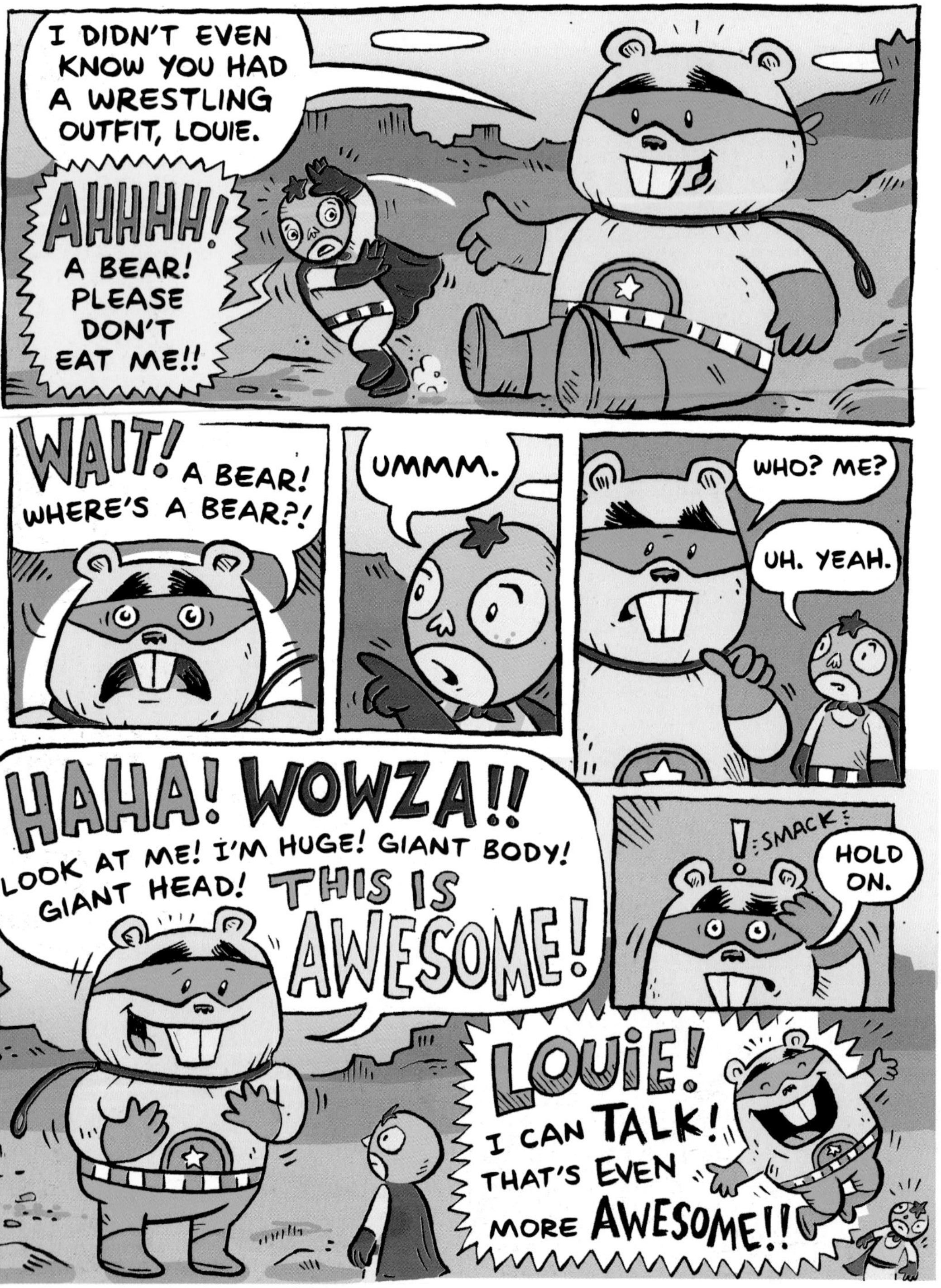
I DIDN'T EVEN KNOW YOU HAD A WRESTLING OUTFIT, LOUIE.
AHHHH! A BEAR! PLEASE DON'T EAT ME!!
WAIT! A BEAR! WHERE'S A BEAR?!
UMMM.
WHO? ME?
UH. YEAH.
HAHA! WOWZA!! LOOK AT ME! I'M HUGE! GIANT BODY! GIANT HEAD! THIS IS AWESOME!
SMACK
HOLD ON.
LOUIE! I CAN TALK! THAT'S EVEN MORE AWESOME!!

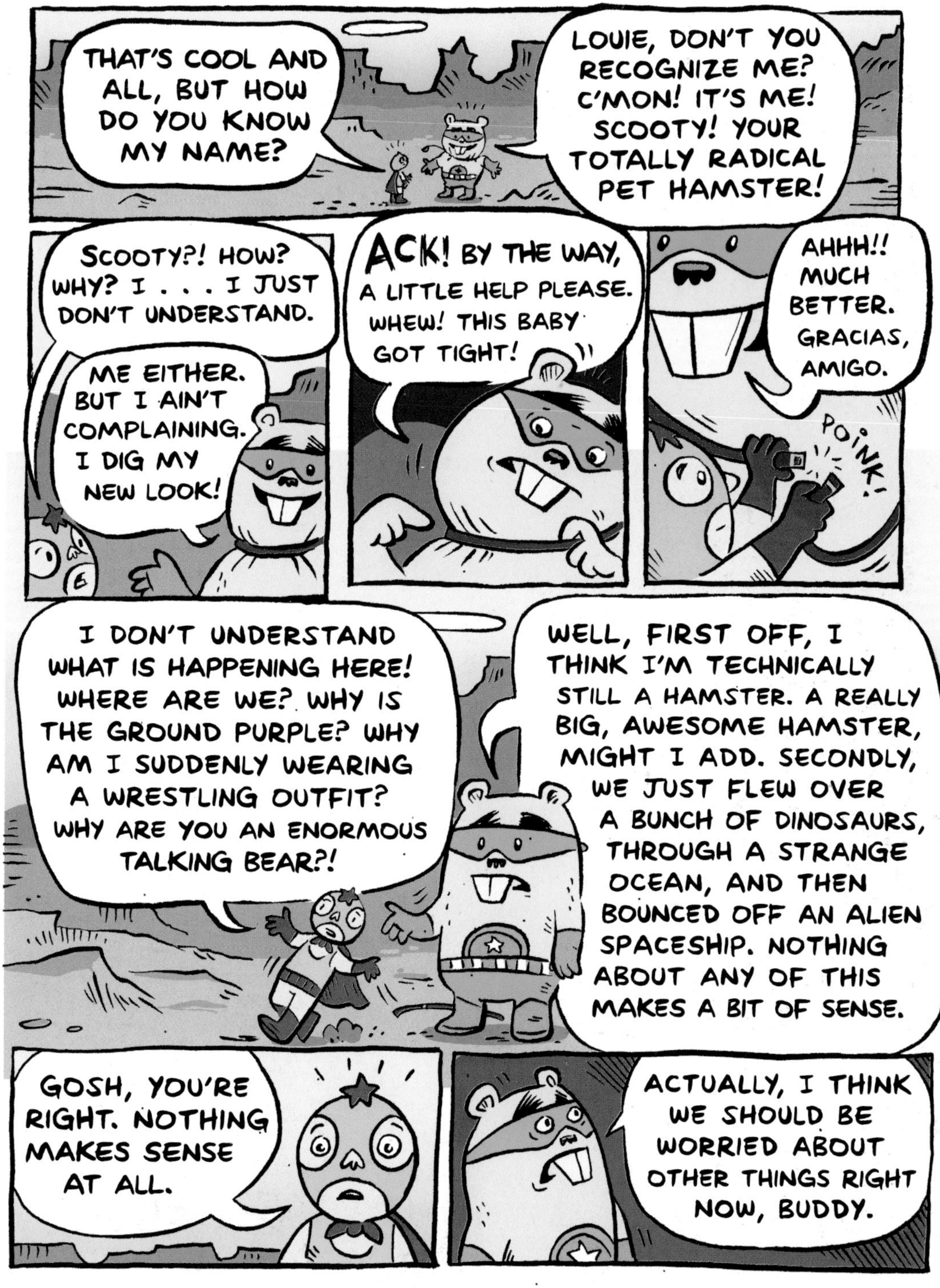
THAT'S COOL AND ALL, BUT HOW DO YOU KNOW MY NAME?
LOUIE, DON'T YOU RECOGNIZE ME? C'MON! IT'S ME! SCOOTY! YOUR TOTALLY RADICAL PET HAMSTER!
SCOOTY?! HOW? WHY? I . . . I JUST DON'T UNDERSTAND.
ME EITHER. BUT I AIN'T COMPLAINING. I DIG MY NEW LOOK!
ACK! BY THE WAY, A LITTLE HELP PLEASE. WHEW! THIS BABY GOT TIGHT!
AHHH!! MUCH BETTER. GRACIAS, AMIGO.
POINK!
I DON'T UNDERSTAND WHAT IS HAPPENING HERE! WHERE ARE WE? WHY IS THE GROUND PURPLE? WHY AM I SUDDENLY WEARING A WRESTLING OUTFIT? WHY ARE YOU AN ENORMOUS TALKING BEAR?!
WELL, FIRST OFF, I THINK I'M TECHNICALLY STILL A HAMSTER. A REALLY BIG, AWESOME HAMSTER, MIGHT I ADD. SECONDLY, WE JUST FLEW OVER A BUNCH OF DINOSAURS, THROUGH A STRANGE OCEAN, AND THEN BOUNCED OFF AN ALIEN SPACESHIP. NOTHING ABOUT ANY OF THIS MAKES A BIT OF SENSE.
GOSH, YOU'RE RIGHT. NOTHING MAKES SENSE AT ALL.
ACTUALLY, I THINK WE SHOULD BE WORRIED ABOUT OTHER THINGS RIGHT NOW, BUDDY.

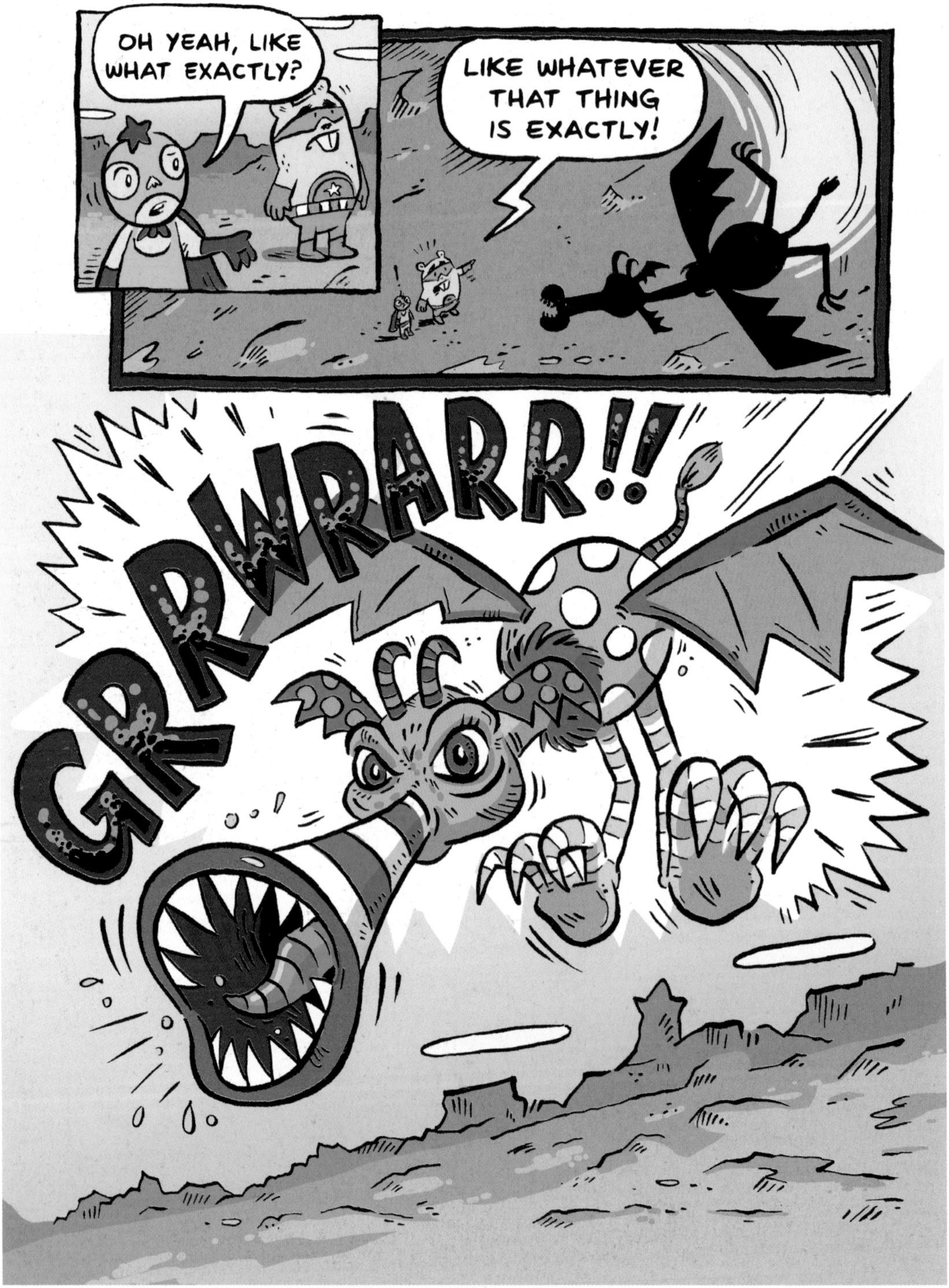
OH YEAH, LIKE WHAT EXACTLY?
LIKE WHATEVER THAT THING IS EXACTLY!
GRRWRARR!!

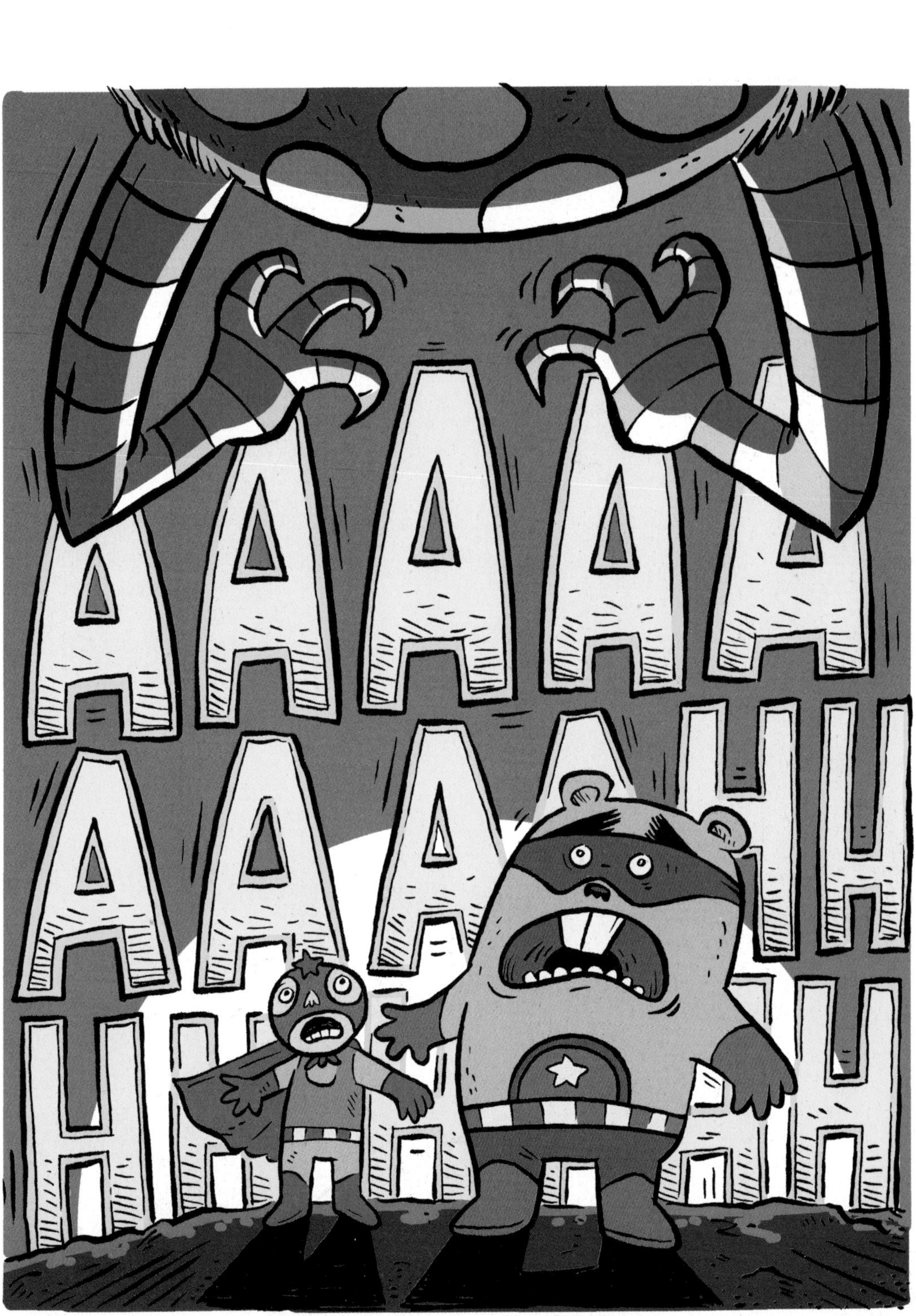
AAAAAAAAAHHHHHH

Chapter 2

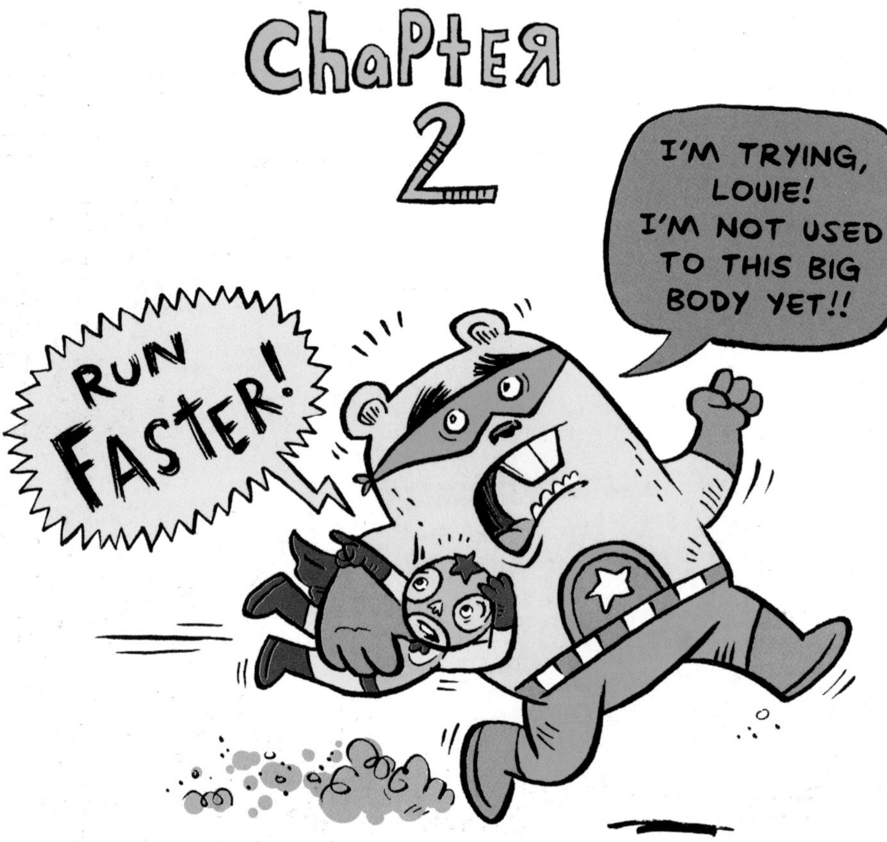
I'M TRYING, LOUIE! I'M NOT USED TO THIS BIG BODY YET!!
RUN FASTER!

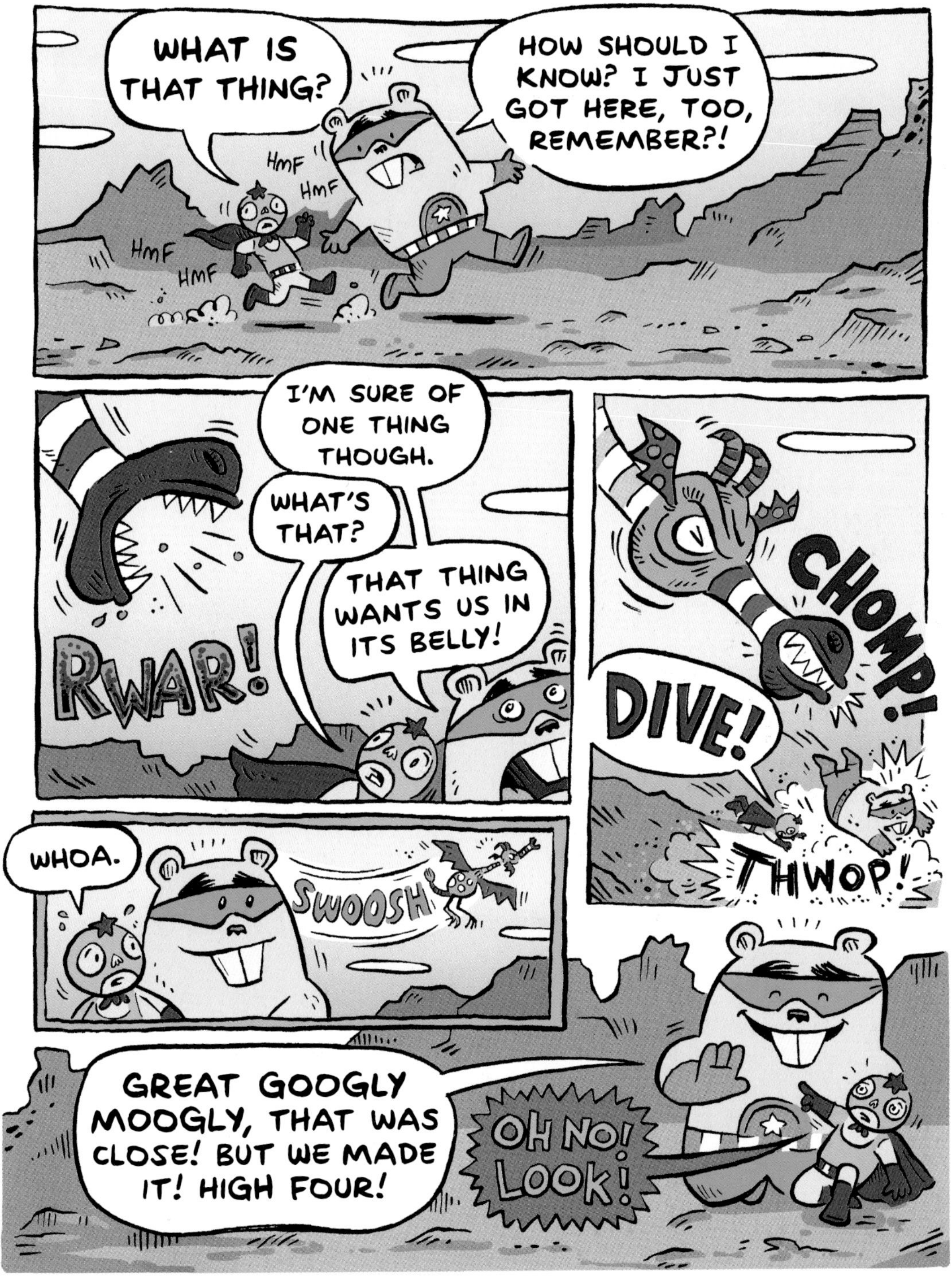
WHAT IS THAT THING?
HOW SHOULD I KNOW? I JUST GOT HERE, TOO, REMEMBER?!
HMF HMF
HMF HMF
I'M SURE OF ONE THING THOUGH.
WHAT'S THAT?
THAT THING WANTS US IN ITS BELLY!
RWAR!
CHOMP!
DIVE!
THWOP!
WHOA.
SWOOSH
GREAT GOOGLY MOOGLY, THAT WAS CLOSE! BUT WE MADE IT! HIGH FOUR!
OH NO! LOOK!

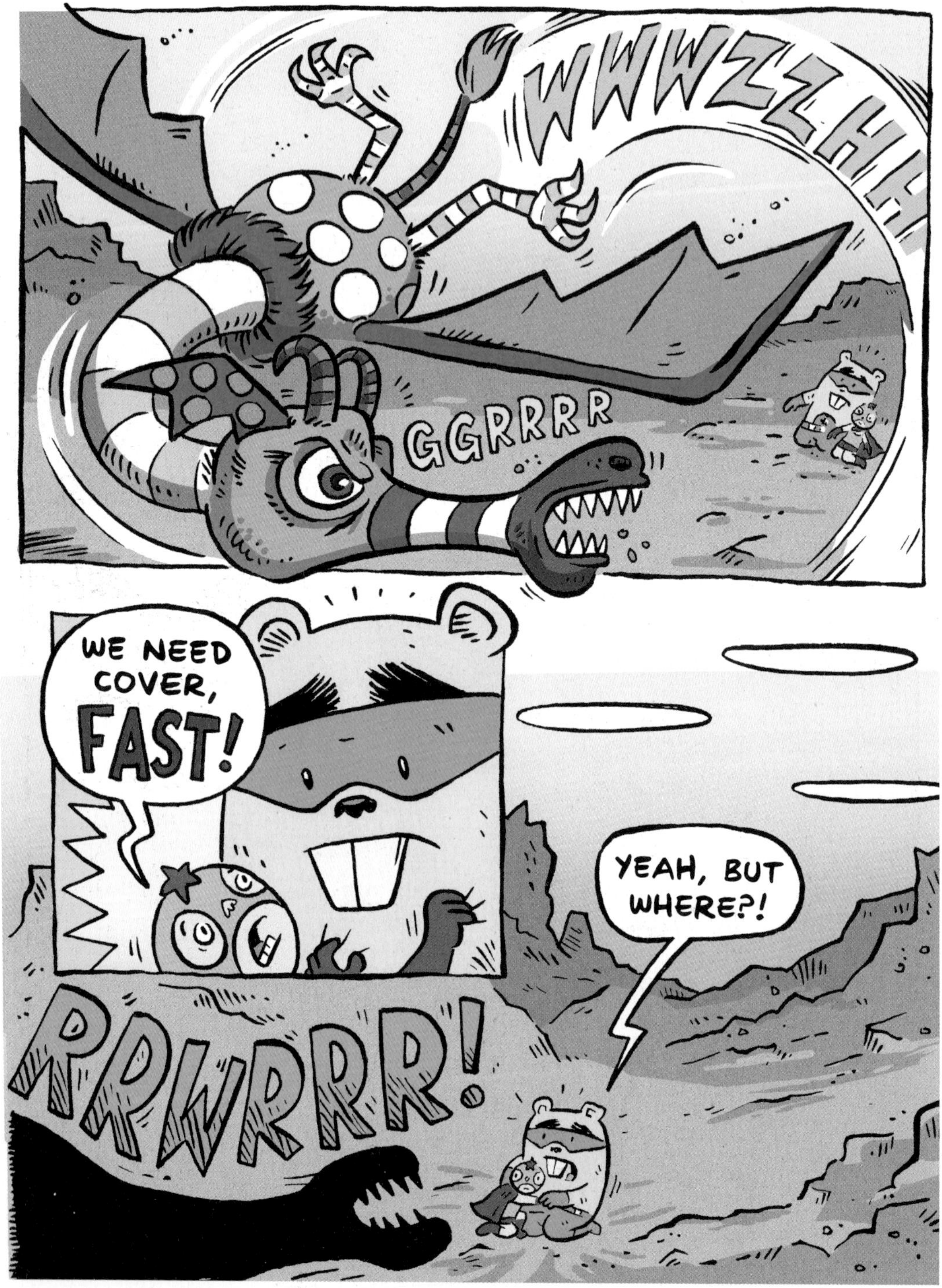
WWWZZHH
GGRRRR
WE NEED COVER, FAST!
RRWRRR!
YEAH, BUT WHERE?!

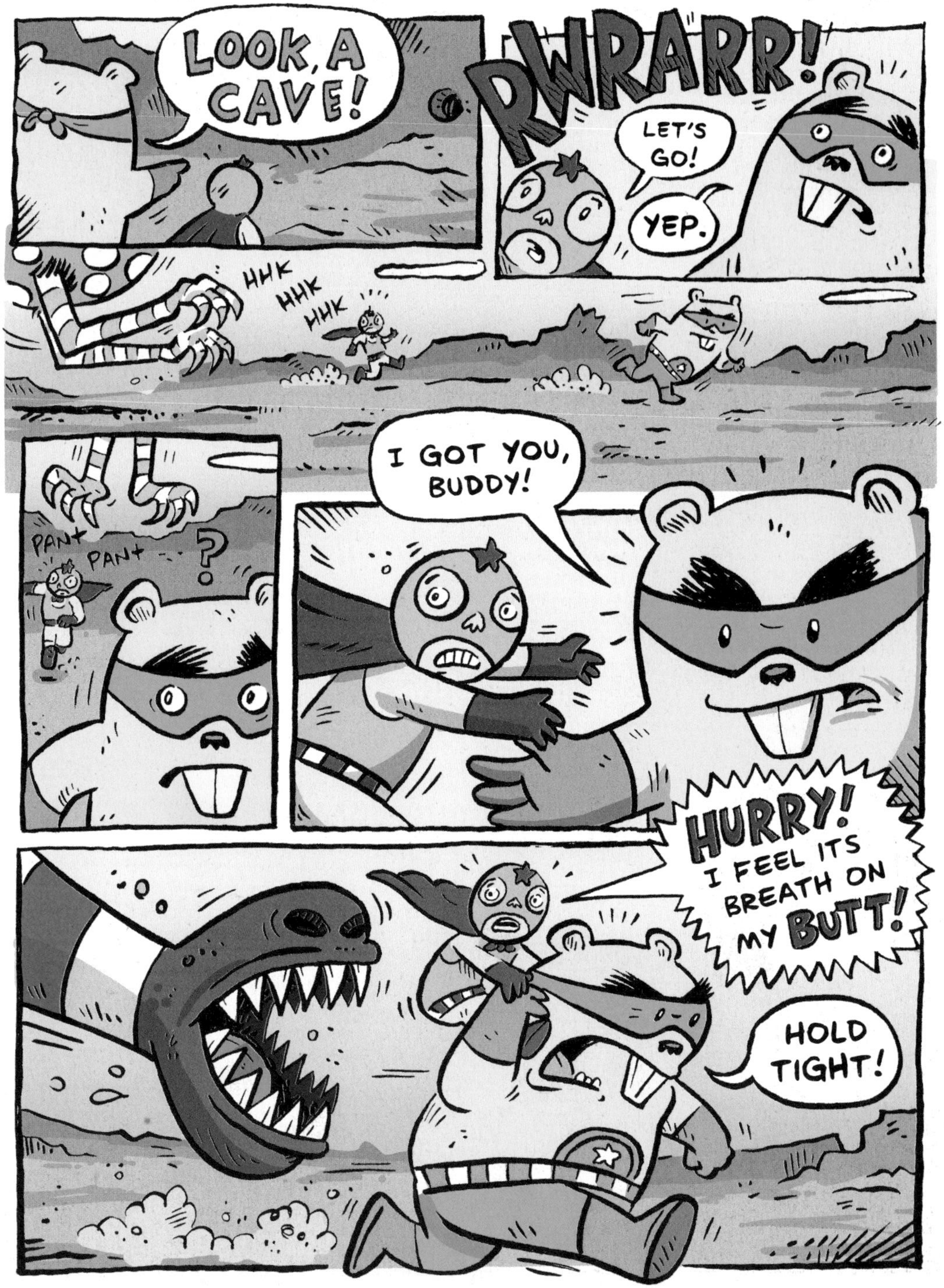
LOOK, A CAVE!
RWRARR!
LET'S GO!
YEP.
HHK HHK HHK
PANT PANT
?
I GOT YOU, BUDDY!
HURRY! I FEEL ITS BREATH ON MY BUTT!
HOLD TIGHT!

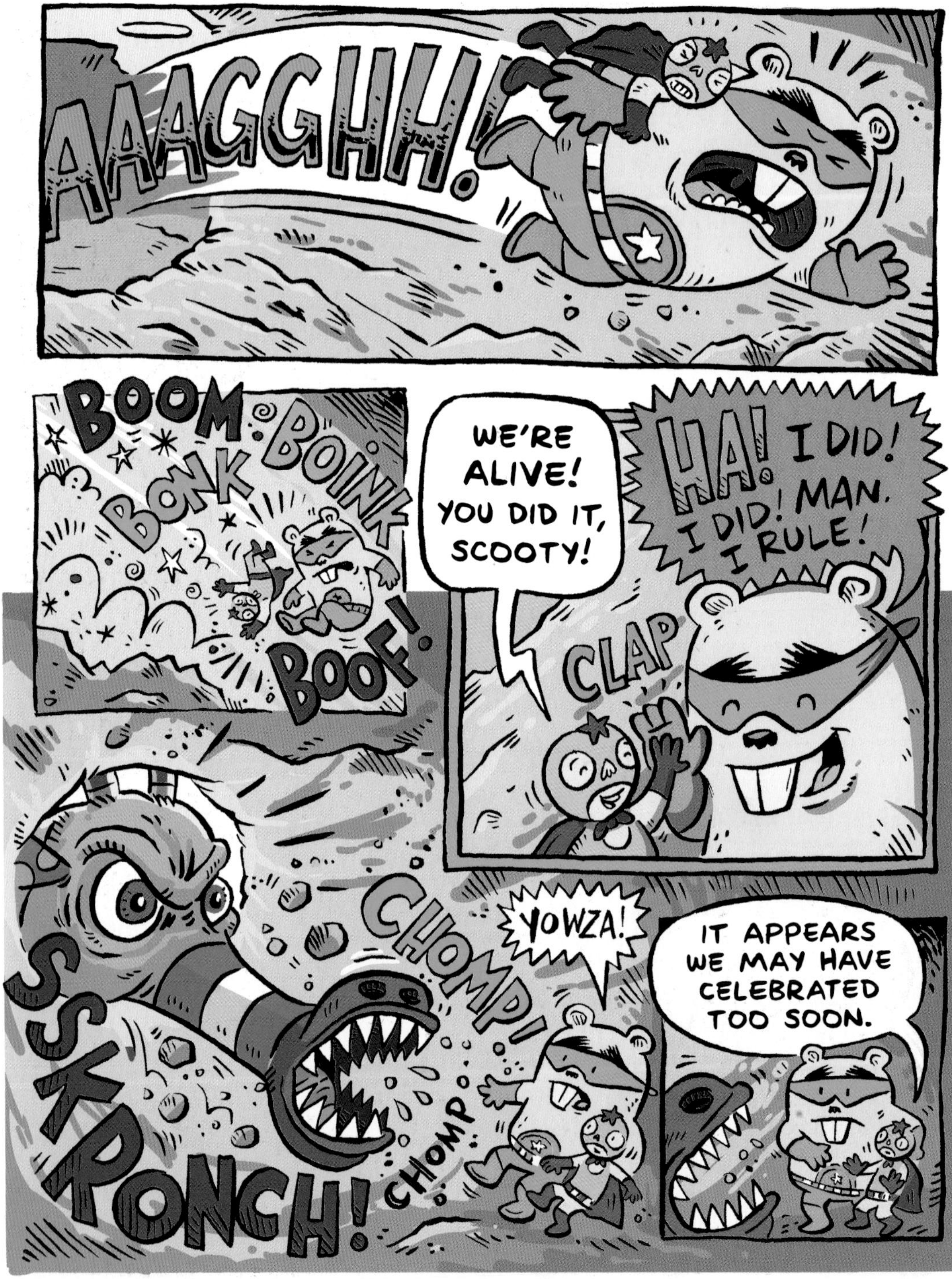
AAAGGHH!
BOOM
BONK
BOINK
BOOF!
WE'RE ALIVE! YOU DID IT, SCOOTY!
HA! I DID! I DID! MAN. I RULE!
CLAP
SSKRONCH!
CHOMP!
CHOMP
YOWZA!
IT APPEARS WE MAY HAVE CELEBRATED TOO SOON.

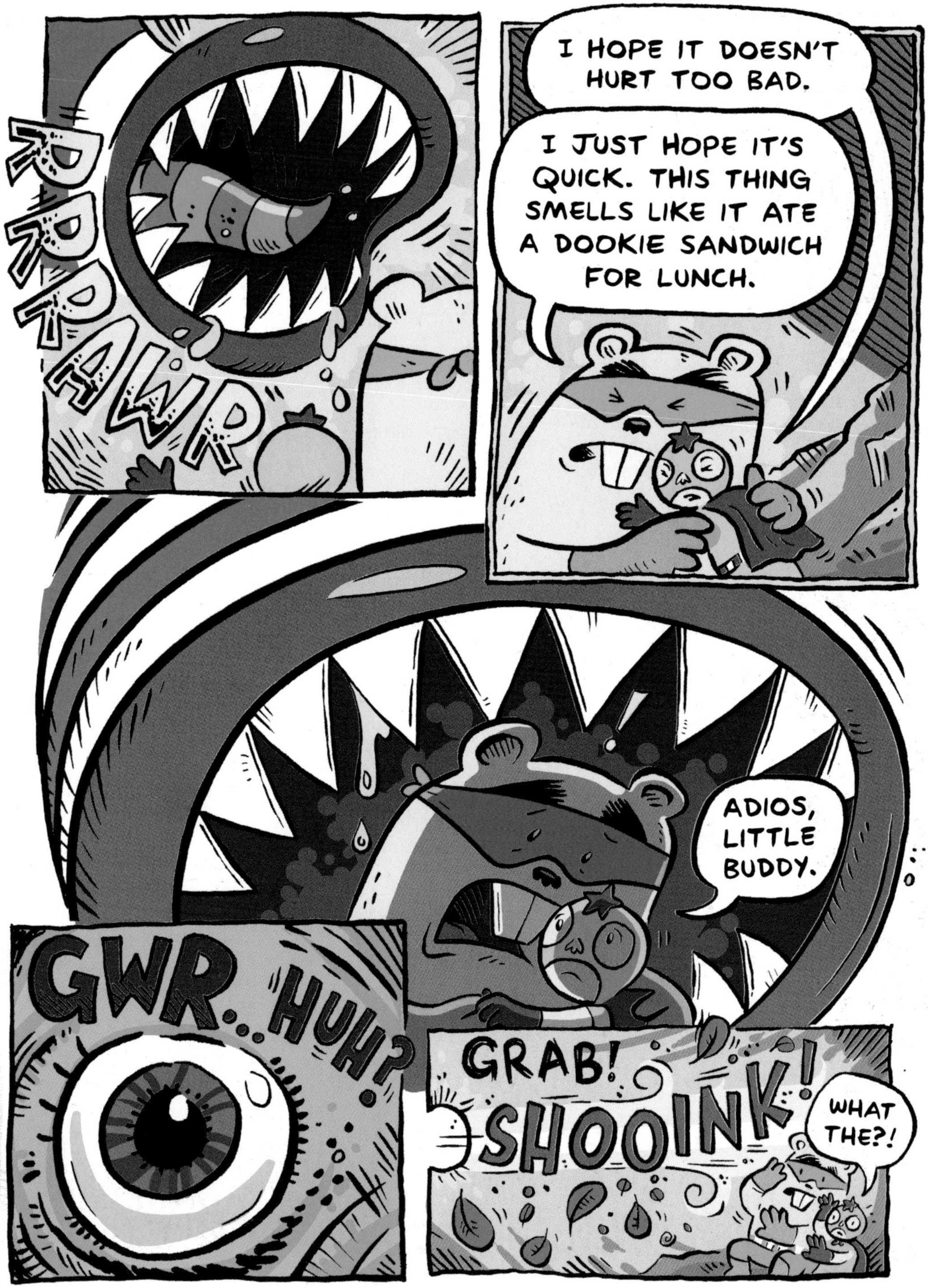
RRRAWR
I HOPE IT DOESN'T HURT TOO BAD.
I JUST HOPE IT'S QUICK. THIS THING SMELLS LIKE IT ATE A DOOKIE SANDWICH FOR LUNCH.
ADIOS, LITTLE BUDDY.
GWR... HUH?
GRAB!
SHOOINK!
WHAT THE?!

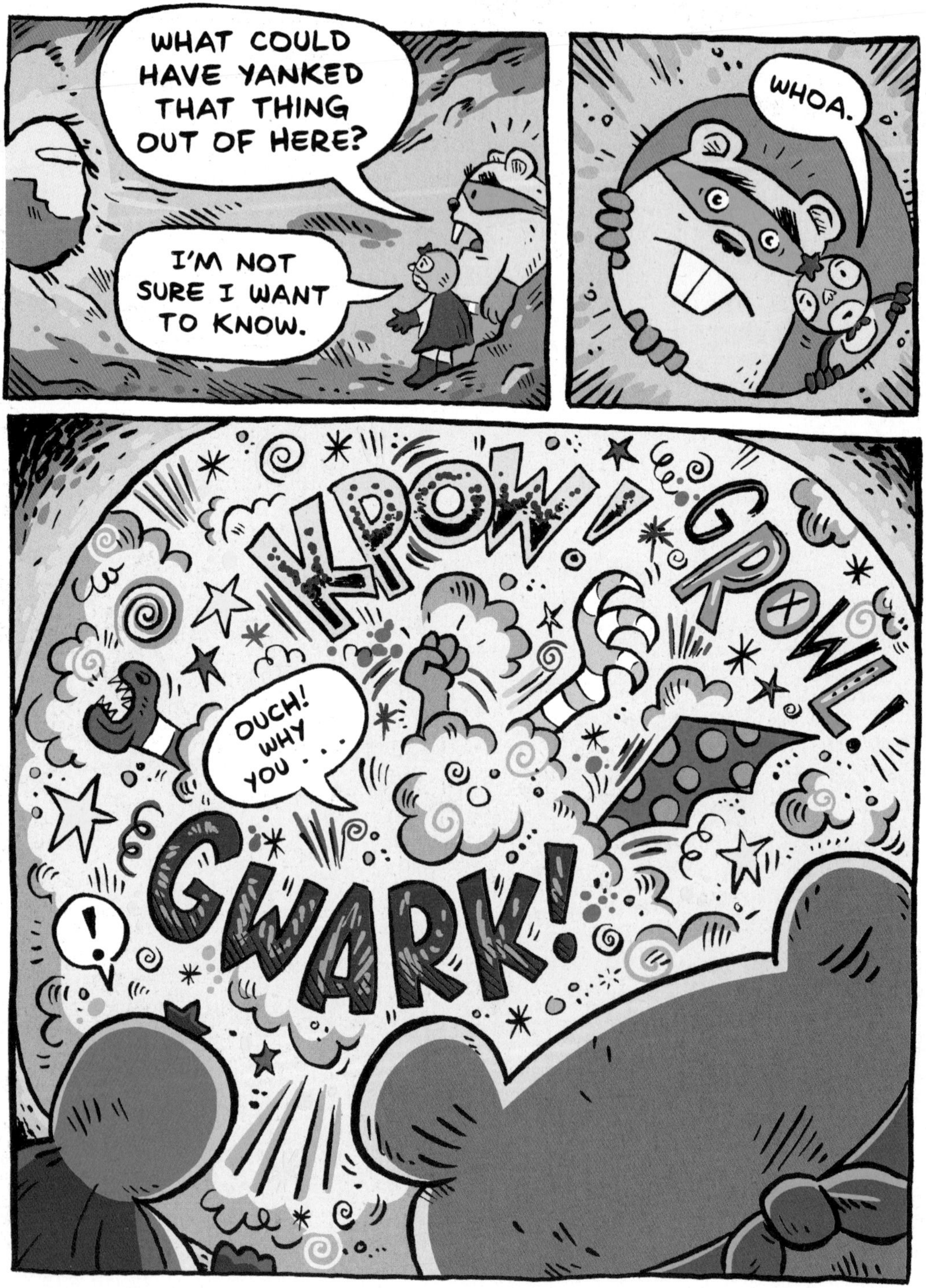
WHAT COULD HAVE YANKED THAT THING OUT OF HERE?
I'M NOT SURE I WANT TO KNOW.
WHOA.
KPOW!
GROWL!
OUCH! WHY YOU . . .
GWARK!
!

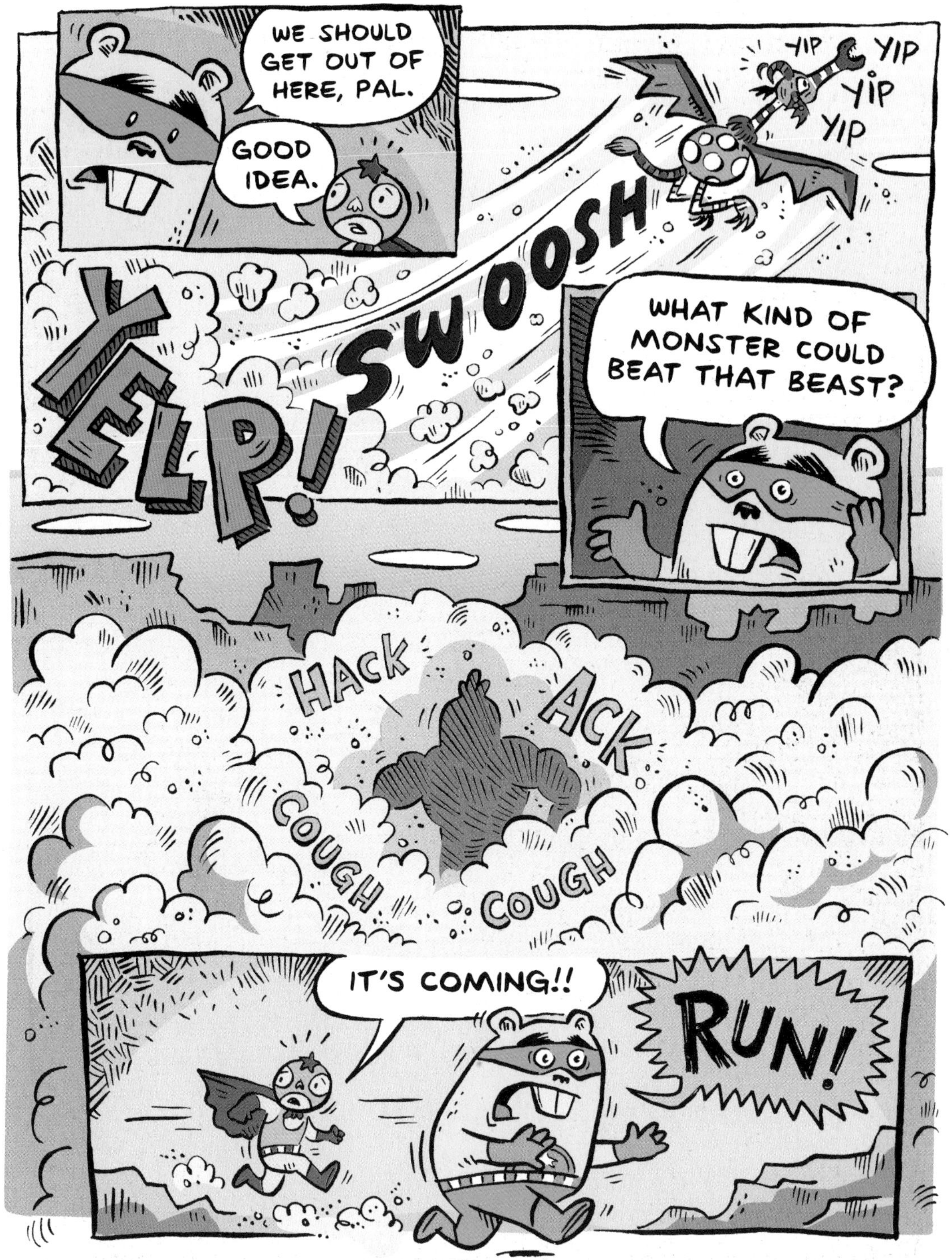
WE SHOULD GET OUT OF HERE, PAL.
GOOD IDEA.
YIP YIP YIP YIP
SWOOSH
YELP!
WHAT KIND OF MONSTER COULD BEAT THAT BEAST?
HACK
ACK
COUGH
COUGH
IT'S COMING!!
RUN!

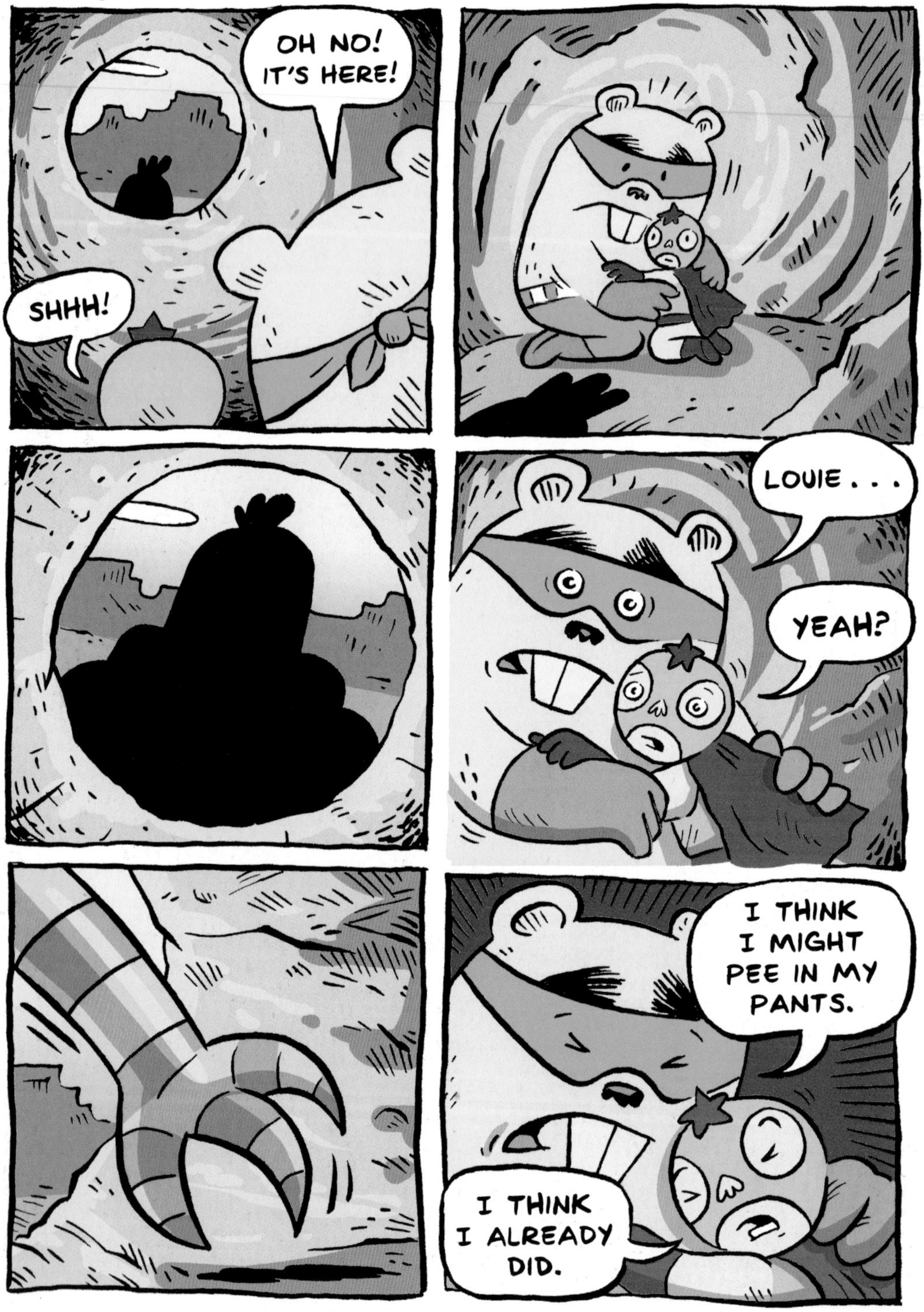
OH NO! IT'S HERE!
SHHH!
LOUIE . . .
YEAH?
I THINK I MIGHT PEE IN MY PANTS.
I THINK I ALREADY DID.

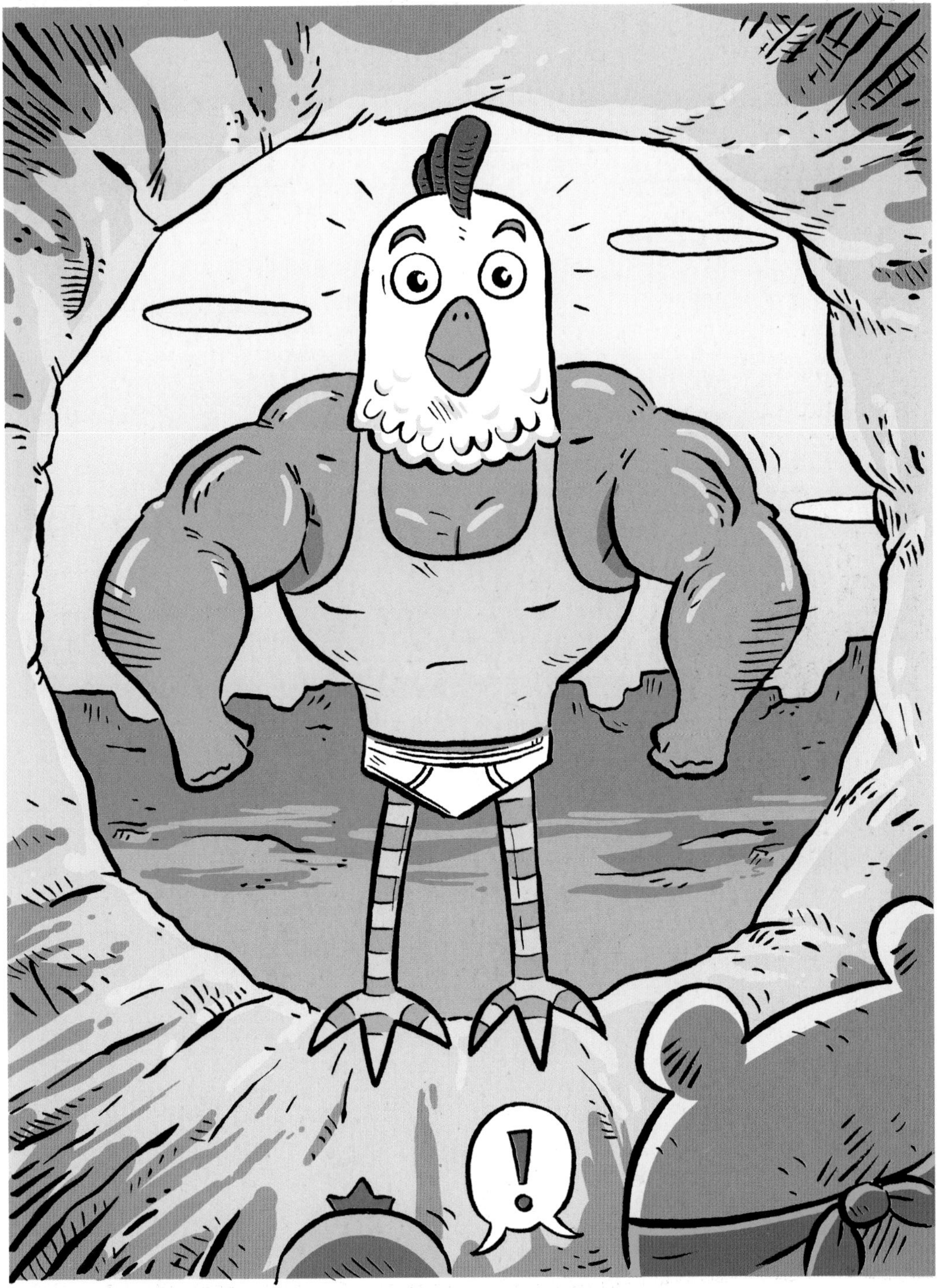
!

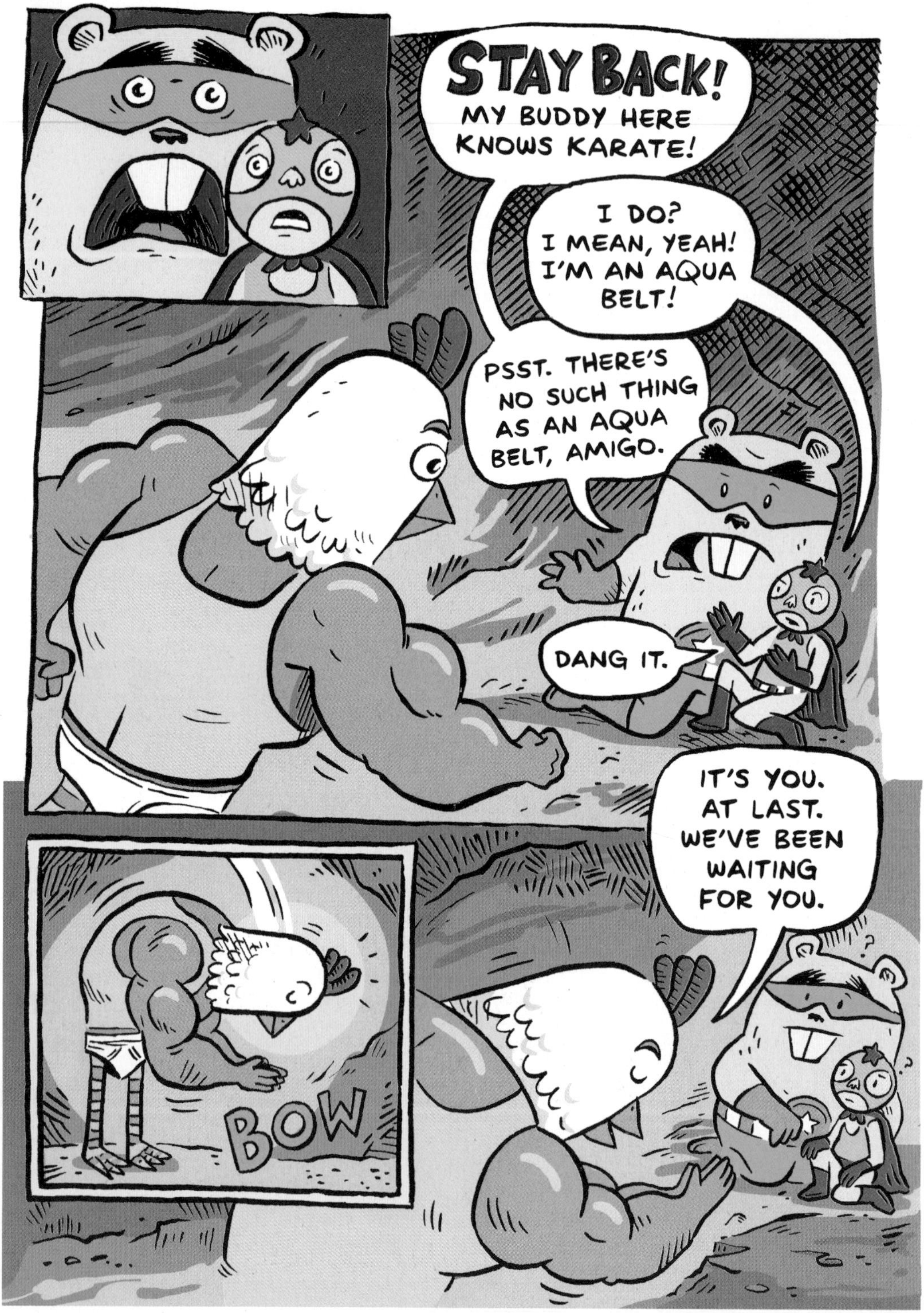
STAY BACK! MY BUDDY HERE KNOWS KARATE!
I DO? I MEAN, YEAH! I'M AN AQUA BELT!
PSST. THERE'S NO SUCH THING AS AN AQUA BELT, AMIGO.
DANG IT.
IT'S YOU. AT LAST. WE'VE BEEN WAITING FOR YOU.
BOW

CHAPTER 3

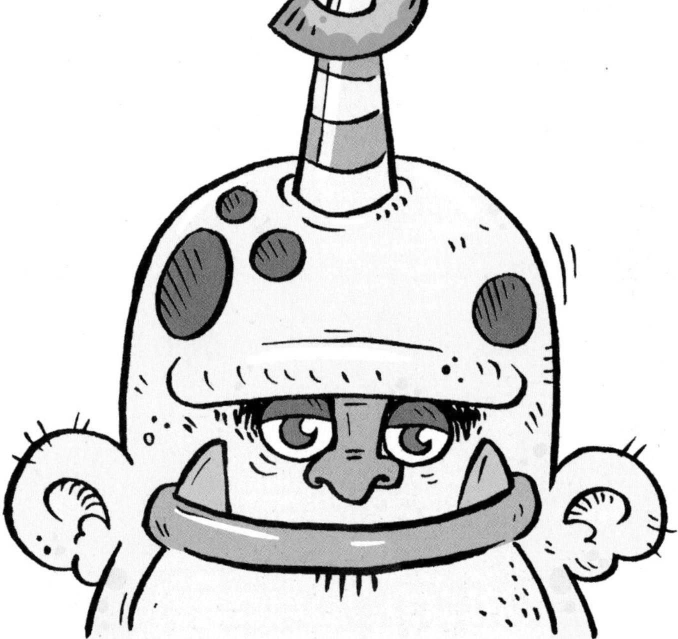

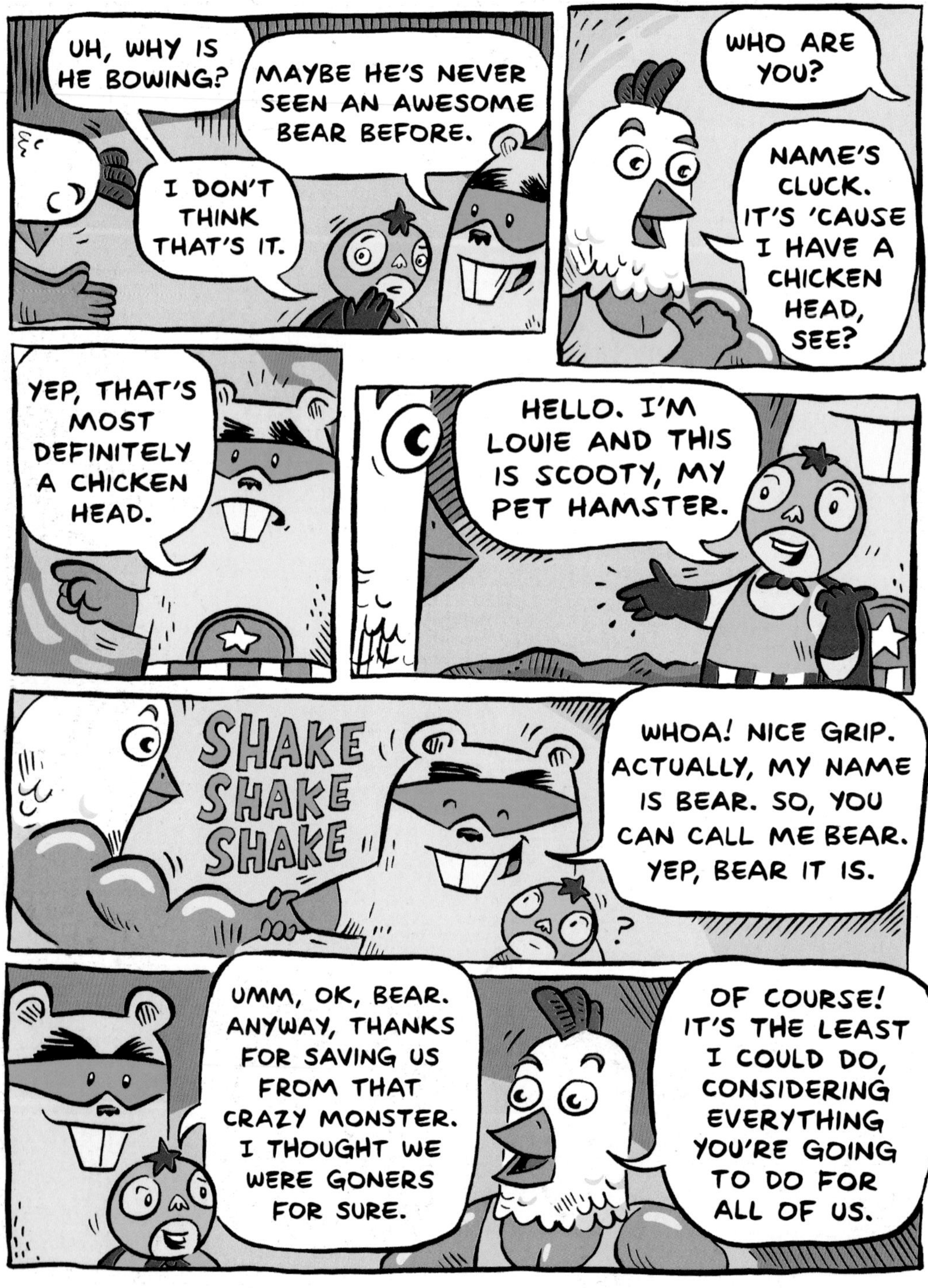
UH, WHY IS HE BOWING?
MAYBE HE'S NEVER SEEN AN AWESOME BEAR BEFORE.
I DON'T THINK THAT'S IT.
WHO ARE YOU?
NAME'S CLUCK. IT'S 'CAUSE I HAVE A CHICKEN HEAD, SEE?
YEP, THAT'S MOST DEFINITELY A CHICKEN HEAD.
HELLO. I'M LOUIE AND THIS IS SCOOTY, MY PET HAMSTER.
SHAKE SHAKE SHAKE
WHOA! NICE GRIP. ACTUALLY, MY NAME IS BEAR. SO, YOU CAN CALL ME BEAR. YEP, BEAR IT IS.
?
UMM, OK, BEAR. ANYWAY, THANKS FOR SAVING US FROM THAT CRAZY MONSTER. I THOUGHT WE WERE GONERS FOR SURE.
OF COURSE! IT'S THE LEAST I COULD DO, CONSIDERING EVERYTHING YOU'RE GOING TO DO FOR ALL OF US.

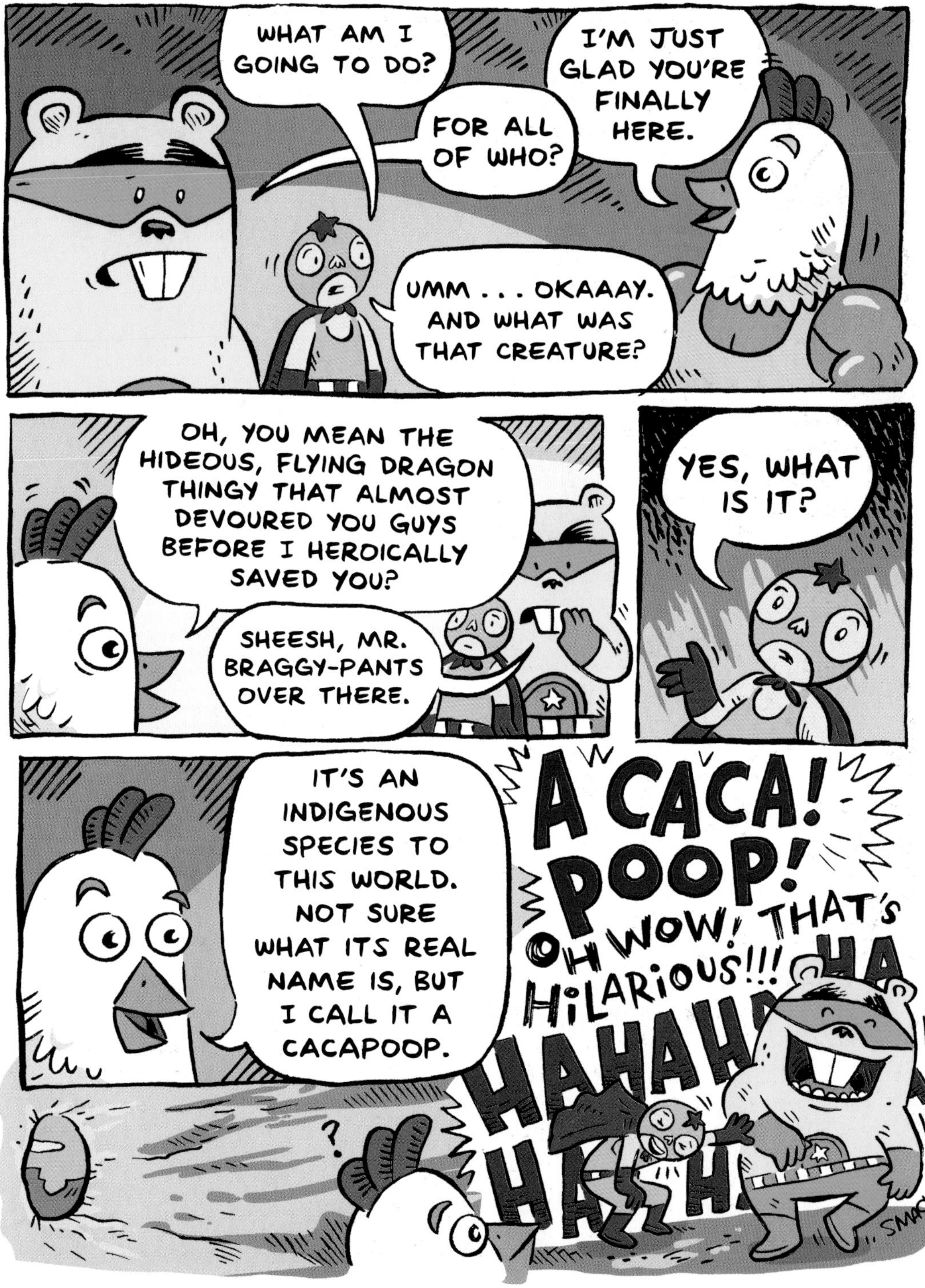
WHAT AM I GOING TO DO?
I'M JUST GLAD YOU'RE FINALLY HERE.
FOR ALL OF WHO?
UMM . . . OKAAAY. AND WHAT WAS THAT CREATURE?
OH, YOU MEAN THE HIDEOUS, FLYING DRAGON THINGY THAT ALMOST DEVOURED YOU GUYS BEFORE I HEROICALLY SAVED YOU?
SHEESH, MR. BRAGGY-PANTS OVER THERE.
YES, WHAT IS IT?
IT'S AN INDIGENOUS SPECIES TO THIS WORLD. NOT SURE WHAT ITS REAL NAME IS, BUT I CALL IT A CACAPOOP.
A CACA! POOP!
OH WOW! THAT'S HILARIOUS!!!
HA
HAHAH
HAHAH
?
SMACK!

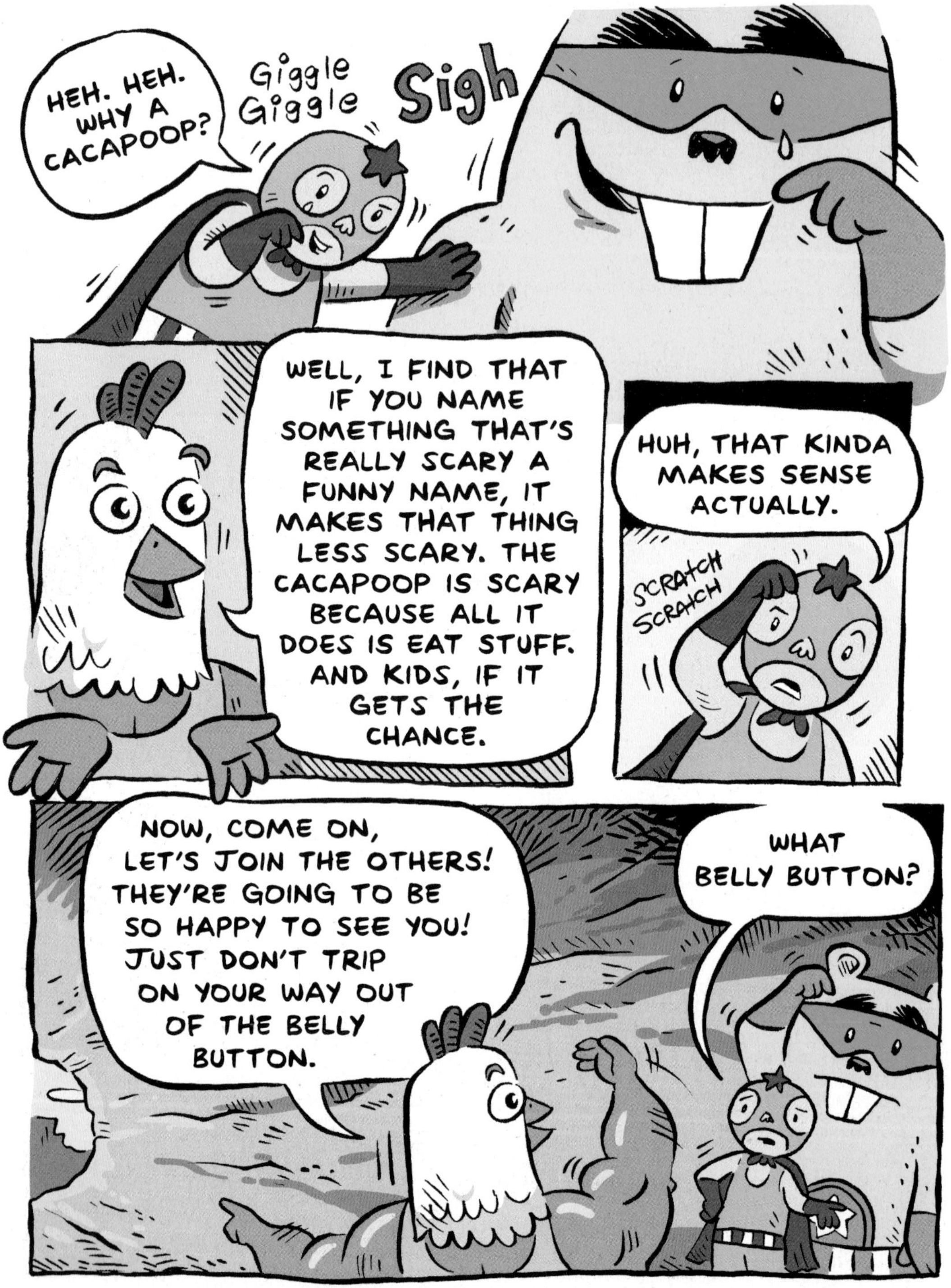

HEH. HEH. WHY A CACAPOOP?
Giggle Giggle
Sigh
WELL, I FIND THAT IF YOU NAME SOMETHING THAT'S REALLY SCARY A FUNNY NAME, IT MAKES THAT THING LESS SCARY. THE CACAPOOP IS SCARY BECAUSE ALL IT DOES IS EAT STUFF. AND KIDS, IF IT GETS THE CHANCE.
HUH, THAT KINDA MAKES SENSE ACTUALLY.
SCRATCH SCRATCH
NOW, COME ON, LET'S JOIN THE OTHERS! THEY'RE GOING TO BE SO HAPPY TO SEE YOU! JUST DON'T TRIP ON YOUR WAY OUT OF THE BELLY BUTTON.
WHAT BELLY BUTTON?

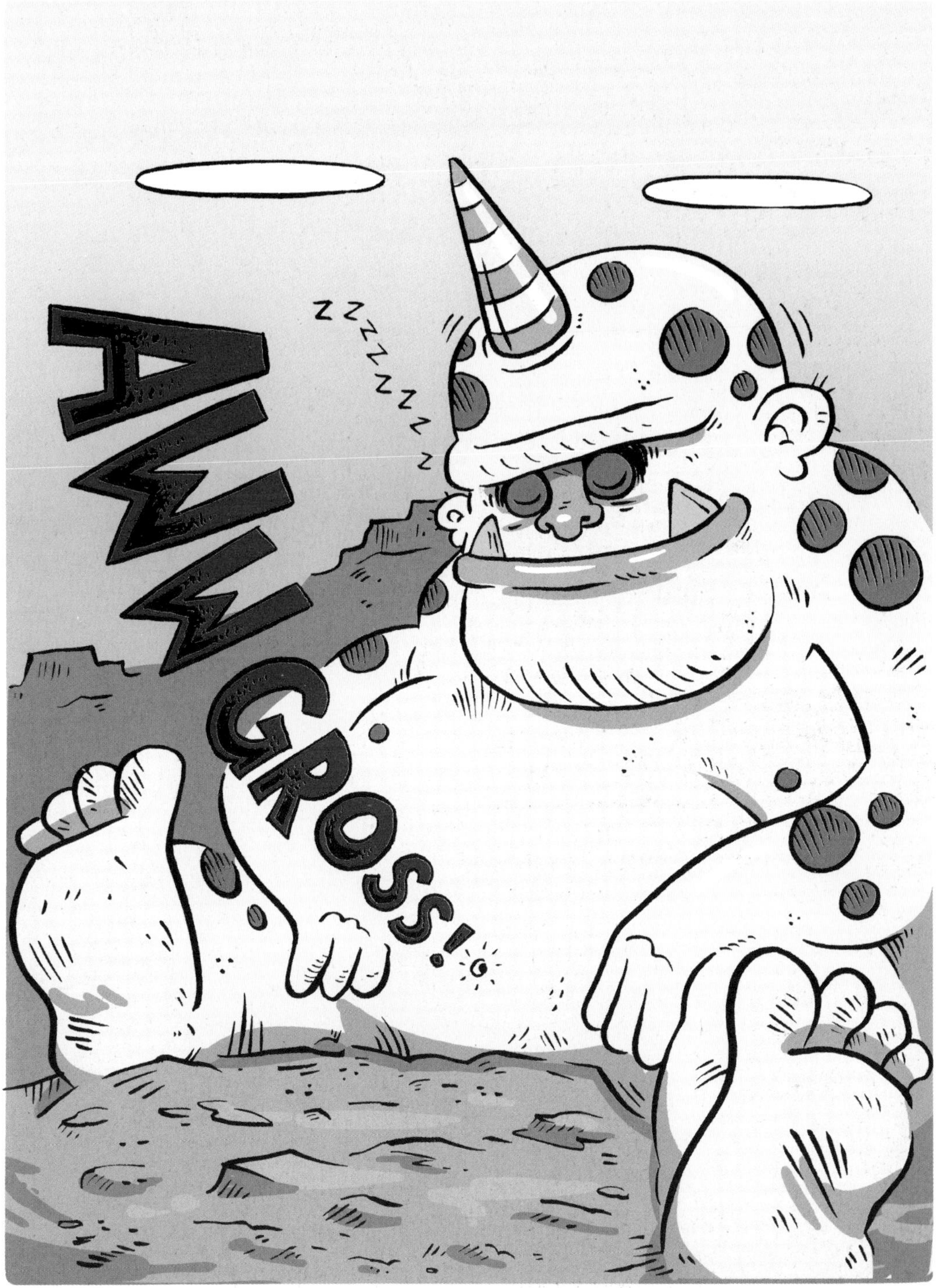

Z Z Z Z Z Z Z Z Z
AWW GROSS!

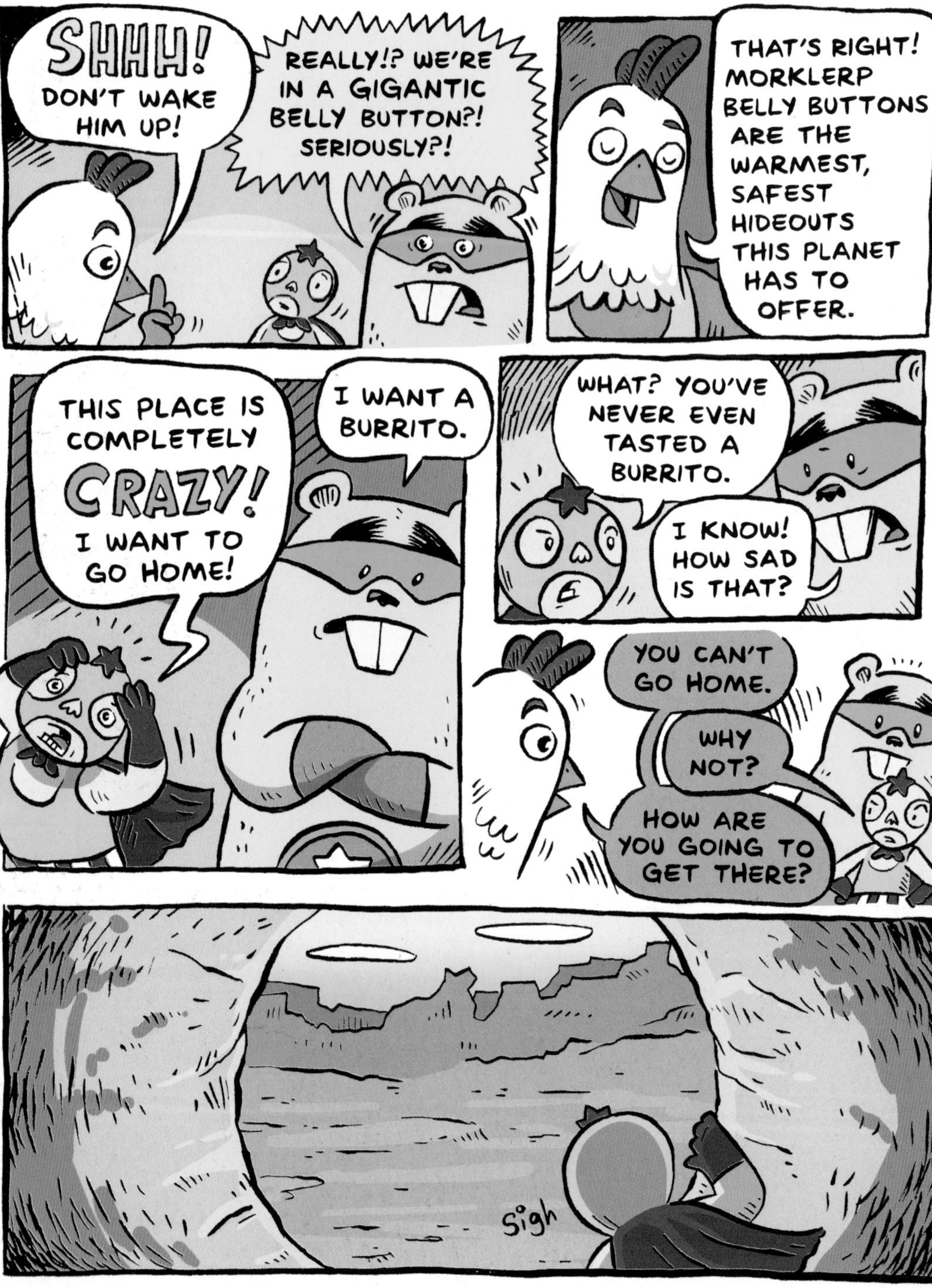
SHHH! DON'T WAKE HIM UP!
REALLY!? WE'RE IN A GIGANTIC BELLY BUTTON?! SERIOUSLY?!
THAT'S RIGHT! MORKLERP BELLY BUTTONS ARE THE WARMEST, SAFEST HIDEOUTS THIS PLANET HAS TO OFFER.
THIS PLACE IS COMPLETELY CRAZY! I WANT TO GO HOME!
I WANT A BURRITO.
WHAT? YOU'VE NEVER EVEN TASTED A BURRITO.
I KNOW! HOW SAD IS THAT?
YOU CAN'T GO HOME.
WHY NOT?
HOW ARE YOU GOING TO GET THERE?
Sigh

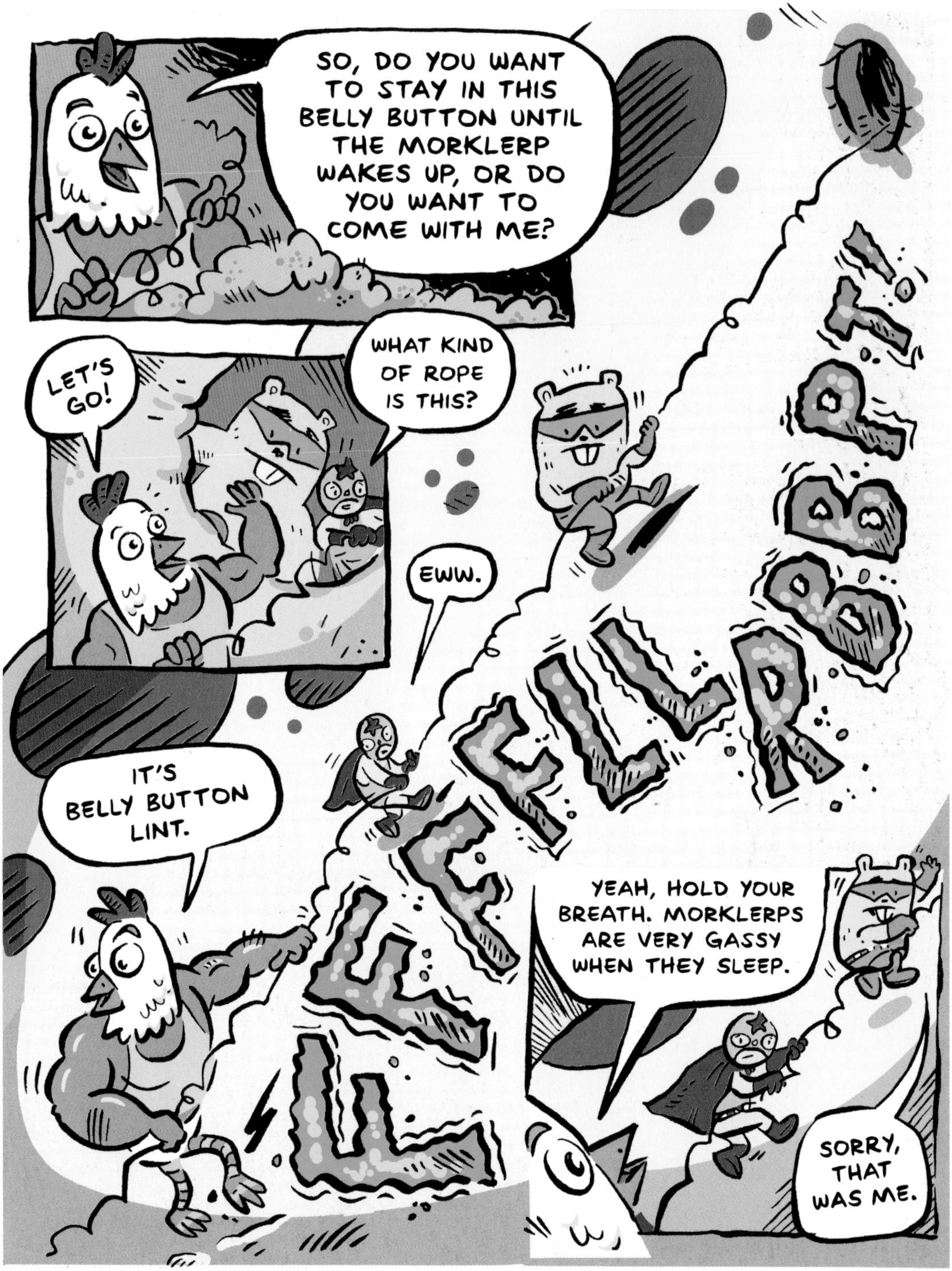
SO, DO YOU WANT TO STAY IN THIS BELLY BUTTON UNTIL THE MORKLERP WAKES UP, OR DO YOU WANT TO COME WITH ME?
LET'S GO!
WHAT KIND OF ROPE IS THIS?
EWW.
IT'S BELLY BUTTON LINT.
EEFFLLRBBBPT!!
YEAH, HOLD YOUR BREATH. MORKLERPS ARE VERY GASSY WHEN THEY SLEEP.
SORRY, THAT WAS ME.

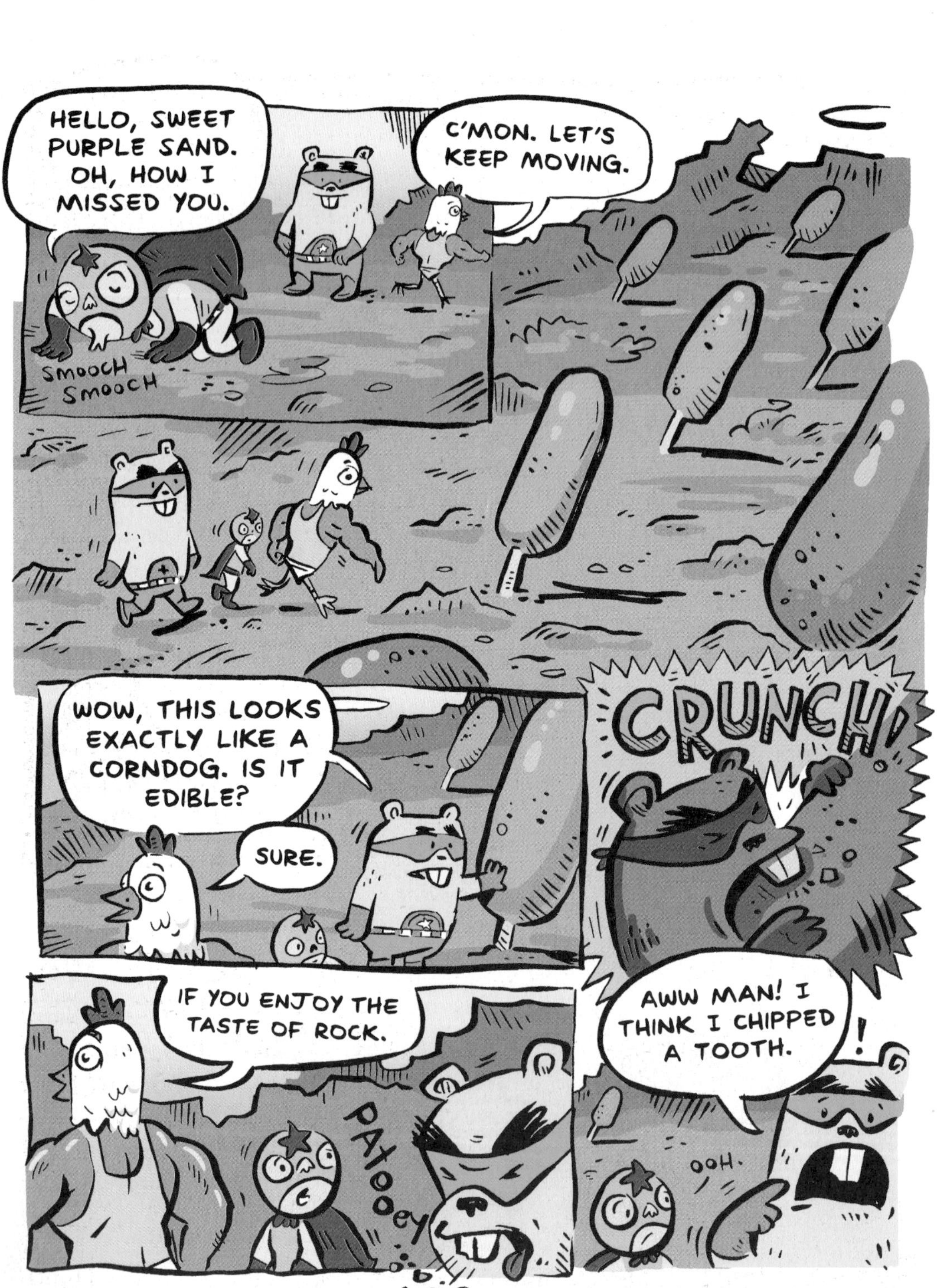

HELLO, SWEET PURPLE SAND. OH, HOW I MISSED YOU.
C'MON. LET'S KEEP MOVING.
SMOOCH SMOOCH
WOW, THIS LOOKS EXACTLY LIKE A CORNDOG. IS IT EDIBLE?
SURE.
CRUNCH!
IF YOU ENJOY THE TASTE OF ROCK.
PATOOEY
AWW MAN! I THINK I CHIPPED A TOOTH.
OOH.
!

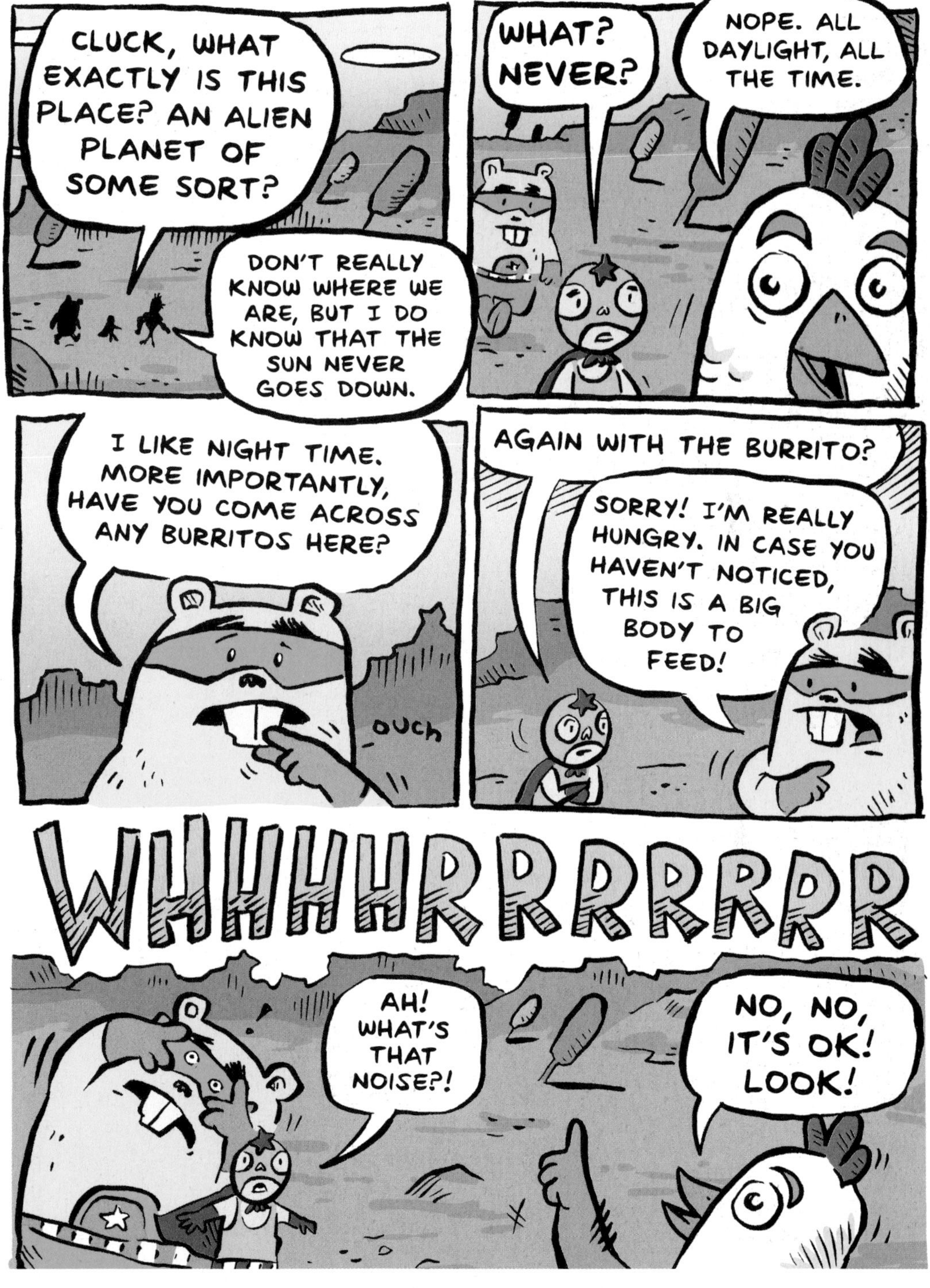
CLUCK, WHAT EXACTLY IS THIS PLACE? AN ALIEN PLANET OF SOME SORT?
DON'T REALLY KNOW WHERE WE ARE, BUT I DO KNOW THAT THE SUN NEVER GOES DOWN.
WHAT? NEVER?
NOPE. ALL DAYLIGHT, ALL THE TIME.
I LIKE NIGHT TIME. MORE IMPORTANTLY, HAVE YOU COME ACROSS ANY BURRITOS HERE?
ouch
AGAIN WITH THE BURRITO?
SORRY! I'M REALLY HUNGRY. IN CASE YOU HAVEN'T NOTICED, THIS IS A BIG BODY TO FEED!
WHHHHRRRRRRR
AH! WHAT'S THAT NOISE?!
NO, NO, IT'S OK! LOOK!

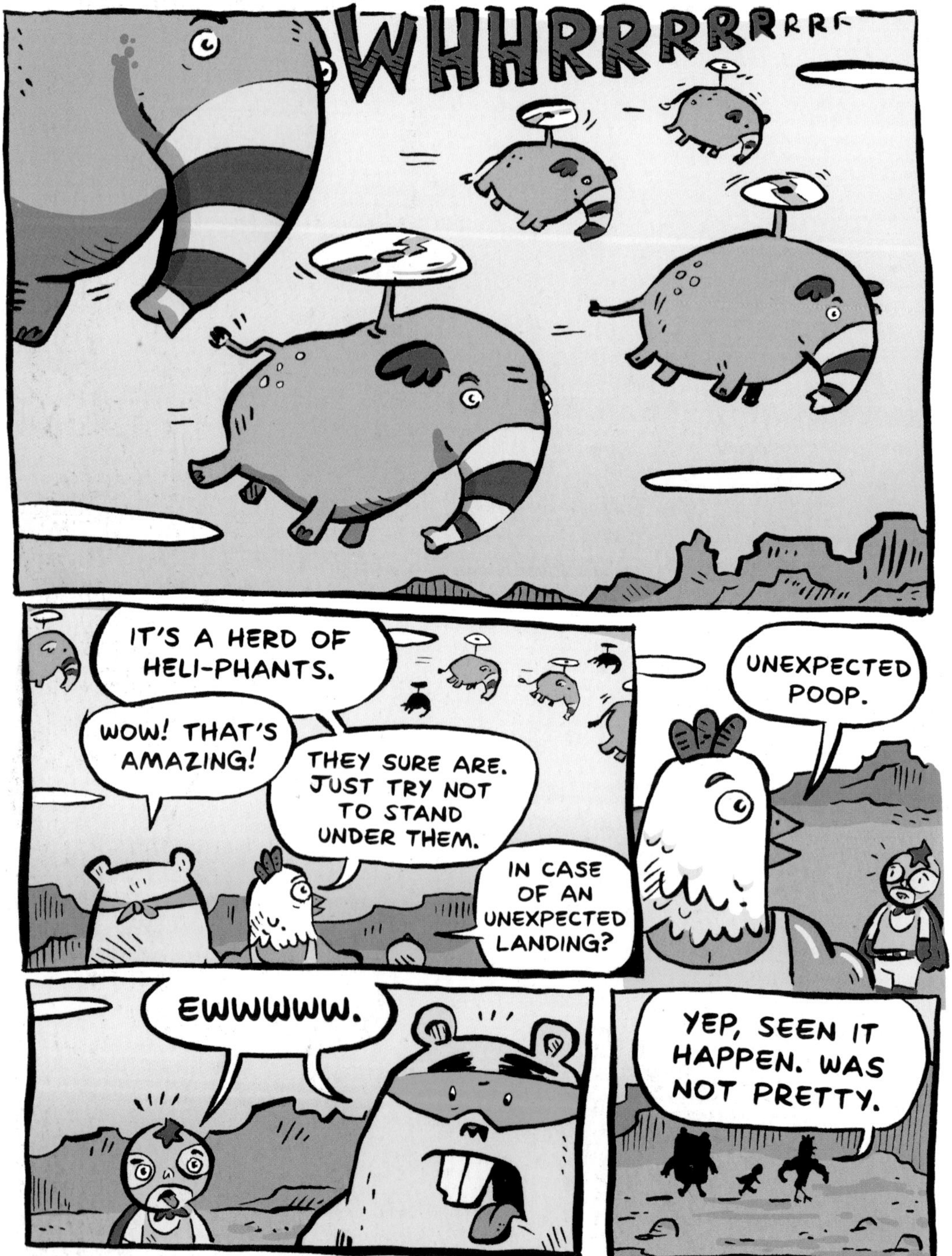
WHHRRRRRRRF
IT'S A HERD OF HELI-PHANTS.
WOW! THAT'S AMAZING!
THEY SURE ARE. JUST TRY NOT TO STAND UNDER THEM.
IN CASE OF AN UNEXPECTED LANDING?
UNEXPECTED POOP.
EWWWWW.
YEP, SEEN IT HAPPEN. WAS NOT PRETTY.

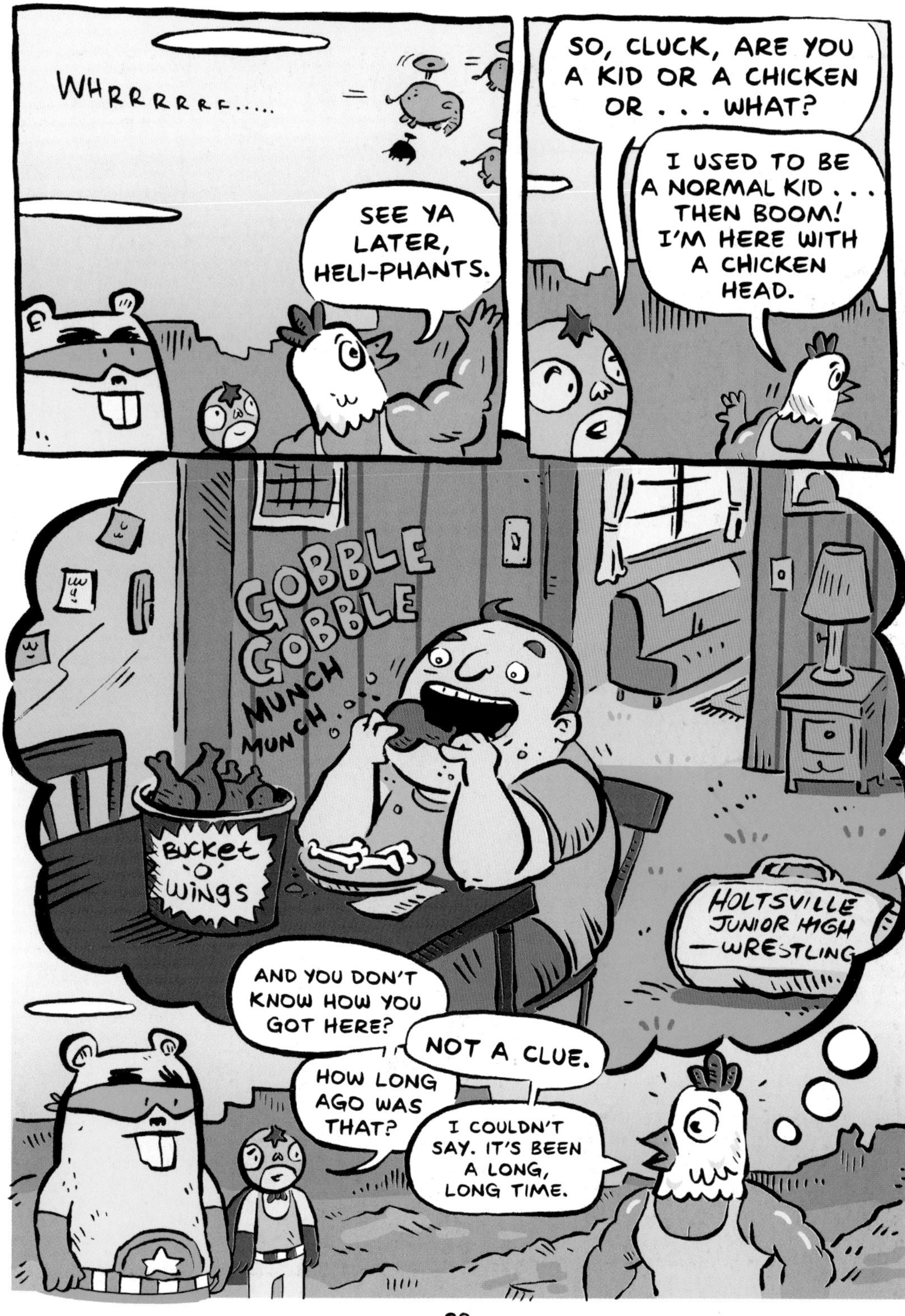
WHRRRRRF.....
SEE YA LATER, HELI-PHANTS.
SO, CLUCK, ARE YOU A KID OR A CHICKEN OR . . . WHAT?
I USED TO BE A NORMAL KID . . . THEN BOOM! I'M HERE WITH A CHICKEN HEAD.
GOBBLE GOBBLE
MUNCH MUNCH
BUCKET-O-WINGS
HOLTSVILLE JUNIOR HIGH —WRESTLING
AND YOU DON'T KNOW HOW YOU GOT HERE?
NOT A CLUE.
HOW LONG AGO WAS THAT?
I COULDN'T SAY. IT'S BEEN A LONG, LONG TIME.

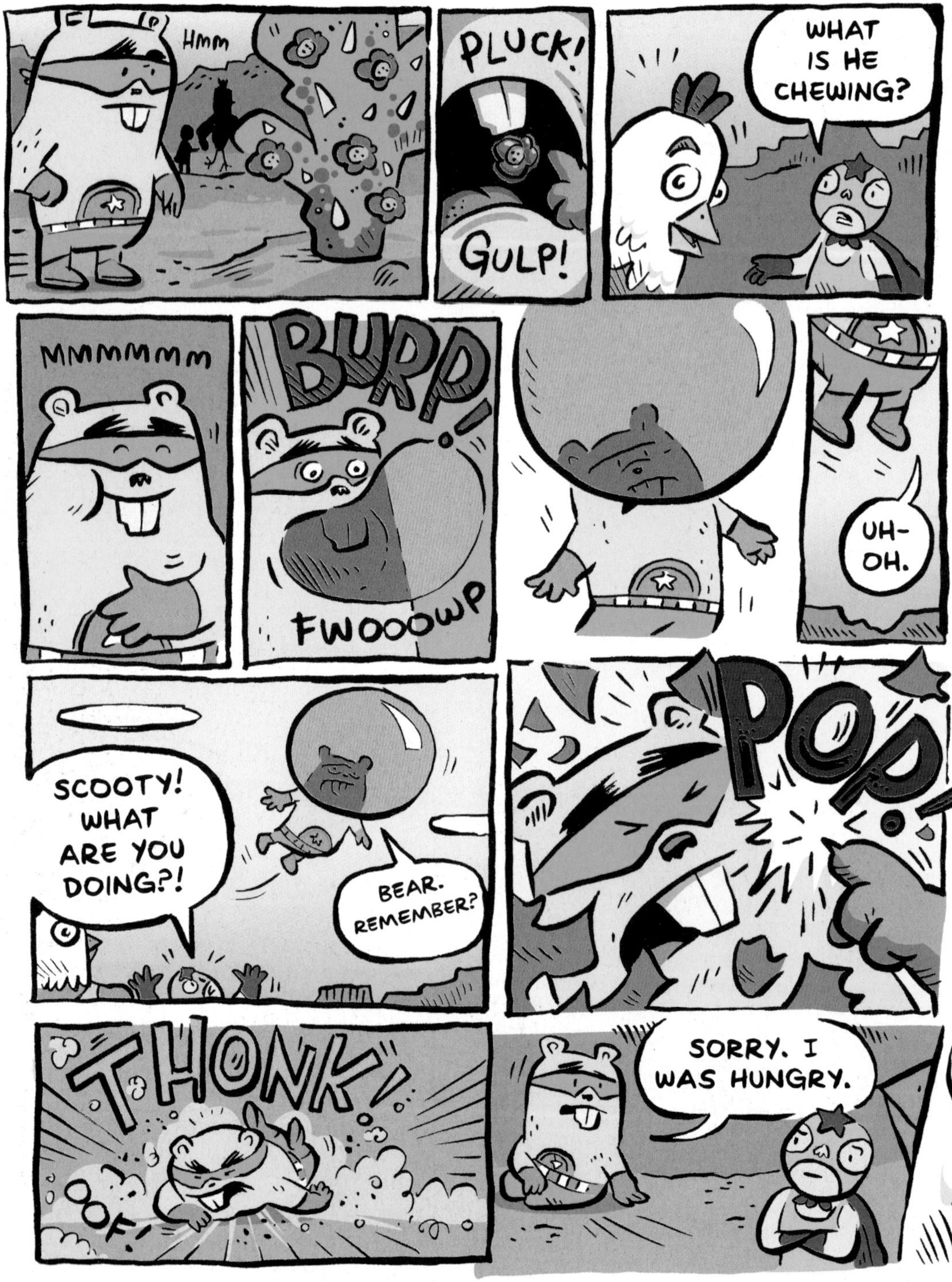
HMM
PLUCK!
GULP!
WHAT IS HE CHEWING?
MMMMMMM
BURP!
FWOOOWP
UH-OH.
SCOOTY! WHAT ARE YOU DOING?!
BEAR. REMEMBER?
POP!
THONK!
OOF!
SORRY. I WAS HUNGRY.

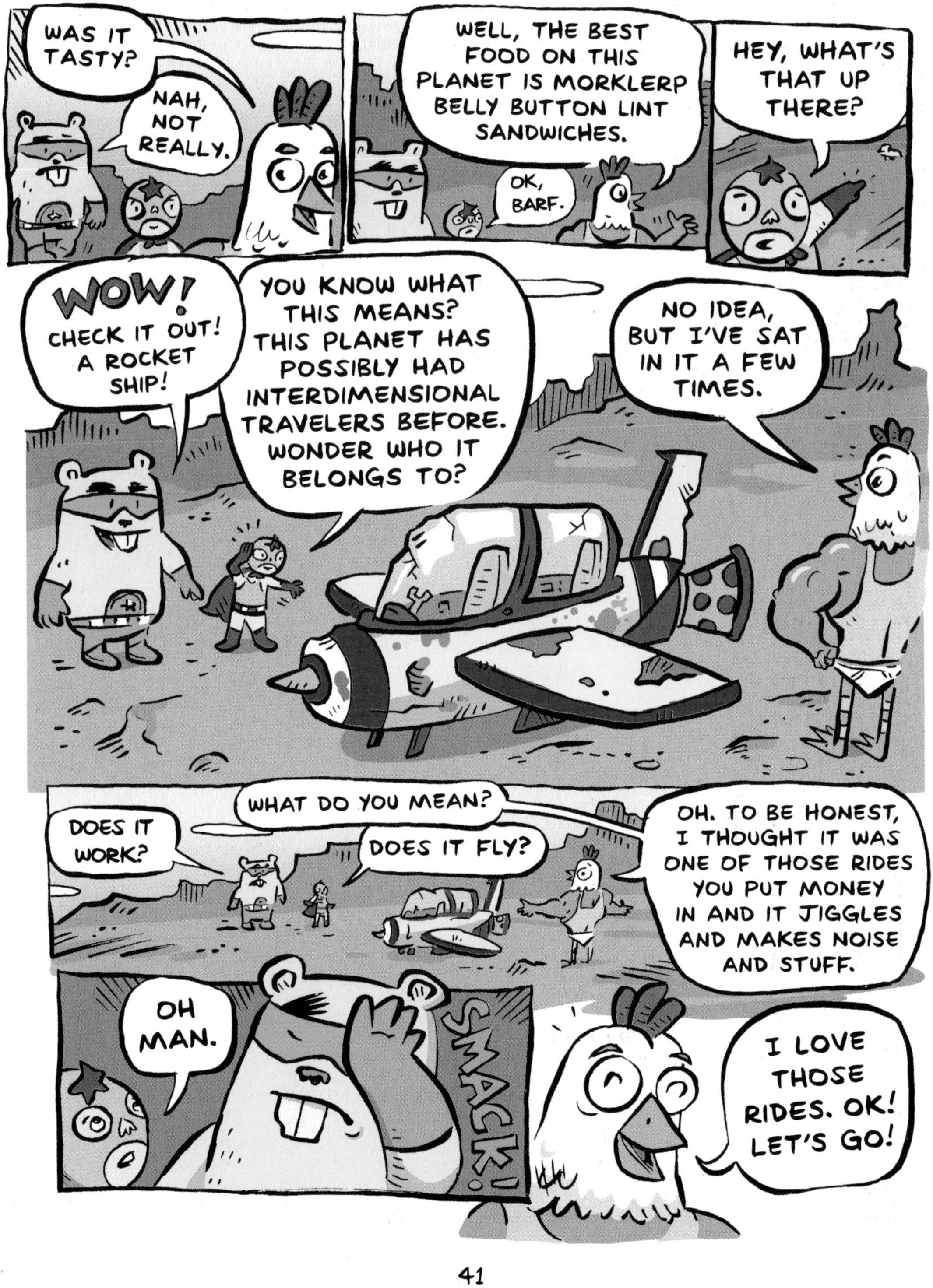

WAS IT TASTY?
NAH, NOT REALLY.
WELL, THE BEST FOOD ON THIS PLANET IS MORKLERP BELLY BUTTON LINT SANDWICHES.
OK, BARF.
HEY, WHAT'S THAT UP THERE?
WOW! CHECK IT OUT! A ROCKET SHIP!
YOU KNOW WHAT THIS MEANS? THIS PLANET HAS POSSIBLY HAD INTERDIMENSIONAL TRAVELERS BEFORE. WONDER WHO IT BELONGS TO?
NO IDEA, BUT I'VE SAT IN IT A FEW TIMES.
DOES IT WORK?
WHAT DO YOU MEAN?
DOES IT FLY?
OH. TO BE HONEST, I THOUGHT IT WAS ONE OF THOSE RIDES YOU PUT MONEY IN AND IT JIGGLES AND MAKES NOISE AND STUFF.
OH MAN.
SMACK!
I LOVE THOSE RIDES. OK! LET'S GO!

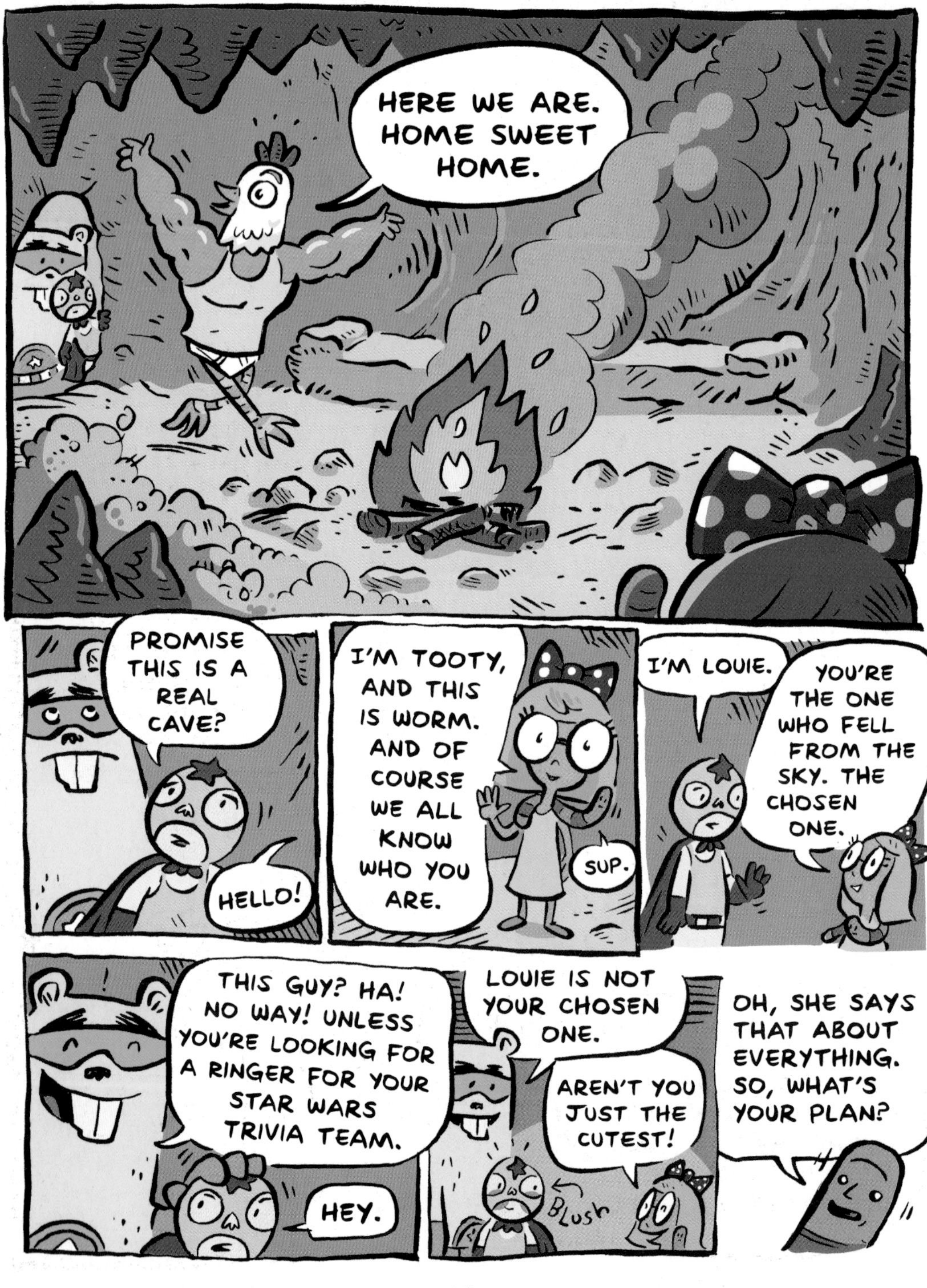
HERE WE ARE. HOME SWEET HOME.
PROMISE THIS IS A REAL CAVE?
HELLO!
I'M TOOTY, AND THIS IS WORM. AND OF COURSE WE ALL KNOW WHO YOU ARE.
SUP.
I'M LOUIE.
YOU'RE THE ONE WHO FELL FROM THE SKY. THE CHOSEN ONE.
THIS GUY? HA! NO WAY! UNLESS YOU'RE LOOKING FOR A RINGER FOR YOUR STAR WARS TRIVIA TEAM.
HEY.
LOUIE IS NOT YOUR CHOSEN ONE.
AREN'T YOU JUST THE CUTEST!
BLUSH
OH, SHE SAYS THAT ABOUT EVERYTHING. SO, WHAT'S YOUR PLAN?

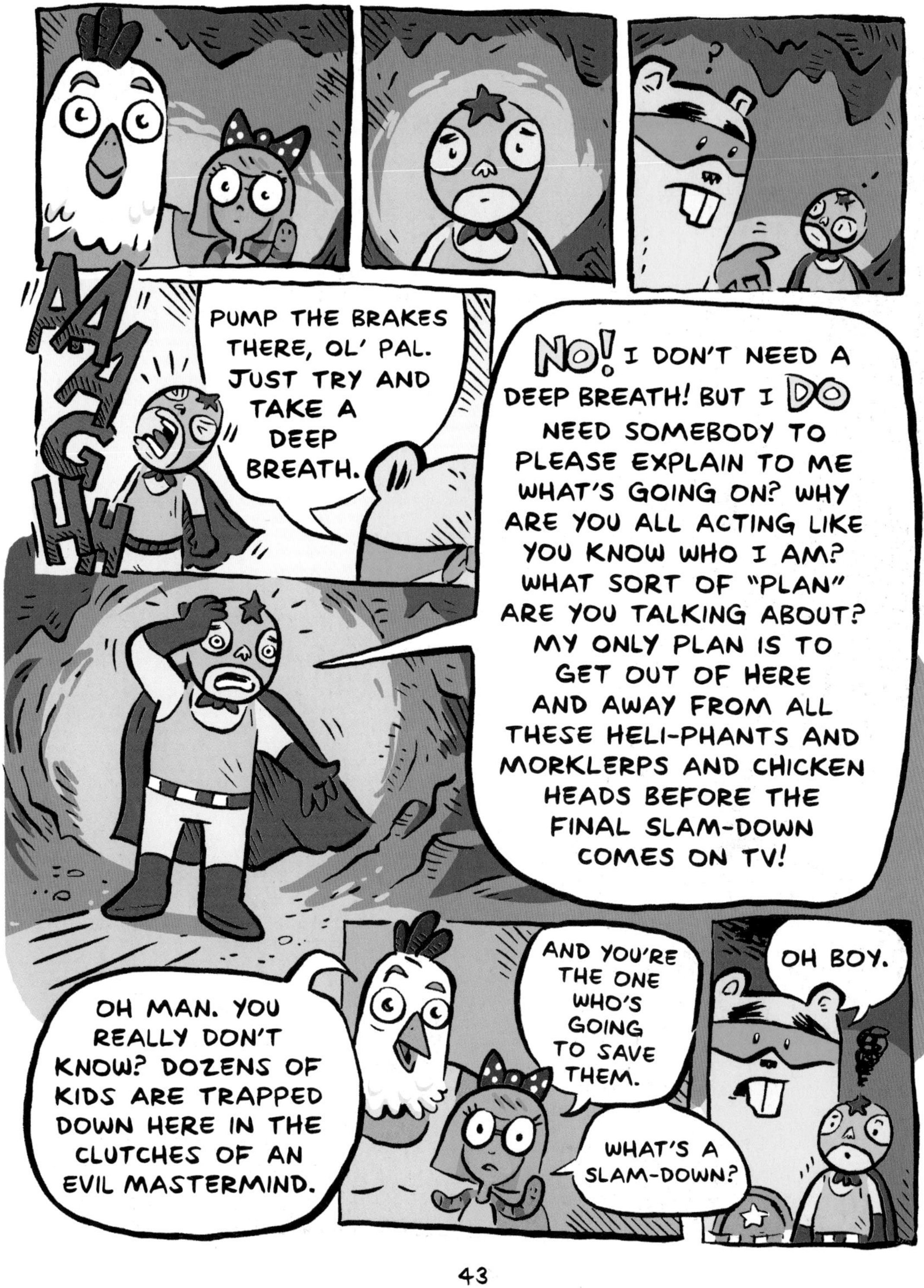
AAAGHH
PUMP THE BRAKES THERE, OL' PAL. JUST TRY AND TAKE A DEEP BREATH.
NO! I DON'T NEED A DEEP BREATH! BUT I DO NEED SOMEBODY TO PLEASE EXPLAIN TO ME WHAT'S GOING ON? WHY ARE YOU ALL ACTING LIKE YOU KNOW WHO I AM? WHAT SORT OF "PLAN" ARE YOU TALKING ABOUT? MY ONLY PLAN IS TO GET OUT OF HERE AND AWAY FROM ALL THESE HELI-PHANTS AND MORKLERPS AND CHICKEN HEADS BEFORE THE FINAL SLAM-DOWN COMES ON TV!
OH MAN. YOU REALLY DON'T KNOW? DOZENS OF KIDS ARE TRAPPED DOWN HERE IN THE CLUTCHES OF AN EVIL MASTERMIND.
AND YOU'RE THE ONE WHO'S GOING TO SAVE THEM.
WHAT'S A SLAM-DOWN?
OH BOY.

CHAPTER 4

MOO.

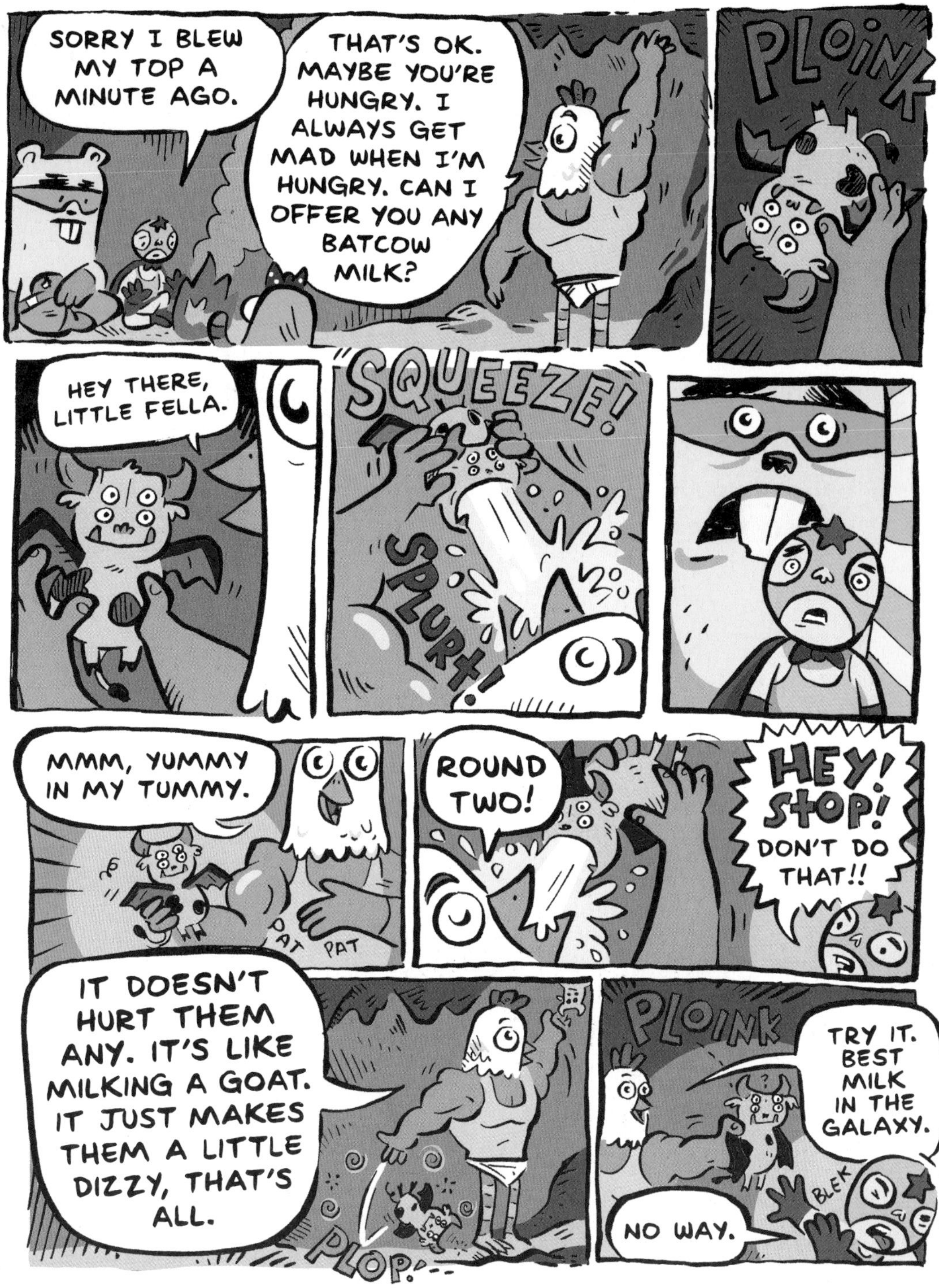
SORRY I BLEW MY TOP A MINUTE AGO.
THAT'S OK. MAYBE YOU'RE HUNGRY. I ALWAYS GET MAD WHEN I'M HUNGRY. CAN I OFFER YOU ANY BATCOW MILK?
PLOINK
HEY THERE, LITTLE FELLA.
SQUEEZE!
SPLURT!
MMM, YUMMY IN MY TUMMY.
PAT PAT
ROUND TWO!
HEY! STOP! DON'T DO THAT!!
IT DOESN'T HURT THEM ANY. IT'S LIKE MILKING A GOAT. IT JUST MAKES THEM A LITTLE DIZZY, THAT'S ALL.
PLOP!
PLOINK
TRY IT. BEST MILK IN THE GALAXY.
BLEK
NO WAY.

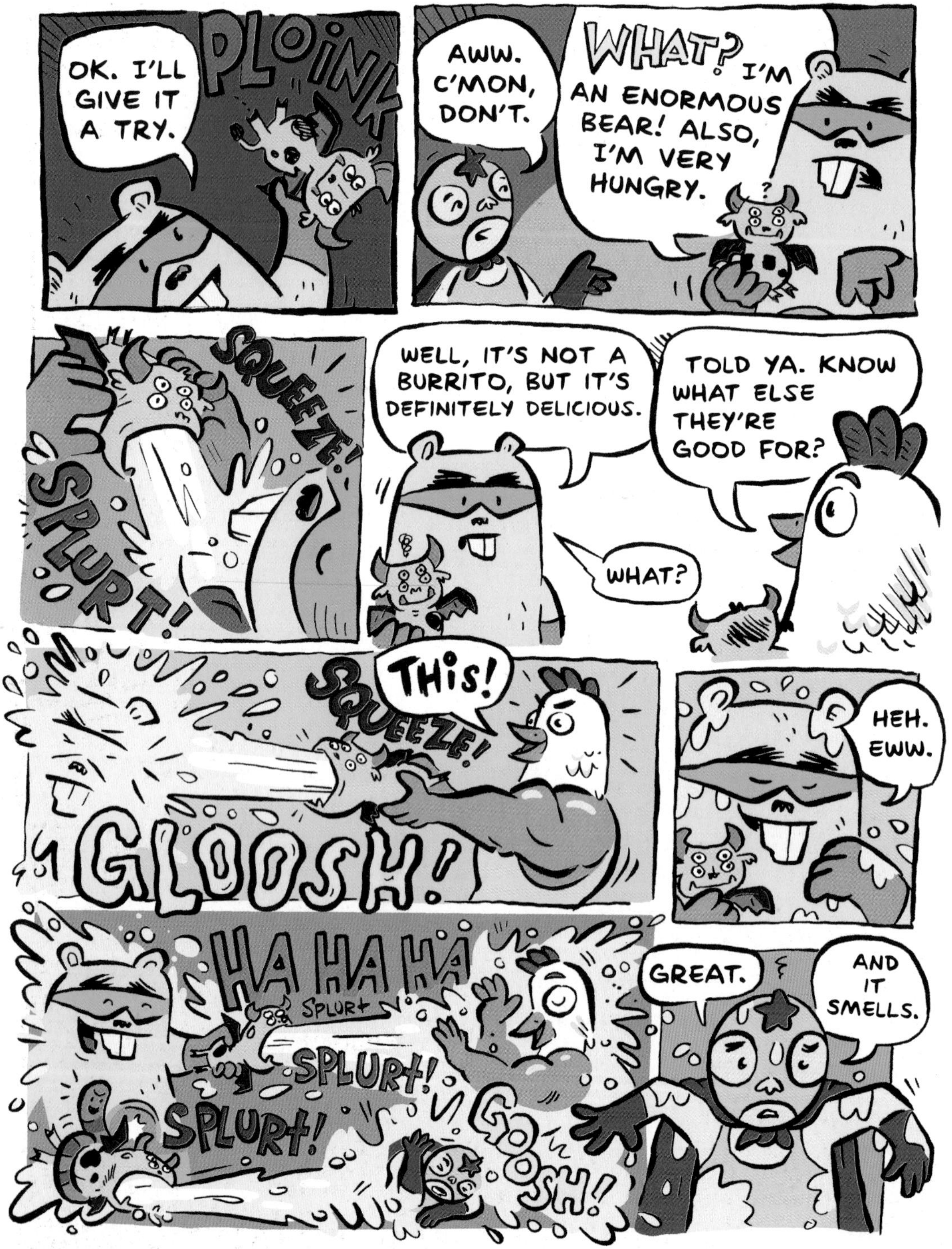
OK. I'LL GIVE IT A TRY.
PLOINK
AWW. C'MON, DON'T.
WHAT? I'M AN ENORMOUS BEAR! ALSO, I'M VERY HUNGRY.
SQUEEEZE!
SPLURT!
WELL, IT'S NOT A BURRITO, BUT IT'S DEFINITELY DELICIOUS.
TOLD YA. KNOW WHAT ELSE THEY'RE GOOD FOR?
WHAT?
THIS!
SQUEEEZE!
GLOOSH!
HEH. EWW.
HA HA HA
SPLURT
SPLURT!
SPLURT!
GLOOSH!
GREAT.
AND IT SMELLS.

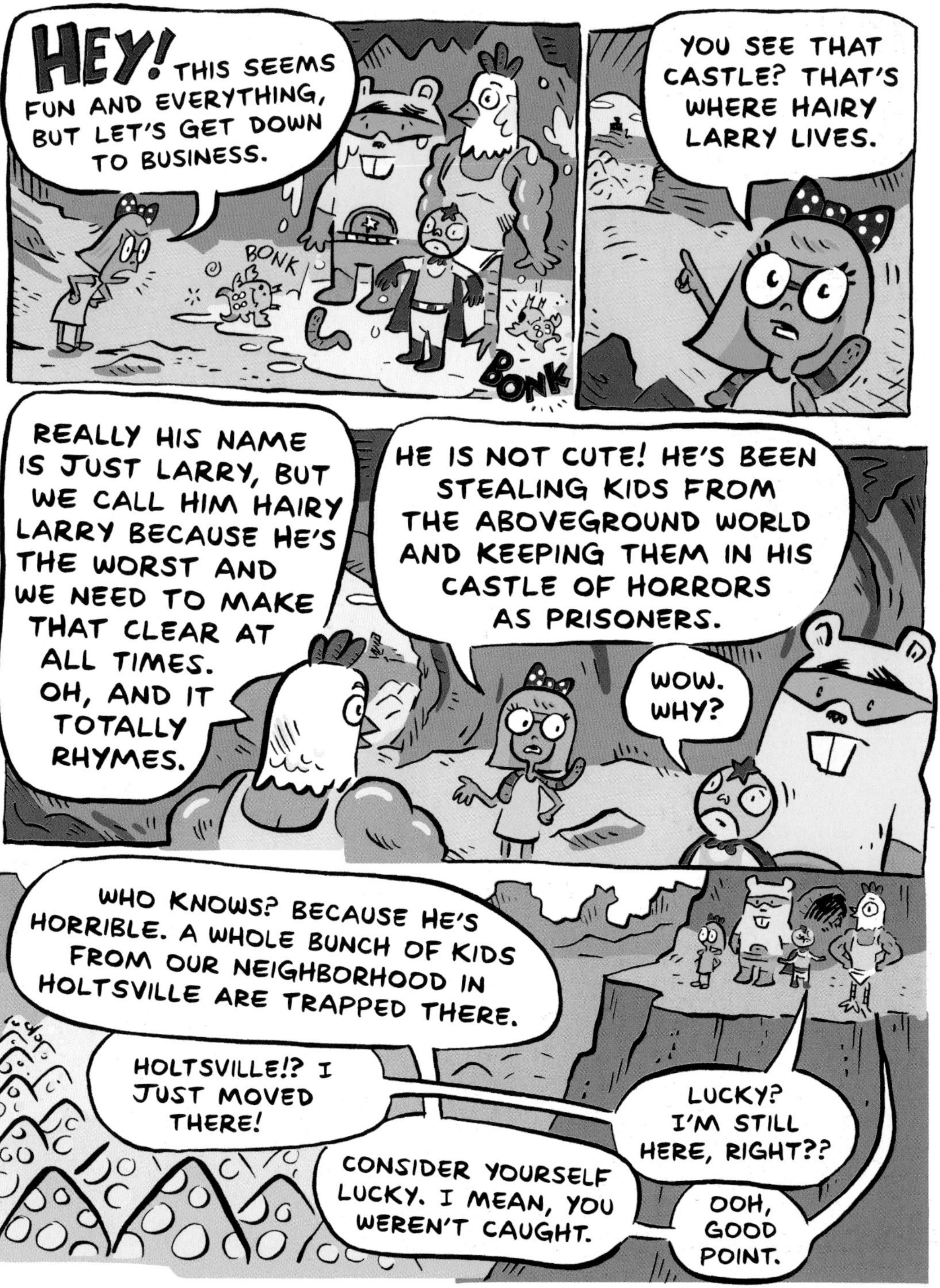
HEY! THIS SEEMS FUN AND EVERYTHING, BUT LET'S GET DOWN TO BUSINESS.
BONK
BONK
YOU SEE THAT CASTLE? THAT'S WHERE HAIRY LARRY LIVES.
REALLY HIS NAME IS JUST LARRY, BUT WE CALL HIM HAIRY LARRY BECAUSE HE'S THE WORST AND WE NEED TO MAKE THAT CLEAR AT ALL TIMES. OH, AND IT TOTALLY RHYMES.
HE IS NOT CUTE! HE'S BEEN STEALING KIDS FROM THE ABOVEGROUND WORLD AND KEEPING THEM IN HIS CASTLE OF HORRORS AS PRISONERS.
WOW. WHY?
WHO KNOWS? BECAUSE HE'S HORRIBLE. A WHOLE BUNCH OF KIDS FROM OUR NEIGHBORHOOD IN HOLTSVILLE ARE TRAPPED THERE.
HOLTSVILLE!? I JUST MOVED THERE!
CONSIDER YOURSELF LUCKY. I MEAN, YOU WEREN'T CAUGHT.
LUCKY? I'M STILL HERE, RIGHT??
OOH, GOOD POINT.

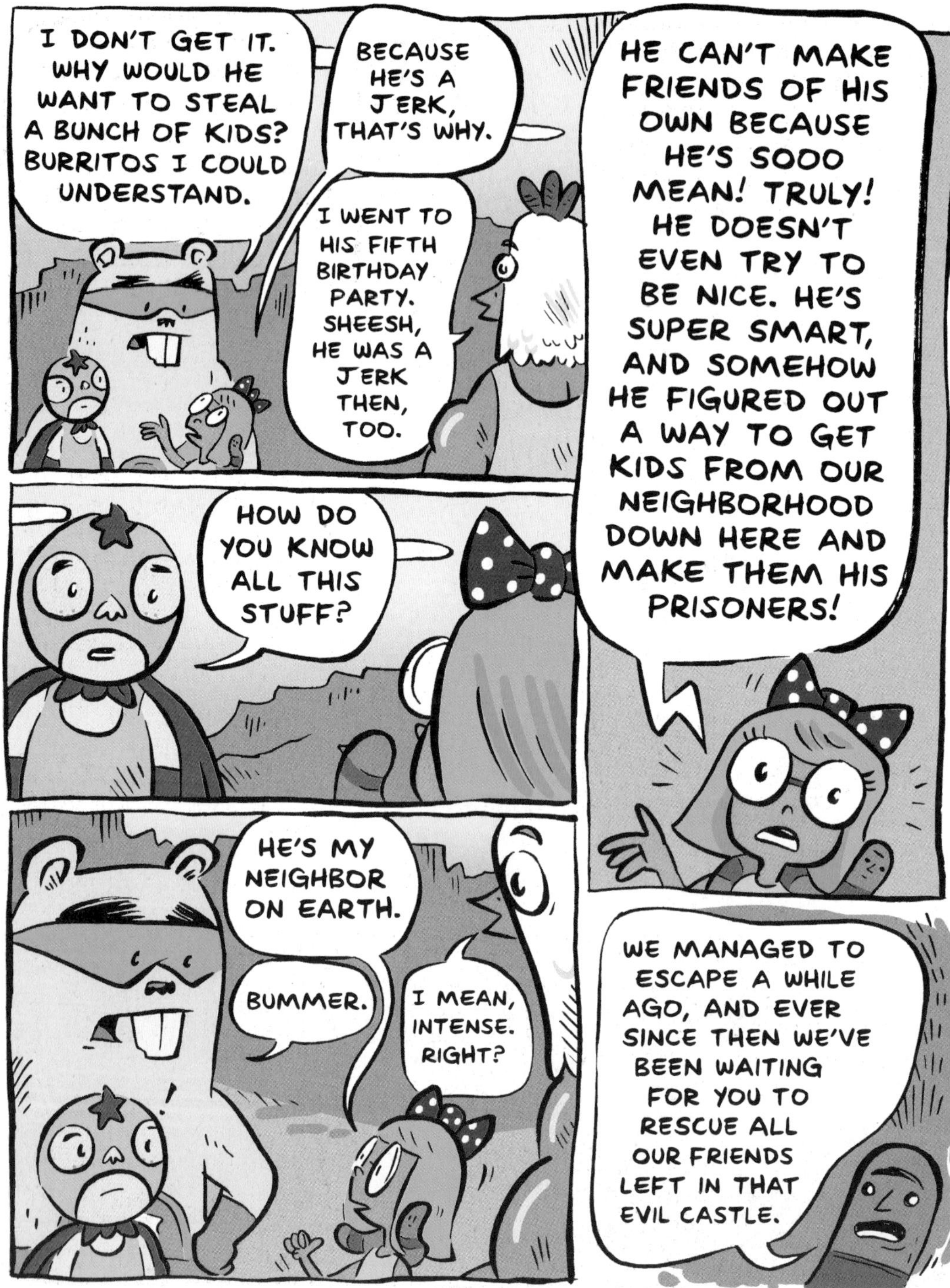
I DON'T GET IT. WHY WOULD HE WANT TO STEAL A BUNCH OF KIDS? BURRITOS I COULD UNDERSTAND.
BECAUSE HE'S A JERK, THAT'S WHY.
I WENT TO HIS FIFTH BIRTHDAY PARTY. SHEESH, HE WAS A JERK THEN, TOO.
HOW DO YOU KNOW ALL THIS STUFF?
HE'S MY NEIGHBOR ON EARTH.
BUMMER.
I MEAN, INTENSE. RIGHT?
HE CAN'T MAKE FRIENDS OF HIS OWN BECAUSE HE'S SOOO MEAN! TRULY! HE DOESN'T EVEN TRY TO BE NICE. HE'S SUPER SMART, AND SOMEHOW HE FIGURED OUT A WAY TO GET KIDS FROM OUR NEIGHBORHOOD DOWN HERE AND MAKE THEM HIS PRISONERS!
WE MANAGED TO ESCAPE A WHILE AGO, AND EVER SINCE THEN WE'VE BEEN WAITING FOR YOU TO RESCUE ALL OUR FRIENDS LEFT IN THAT EVIL CASTLE.

LOOK, IT'S SAD THAT A TON OF KIDS ARE BEING HELD CAPTIVE BY A HAIRY MANIAC, BUT I HAVE NO IDEA WHAT I COULD DO ABOUT IT. YOU MUST BE WAITING FOR SOMEBODY ELSE.

NOPE, IT'S DEFINITELY YOU. WE SAW IT IN THE BERRYPOP ORBS.

I'M SORRY. COME AGAIN?

BERRYPOPS ARE THESE CRITTERS WHO PROPHESIZE THE FUTURE WITH THESE FLOATING SPHERE THINGS. A WHILE AGO, THEY PREDICTED AN EXACT IMAGE OF YOUR FACE. THEY EVEN SHOWED A PICTURE OF A BEAR SIDEKICK, AND THEY SHOWED YOU DEFEATING HAIRY LARRY AND FREEING ALL OUR FRIENDS.

HA! RIGHT, AND WHO WOULDN'T TRUST PICTURES IN RANDOM SPHERE THINGS?

AND WHO'S TO SAY I'M HIS SIDEKICK?

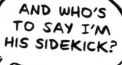

IT DOESN'T MATTER. THE BERRYPOPS ARE NEVER EVER WRONG.

DID THE ORBS SHOW YOU HOW I'M SUPPOSED TO DO ALL THAT?

NO.

HMPH

SPLURT!

WELL, IT SOUNDS NUTTY IF YOU ASK ME.

owie

BONK!

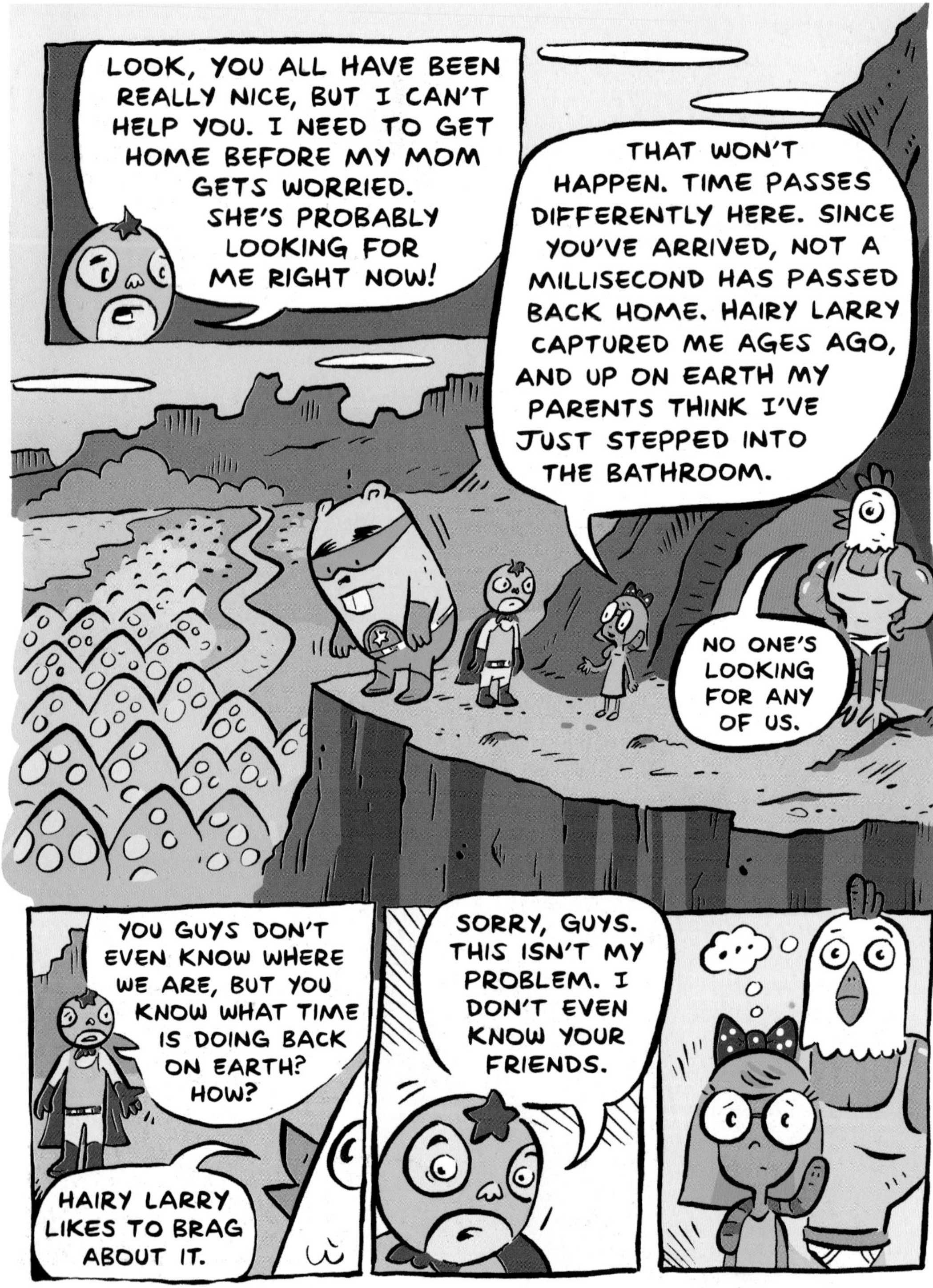
LOOK, YOU ALL HAVE BEEN REALLY NICE, BUT I CAN'T HELP YOU. I NEED TO GET HOME BEFORE MY MOM GETS WORRIED. SHE'S PROBABLY LOOKING FOR ME RIGHT NOW!
THAT WON'T HAPPEN. TIME PASSES DIFFERENTLY HERE. SINCE YOU'VE ARRIVED, NOT A MILLISECOND HAS PASSED BACK HOME. HAIRY LARRY CAPTURED ME AGES AGO, AND UP ON EARTH MY PARENTS THINK I'VE JUST STEPPED INTO THE BATHROOM.
NO ONE'S LOOKING FOR ANY OF US.
YOU GUYS DON'T EVEN KNOW WHERE WE ARE, BUT YOU KNOW WHAT TIME IS DOING BACK ON EARTH? HOW?
HAIRY LARRY LIKES TO BRAG ABOUT IT.
SORRY, GUYS. THIS ISN'T MY PROBLEM. I DON'T EVEN KNOW YOUR FRIENDS.

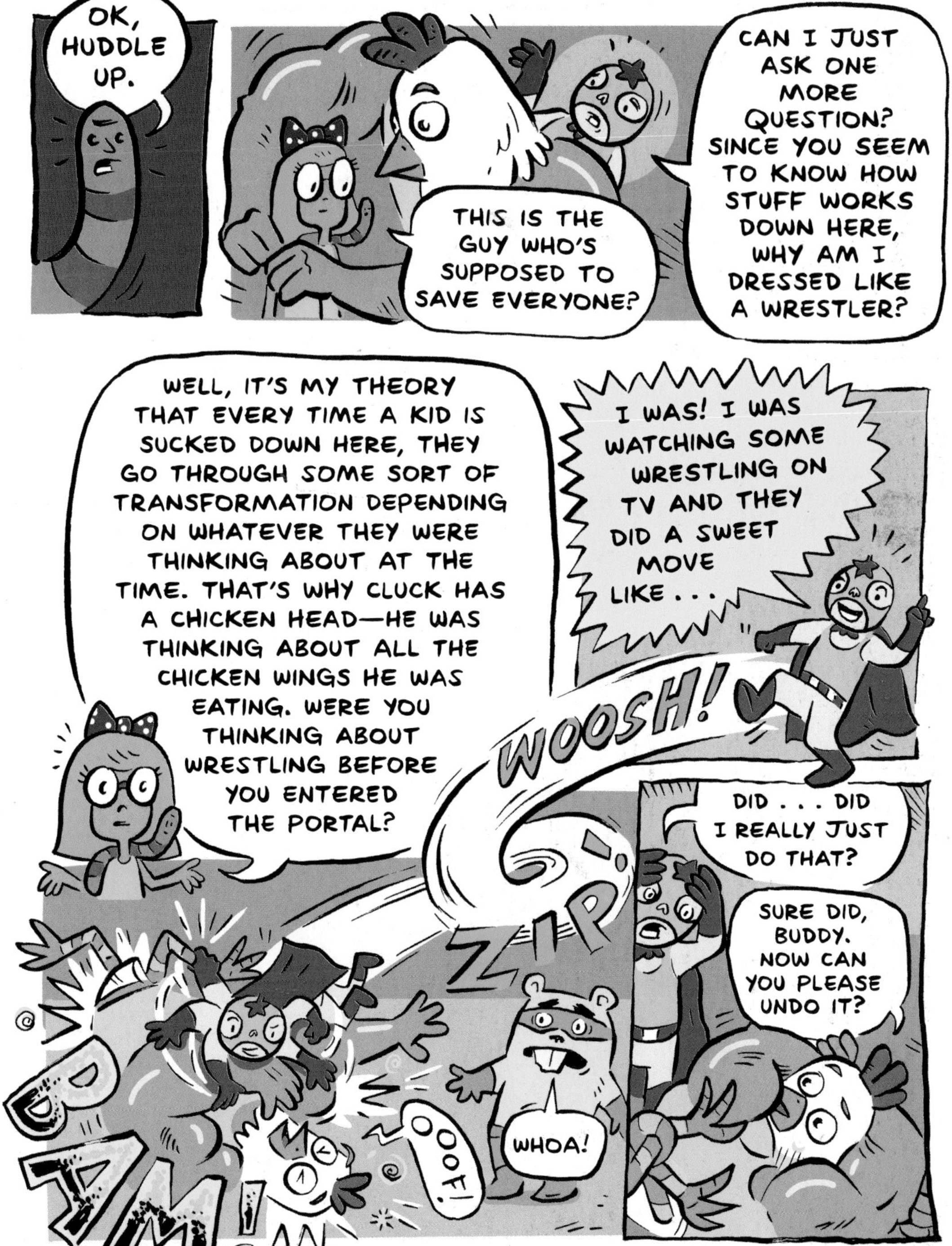
OK, HUDDLE UP.
THIS IS THE GUY WHO'S SUPPOSED TO SAVE EVERYONE?
CAN I JUST ASK ONE MORE QUESTION? SINCE YOU SEEM TO KNOW HOW STUFF WORKS DOWN HERE, WHY AM I DRESSED LIKE A WRESTLER?
WELL, IT'S MY THEORY THAT EVERY TIME A KID IS SUCKED DOWN HERE, THEY GO THROUGH SOME SORT OF TRANSFORMATION DEPENDING ON WHATEVER THEY WERE THINKING ABOUT AT THE TIME. THAT'S WHY CLUCK HAS A CHICKEN HEAD—HE WAS THINKING ABOUT ALL THE CHICKEN WINGS HE WAS EATING. WERE YOU THINKING ABOUT WRESTLING BEFORE YOU ENTERED THE PORTAL?
I WAS! I WAS WATCHING SOME WRESTLING ON TV AND THEY DID A SWEET MOVE LIKE . . .
WOOSH!
ZIP!
BAM!
OOOF!
WHOA!
DID . . . DID I REALLY JUST DO THAT?
SURE DID, BUDDY. NOW CAN YOU PLEASE UNDO IT?

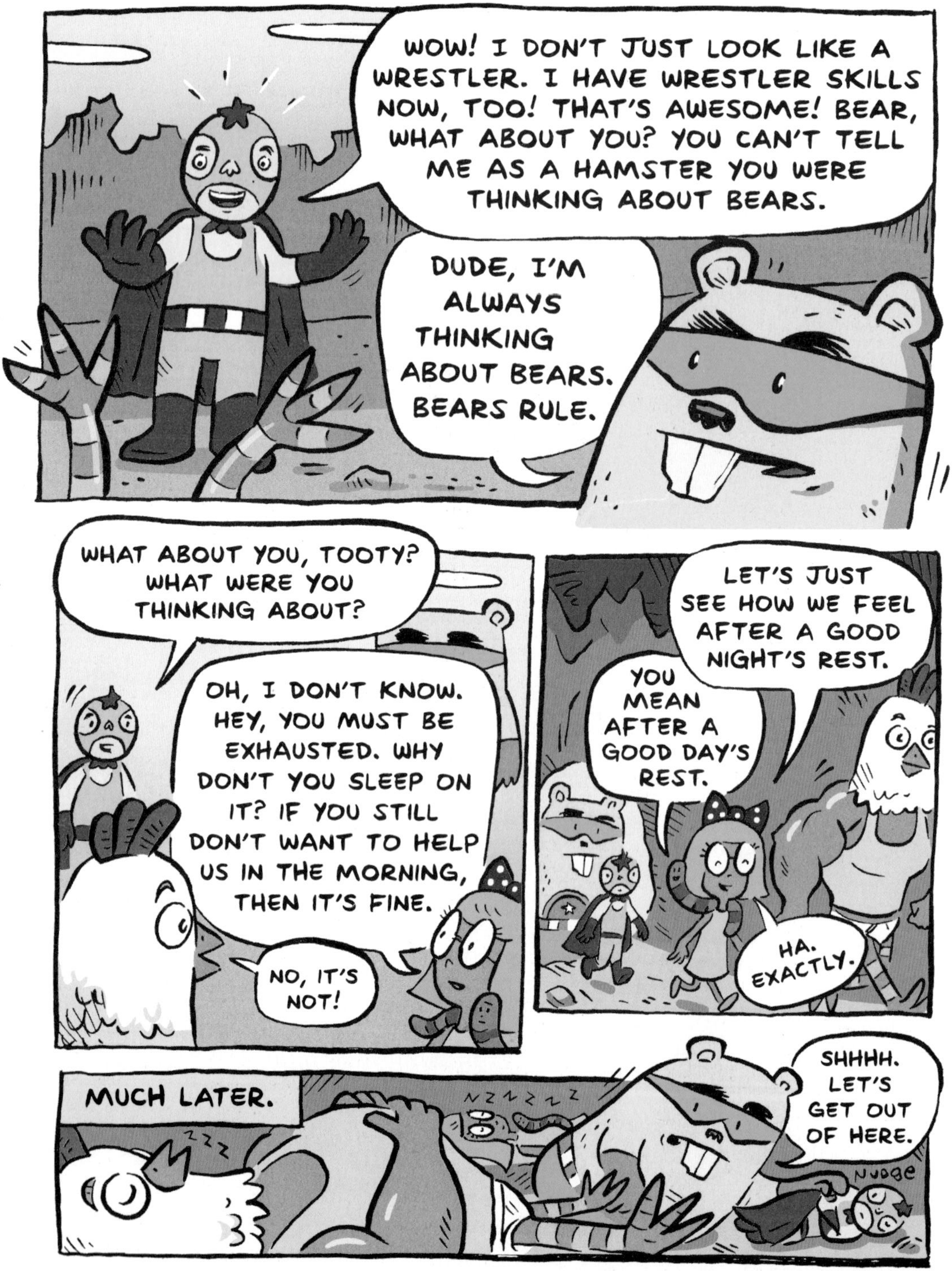
WOW! I DON'T JUST LOOK LIKE A WRESTLER. I HAVE WRESTLER SKILLS NOW, TOO! THAT'S AWESOME! BEAR, WHAT ABOUT YOU? YOU CAN'T TELL ME AS A HAMSTER YOU WERE THINKING ABOUT BEARS.
DUDE, I'M ALWAYS THINKING ABOUT BEARS. BEARS RULE.
WHAT ABOUT YOU, TOOTY? WHAT WERE YOU THINKING ABOUT?
OH, I DON'T KNOW. HEY, YOU MUST BE EXHAUSTED. WHY DON'T YOU SLEEP ON IT? IF YOU STILL DON'T WANT TO HELP US IN THE MORNING, THEN IT'S FINE.
NO, IT'S NOT!
LET'S JUST SEE HOW WE FEEL AFTER A GOOD NIGHT'S REST.
YOU MEAN AFTER A GOOD DAY'S REST.
HA. EXACTLY.
MUCH LATER.
SHHHH. LET'S GET OUT OF HERE.
NUDGE

CHAPTER 5

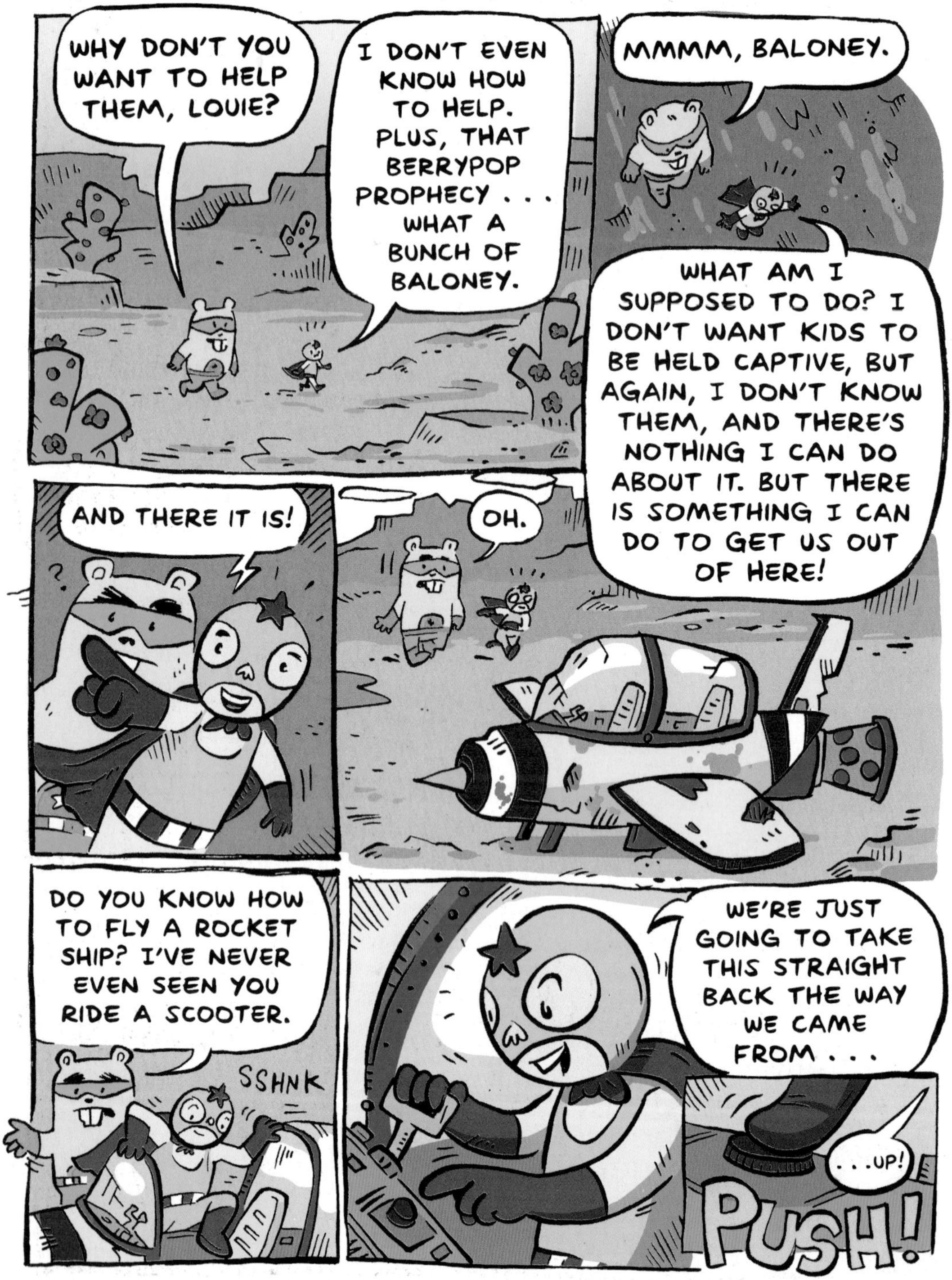
WHY DON'T YOU WANT TO HELP THEM, LOUIE?
I DON'T EVEN KNOW HOW TO HELP. PLUS, THAT BERRYPOP PROPHECY . . . WHAT A BUNCH OF BALONEY.
MMMM, BALONEY.
WHAT AM I SUPPOSED TO DO? I DON'T WANT KIDS TO BE HELD CAPTIVE, BUT AGAIN, I DON'T KNOW THEM, AND THERE'S NOTHING I CAN DO ABOUT IT. BUT THERE IS SOMETHING I CAN DO TO GET US OUT OF HERE!
AND THERE IT IS!
OH.
DO YOU KNOW HOW TO FLY A ROCKET SHIP? I'VE NEVER EVEN SEEN YOU RIDE A SCOOTER.
SSHNK
WE'RE JUST GOING TO TAKE THIS STRAIGHT BACK THE WAY WE CAME FROM . . .
. . .UP!
PUSH!

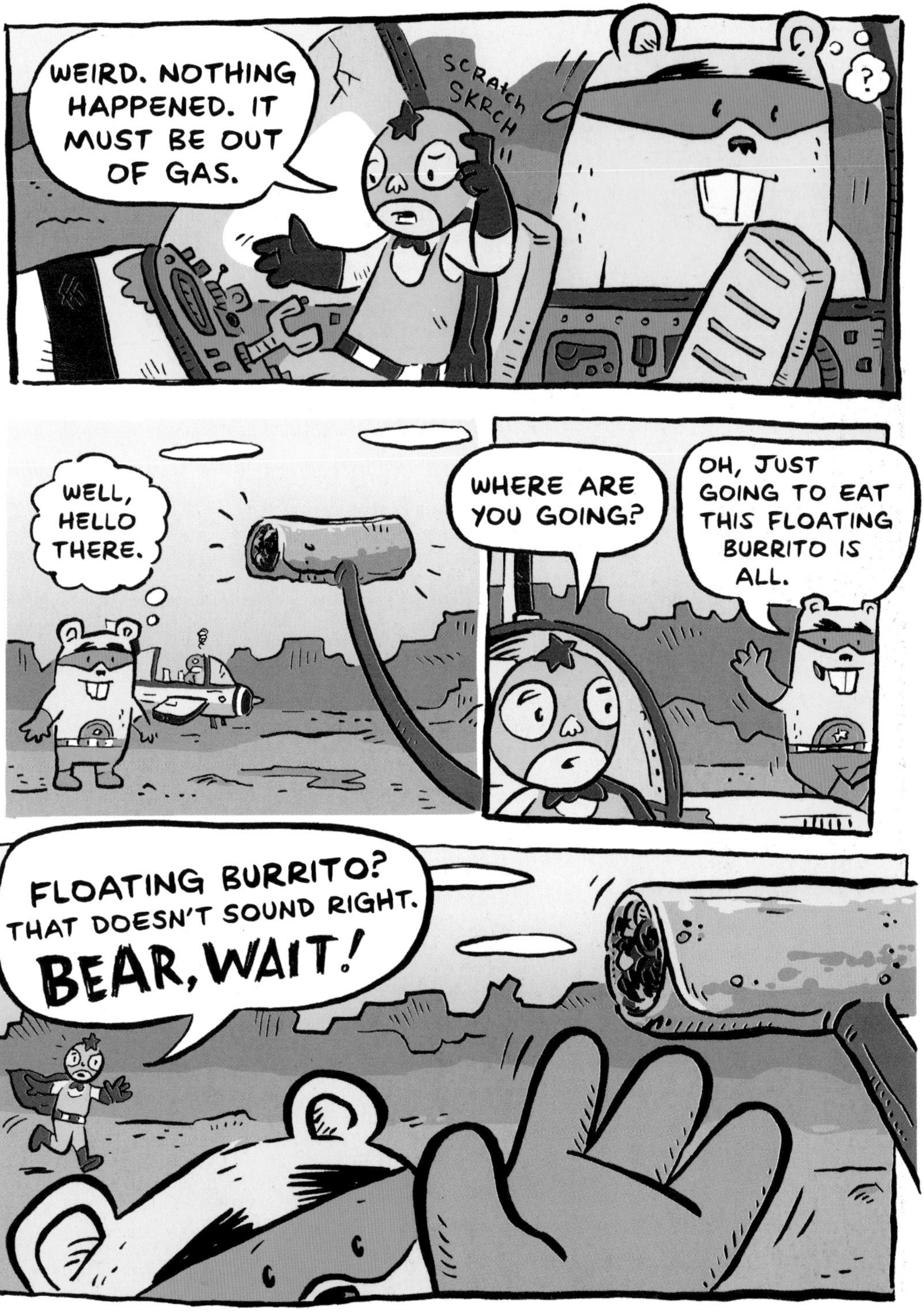

WEIRD. NOTHING HAPPENED. IT MUST BE OUT OF GAS.
SCRATCH SKRCH
?
WELL, HELLO THERE.
WHERE ARE YOU GOING?
OH, JUST GOING TO EAT THIS FLOATING BURRITO IS ALL.
FLOATING BURRITO? THAT DOESN'T SOUND RIGHT. BEAR, WAIT!

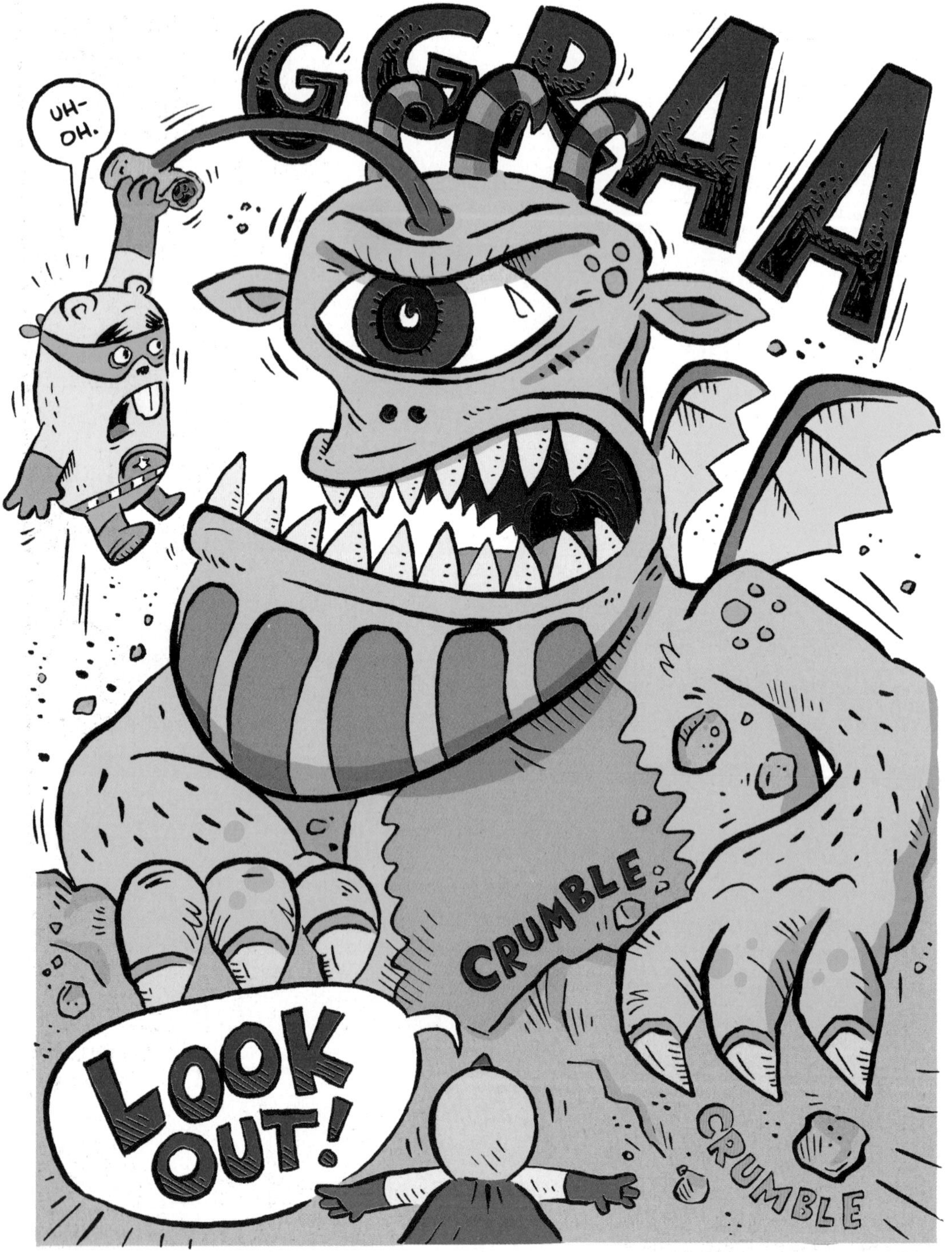
GGRAA
UH-OH.
CRUMBLE
LOOK OUT!
CRUMBLE

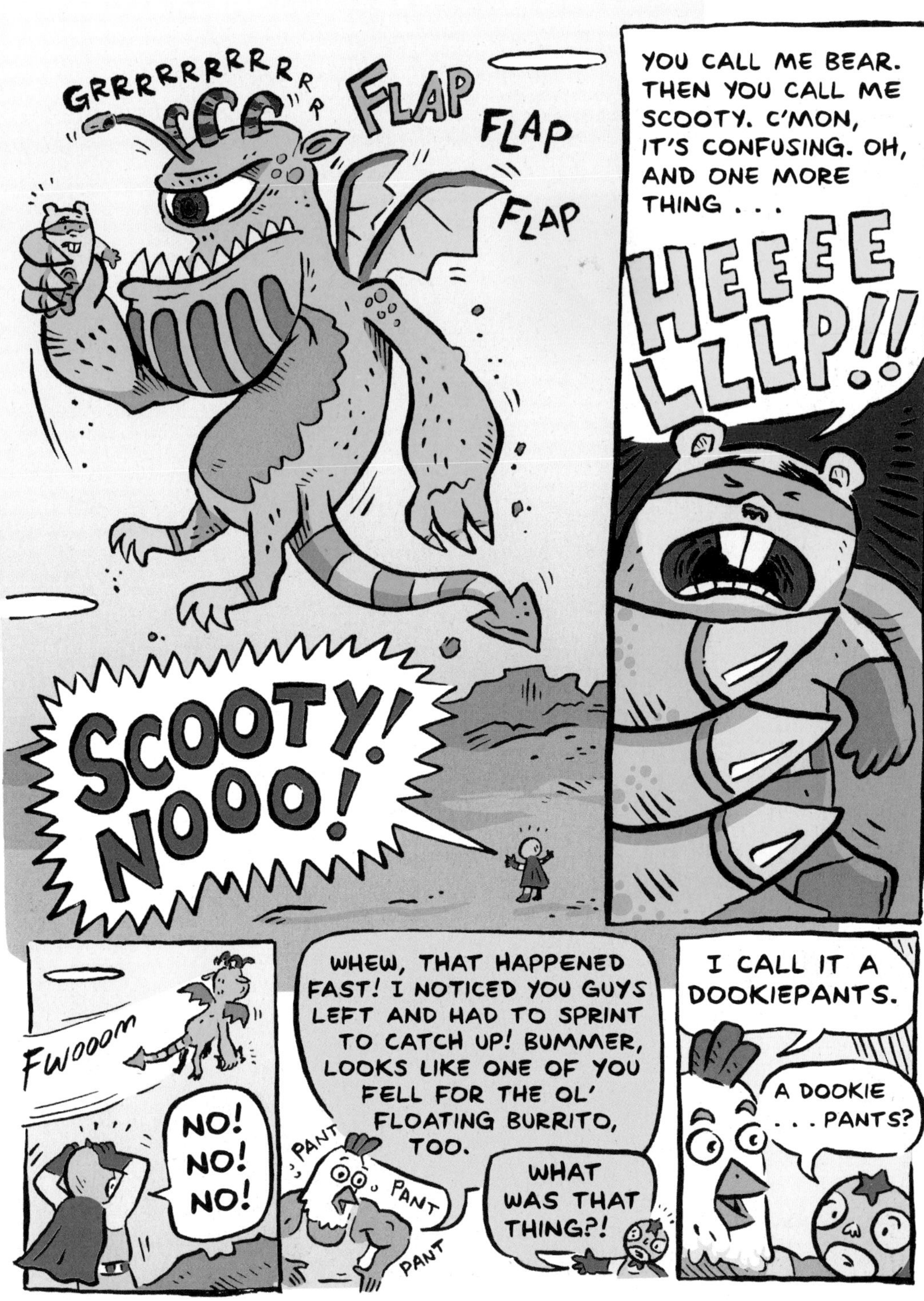
GRRRRRRRRRRR
FLAP
FLAP
FLAP
SCOOTY! NOOO!
YOU CALL ME BEAR. THEN YOU CALL ME SCOOTY. C'MON, IT'S CONFUSING. OH, AND ONE MORE THING . . .
HEEEE LLLP!!
FWOOOM
NO! NO! NO!
WHEW, THAT HAPPENED FAST! I NOTICED YOU GUYS LEFT AND HAD TO SPRINT TO CATCH UP! BUMMER, LOOKS LIKE ONE OF YOU FELL FOR THE OL' FLOATING BURRITO, TOO.
PANT
PANT
PANT
WHAT WAS THAT THING?!
I CALL IT A DOOKIEPANTS.
A DOOKIE . . . PANTS?

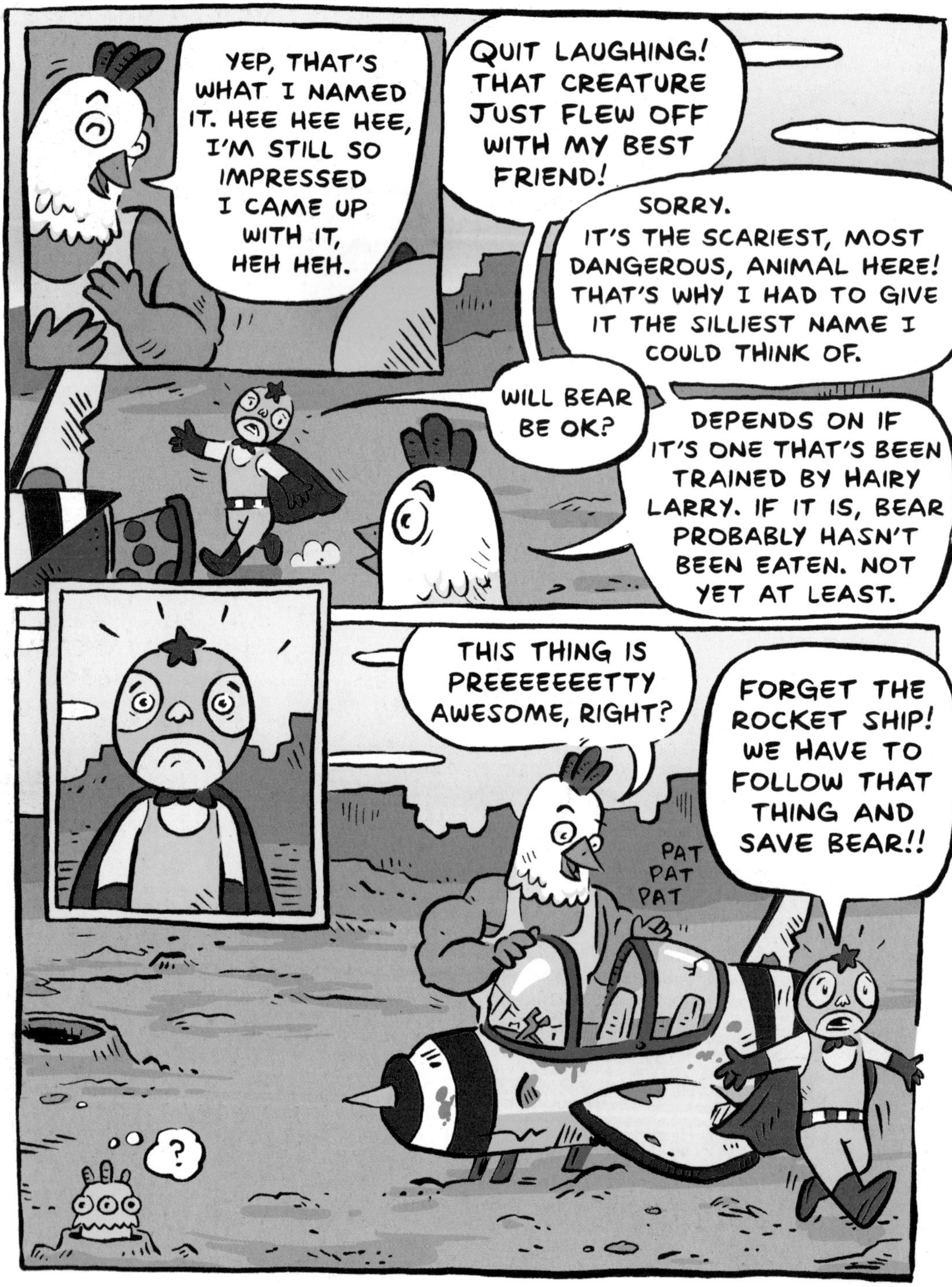
YEP, THAT'S WHAT I NAMED IT. HEE HEE HEE, I'M STILL SO IMPRESSED I CAME UP WITH IT, HEH HEH.
QUIT LAUGHING! THAT CREATURE JUST FLEW OFF WITH MY BEST FRIEND!
SORRY. IT'S THE SCARIEST, MOST DANGEROUS, ANIMAL HERE! THAT'S WHY I HAD TO GIVE IT THE SILLIEST NAME I COULD THINK OF.
WILL BEAR BE OK?
DEPENDS ON IF IT'S ONE THAT'S BEEN TRAINED BY HAIRY LARRY. IF IT IS, BEAR PROBABLY HASN'T BEEN EATEN. NOT YET AT LEAST.
THIS THING IS PREEEEEEETTY AWESOME, RIGHT?
PAT PAT PAT
FORGET THE ROCKET SHIP! WE HAVE TO FOLLOW THAT THING AND SAVE BEAR!!
?

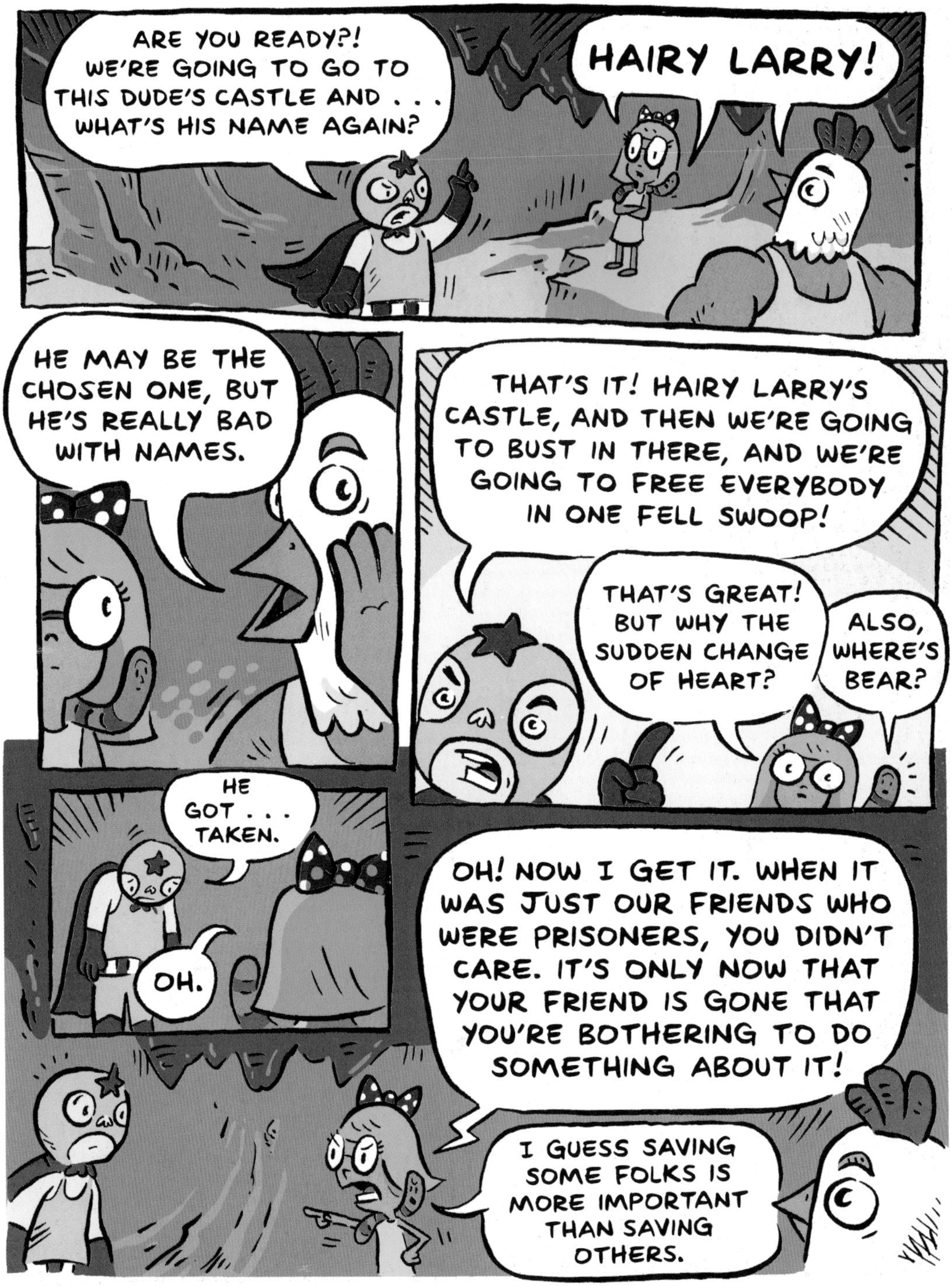

ARE YOU READY?! WE'RE GOING TO GO TO THIS DUDE'S CASTLE AND . . . WHAT'S HIS NAME AGAIN?
HAIRY LARRY!
HE MAY BE THE CHOSEN ONE, BUT HE'S REALLY BAD WITH NAMES.
THAT'S IT! HAIRY LARRY'S CASTLE, AND THEN WE'RE GOING TO BUST IN THERE, AND WE'RE GOING TO FREE EVERYBODY IN ONE FELL SWOOP!
THAT'S GREAT! BUT WHY THE SUDDEN CHANGE OF HEART?
ALSO, WHERE'S BEAR?
HE GOT . . . TAKEN.
OH.
OH! NOW I GET IT. WHEN IT WAS JUST OUR FRIENDS WHO WERE PRISONERS, YOU DIDN'T CARE. IT'S ONLY NOW THAT YOUR FRIEND IS GONE THAT YOU'RE BOTHERING TO DO SOMETHING ABOUT IT!
I GUESS SAVING SOME FOLKS IS MORE IMPORTANT THAN SAVING OTHERS.

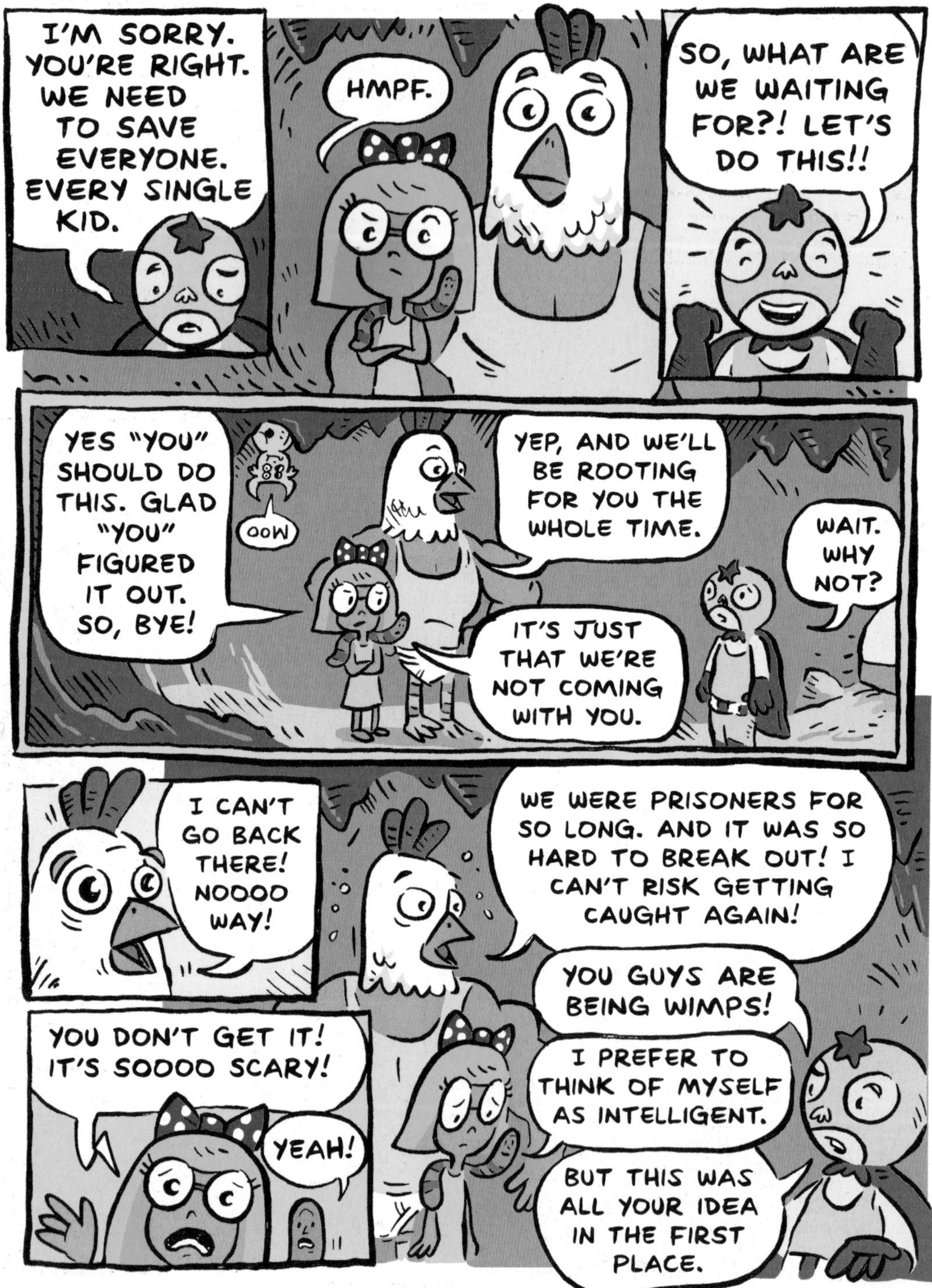

I'M SORRY. YOU'RE RIGHT. WE NEED TO SAVE EVERYONE. EVERY SINGLE KID.
HMPF.
SO, WHAT ARE WE WAITING FOR?! LET'S DO THIS!!
YES "YOU" SHOULD DO THIS. GLAD "YOU" FIGURED IT OUT. SO, BYE!
OOW
YEP, AND WE'LL BE ROOTING FOR YOU THE WHOLE TIME.
WAIT. WHY NOT?
IT'S JUST THAT WE'RE NOT COMING WITH YOU.
I CAN'T GO BACK THERE! NOOOO WAY!
WE WERE PRISONERS FOR SO LONG. AND IT WAS SO HARD TO BREAK OUT! I CAN'T RISK GETTING CAUGHT AGAIN!
YOU GUYS ARE BEING WIMPS!
YOU DON'T GET IT! IT'S SOOOO SCARY!
YEAH!
I PREFER TO THINK OF MYSELF AS INTELLIGENT.
BUT THIS WAS ALL YOUR IDEA IN THE FIRST PLACE.

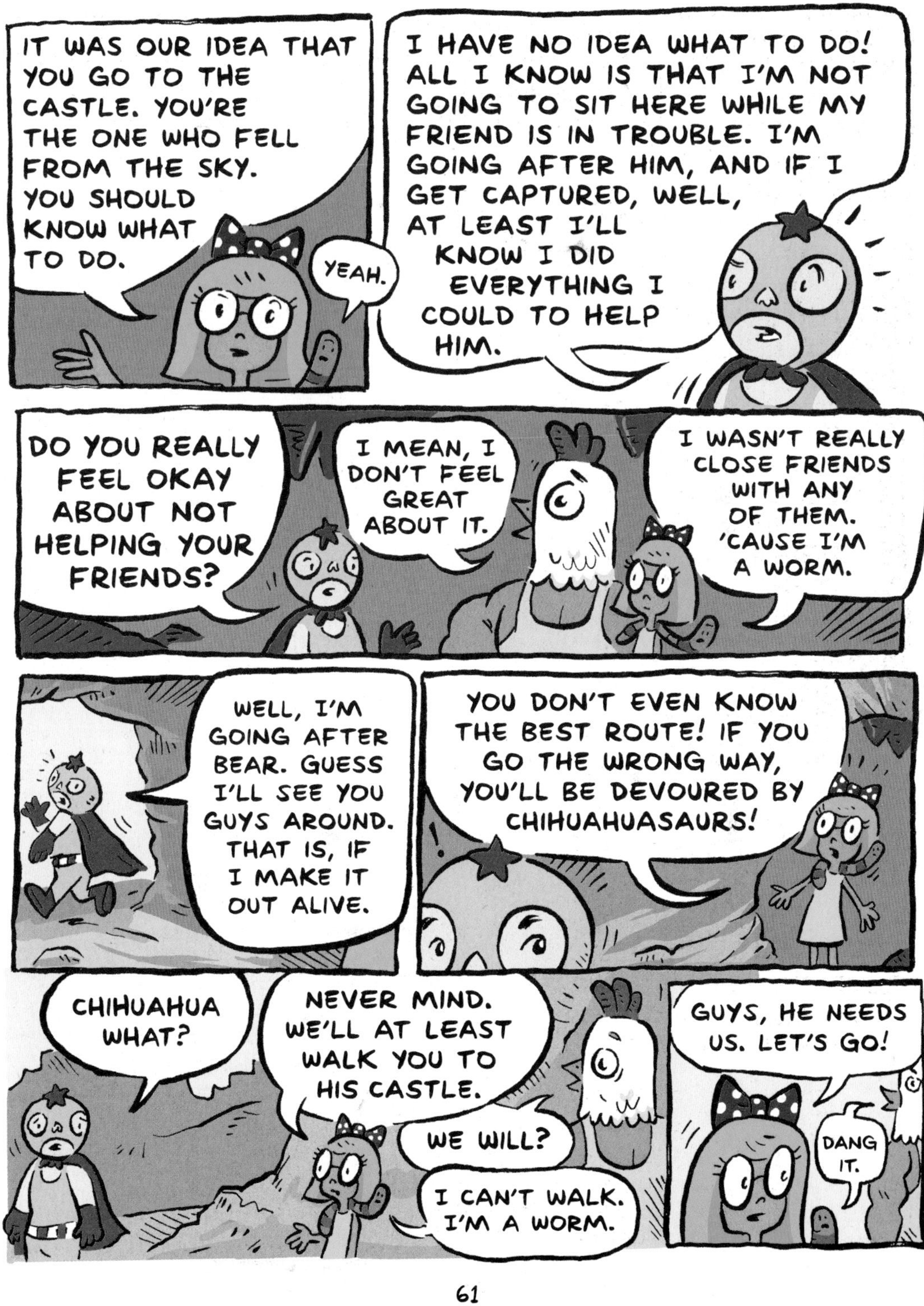
IT WAS OUR IDEA THAT YOU GO TO THE CASTLE. YOU'RE THE ONE WHO FELL FROM THE SKY. YOU SHOULD KNOW WHAT TO DO.
YEAH.
I HAVE NO IDEA WHAT TO DO! ALL I KNOW IS THAT I'M NOT GOING TO SIT HERE WHILE MY FRIEND IS IN TROUBLE. I'M GOING AFTER HIM, AND IF I GET CAPTURED, WELL, AT LEAST I'LL KNOW I DID EVERYTHING I COULD TO HELP HIM.
DO YOU REALLY FEEL OKAY ABOUT NOT HELPING YOUR FRIENDS?
I MEAN, I DON'T FEEL GREAT ABOUT IT.
I WASN'T REALLY CLOSE FRIENDS WITH ANY OF THEM. 'CAUSE I'M A WORM.
WELL, I'M GOING AFTER BEAR. GUESS I'LL SEE YOU GUYS AROUND. THAT IS, IF I MAKE IT OUT ALIVE.
YOU DON'T EVEN KNOW THE BEST ROUTE! IF YOU GO THE WRONG WAY, YOU'LL BE DEVOURED BY CHIHUAHUASAURS!
!
CHIHUAHUA WHAT?
NEVER MIND. WE'LL AT LEAST WALK YOU TO HIS CASTLE.
WE WILL?
I CAN'T WALK. I'M A WORM.
GUYS, HE NEEDS US. LET'S GO!
DANG IT.

CHAPTER 6

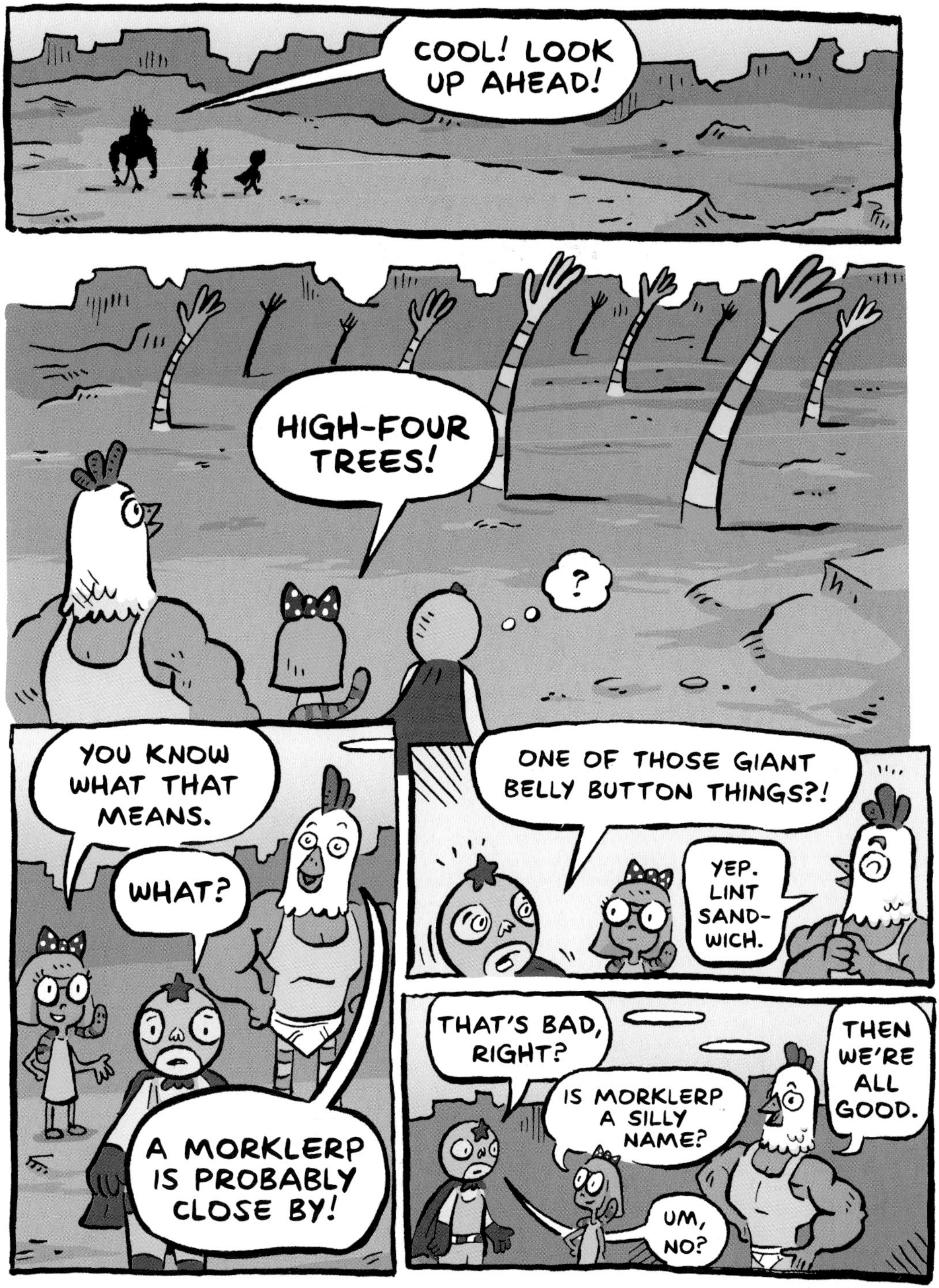
COOL! LOOK UP AHEAD!
HIGH-FOUR TREES!
?
YOU KNOW WHAT THAT MEANS.
WHAT?
A MORKLERP IS PROBABLY CLOSE BY!
ONE OF THOSE GIANT BELLY BUTTON THINGS?!
YEP. LINT SAND-WICH.
THAT'S BAD, RIGHT?
IS MORKLERP A SILLY NAME?
UM, NO?
THEN WE'RE ALL GOOD.

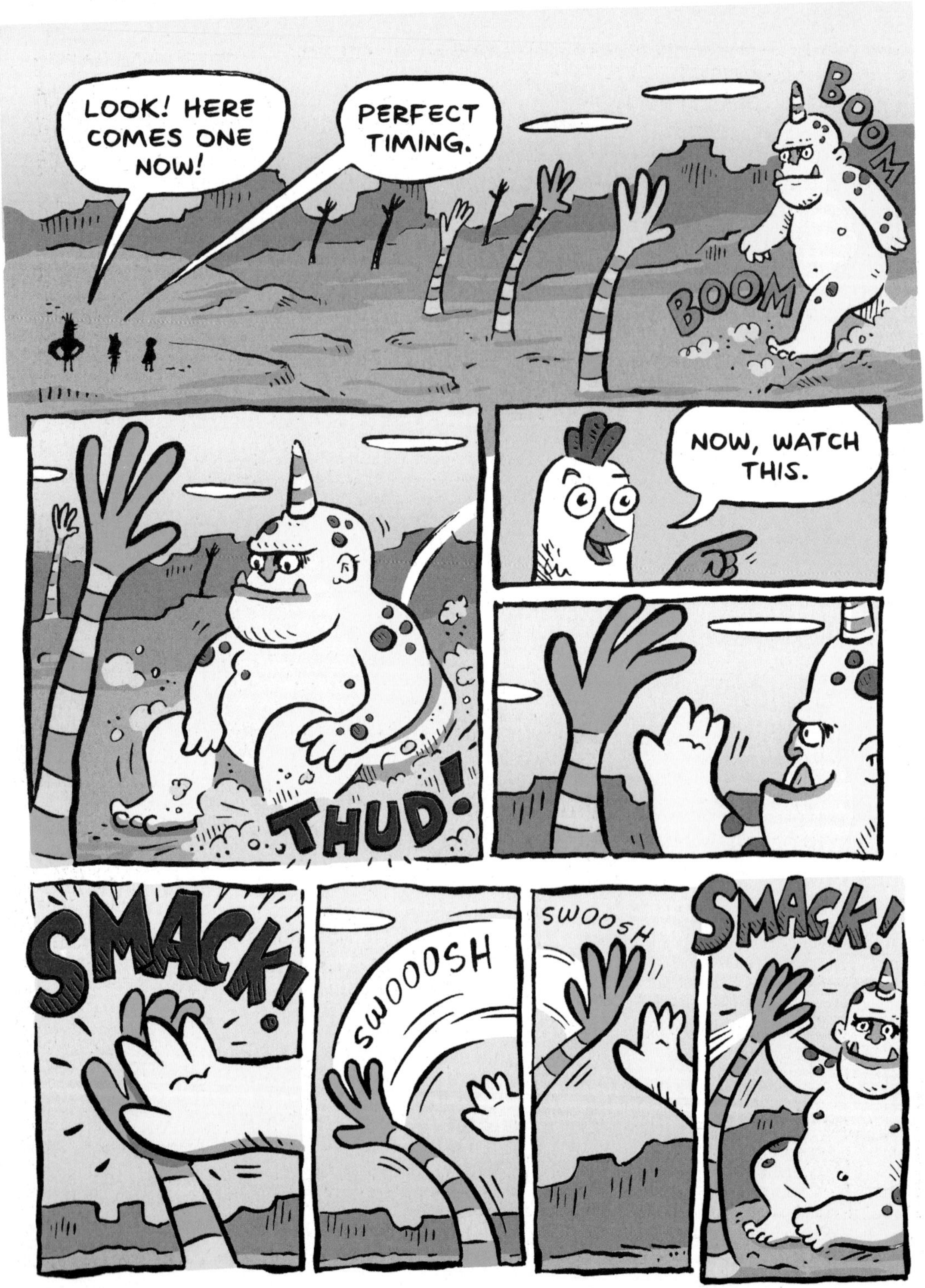
LOOK! HERE COMES ONE NOW!
PERFECT TIMING.
BOOM
BOOM
THUD!
NOW, WATCH THIS.
SMACK!
SWOOOSH
SWOOSH
SMACK!

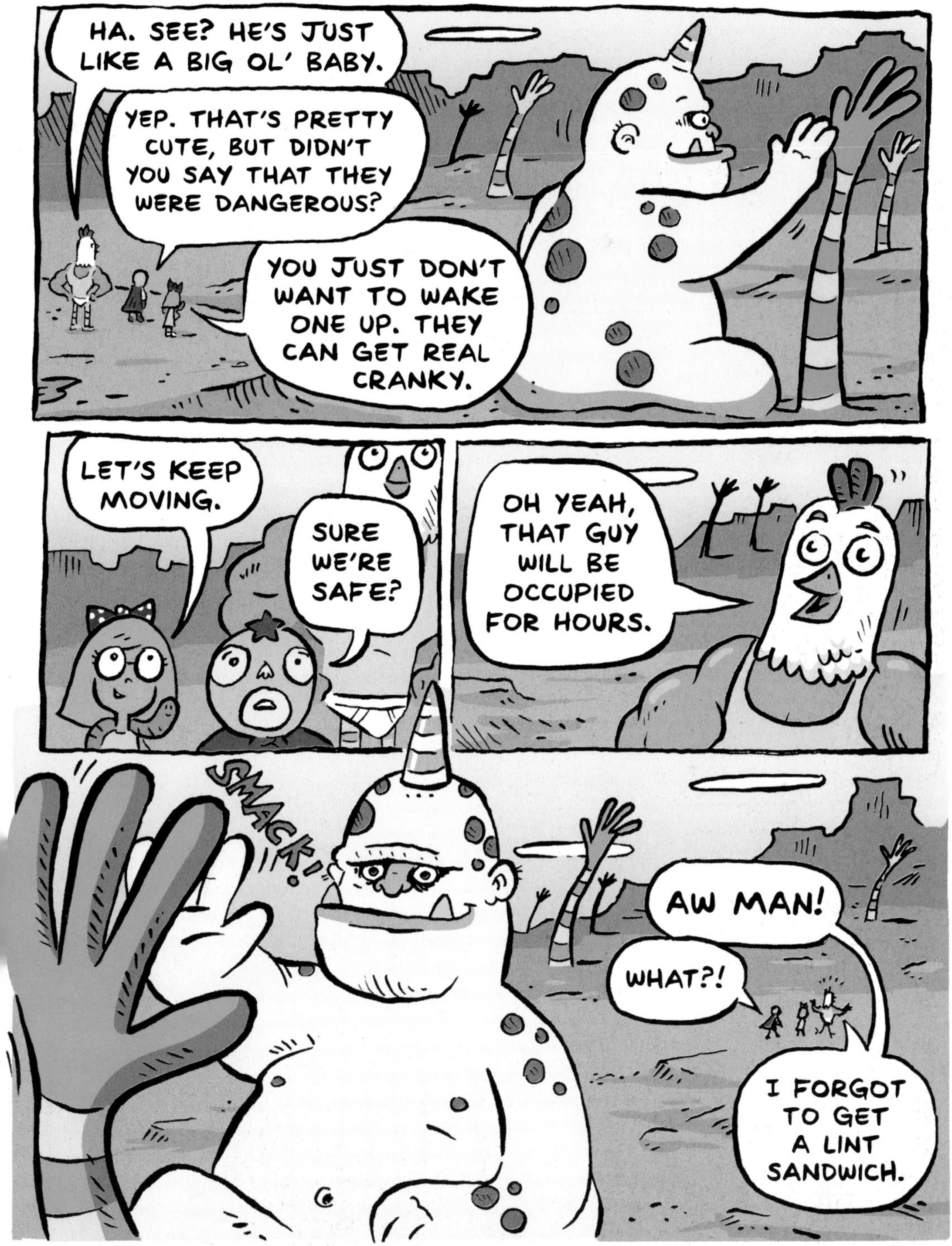
HA. SEE? HE'S JUST LIKE A BIG OL' BABY.
YEP. THAT'S PRETTY CUTE, BUT DIDN'T YOU SAY THAT THEY WERE DANGEROUS?
YOU JUST DON'T WANT TO WAKE ONE UP. THEY CAN GET REAL CRANKY.
LET'S KEEP MOVING.
SURE WE'RE SAFE?
OH YEAH, THAT GUY WILL BE OCCUPIED FOR HOURS.
SMACK!
AW MAN!
WHAT?!
I FORGOT TO GET A LINT SANDWICH.

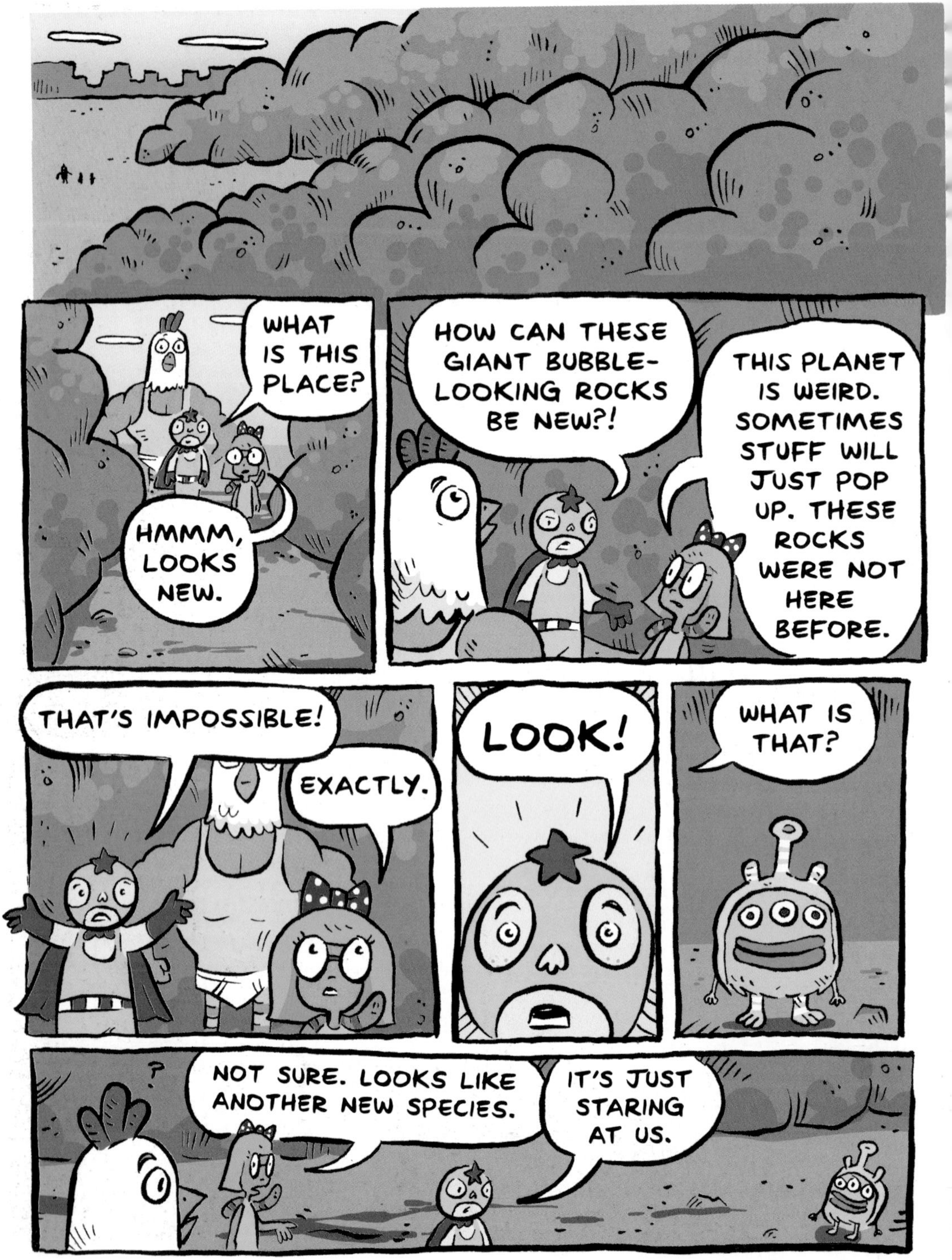
WHAT IS THIS PLACE?
HMMM, LOOKS NEW.
HOW CAN THESE GIANT BUBBLE-LOOKING ROCKS BE NEW?!
THIS PLANET IS WEIRD. SOMETIMES STUFF WILL JUST POP UP. THESE ROCKS WERE NOT HERE BEFORE.
THAT'S IMPOSSIBLE!
EXACTLY.
LOOK!
WHAT IS THAT?
NOT SURE. LOOKS LIKE ANOTHER NEW SPECIES.
IT'S JUST STARING AT US.

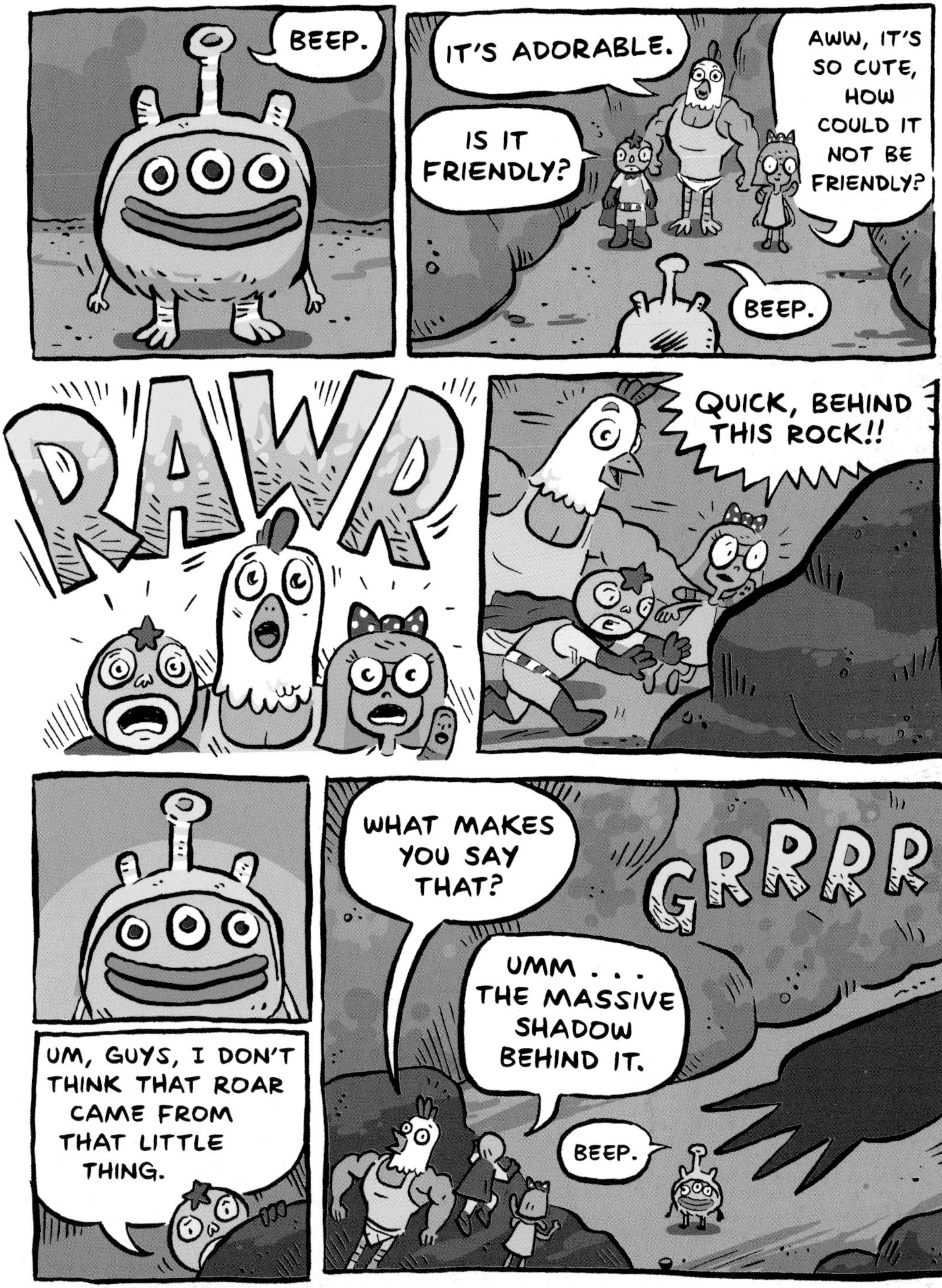
BEEP.
IT'S ADORABLE.
IS IT FRIENDLY?
AWW, IT'S SO CUTE, HOW COULD IT NOT BE FRIENDLY?
BEEP.
RAWR
QUICK, BEHIND THIS ROCK!!
UM, GUYS, I DON'T THINK THAT ROAR CAME FROM THAT LITTLE THING.
WHAT MAKES YOU SAY THAT?
GRRRR
UMM . . . THE MASSIVE SHADOW BEHIND IT.
BEEP.

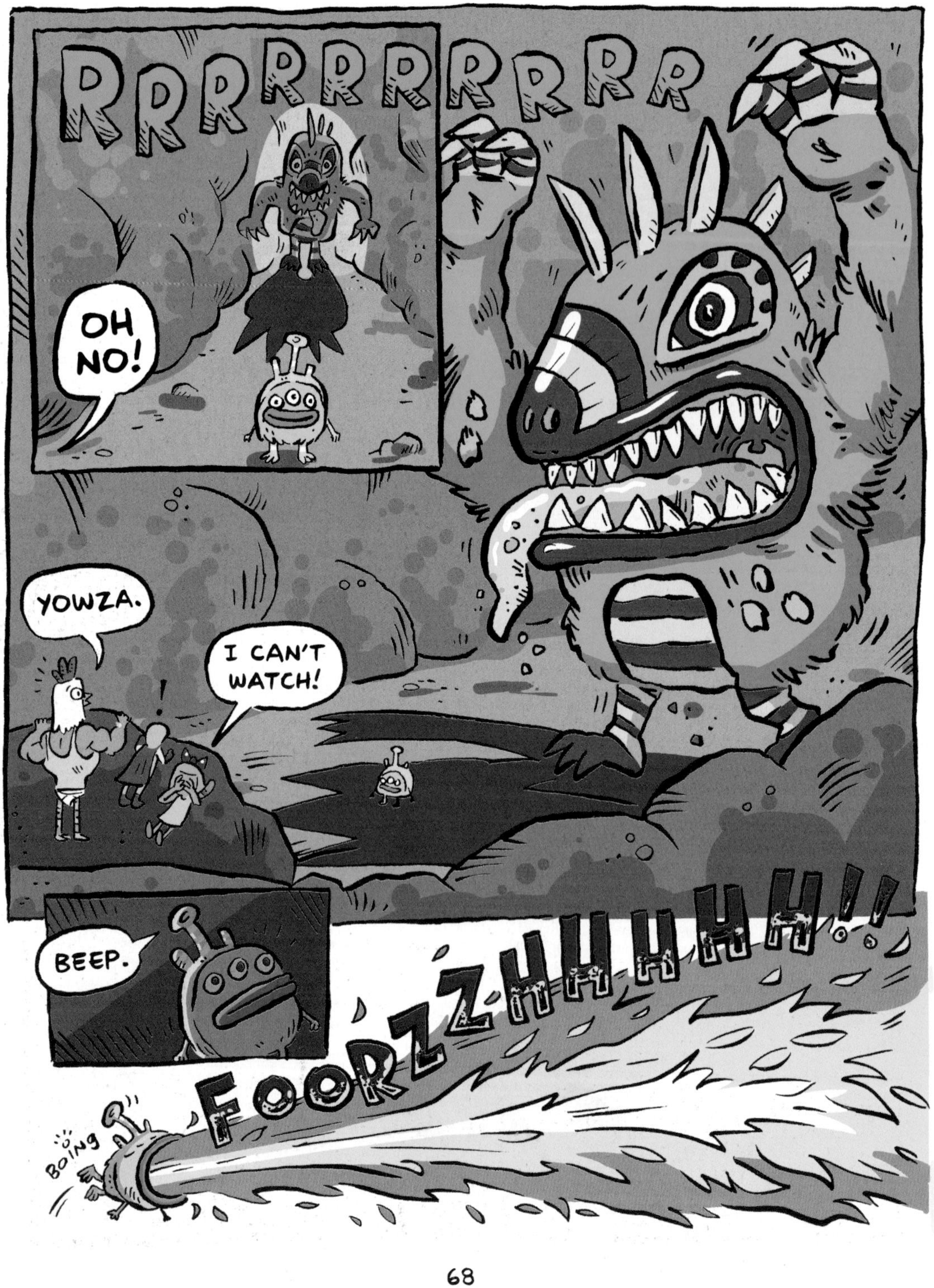
RRRRRRRRRRR
OH NO!
YOWZA.
I CAN'T WATCH!
BEEP.
FOORZZHHHHHH!!
BOING

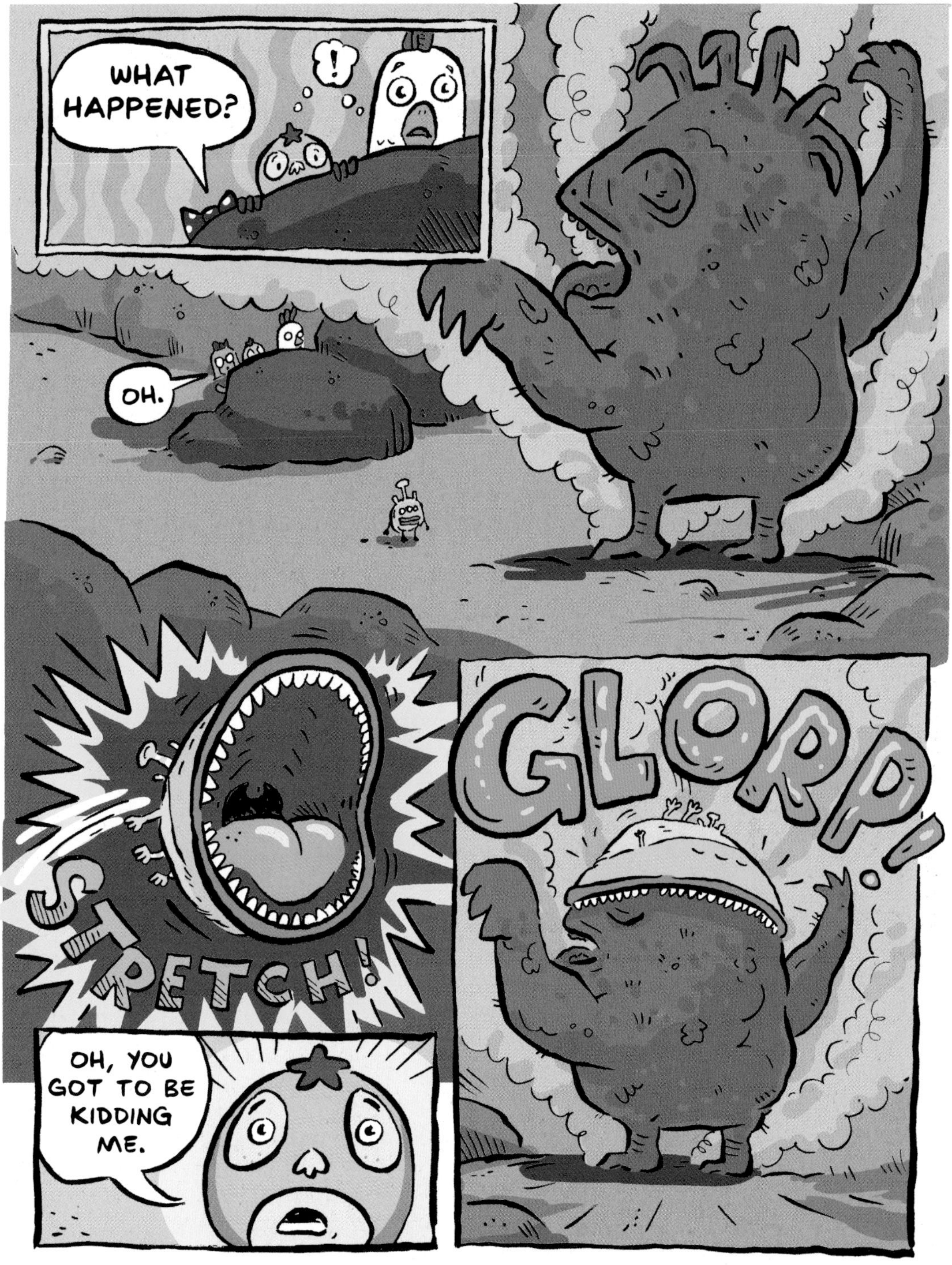
WHAT HAPPENED?
!
OH.
STRETCH!
GLORP!
OH, YOU GOT TO BE KIDDING ME.

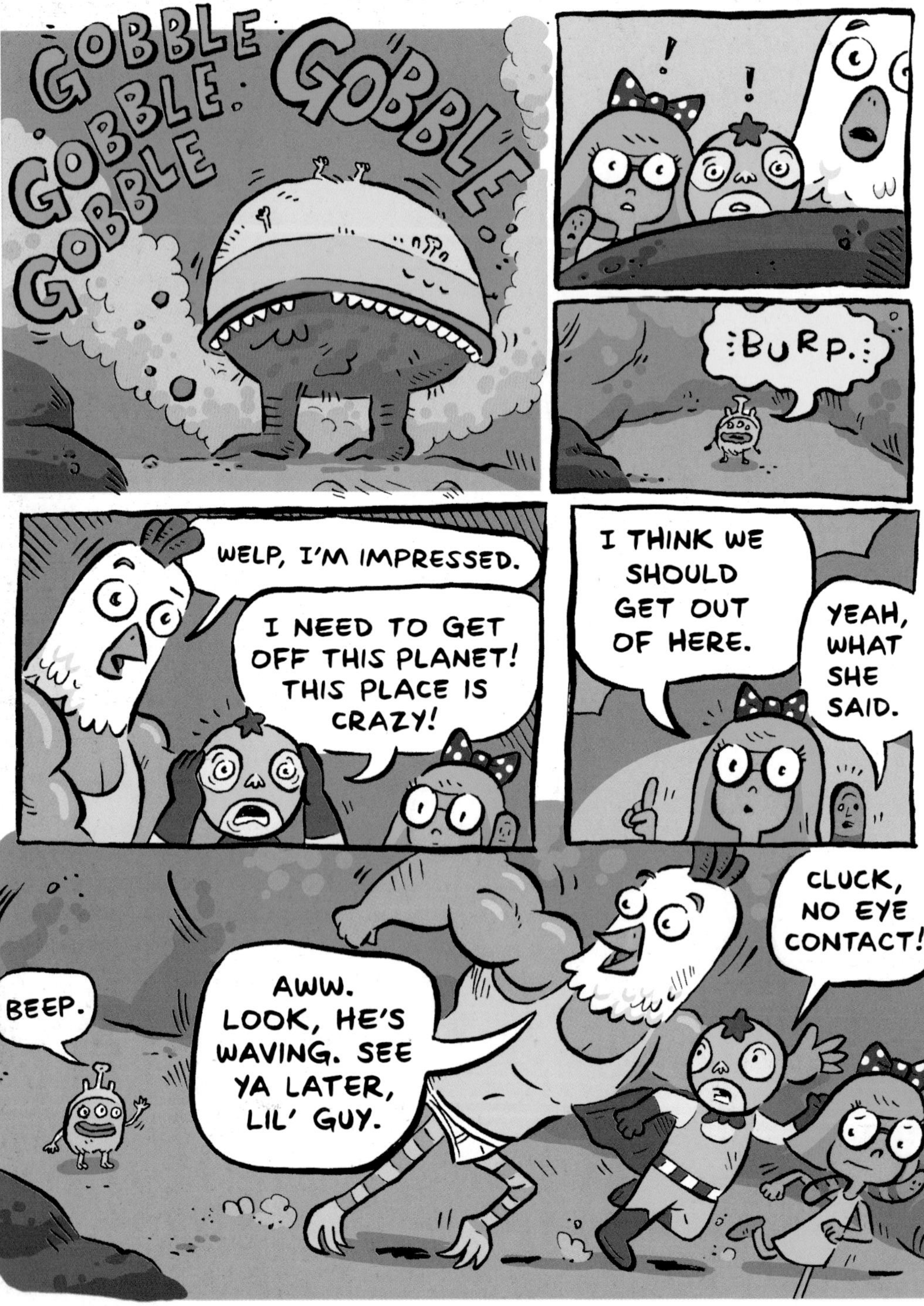
GOBBLE
GOBBLE
GOBBLE
GOBBLE
GOBBLE
!
!
BURP.
WELP, I'M IMPRESSED.
I NEED TO GET OFF THIS PLANET! THIS PLACE IS CRAZY!
I THINK WE SHOULD GET OUT OF HERE.
YEAH, WHAT SHE SAID.
BEEP.
AWW. LOOK, HE'S WAVING. SEE YA LATER, LIL' GUY.
CLUCK, NO EYE CONTACT!

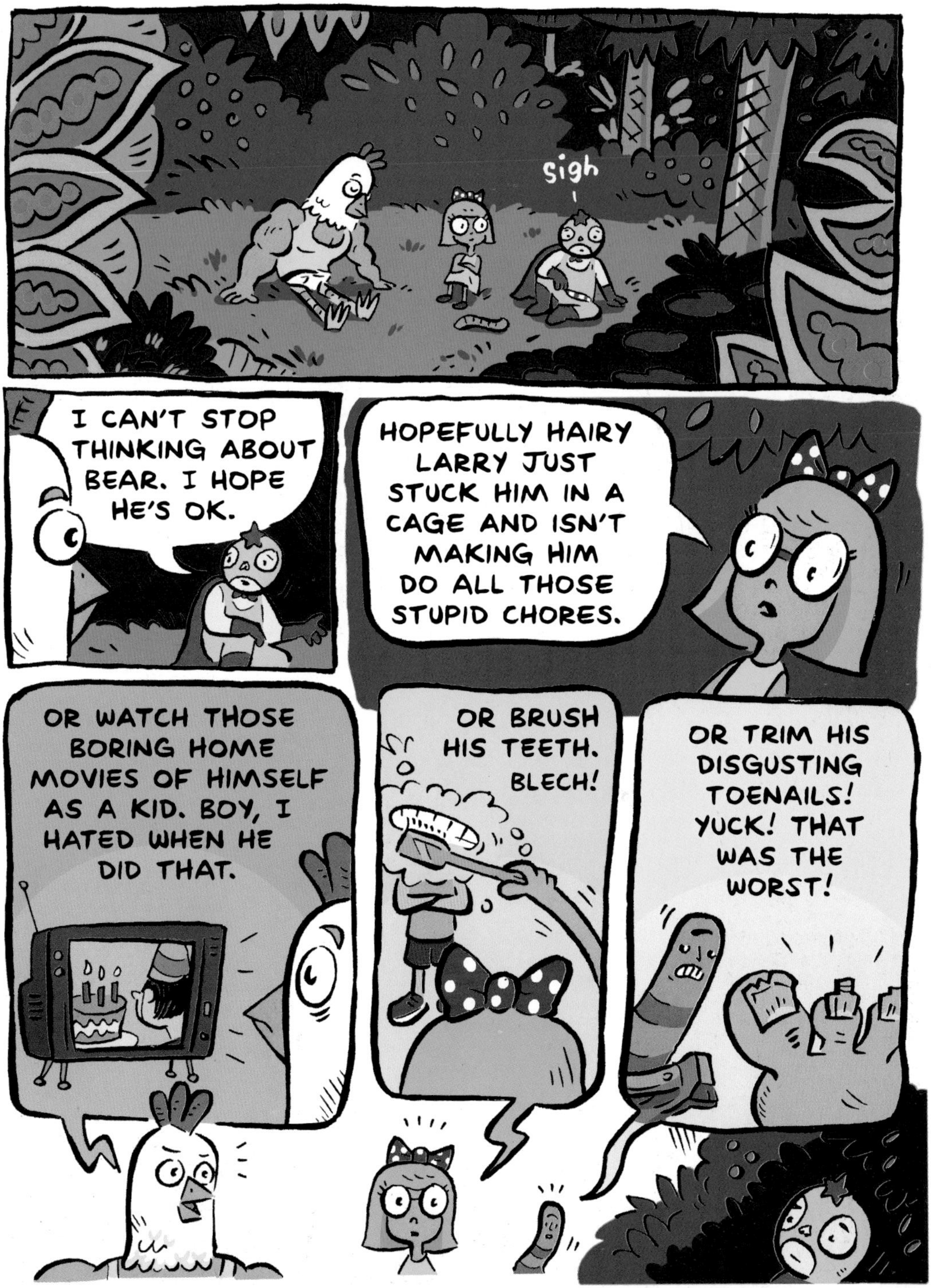
sigh
I CAN'T STOP THINKING ABOUT BEAR. I HOPE HE'S OK.
HOPEFULLY HAIRY LARRY JUST STUCK HIM IN A CAGE AND ISN'T MAKING HIM DO ALL THOSE STUPID CHORES.
OR WATCH THOSE BORING HOME MOVIES OF HIMSELF AS A KID. BOY, I HATED WHEN HE DID THAT.
OR BRUSH HIS TEETH.
BLECH!
OR TRIM HIS DISGUSTING TOENAILS! YUCK! THAT WAS THE WORST!

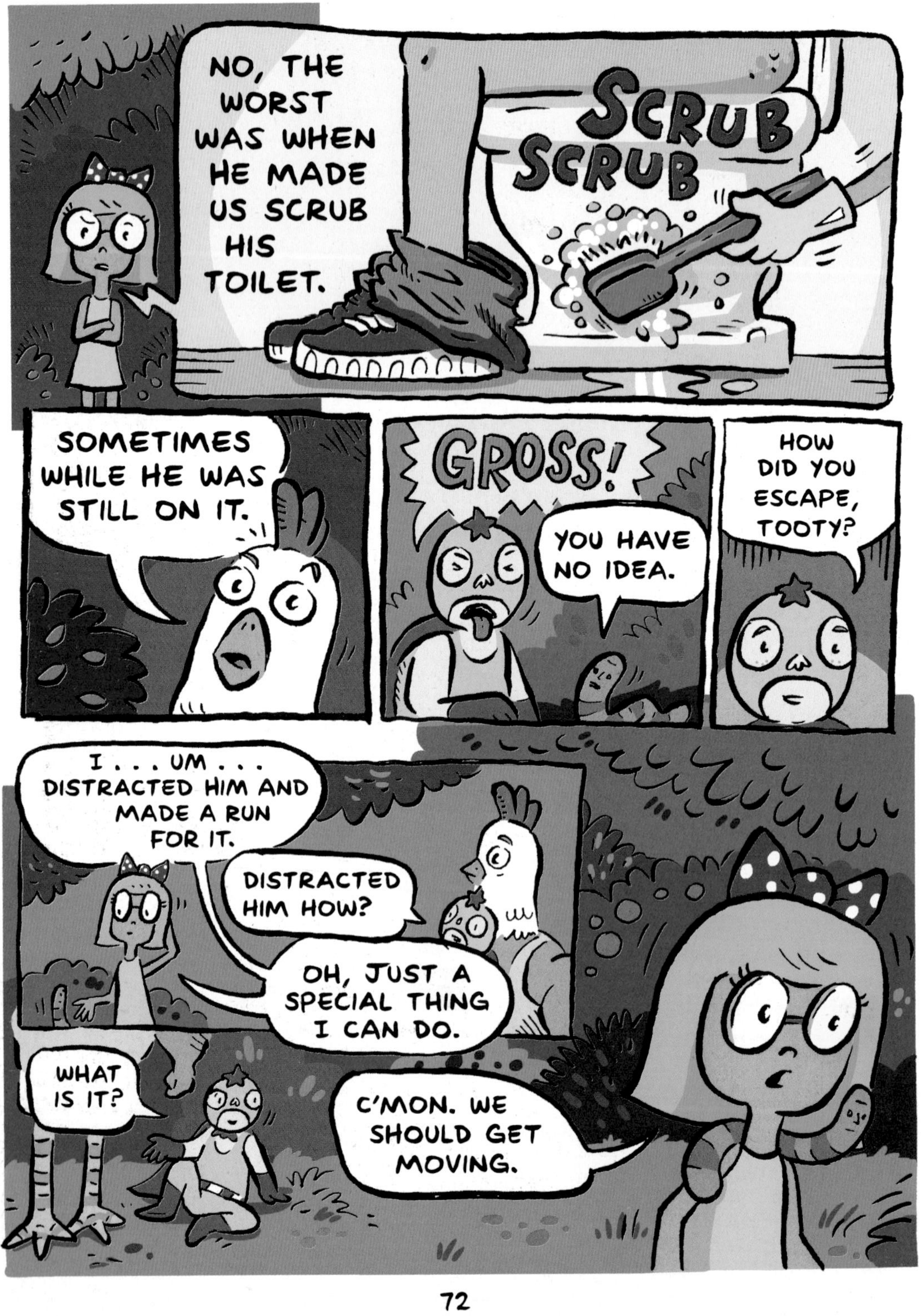
NO, THE WORST WAS WHEN HE MADE US SCRUB HIS TOILET.
SCRUB
SCRUB
SOMETIMES WHILE HE WAS STILL ON IT.
GROSS!
YOU HAVE NO IDEA.
HOW DID YOU ESCAPE, TOOTY?
I . . . UM . . . DISTRACTED HIM AND MADE A RUN FOR IT.
DISTRACTED HIM HOW?
OH, JUST A SPECIAL THING I CAN DO.
WHAT IS IT?
C'MON. WE SHOULD GET MOVING.

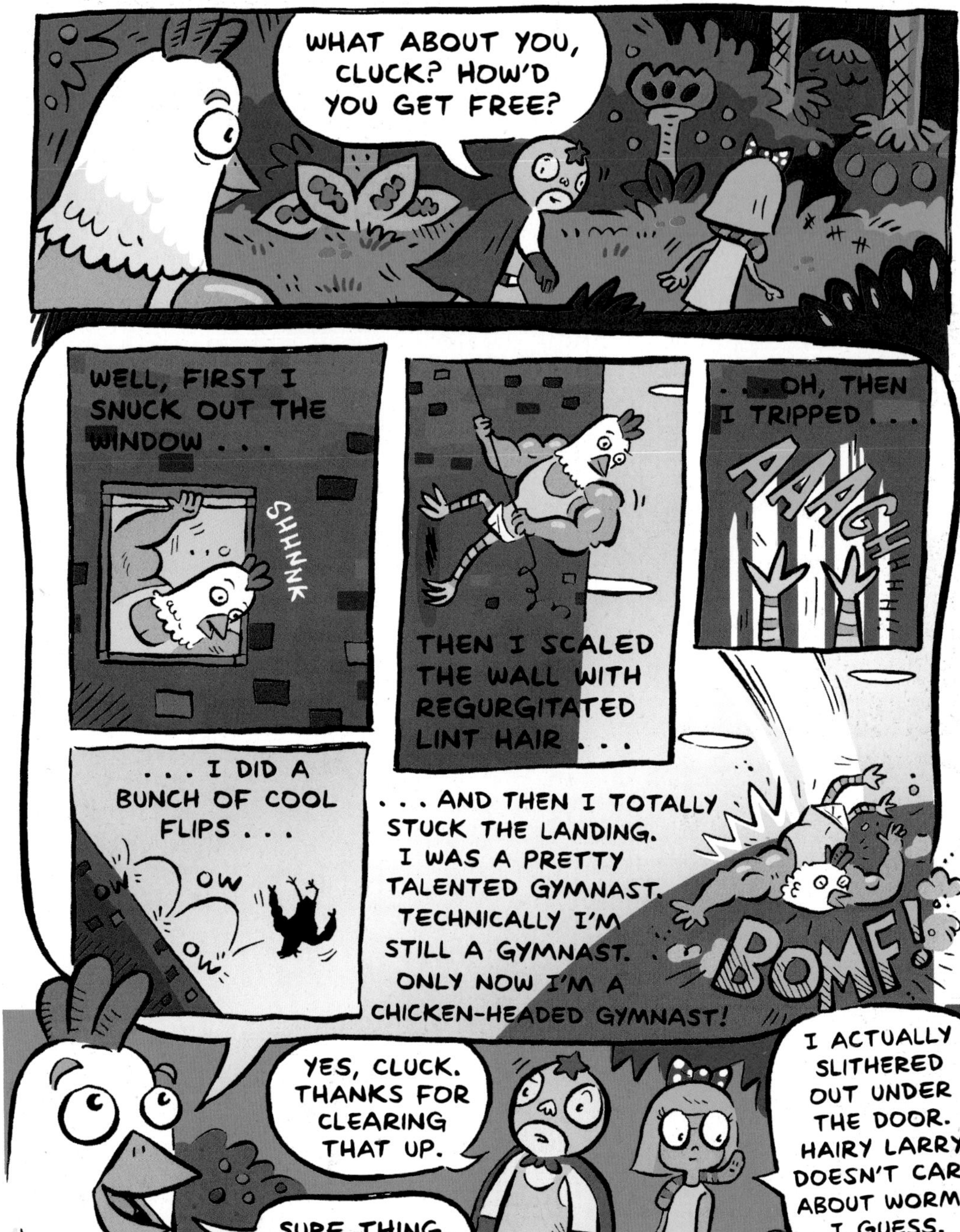
WHAT ABOUT YOU, CLUCK? HOW'D YOU GET FREE?
WELL, FIRST I SNUCK OUT THE WINDOW . . .
SHHNNK
THEN I SCALED THE WALL WITH REGURGITATED LINT HAIR . . .
. . . OH, THEN I TRIPPED . . .
AAAGH
. . . I DID A BUNCH OF COOL FLIPS . . .
OW
OW
OW
. . . AND THEN I TOTALLY STUCK THE LANDING. I WAS A PRETTY TALENTED GYMNAST. TECHNICALLY I'M STILL A GYMNAST. ONLY NOW I'M A CHICKEN-HEADED GYMNAST!
BOMF!
YES, CLUCK. THANKS FOR CLEARING THAT UP.
SURE THING, BUDDY.
I ACTUALLY SLITHERED OUT UNDER THE DOOR. HAIRY LARRY DOESN'T CARE ABOUT WORMS I GUESS.

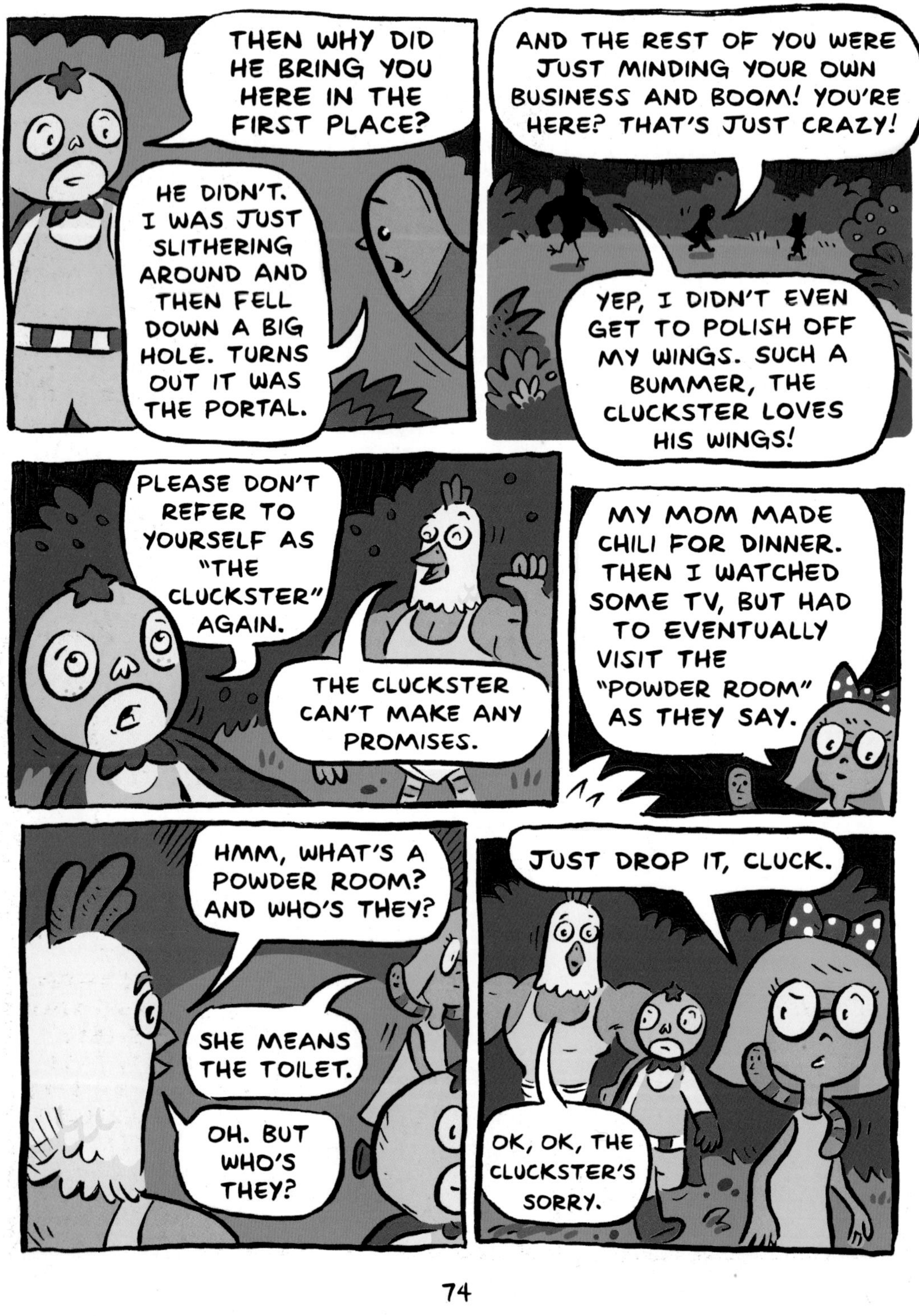
THEN WHY DID HE BRING YOU HERE IN THE FIRST PLACE?
HE DIDN'T. I WAS JUST SLITHERING AROUND AND THEN FELL DOWN A BIG HOLE. TURNS OUT IT WAS THE PORTAL.
AND THE REST OF YOU WERE JUST MINDING YOUR OWN BUSINESS AND BOOM! YOU'RE HERE? THAT'S JUST CRAZY!
YEP, I DIDN'T EVEN GET TO POLISH OFF MY WINGS. SUCH A BUMMER, THE CLUCKSTER LOVES HIS WINGS!
PLEASE DON'T REFER TO YOURSELF AS "THE CLUCKSTER" AGAIN.
THE CLUCKSTER CAN'T MAKE ANY PROMISES.
MY MOM MADE CHILI FOR DINNER. THEN I WATCHED SOME TV, BUT HAD TO EVENTUALLY VISIT THE "POWDER ROOM" AS THEY SAY.
HMM, WHAT'S A POWDER ROOM? AND WHO'S THEY?
SHE MEANS THE TOILET.
OH. BUT WHO'S THEY?
JUST DROP IT, CLUCK.
OK, OK, THE CLUCKSTER'S SORRY.

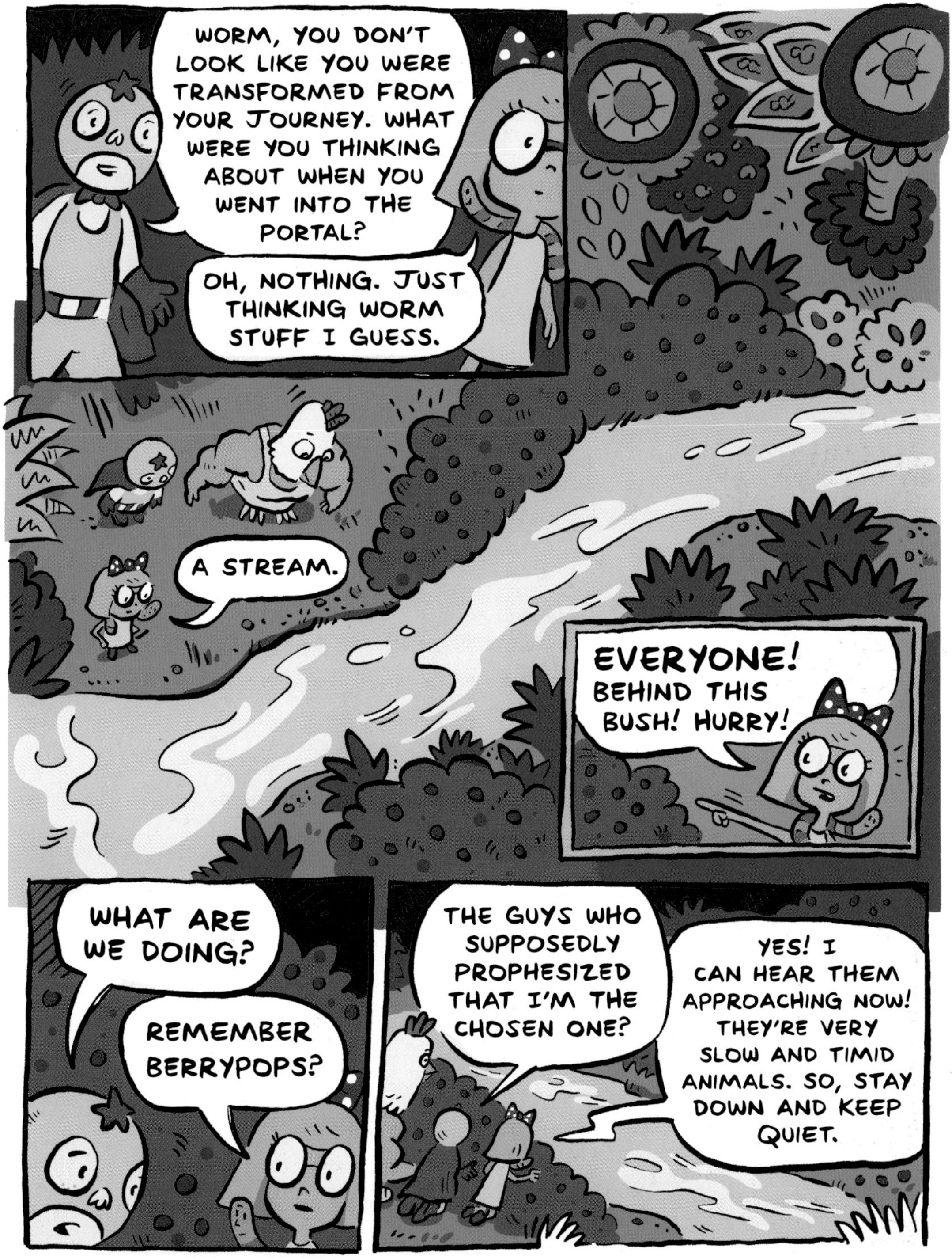
WORM, YOU DON'T LOOK LIKE YOU WERE TRANSFORMED FROM YOUR JOURNEY. WHAT WERE YOU THINKING ABOUT WHEN YOU WENT INTO THE PORTAL?
OH, NOTHING. JUST THINKING WORM STUFF I GUESS.
A STREAM.
EVERYONE! BEHIND THIS BUSH! HURRY!
WHAT ARE WE DOING?
REMEMBER BERRYPOPS?
THE GUYS WHO SUPPOSEDLY PROPHESIZED THAT I'M THE CHOSEN ONE?
YES! I CAN HEAR THEM APPROACHING NOW! THEY'RE VERY SLOW AND TIMID ANIMALS. SO, STAY DOWN AND KEEP QUIET.

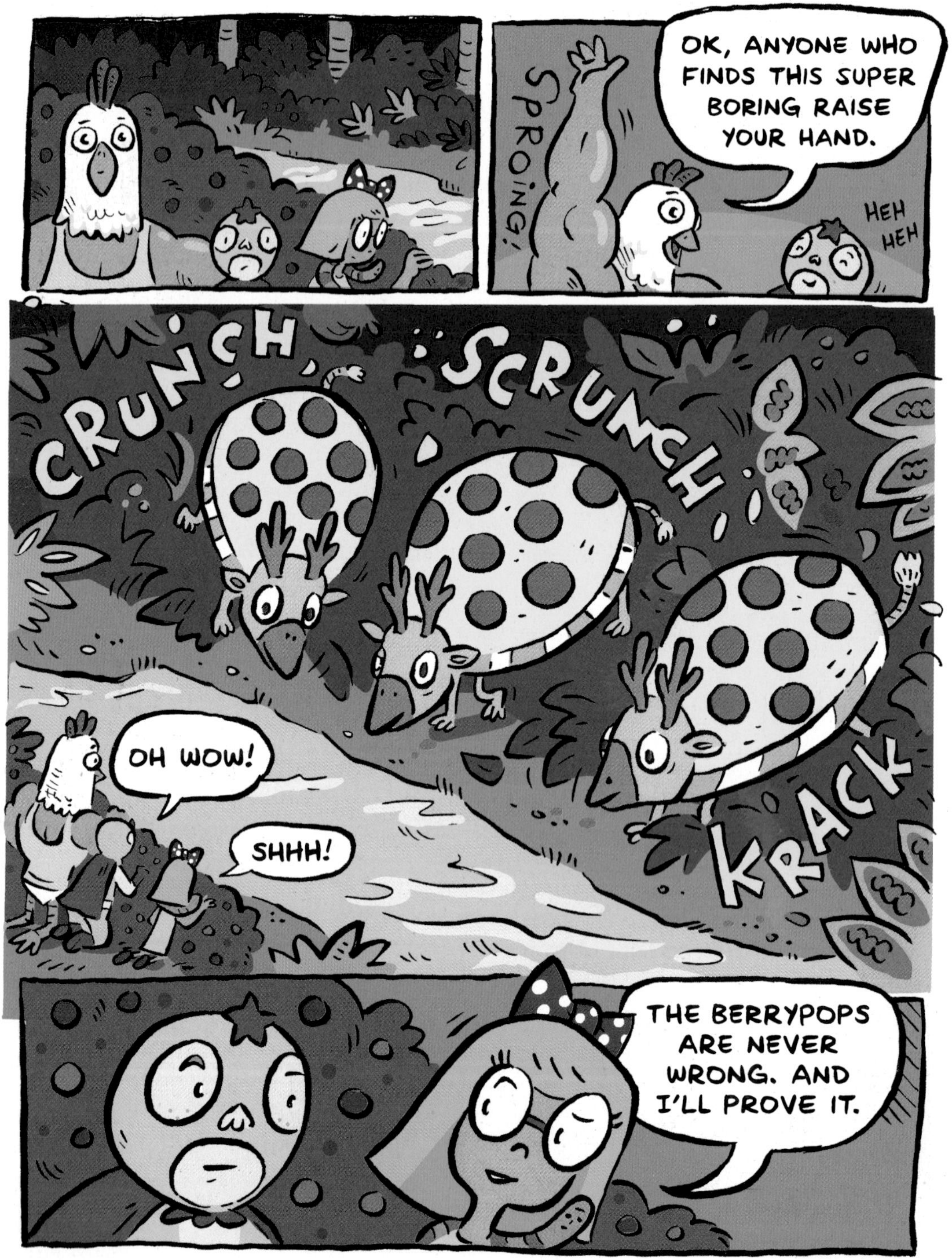
SPROING!
OK, ANYONE WHO FINDS THIS SUPER BORING RAISE YOUR HAND.
HEH HEH
CRUNCH
SCRUNCH
KRACK
OH WOW!
SHHH!
THE BERRYPOPS ARE NEVER WRONG. AND I'LL PROVE IT.

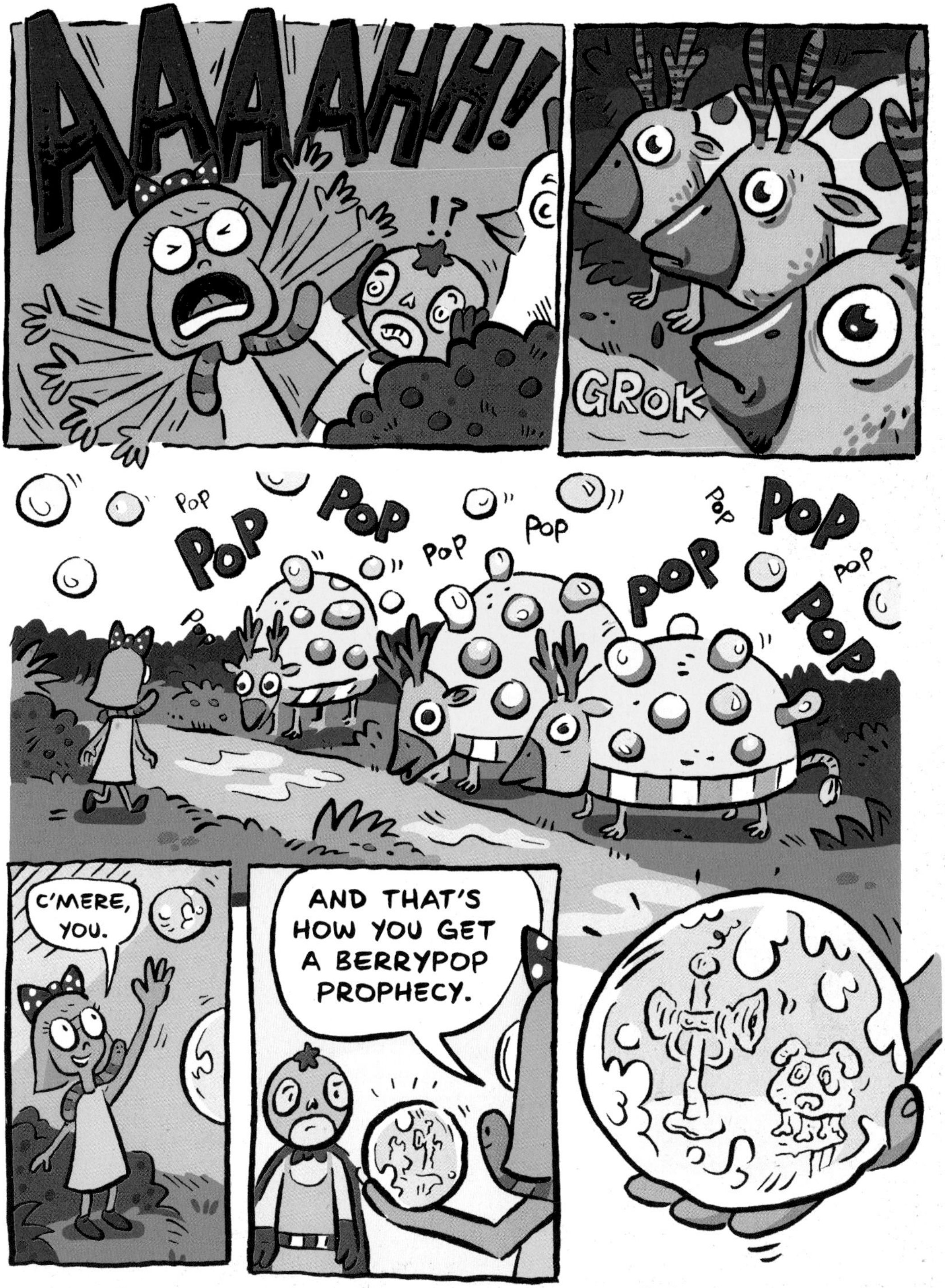
AAAAHH!
!?
GROK
POP
POP
POP
POP
POP
POP
POP
POP
POP
POP
POP
POP
C'MERE, YOU.
AND THAT'S HOW YOU GET A BERRYPOP PROPHECY.

WHAT! THAT'S THE PROPHECY? A WEIRD, TINY CRITTER JUST LOOKING AT SOME OTHER WEIRD THING? AND IS THAT A CLIFF?

ISN'T IT AMAZING? THOSE BERRYPOPS ARE BRILLIANT. IS THERE ANYTHING THEY DON'T KNOW?

HMPF

THAT TELLS US NOTHING! AND HOW DO YOU KNOW YOU EVEN GRABBED THE RIGHT ORB?!?

BOOP

SLURP

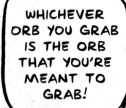

WHICHEVER ORB YOU GRAB IS THE ORB THAT YOU'RE MEANT TO GRAB!

WOW! HOW CONVENIENT! HOW ABOUT AN ORB THAT TELLS ME WHERE BEAR IS?

WE KNOW WHERE HE IS.

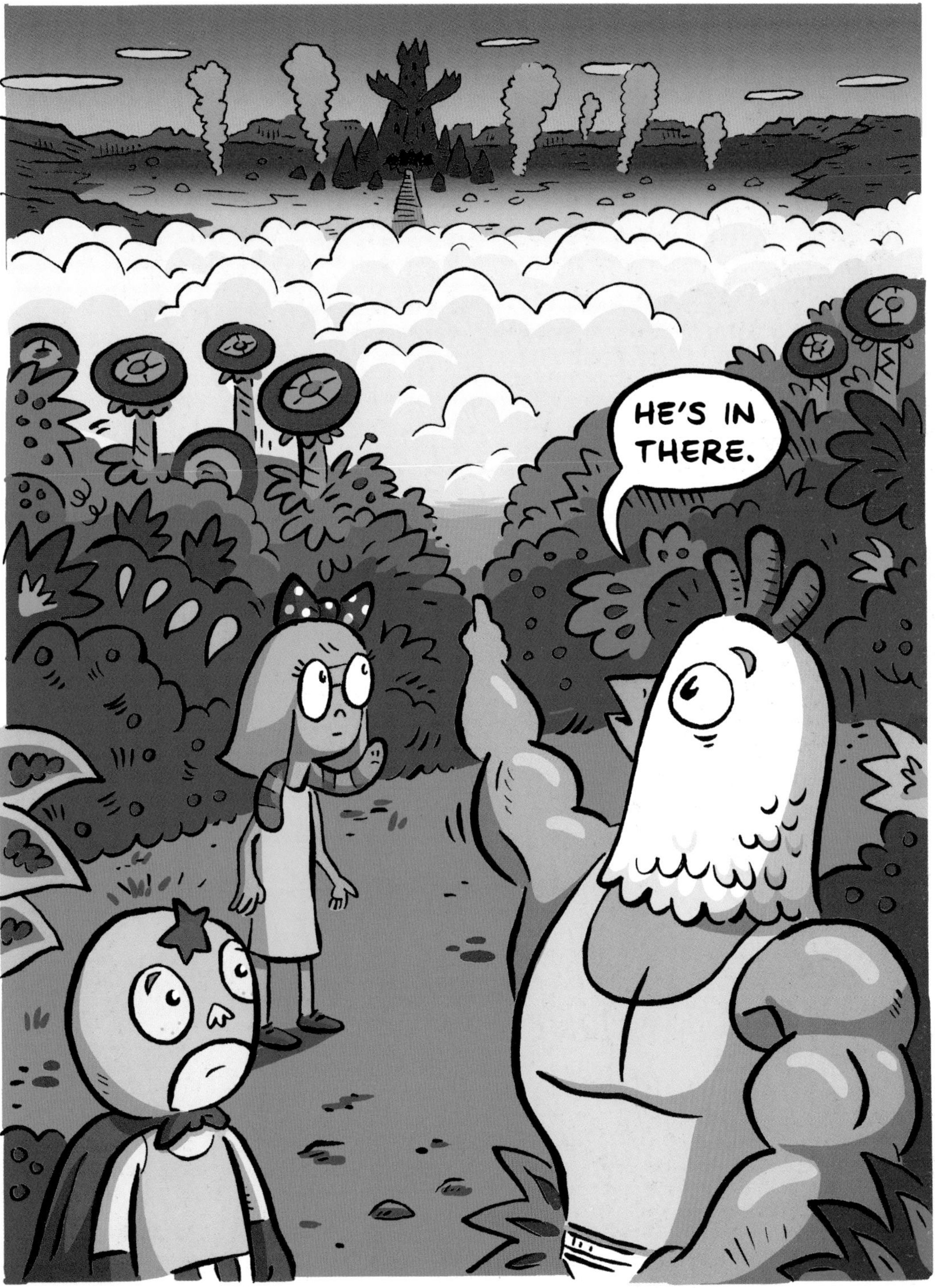
HE'S IN THERE.

Chapter

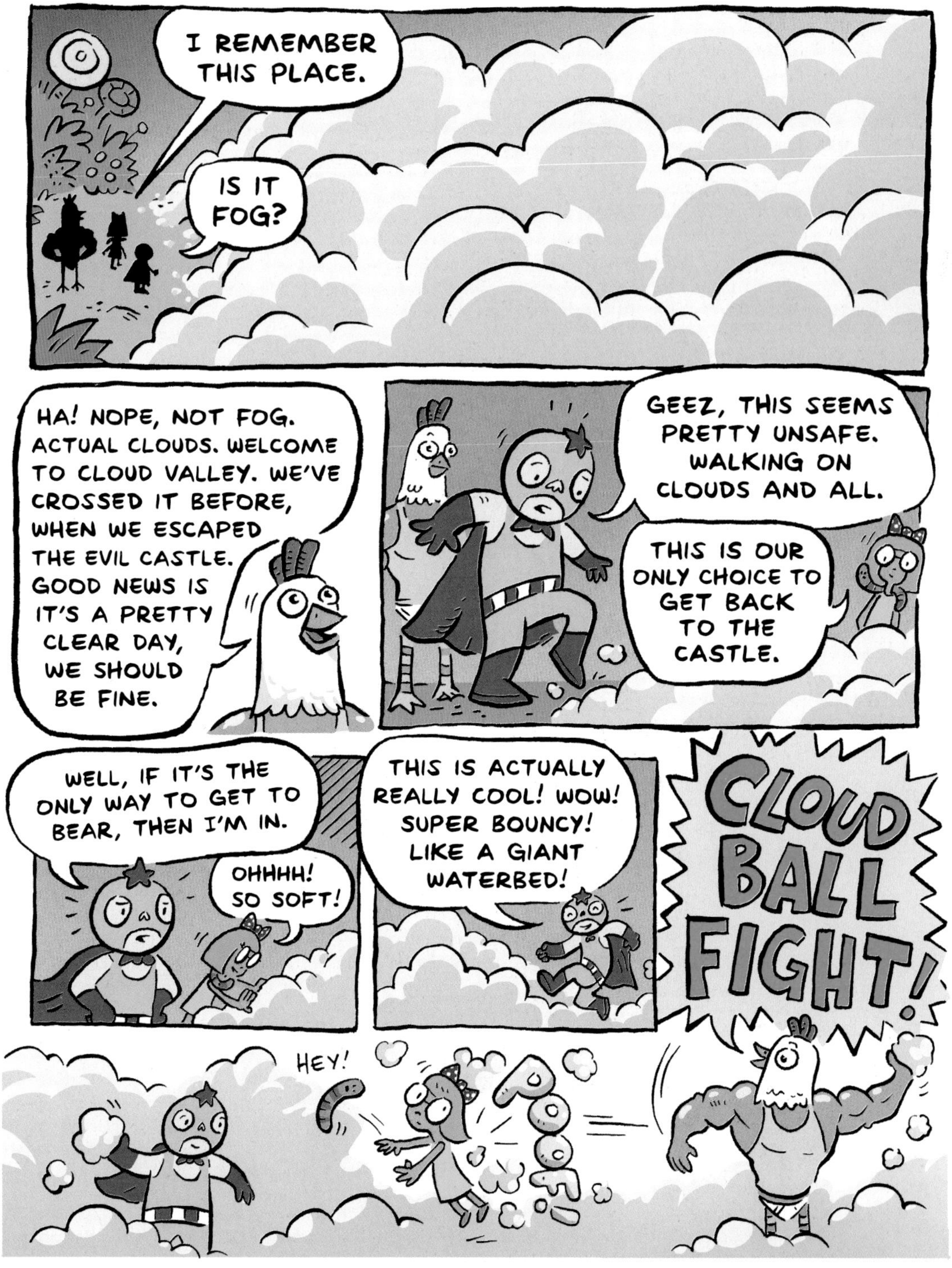
I REMEMBER THIS PLACE.
IS IT FOG?
HA! NOPE, NOT FOG. ACTUAL CLOUDS. WELCOME TO CLOUD VALLEY. WE'VE CROSSED IT BEFORE, WHEN WE ESCAPED THE EVIL CASTLE. GOOD NEWS IS IT'S A PRETTY CLEAR DAY, WE SHOULD BE FINE.
GEEZ, THIS SEEMS PRETTY UNSAFE. WALKING ON CLOUDS AND ALL.
THIS IS OUR ONLY CHOICE TO GET BACK TO THE CASTLE.
WELL, IF IT'S THE ONLY WAY TO GET TO BEAR, THEN I'M IN.
OHHHH! SO SOFT!
THIS IS ACTUALLY REALLY COOL! WOW! SUPER BOUNCY! LIKE A GIANT WATERBED!
CLOUD BALL FIGHT!
HEY!
POOF

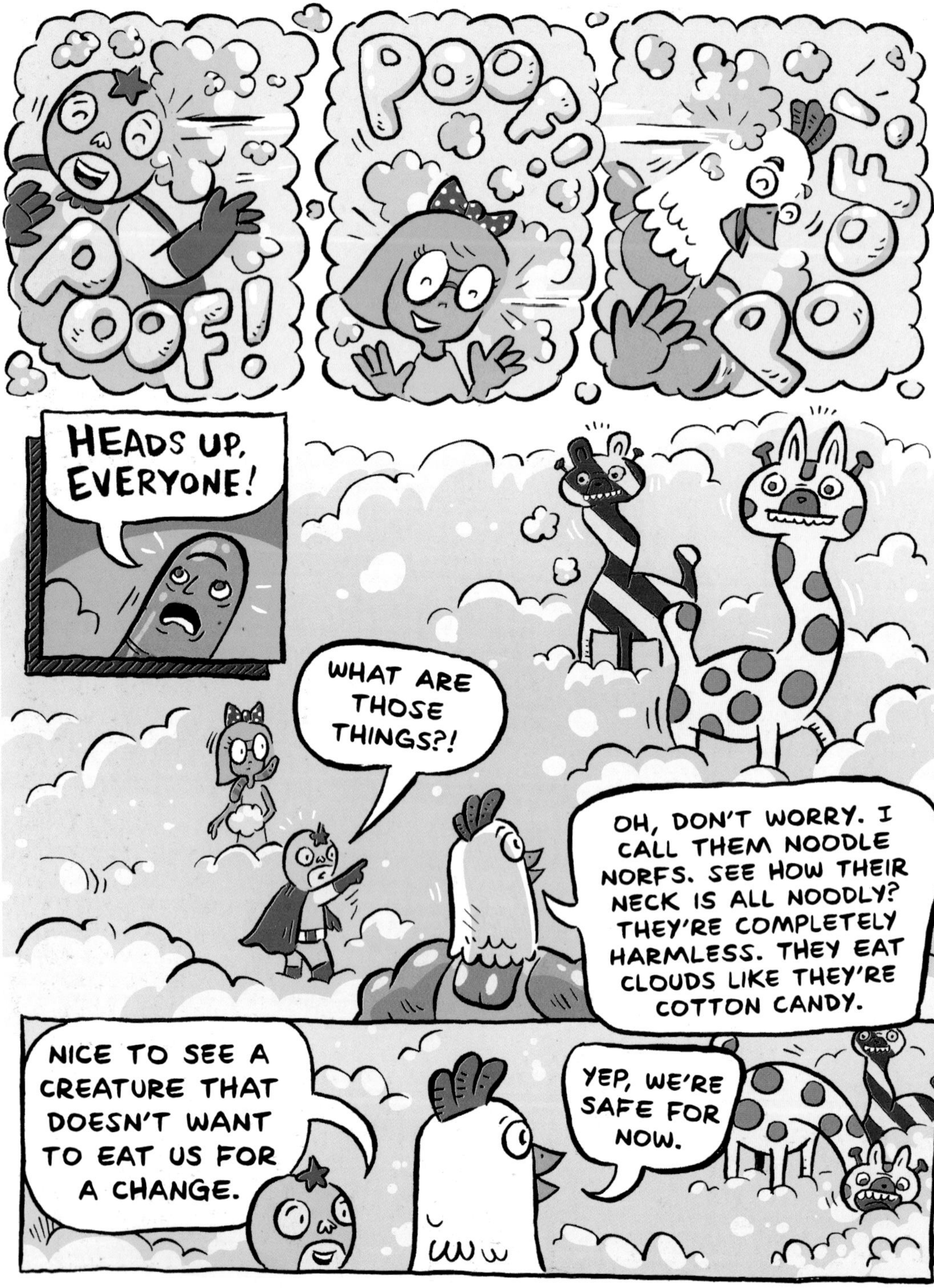
POOF!
POOF!
POOF!
HEADS UP, EVERYONE!
WHAT ARE THOSE THINGS?!
OH, DON'T WORRY. I CALL THEM NOODLE NORFS. SEE HOW THEIR NECK IS ALL NOODLY? THEY'RE COMPLETELY HARMLESS. THEY EAT CLOUDS LIKE THEY'RE COTTON CANDY.
NICE TO SEE A CREATURE THAT DOESN'T WANT TO EAT US FOR A CHANGE.
YEP, WE'RE SAFE FOR NOW.

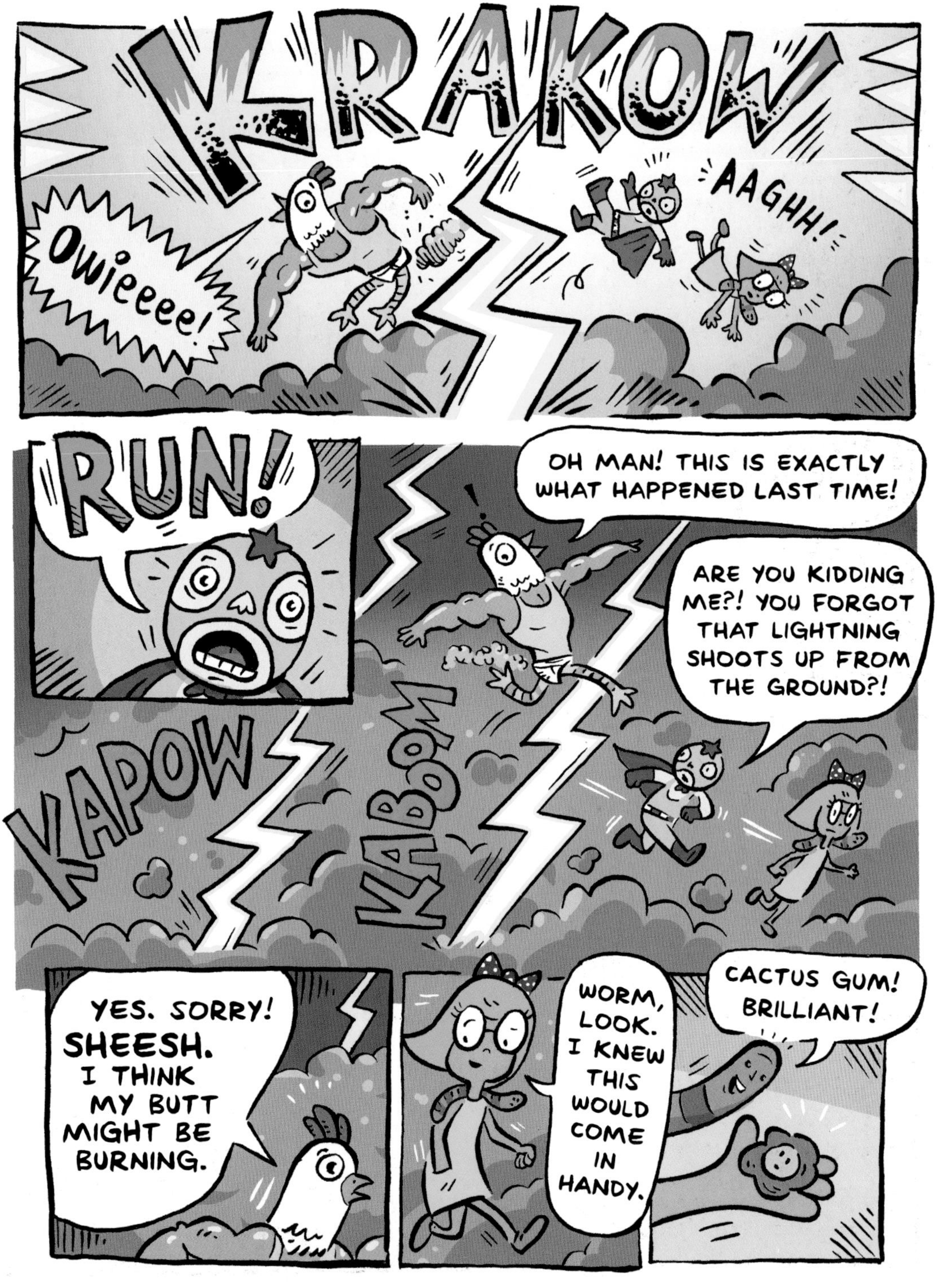
KRAKOW
Owieeeee!
AAGHH!
RUN!
OH MAN! THIS IS EXACTLY WHAT HAPPENED LAST TIME!
ARE YOU KIDDING ME?! YOU FORGOT THAT LIGHTNING SHOOTS UP FROM THE GROUND?!
KAPOW
KABOOM
YES. SORRY! SHEESH. I THINK MY BUTT MIGHT BE BURNING.
WORM, LOOK. I KNEW THIS WOULD COME IN HANDY.
CACTUS GUM! BRILLIANT!

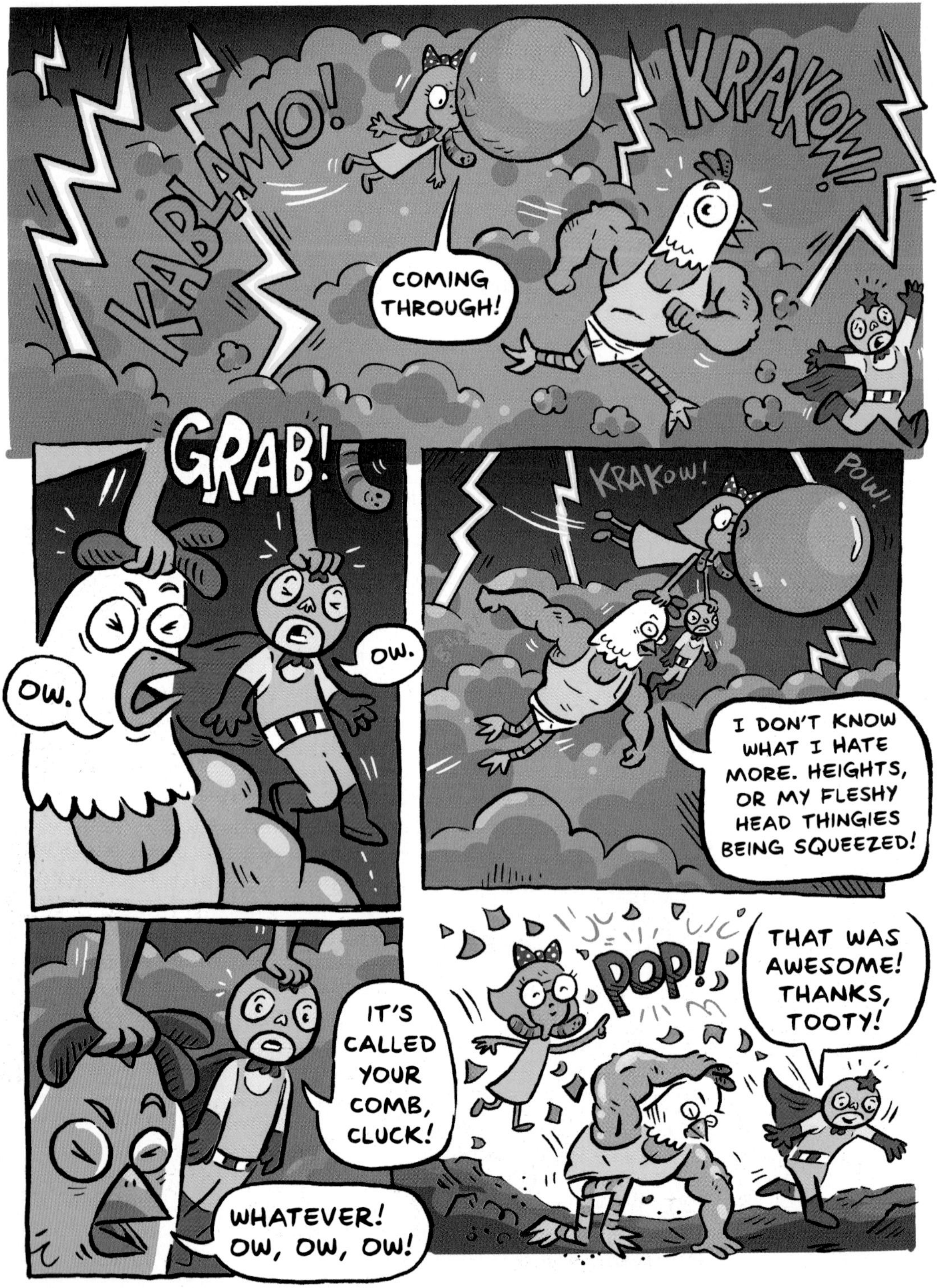
KABLAMO!
KRAKOW!
COMING THROUGH!
GRAB!
OW.
OW.
KRAKOW!
POW!
I DON'T KNOW WHAT I HATE MORE. HEIGHTS, OR MY FLESHY HEAD THINGIES BEING SQUEEZED!
IT'S CALLED YOUR COMB, CLUCK!
WHATEVER! OW, OW, OW!
POP!
THAT WAS AWESOME! THANKS, TOOTY!

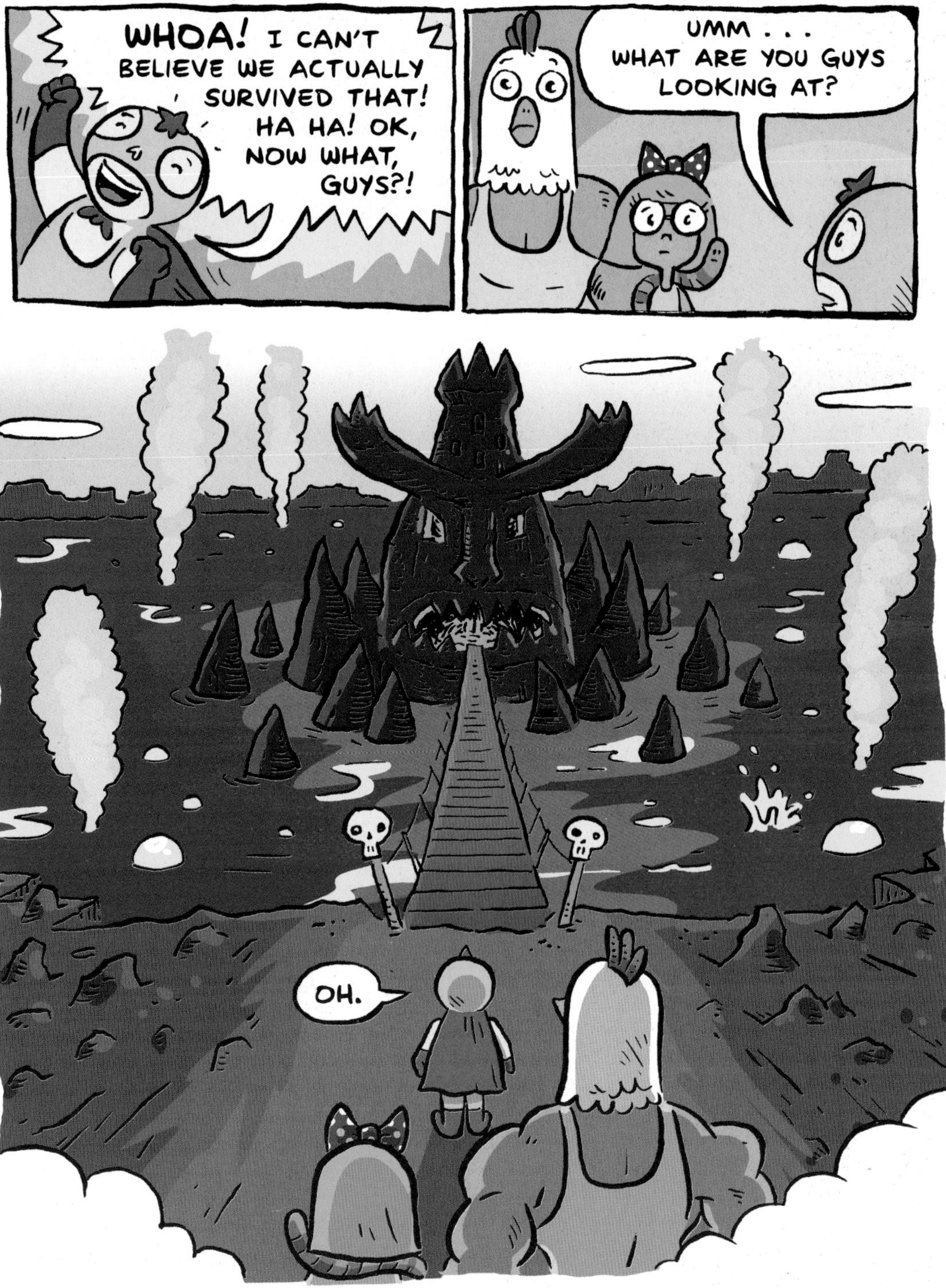
WHOA! I CAN'T BELIEVE WE ACTUALLY SURVIVED THAT! HA HA! OK, NOW WHAT, GUYS?!
UMM . . . WHAT ARE YOU GUYS LOOKING AT?
OH.

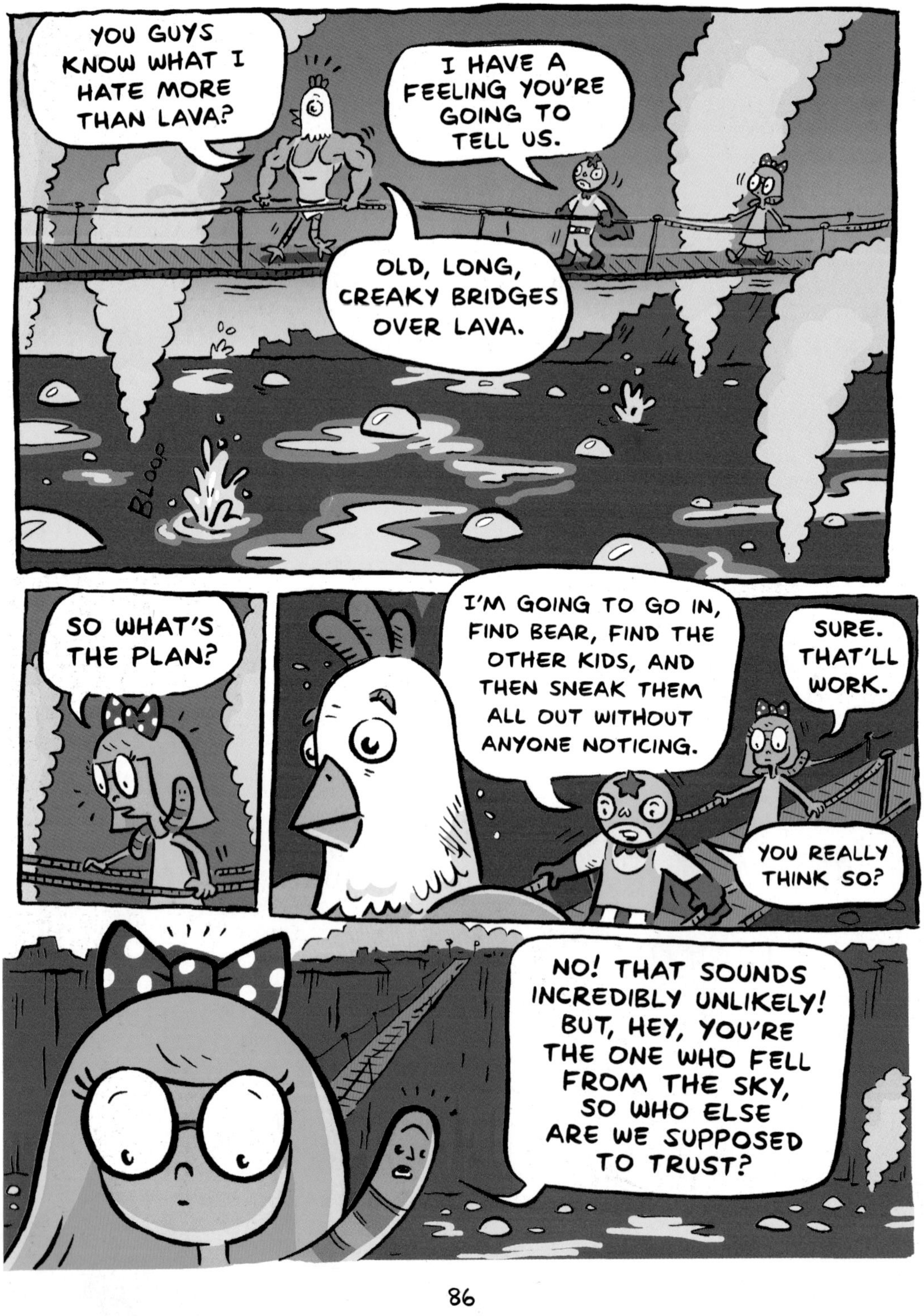
YOU GUYS KNOW WHAT I HATE MORE THAN LAVA?
I HAVE A FEELING YOU'RE GOING TO TELL US.
OLD, LONG, CREAKY BRIDGES OVER LAVA.
BLOOP
SO WHAT'S THE PLAN?
I'M GOING TO GO IN, FIND BEAR, FIND THE OTHER KIDS, AND THEN SNEAK THEM ALL OUT WITHOUT ANYONE NOTICING.
SURE. THAT'LL WORK.
YOU REALLY THINK SO?
NO! THAT SOUNDS INCREDIBLY UNLIKELY! BUT, HEY, YOU'RE THE ONE WHO FELL FROM THE SKY, SO WHO ELSE ARE WE SUPPOSED TO TRUST?

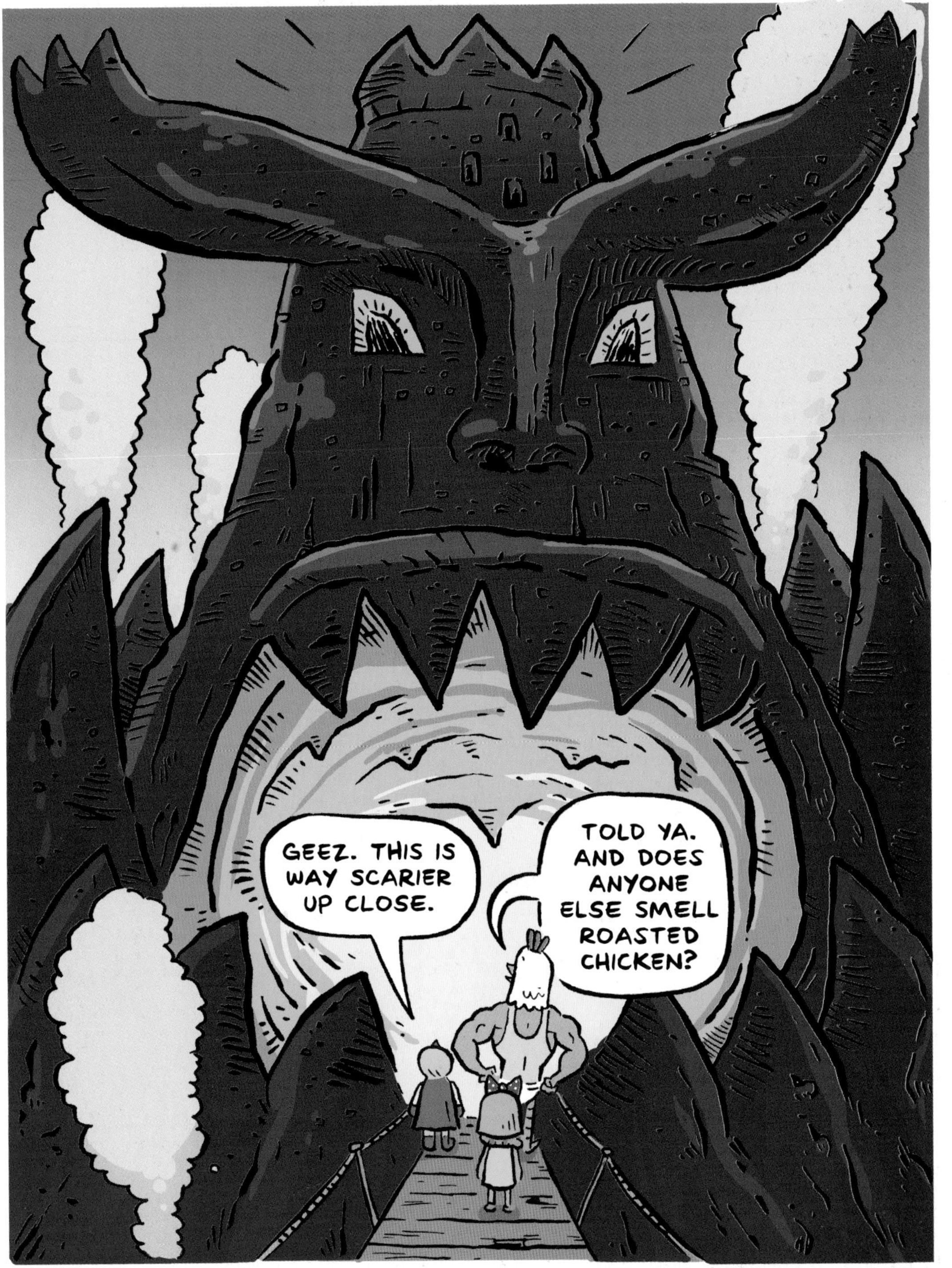
GEEZ. THIS IS WAY SCARIER UP CLOSE.
TOLD YA. AND DOES ANYONE ELSE SMELL ROASTED CHICKEN?

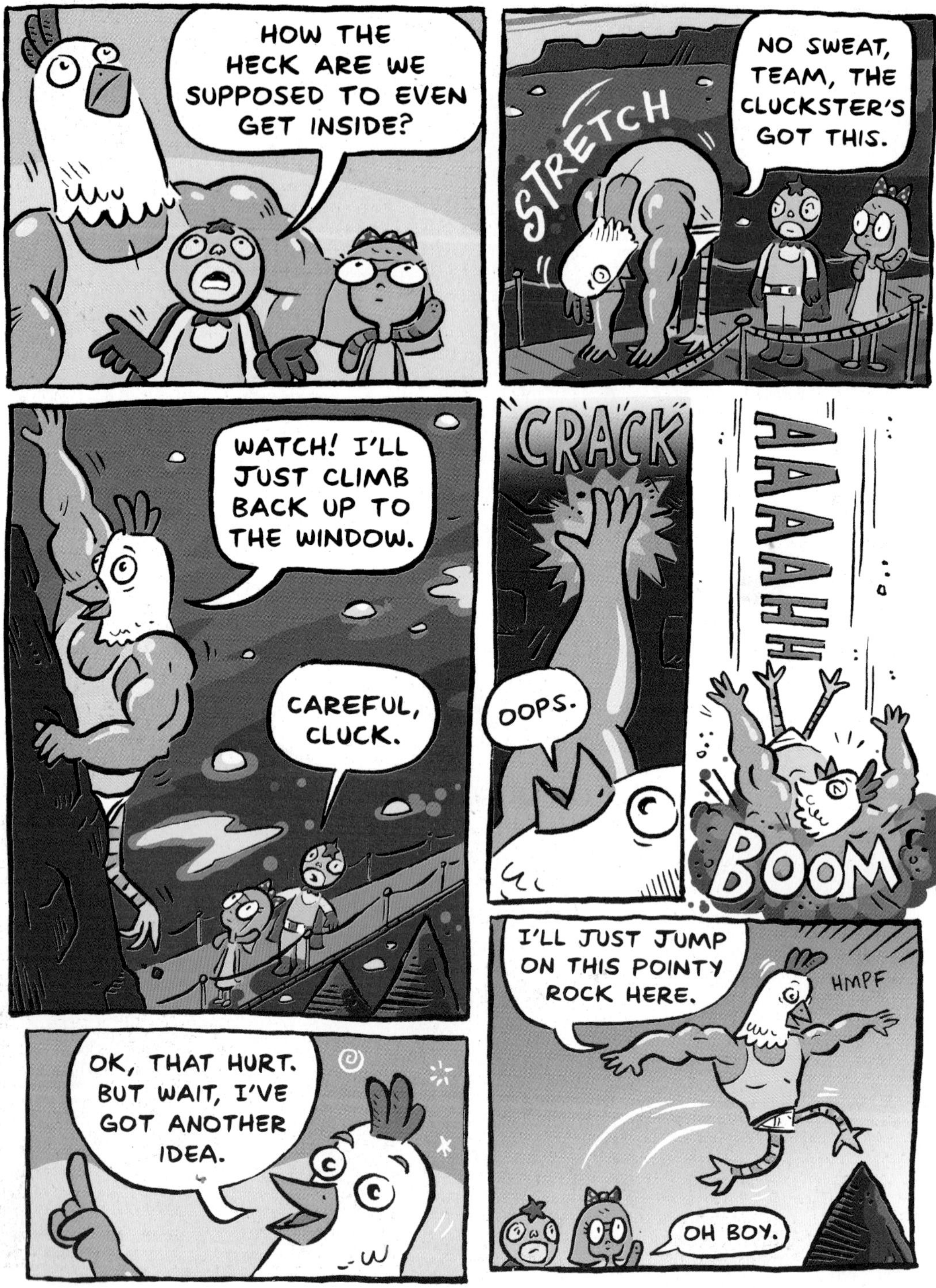
HOW THE HECK ARE WE SUPPOSED TO EVEN GET INSIDE?
NO SWEAT, TEAM, THE CLUCKSTER'S GOT THIS.
STRETCH
WATCH! I'LL JUST CLIMB BACK UP TO THE WINDOW.
CAREFUL, CLUCK.
CRACK
OOPS.
AAAAAHH
BOOM
I'LL JUST JUMP ON THIS POINTY ROCK HERE.
HMPF
OH BOY.
OK, THAT HURT. BUT WAIT, I'VE GOT ANOTHER IDEA.

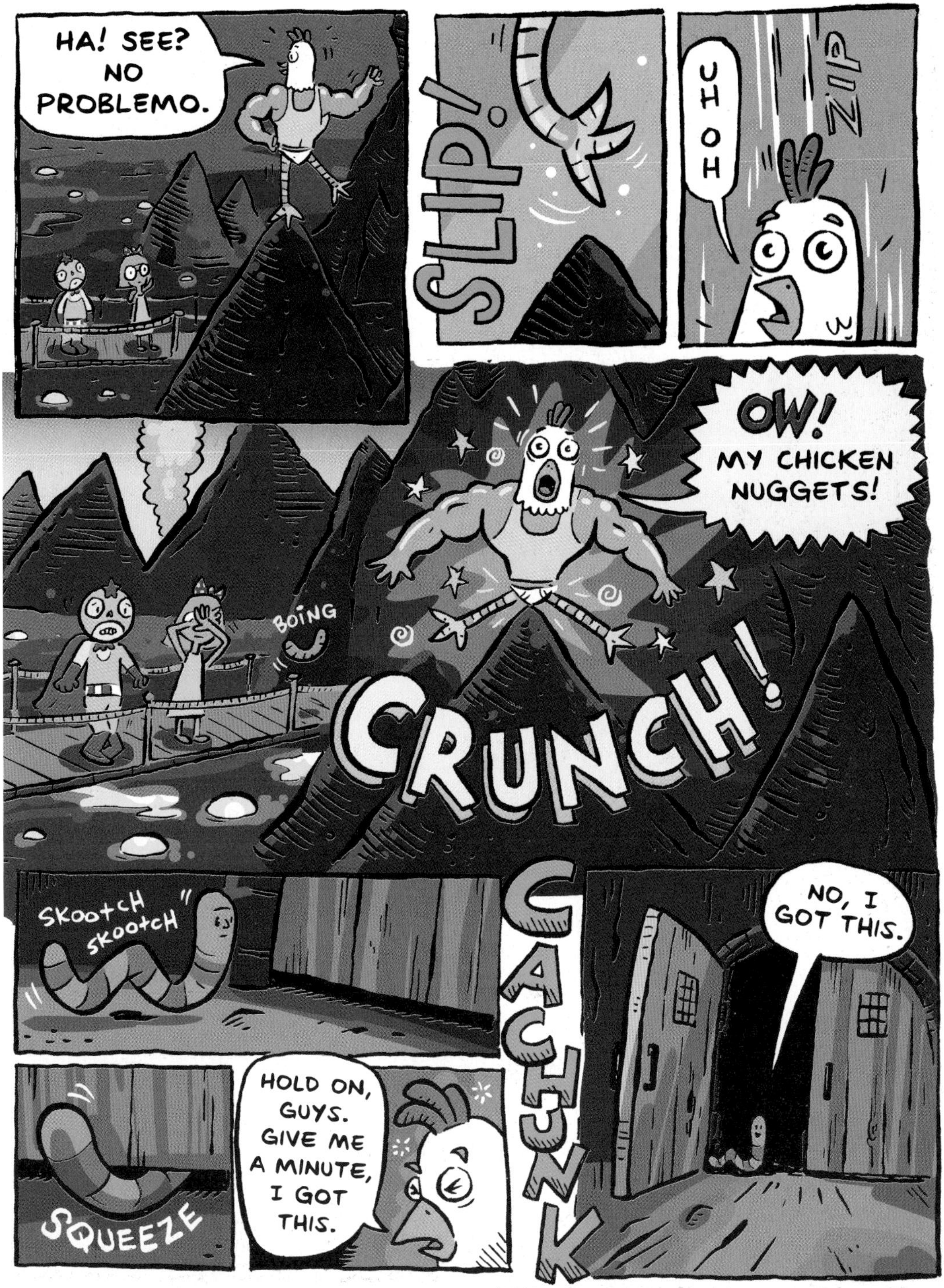
HA! SEE? NO PROBLEMO.
SLIP!
UH OH
ZIP
OW! MY CHICKEN NUGGETS!
BOING
CRUNCH!
SKOOTCH SKOOTCH
CACHUNK
NO, I GOT THIS.
SQUEEZE
HOLD ON, GUYS. GIVE ME A MINUTE, I GOT THIS.

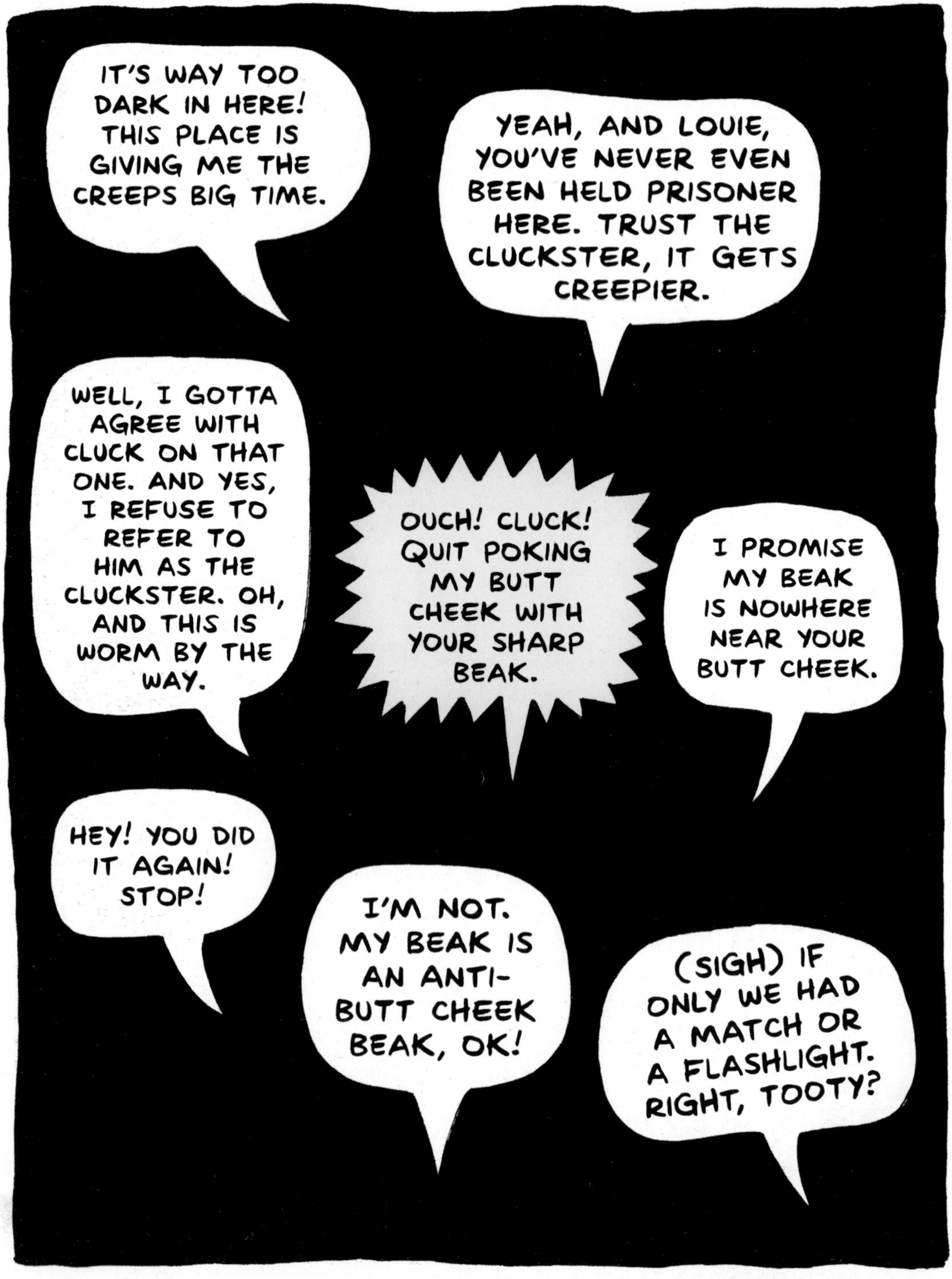

IT'S WAY TOO DARK IN HERE! THIS PLACE IS GIVING ME THE CREEPS BIG TIME.
YEAH, AND LOUIE, YOU'VE NEVER EVEN BEEN HELD PRISONER HERE. TRUST THE CLUCKSTER, IT GETS CREEPIER.
WELL, I GOTTA AGREE WITH CLUCK ON THAT ONE. AND YES, I REFUSE TO REFER TO HIM AS THE CLUCKSTER. OH, AND THIS IS WORM BY THE WAY.
OUCH! CLUCK! QUIT POKING MY BUTT CHEEK WITH YOUR SHARP BEAK.
I PROMISE MY BEAK IS NOWHERE NEAR YOUR BUTT CHEEK.
HEY! YOU DID IT AGAIN! STOP!
I'M NOT. MY BEAK IS AN ANTI-BUTT CHEEK BEAK, OK!
(SIGH) IF ONLY WE HAD A MATCH OR A FLASHLIGHT. RIGHT, TOOTY?

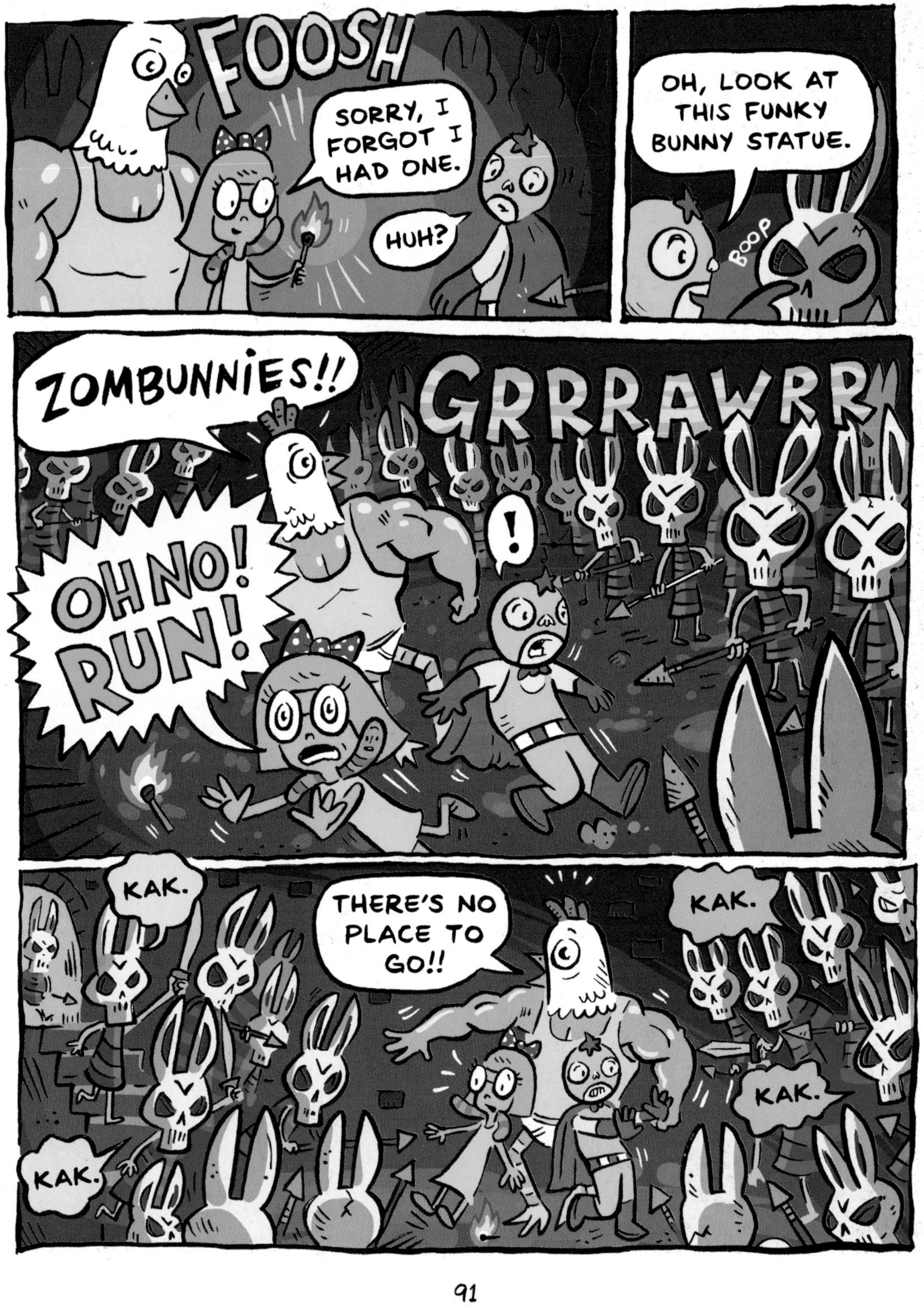

FOOSH
SORRY, I FORGOT I HAD ONE.
HUH?
OH, LOOK AT THIS FUNKY BUNNY STATUE.
BOOP
ZOMBUNNIES!!
GRRRAWRR
!
OH NO! RUN!
KAK.
THERE'S NO PLACE TO GO!!
KAK.
KAK.
KAK.

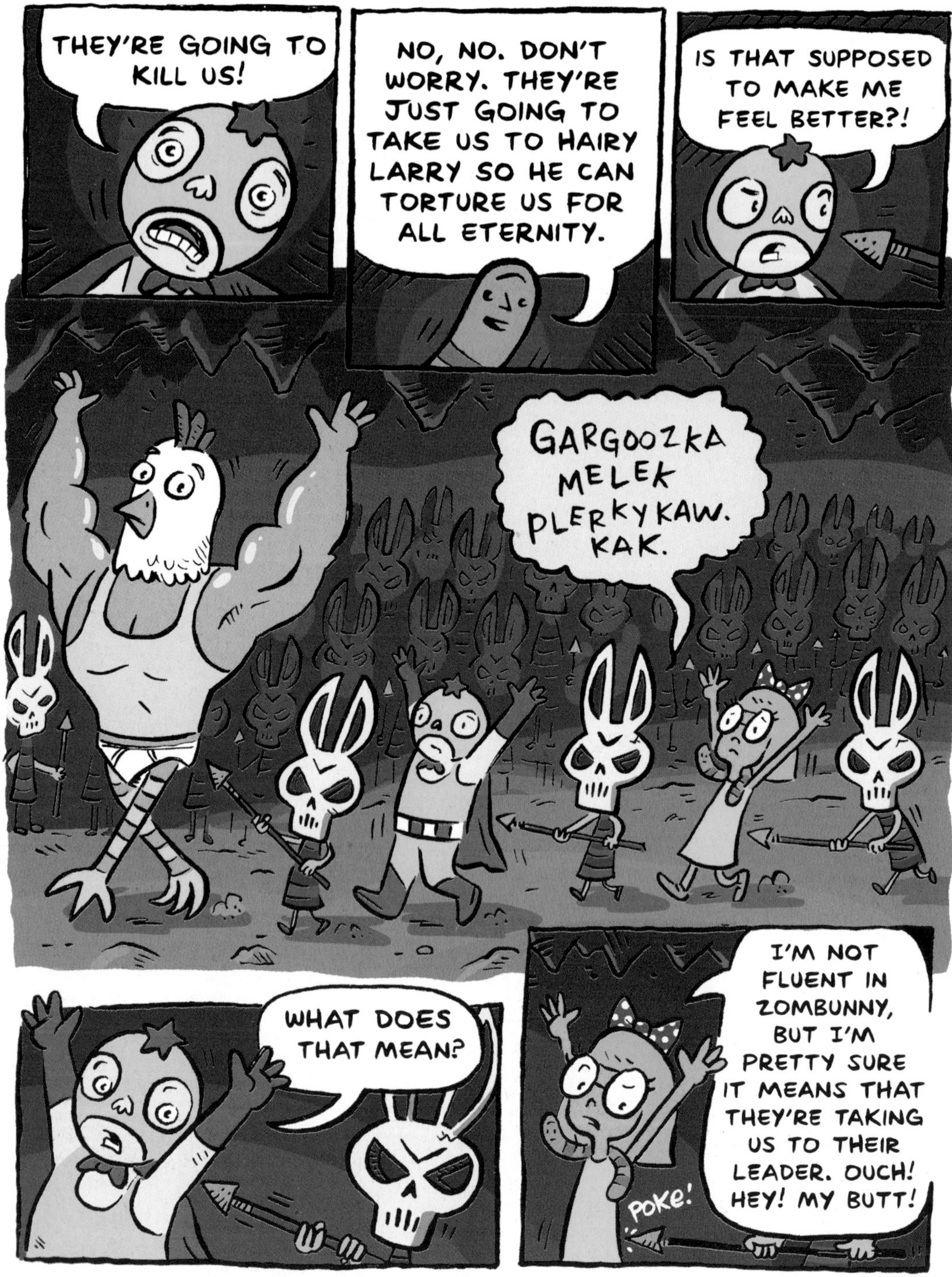
THEY'RE GOING TO KILL US!
NO, NO. DON'T WORRY. THEY'RE JUST GOING TO TAKE US TO HAIRY LARRY SO HE CAN TORTURE US FOR ALL ETERNITY.
IS THAT SUPPOSED TO MAKE ME FEEL BETTER?!
GARGOOZKA MELEK PLERKYKAW. KAK.
WHAT DOES THAT MEAN?
I'M NOT FLUENT IN ZOMBUNNY, BUT I'M PRETTY SURE IT MEANS THAT THEY'RE TAKING US TO THEIR LEADER. OUCH! HEY! MY BUTT!
POKE!

chapter
8

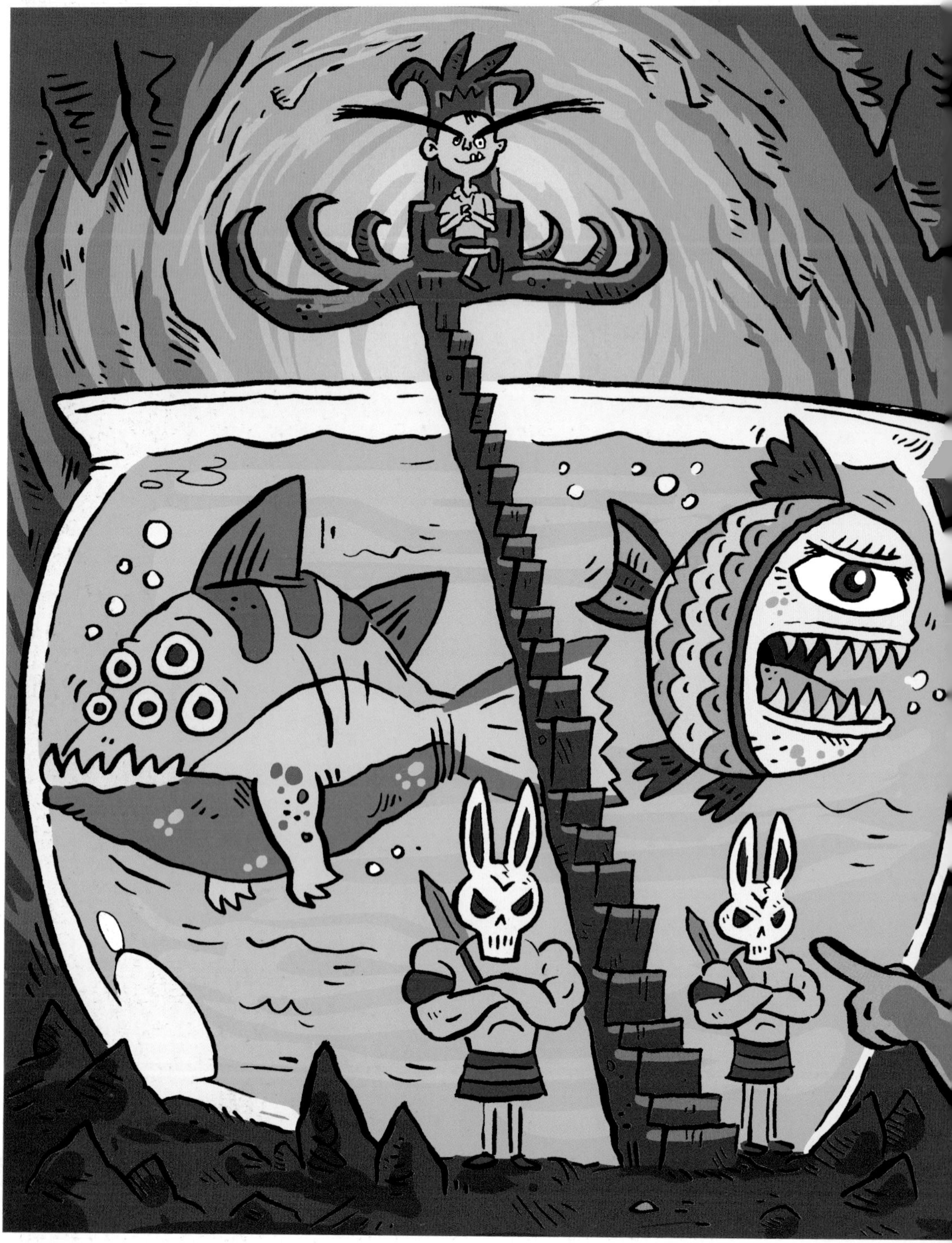

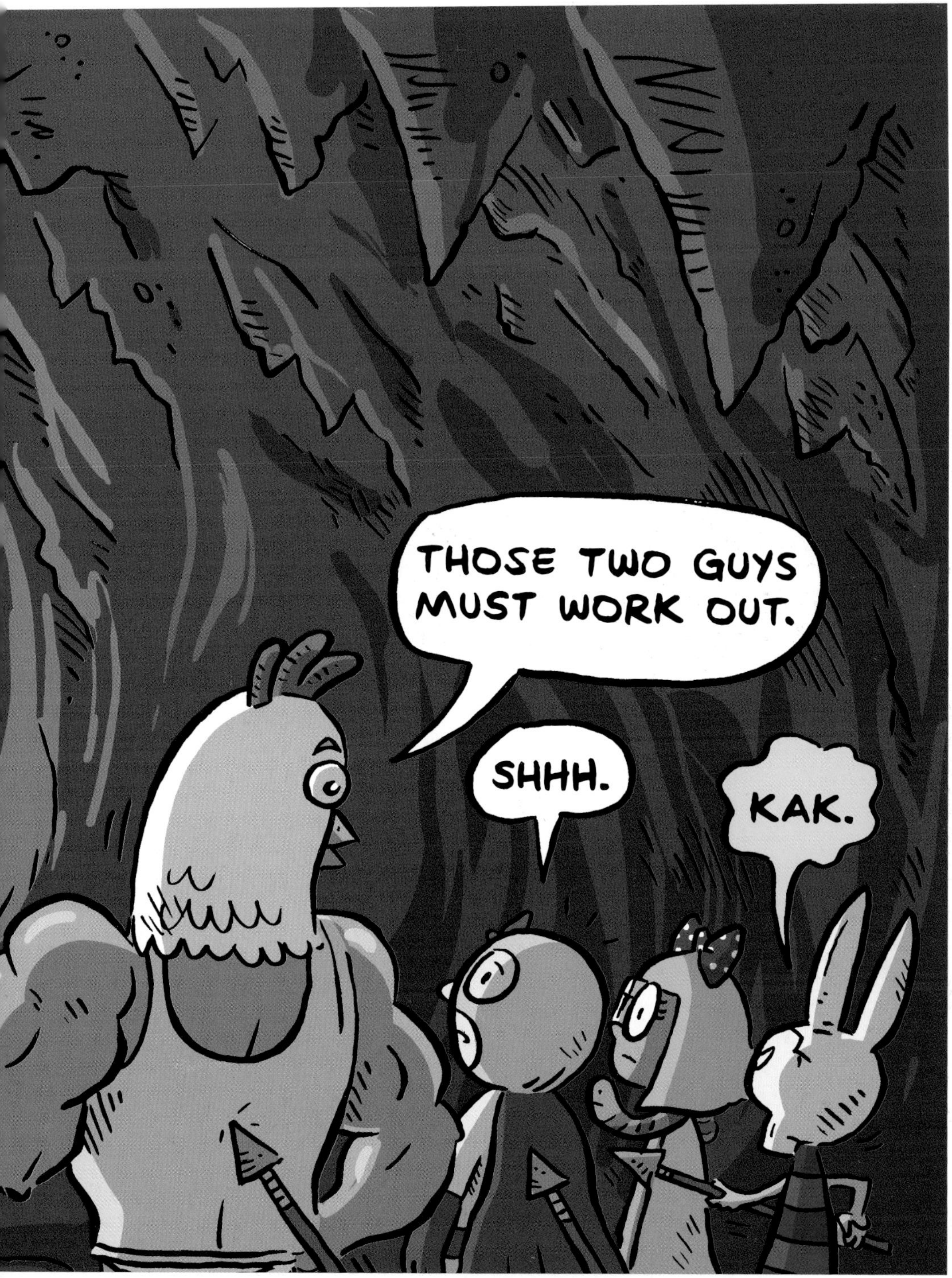
THOSE TWO GUYS MUST WORK OUT.
SHHH.
KAK.

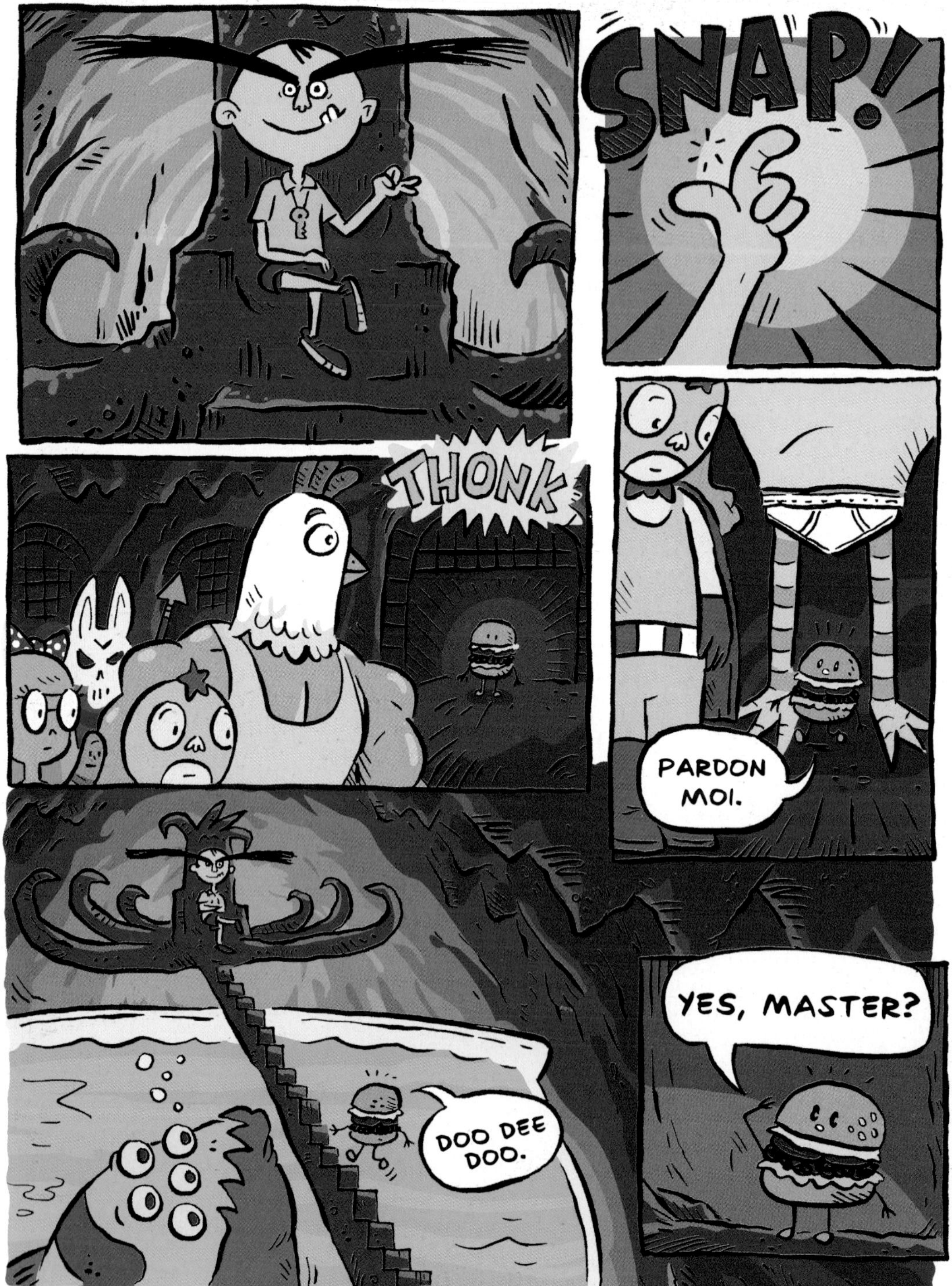
SNAP!
THONK
PARDON MOI.
DOO DEE DOO.
YES, MASTER?

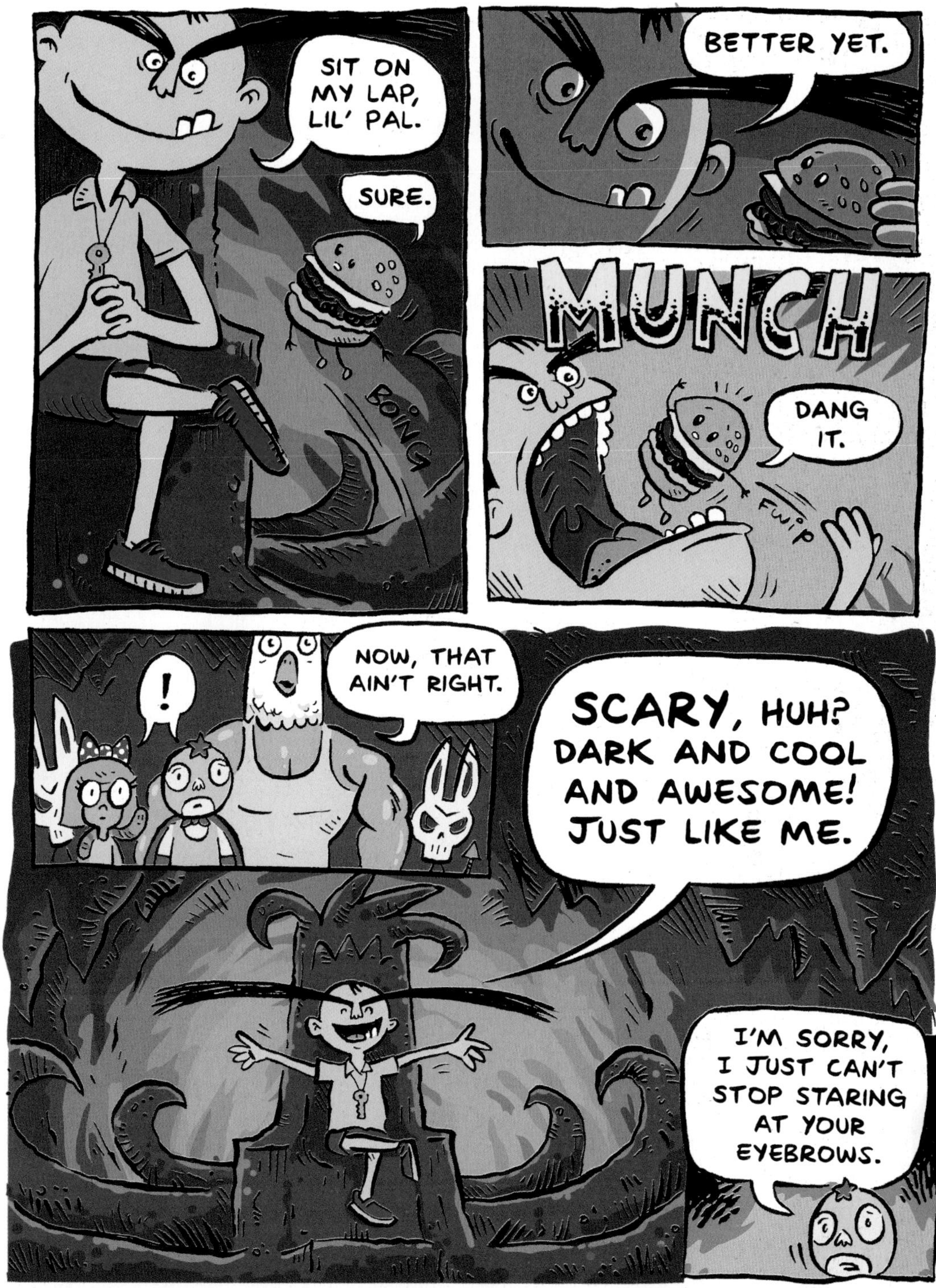
SIT ON MY LAP, LIL' PAL.
SURE.
BOING
BETTER YET.
MUNCH
DANG IT.
FWIP
NOW, THAT AIN'T RIGHT.
!
SCARY, HUH? DARK AND COOL AND AWESOME! JUST LIKE ME.
I'M SORRY, I JUST CAN'T STOP STARING AT YOUR EYEBROWS.

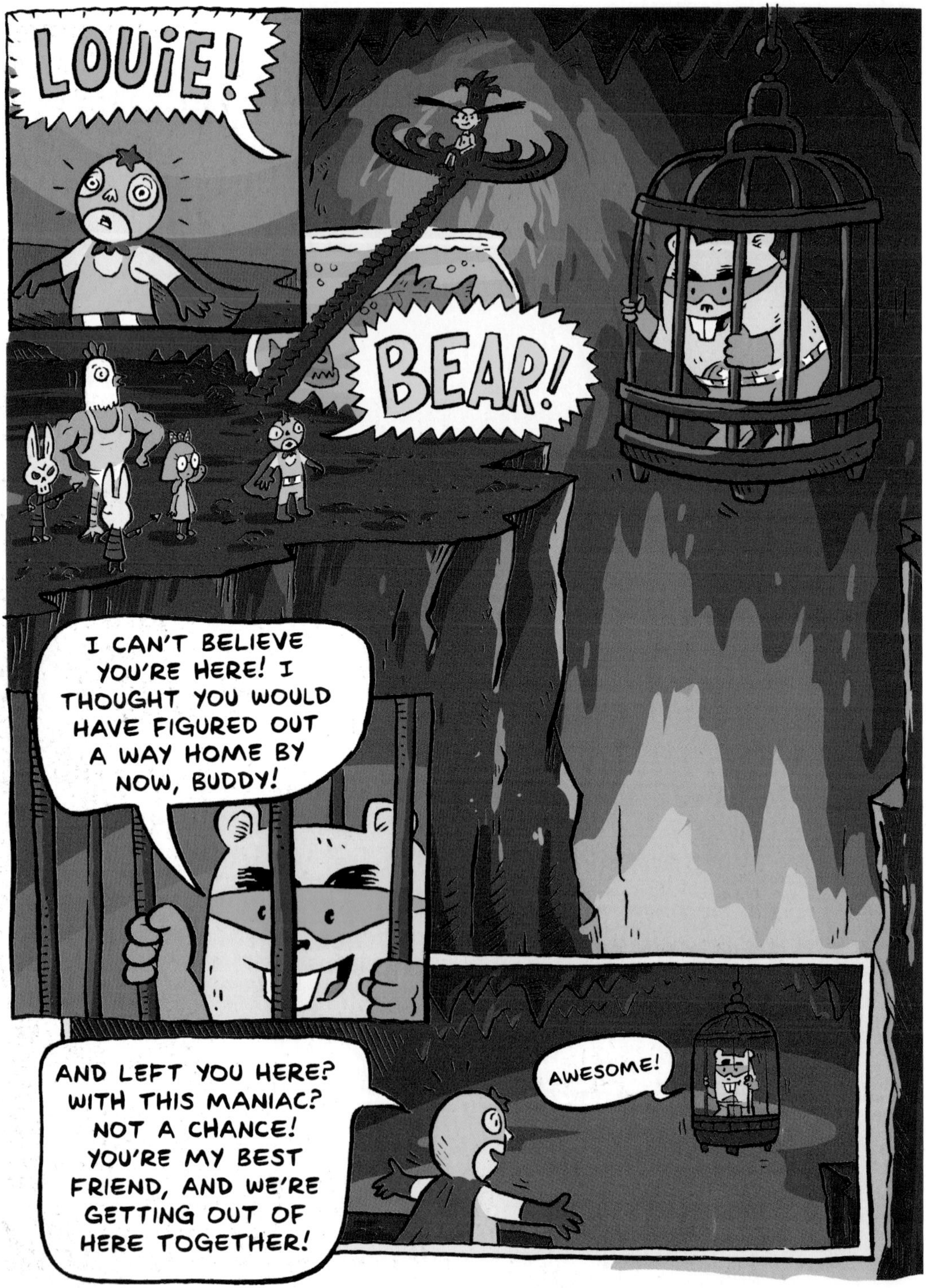
LOUIE!
BEAR!
I CAN'T BELIEVE YOU'RE HERE! I THOUGHT YOU WOULD HAVE FIGURED OUT A WAY HOME BY NOW, BUDDY!
AND LEFT YOU HERE? WITH THIS MANIAC? NOT A CHANCE! YOU'RE MY BEST FRIEND, AND WE'RE GETTING OUT OF HERE TOGETHER!
AWESOME!

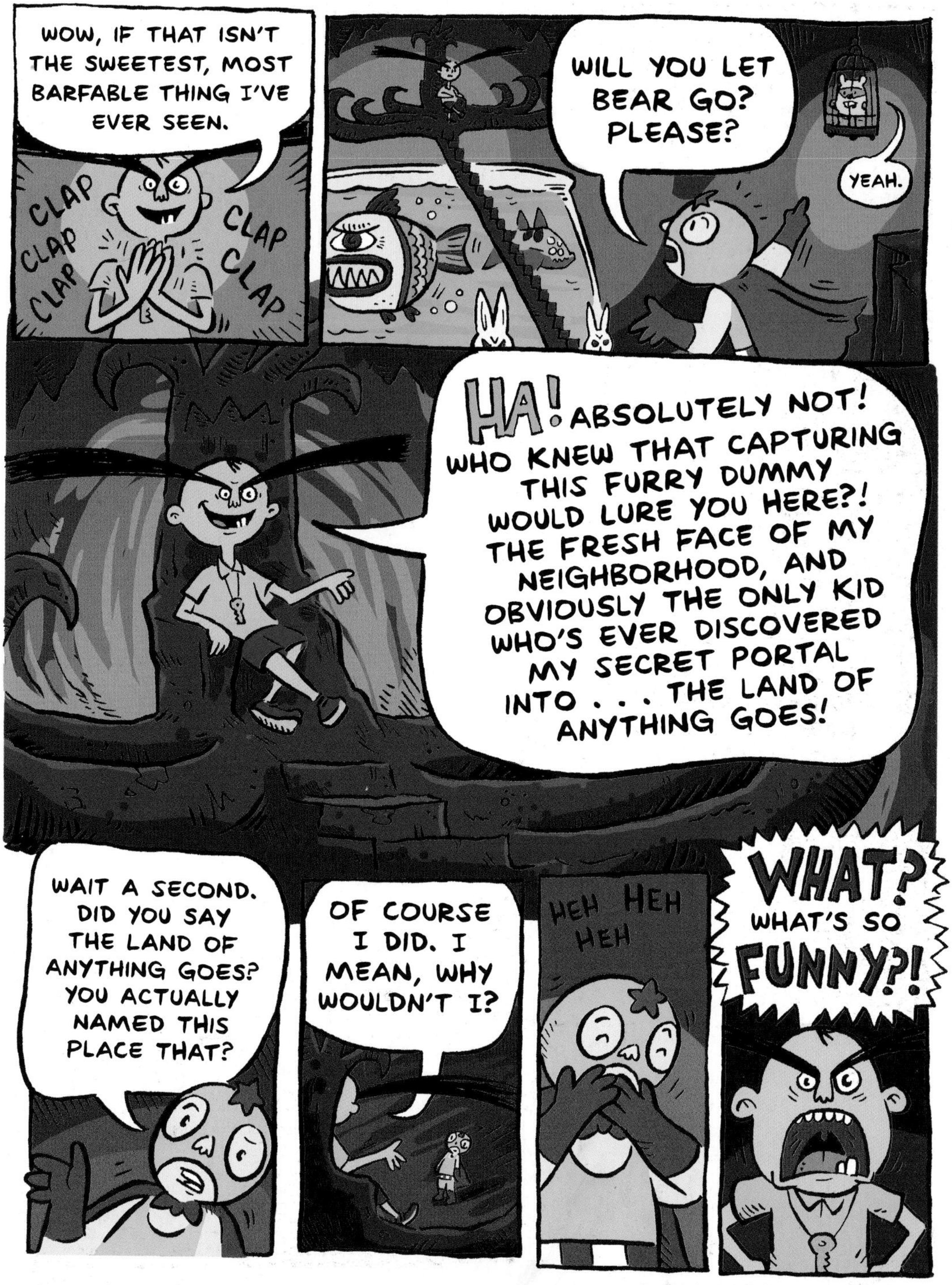
WOW, IF THAT ISN'T THE SWEETEST, MOST BARFABLE THING I'VE EVER SEEN.
CLAP CLAP CLAP
CLAP CLAP CLAP
WILL YOU LET BEAR GO? PLEASE?
YEAH.
HA! ABSOLUTELY NOT! WHO KNEW THAT CAPTURING THIS FURRY DUMMY WOULD LURE YOU HERE?! THE FRESH FACE OF MY NEIGHBORHOOD, AND OBVIOUSLY THE ONLY KID WHO'S EVER DISCOVERED MY SECRET PORTAL INTO . . . THE LAND OF ANYTHING GOES!
WAIT A SECOND. DID YOU SAY THE LAND OF ANYTHING GOES? YOU ACTUALLY NAMED THIS PLACE THAT?
OF COURSE I DID. I MEAN, WHY WOULDN'T I?
HEH HEH HEH
WHAT? WHAT'S SO FUNNY?!

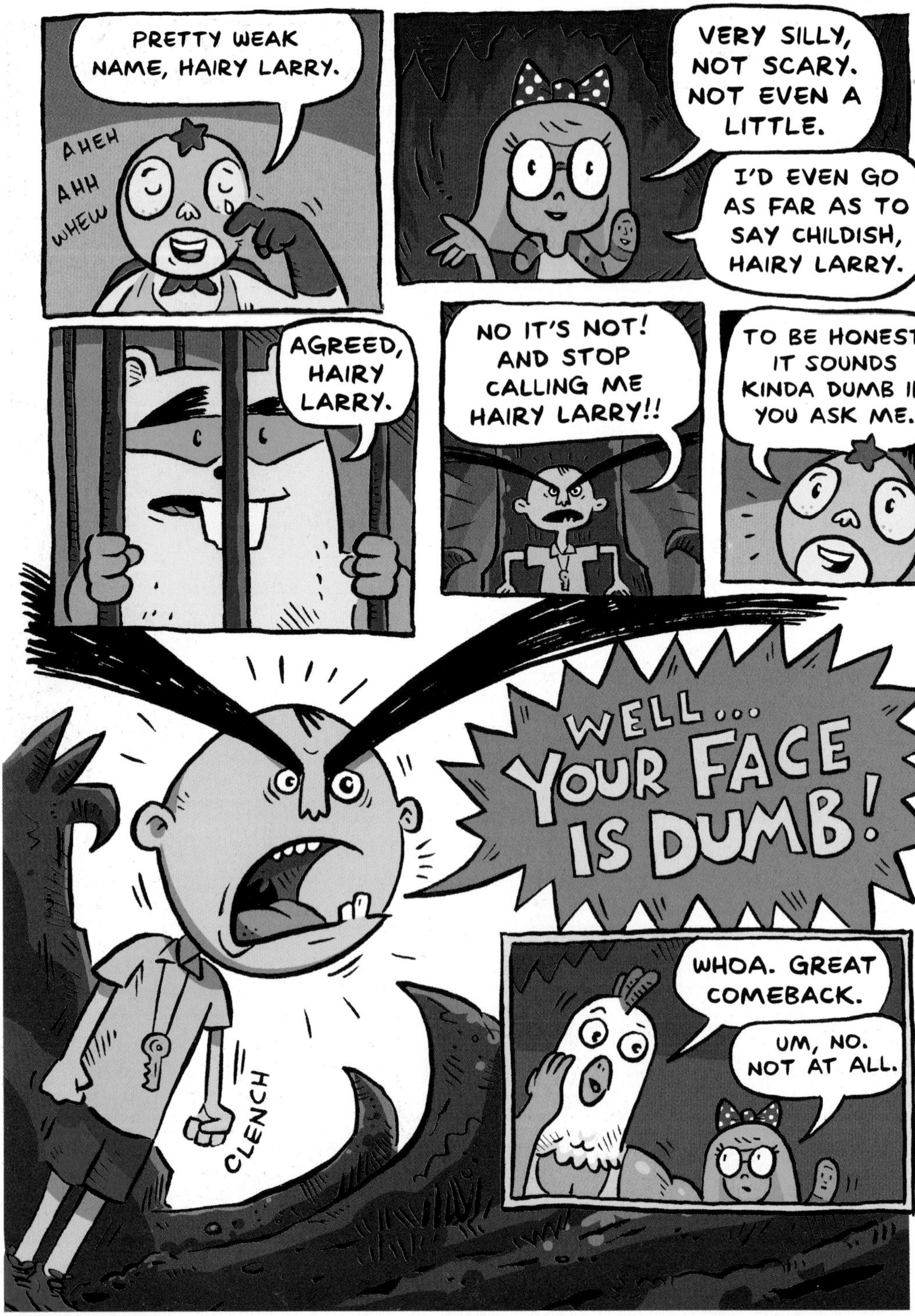
PRETTY WEAK NAME, HAIRY LARRY.
AHEH AHH WHEW
VERY SILLY, NOT SCARY. NOT EVEN A LITTLE.
I'D EVEN GO AS FAR AS TO SAY CHILDISH, HAIRY LARRY.
AGREED, HAIRY LARRY.
NO IT'S NOT! AND STOP CALLING ME HAIRY LARRY!!
TO BE HONEST, IT SOUNDS KINDA DUMB IF YOU ASK ME.
WELL... YOUR FACE IS DUMB!
CLENCH
WHOA. GREAT COMEBACK.
UM, NO. NOT AT ALL.

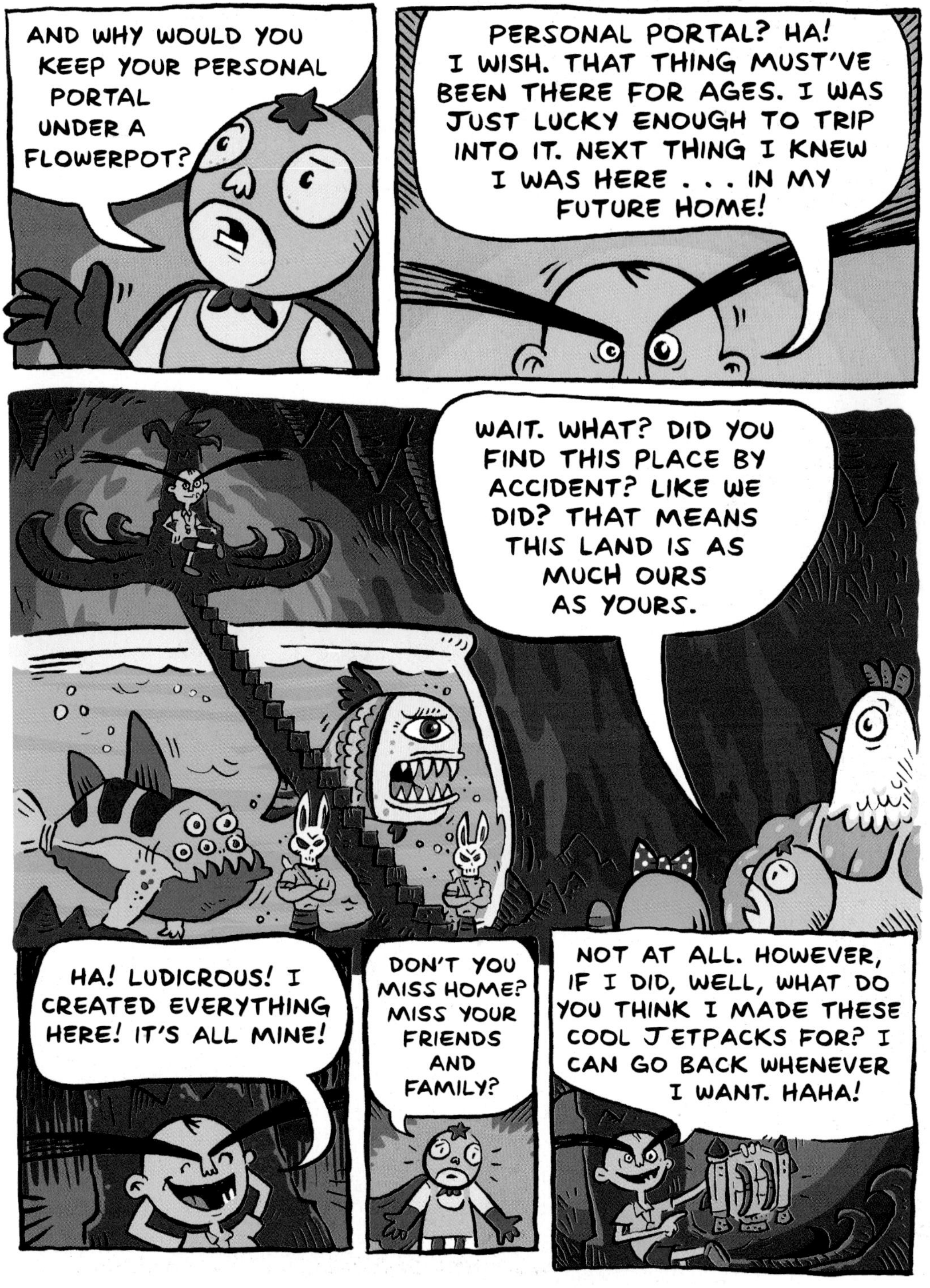
AND WHY WOULD YOU KEEP YOUR PERSONAL PORTAL UNDER A FLOWERPOT?
PERSONAL PORTAL? HA! I WISH. THAT THING MUST'VE BEEN THERE FOR AGES. I WAS JUST LUCKY ENOUGH TO TRIP INTO IT. NEXT THING I KNEW I WAS HERE . . . IN MY FUTURE HOME!
WAIT. WHAT? DID YOU FIND THIS PLACE BY ACCIDENT? LIKE WE DID? THAT MEANS THIS LAND IS AS MUCH OURS AS YOURS.
HA! LUDICROUS! I CREATED EVERYTHING HERE! IT'S ALL MINE!
DON'T YOU MISS HOME? MISS YOUR FRIENDS AND FAMILY?
NOT AT ALL. HOWEVER, IF I DID, WELL, WHAT DO YOU THINK I MADE THESE COOL JETPACKS FOR? I CAN GO BACK WHENEVER I WANT. HAHA!

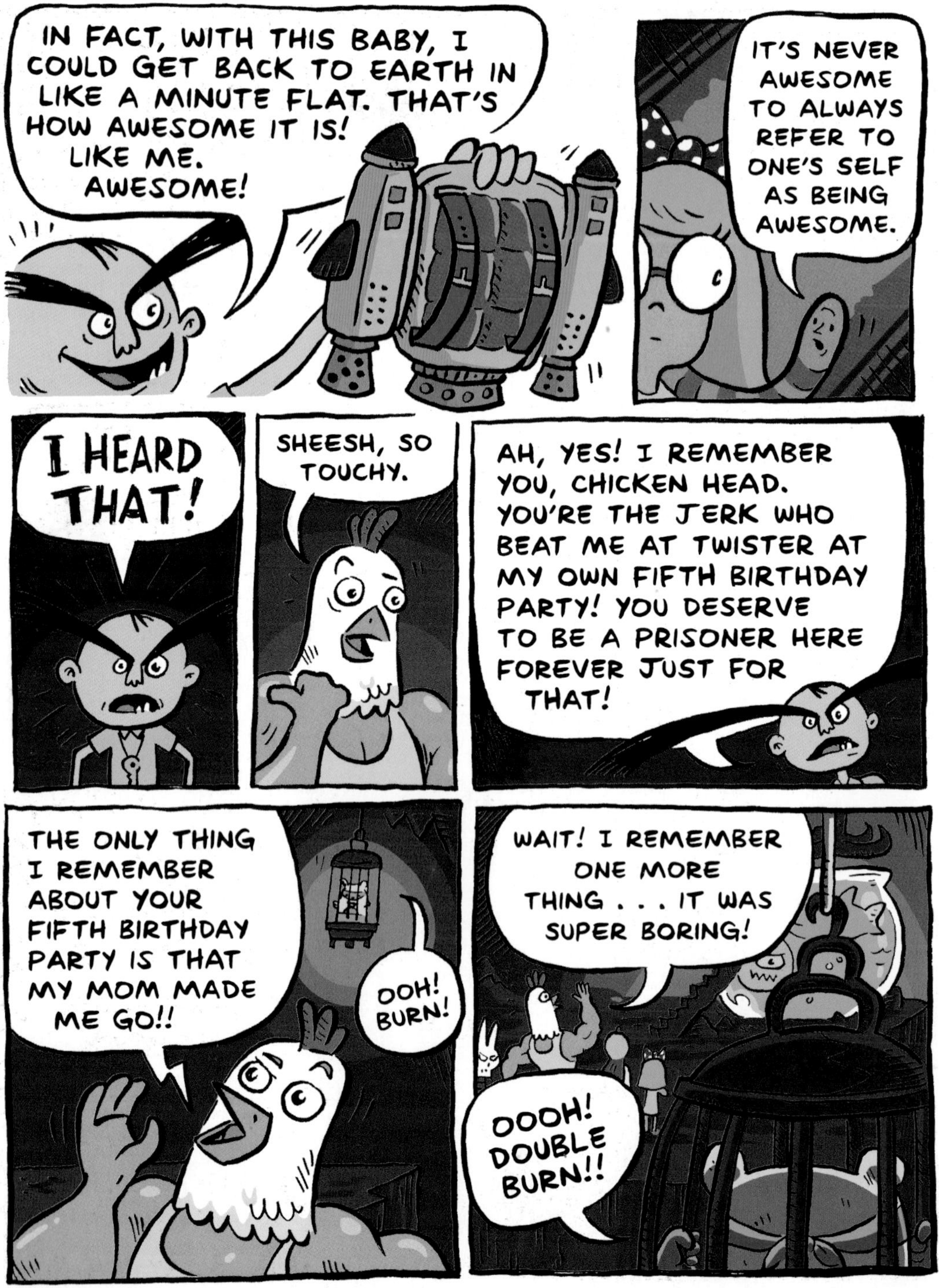
IN FACT, WITH THIS BABY, I COULD GET BACK TO EARTH IN LIKE A MINUTE FLAT. THAT'S HOW AWESOME IT IS! LIKE ME. AWESOME!
IT'S NEVER AWESOME TO ALWAYS REFER TO ONE'S SELF AS BEING AWESOME.
I HEARD THAT!
SHEESH, SO TOUCHY.
AH, YES! I REMEMBER YOU, CHICKEN HEAD. YOU'RE THE JERK WHO BEAT ME AT TWISTER AT MY OWN FIFTH BIRTHDAY PARTY! YOU DESERVE TO BE A PRISONER HERE FOREVER JUST FOR THAT!
THE ONLY THING I REMEMBER ABOUT YOUR FIFTH BIRTHDAY PARTY IS THAT MY MOM MADE ME GO!!
OOH! BURN!
WAIT! I REMEMBER ONE MORE THING . . . IT WAS SUPER BORING!
OOOH! DOUBLE BURN!!

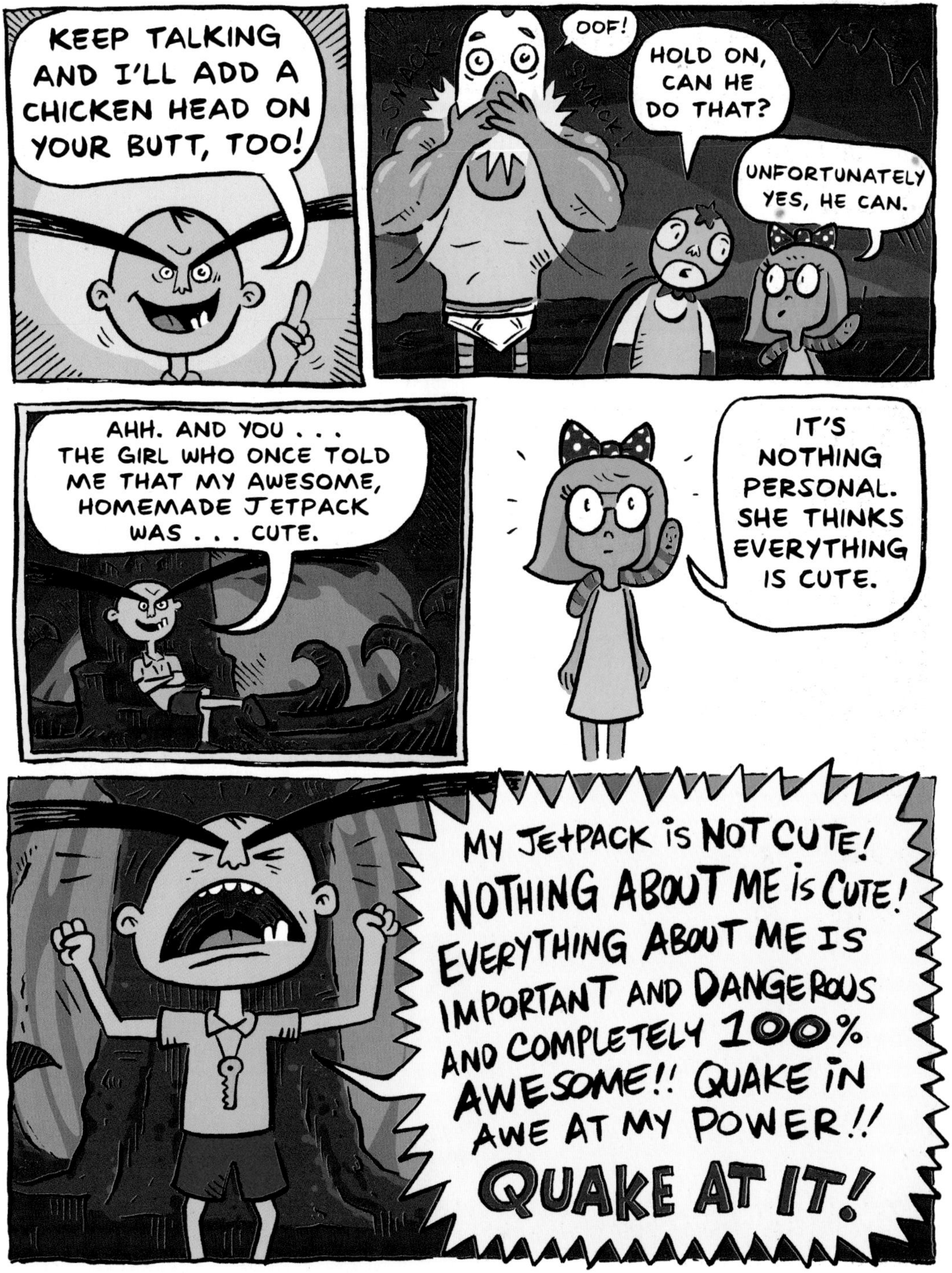
KEEP TALKING AND I'LL ADD A CHICKEN HEAD ON YOUR BUTT, TOO!
SMACK!
SMACK!
OOF!
HOLD ON, CAN HE DO THAT?
UNFORTUNATELY YES, HE CAN.
AHH. AND YOU . . . THE GIRL WHO ONCE TOLD ME THAT MY AWESOME, HOMEMADE JETPACK WAS . . . CUTE.
IT'S NOTHING PERSONAL. SHE THINKS EVERYTHING IS CUTE.
MY JETPACK IS NOT CUTE! NOTHING ABOUT ME IS CUTE! EVERYTHING ABOUT ME IS IMPORTANT AND DANGEROUS AND COMPLETELY 100% AWESOME!! QUAKE IN AWE AT MY POWER!!
QUAKE AT IT!

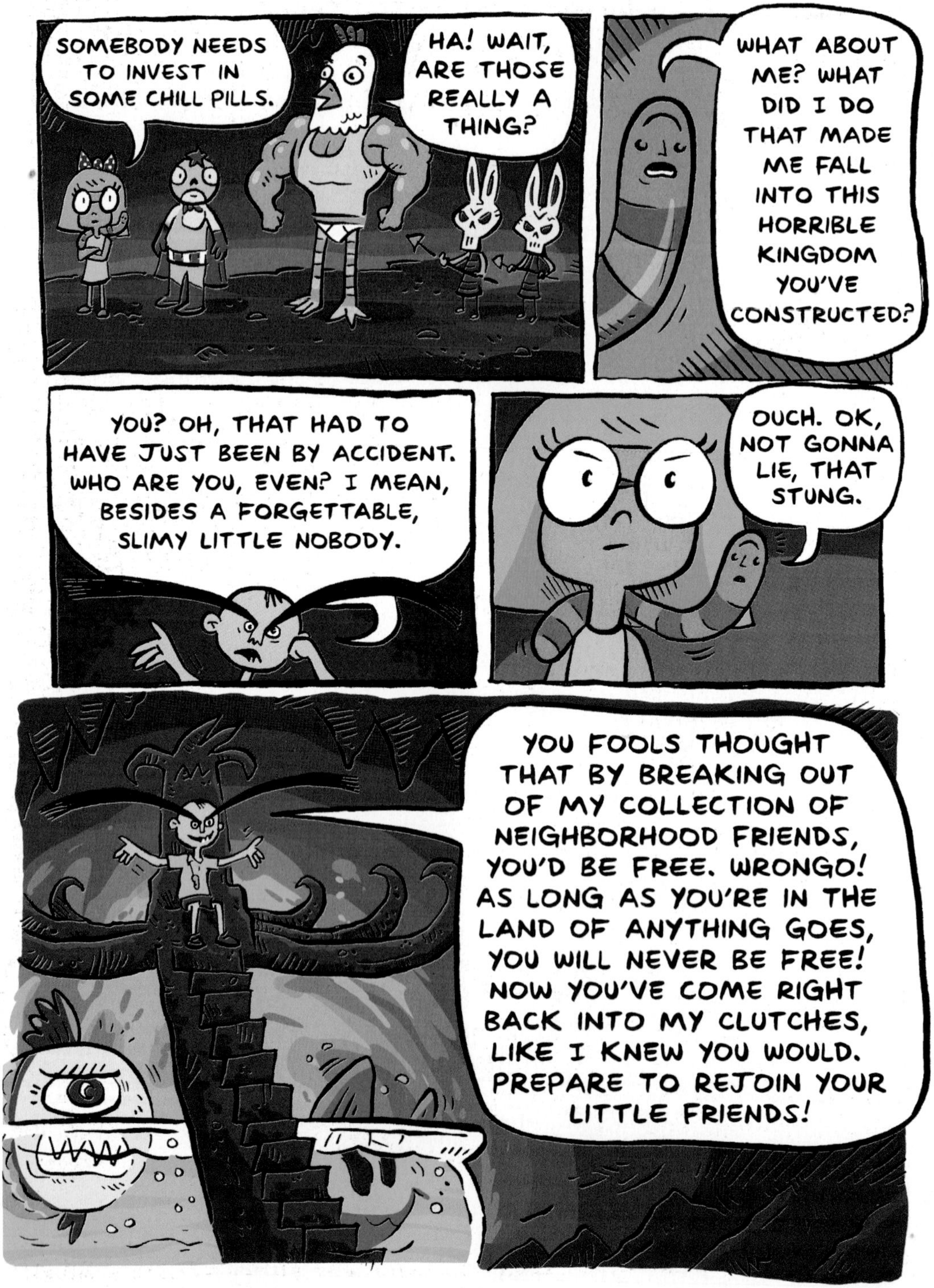
SOMEBODY NEEDS TO INVEST IN SOME CHILL PILLS.
HA! WAIT, ARE THOSE REALLY A THING?
WHAT ABOUT ME? WHAT DID I DO THAT MADE ME FALL INTO THIS HORRIBLE KINGDOM YOU'VE CONSTRUCTED?
YOU? OH, THAT HAD TO HAVE JUST BEEN BY ACCIDENT. WHO ARE YOU, EVEN? I MEAN, BESIDES A FORGETTABLE, SLIMY LITTLE NOBODY.
OUCH. OK, NOT GONNA LIE, THAT STUNG.
YOU FOOLS THOUGHT THAT BY BREAKING OUT OF MY COLLECTION OF NEIGHBORHOOD FRIENDS, YOU'D BE FREE. WRONGO! AS LONG AS YOU'RE IN THE LAND OF ANYTHING GOES, YOU WILL NEVER BE FREE! NOW YOU'VE COME RIGHT BACK INTO MY CLUTCHES, LIKE I KNEW YOU WOULD. PREPARE TO REJOIN YOUR LITTLE FRIENDS!

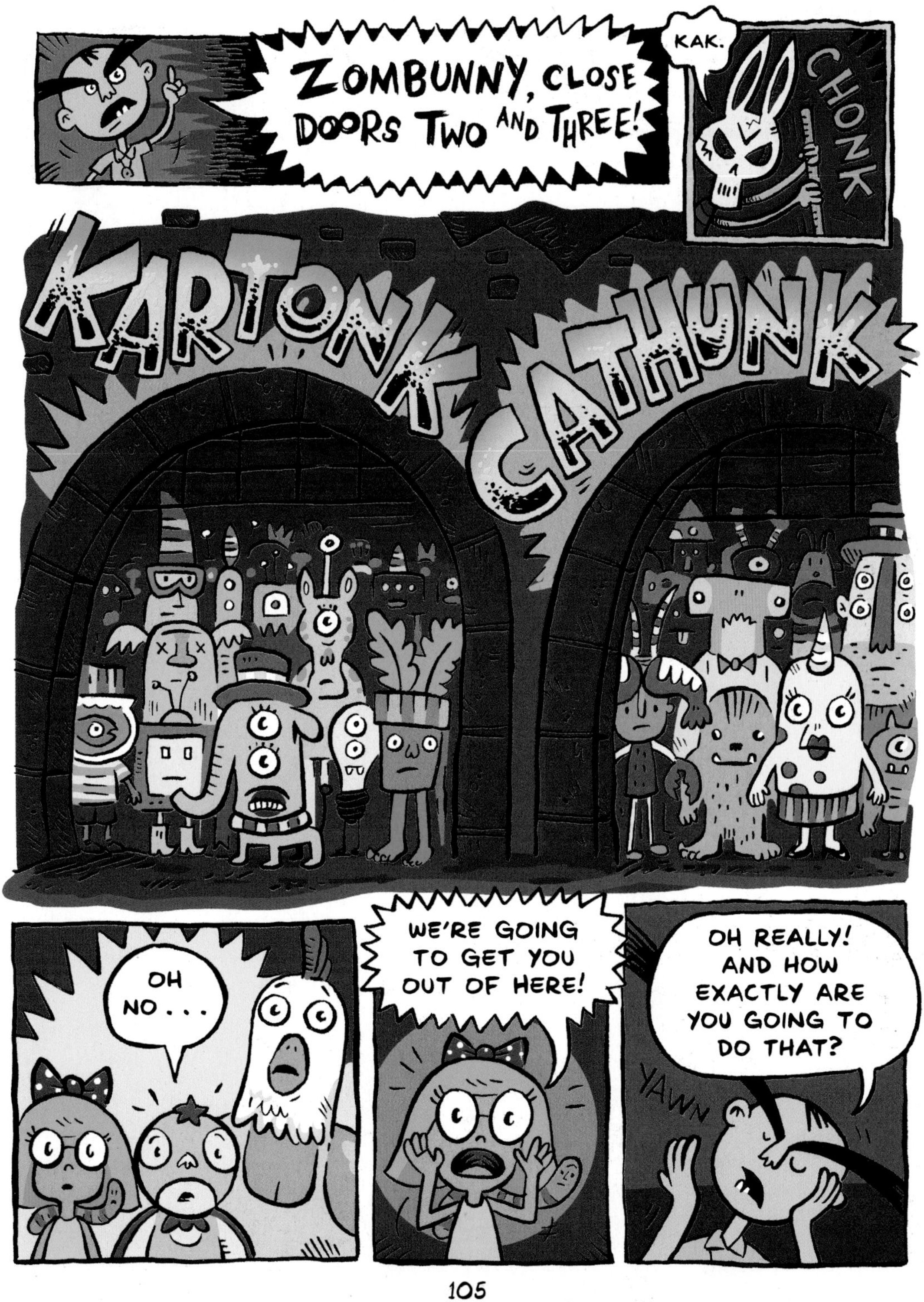
ZOMBUNNY, CLOSE DOORS TWO AND THREE!
KAK.
CHONK
KARTONK
CATHUNK
OH NO . . .
WE'RE GOING TO GET YOU OUT OF HERE!
YAWN
OH REALLY! AND HOW EXACTLY ARE YOU GOING TO DO THAT?

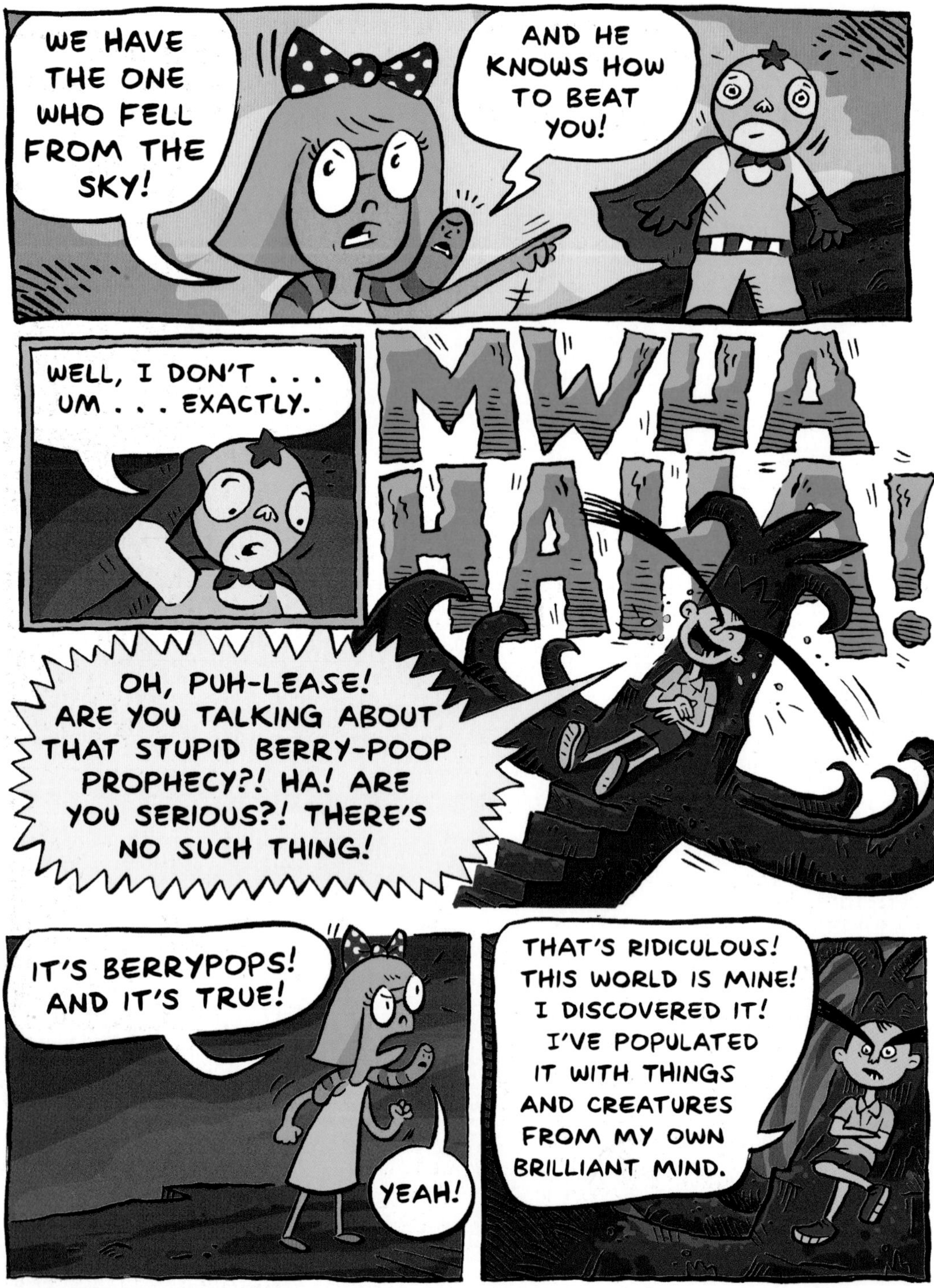

WE HAVE THE ONE WHO FELL FROM THE SKY!
AND HE KNOWS HOW TO BEAT YOU!
WELL, I DON'T . . . UM . . . EXACTLY.
MWHA HAHA!
OH, PUH-LEASE! ARE YOU TALKING ABOUT THAT STUPID BERRY-POOP PROPHECY?! HA! ARE YOU SERIOUS?! THERE'S NO SUCH THING!
IT'S BERRYPOPS! AND IT'S TRUE!
YEAH!
THAT'S RIDICULOUS! THIS WORLD IS MINE! I DISCOVERED IT! I'VE POPULATED IT WITH THINGS AND CREATURES FROM MY OWN BRILLIANT MIND.

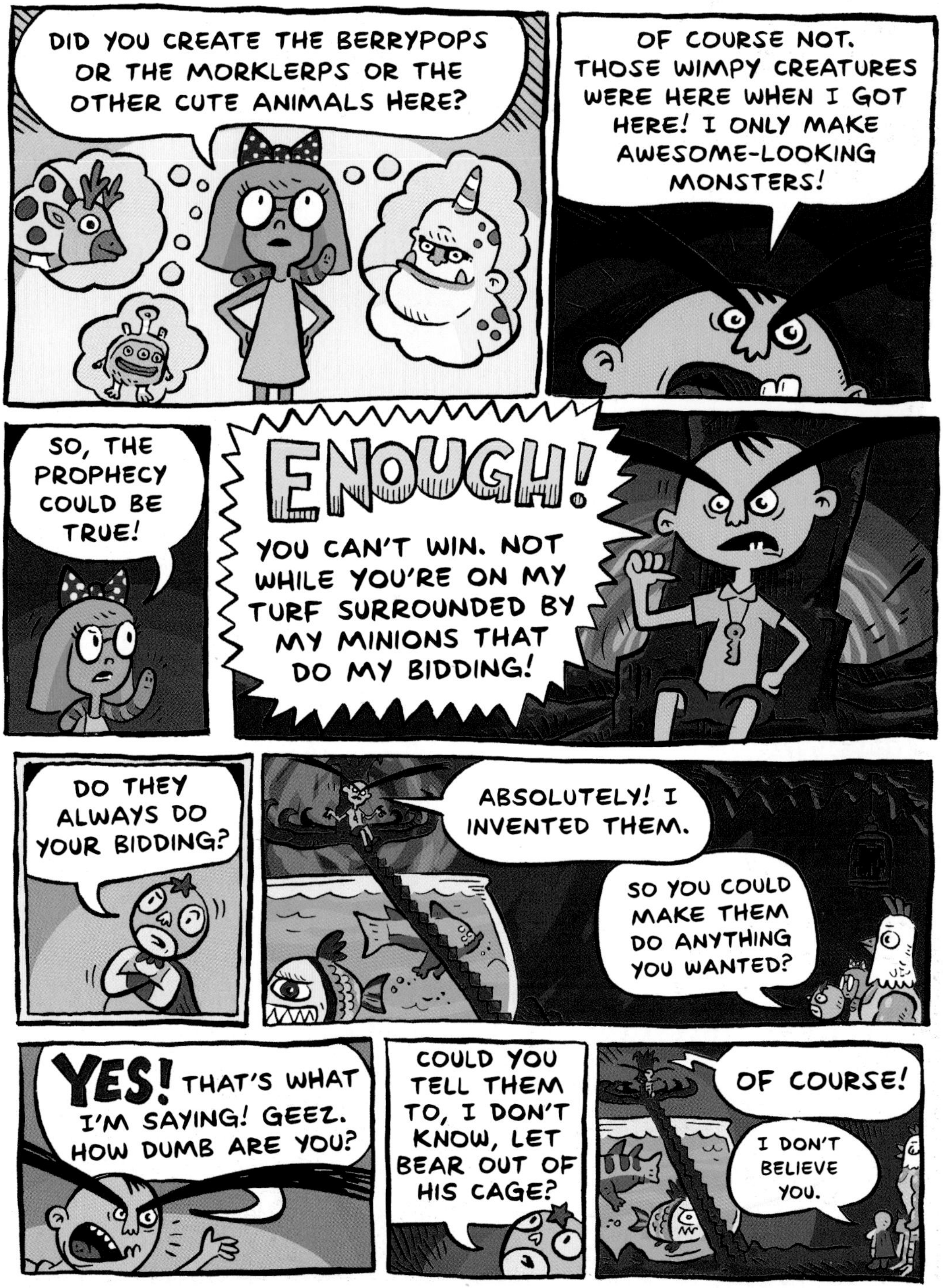

DID YOU CREATE THE BERRYPOPS OR THE MORKLERPS OR THE OTHER CUTE ANIMALS HERE?
OF COURSE NOT. THOSE WIMPY CREATURES WERE HERE WHEN I GOT HERE! I ONLY MAKE AWESOME-LOOKING MONSTERS!
SO, THE PROPHECY COULD BE TRUE!
ENOUGH!
YOU CAN'T WIN. NOT WHILE YOU'RE ON MY TURF SURROUNDED BY MY MINIONS THAT DO MY BIDDING!
DO THEY ALWAYS DO YOUR BIDDING?
ABSOLUTELY! I INVENTED THEM.
SO YOU COULD MAKE THEM DO ANYTHING YOU WANTED?
YES! THAT'S WHAT I'M SAYING! GEEZ. HOW DUMB ARE YOU?
COULD YOU TELL THEM TO, I DON'T KNOW, LET BEAR OUT OF HIS CAGE?
OF COURSE!
I DON'T BELIEVE YOU.

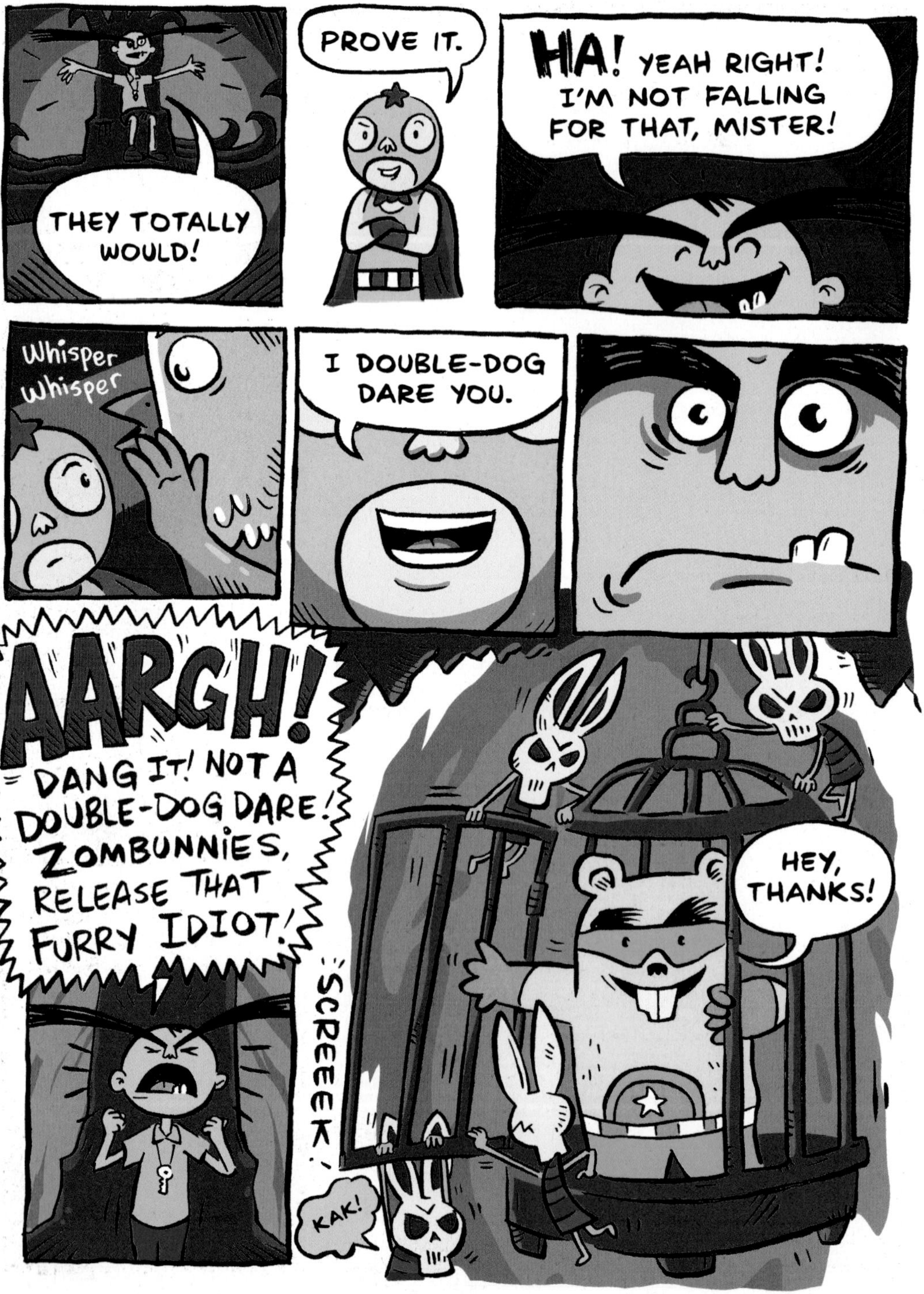
THEY TOTALLY WOULD!
PROVE IT.
HA! YEAH RIGHT! I'M NOT FALLING FOR THAT, MISTER!
Whisper whisper
I DOUBLE-DOG DARE YOU.
AARGH!
DANG IT! NOT A DOUBLE-DOG DARE! ZOMBUNNIES, RELEASE THAT FURRY IDIOT!
SCREEEK!
HEY, THANKS!
KAK!

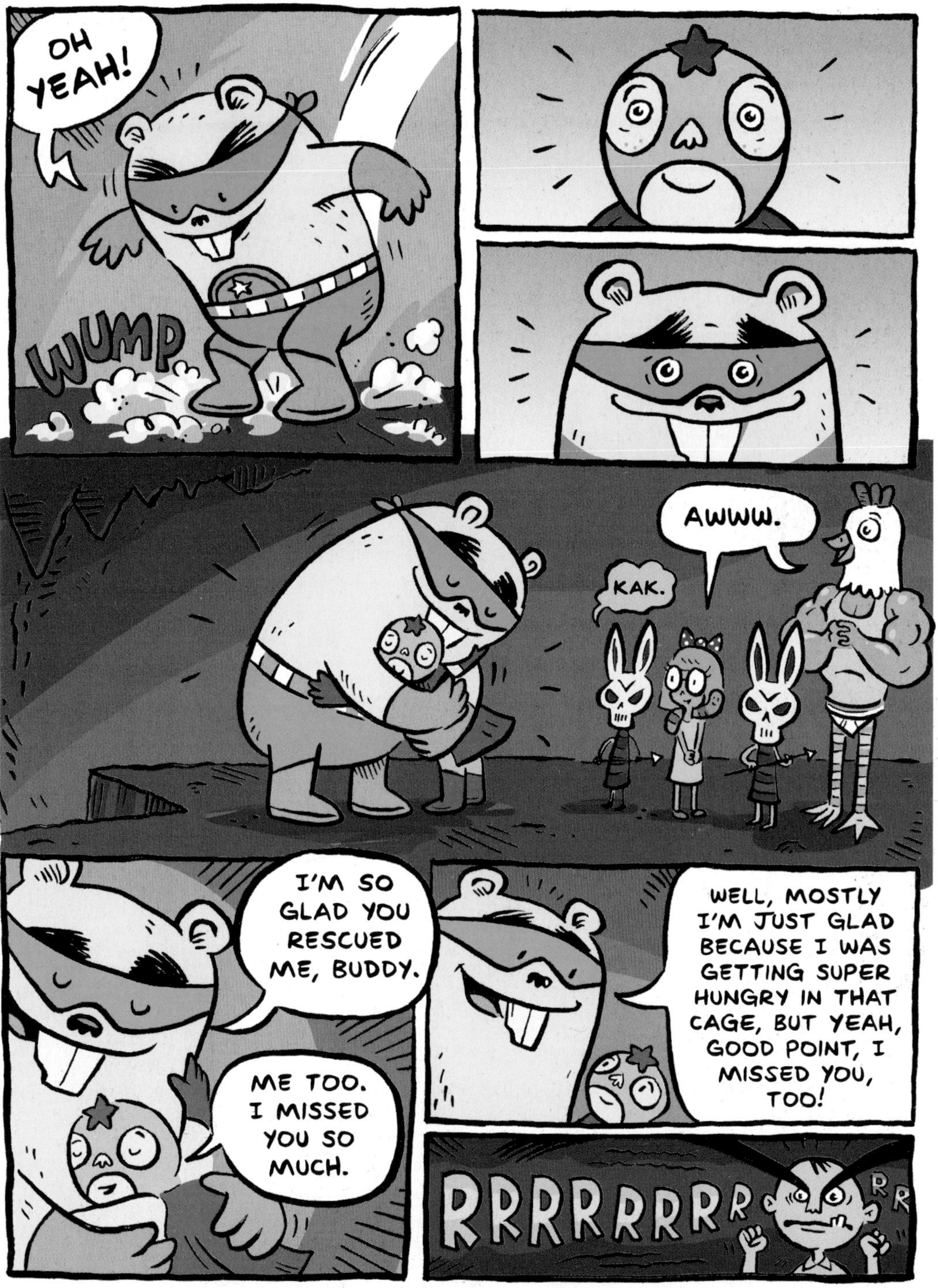
OH YEAH!
WUMP
AWWW.
KAK.
I'M SO GLAD YOU RESCUED ME, BUDDY.
ME TOO. I MISSED YOU SO MUCH.
WELL, MOSTLY I'M JUST GLAD BECAUSE I WAS GETTING SUPER HUNGRY IN THAT CAGE, BUT YEAH, GOOD POINT, I MISSED YOU, TOO!
RRRRRRRRRRR

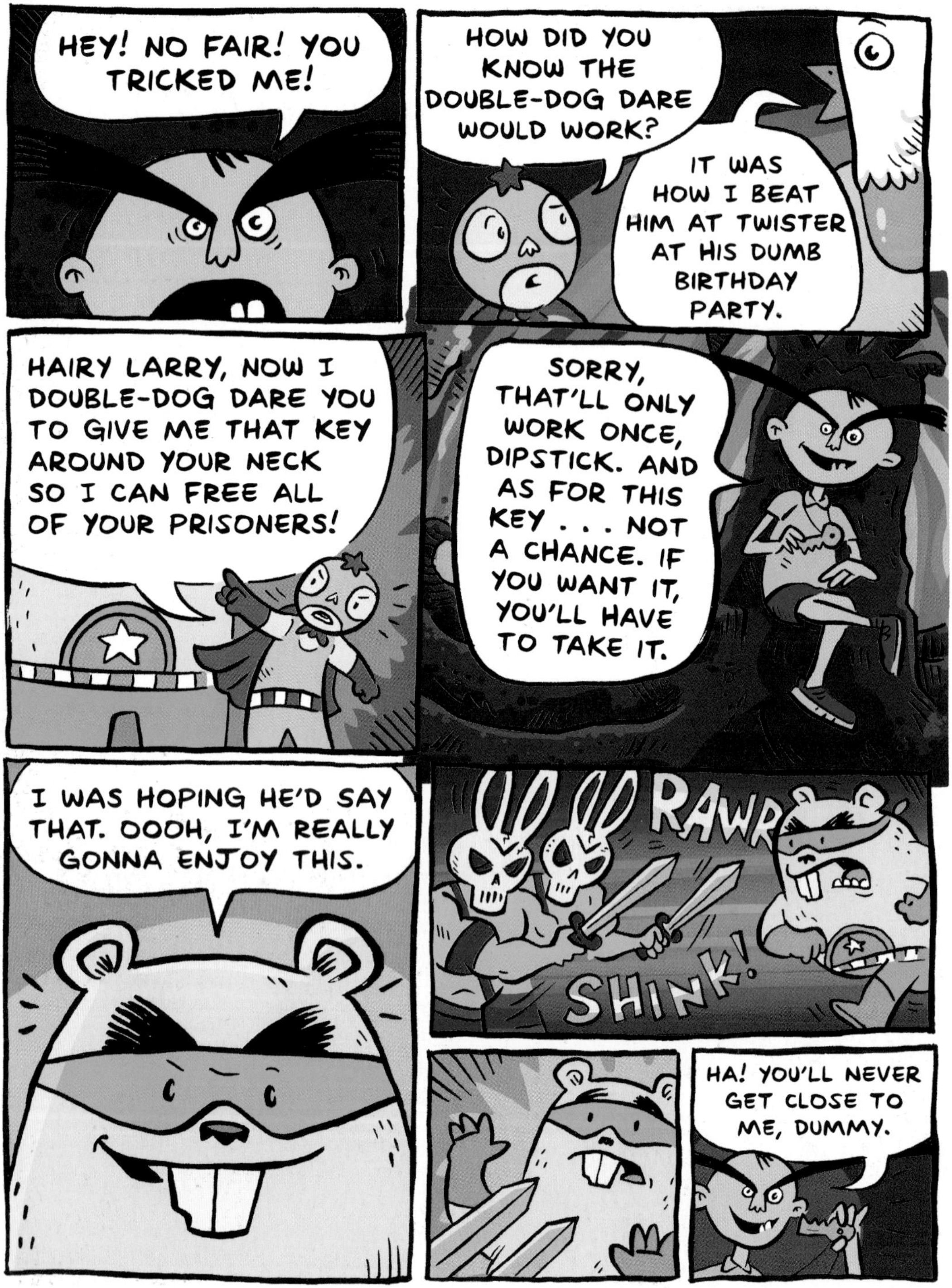
HEY! NO FAIR! YOU TRICKED ME!
HOW DID YOU KNOW THE DOUBLE-DOG DARE WOULD WORK?
IT WAS HOW I BEAT HIM AT TWISTER AT HIS DUMB BIRTHDAY PARTY.
HAIRY LARRY, NOW I DOUBLE-DOG DARE YOU TO GIVE ME THAT KEY AROUND YOUR NECK SO I CAN FREE ALL OF YOUR PRISONERS!
SORRY, THAT'LL ONLY WORK ONCE, DIPSTICK. AND AS FOR THIS KEY . . . NOT A CHANCE. IF YOU WANT IT, YOU'LL HAVE TO TAKE IT.
I WAS HOPING HE'D SAY THAT. OOOH, I'M REALLY GONNA ENJOY THIS.
RAWR
SHINK!
HA! YOU'LL NEVER GET CLOSE TO ME, DUMMY.

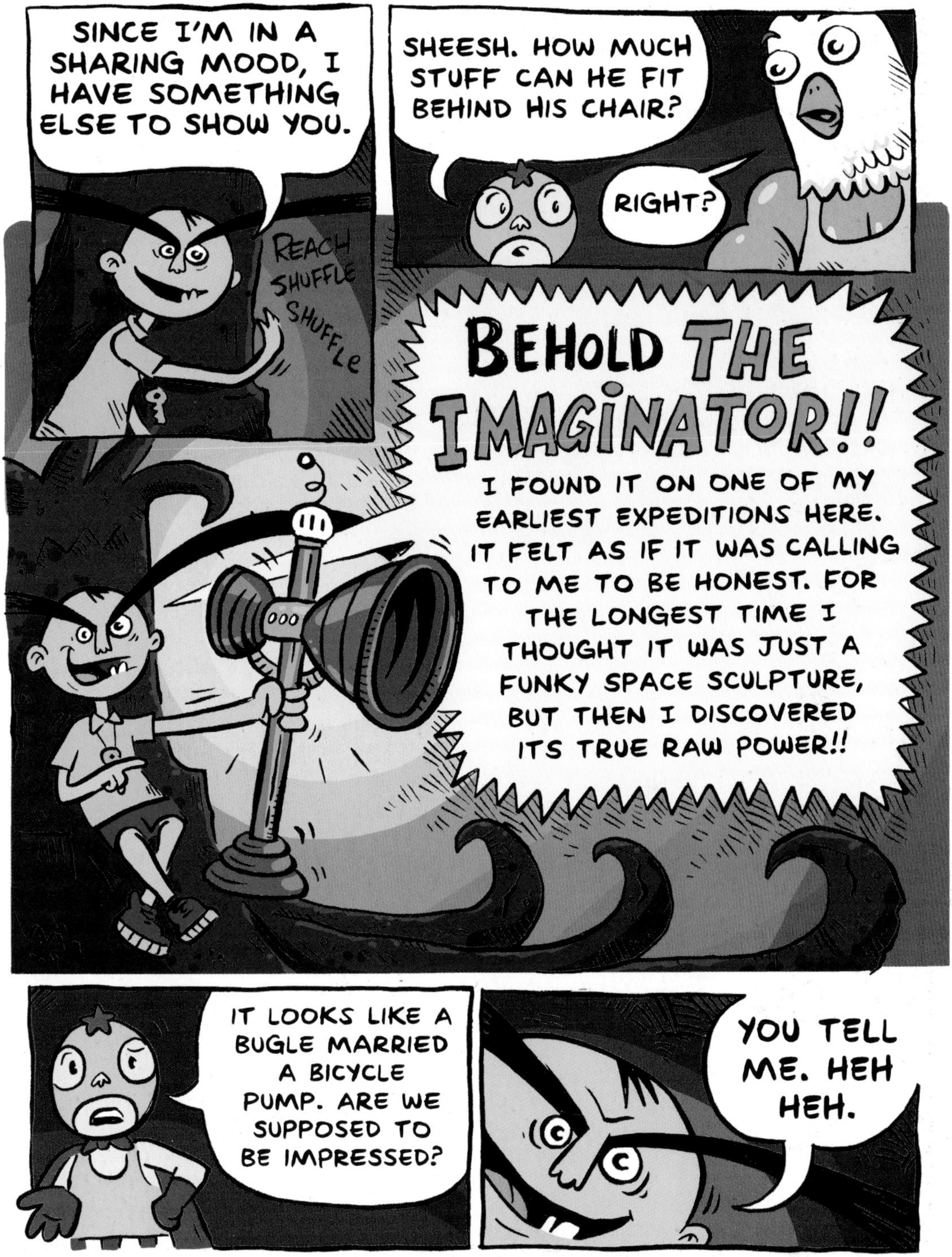
SINCE I'M IN A SHARING MOOD, I HAVE SOMETHING ELSE TO SHOW YOU.
REACH SHUFFLE SHUFFLE
SHEESH. HOW MUCH STUFF CAN HE FIT BEHIND HIS CHAIR?
RIGHT?
BEHOLD THE IMAGINATOR!!
I FOUND IT ON ONE OF MY EARLIEST EXPEDITIONS HERE. IT FELT AS IF IT WAS CALLING TO ME TO BE HONEST. FOR THE LONGEST TIME I THOUGHT IT WAS JUST A FUNKY SPACE SCULPTURE, BUT THEN I DISCOVERED ITS TRUE RAW POWER!!
IT LOOKS LIKE A BUGLE MARRIED A BICYCLE PUMP. ARE WE SUPPOSED TO BE IMPRESSED?
YOU TELL ME. HEH HEH.

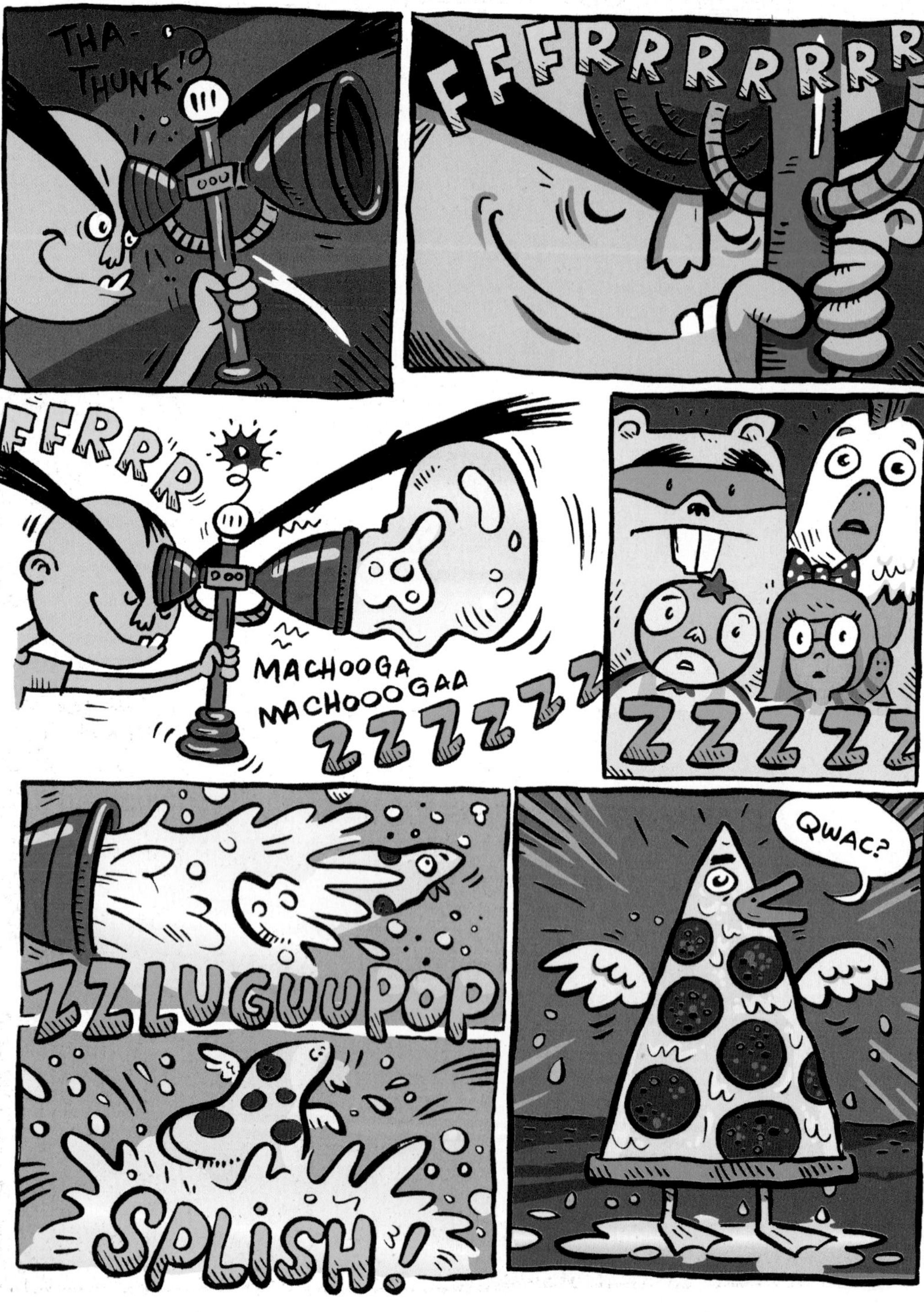
THA-THUNK!
FFFRRRRRRRR
FFRRR
MACHOOGA MACHOOOGAA
ZZZZZZZ
ZZZZZZ
ZZLUGUUPOP
SPLISH!
QWAC?

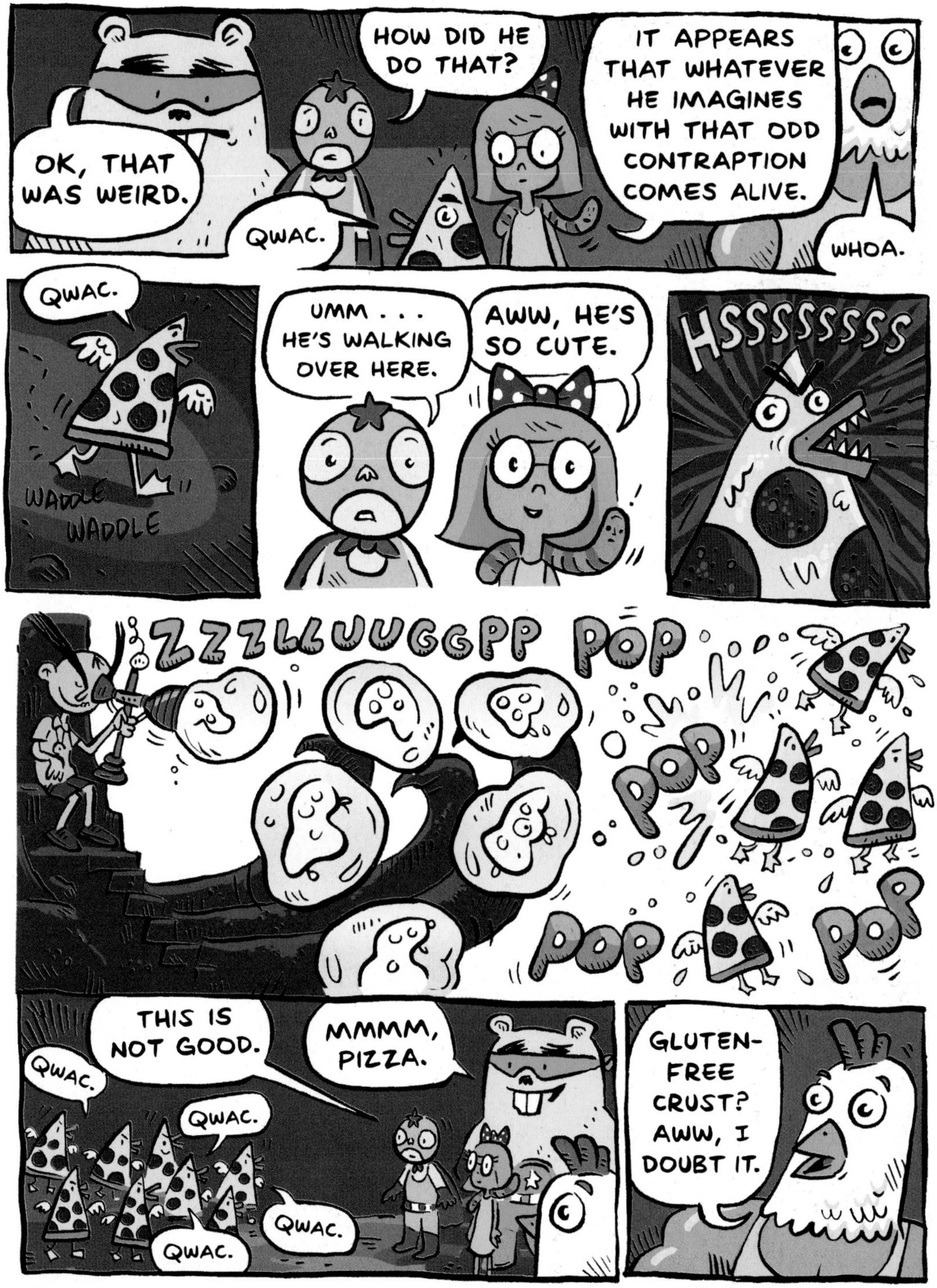
OK, THAT WAS WEIRD.
QWAC.
HOW DID HE DO THAT?
IT APPEARS THAT WHATEVER HE IMAGINES WITH THAT ODD CONTRAPTION COMES ALIVE.
WHOA.
QWAC.
WADDLE WADDLE
UMM . . . HE'S WALKING OVER HERE.
AWW, HE'S SO CUTE.
HSSSSSSSS
ZZZLLUUGGPP POP
POP
POP
POP
THIS IS NOT GOOD.
MMMM, PIZZA.
QWAC.
QWAC.
QWAC.
QWAC.
GLUTEN-FREE CRUST? AWW, I DOUBT IT.

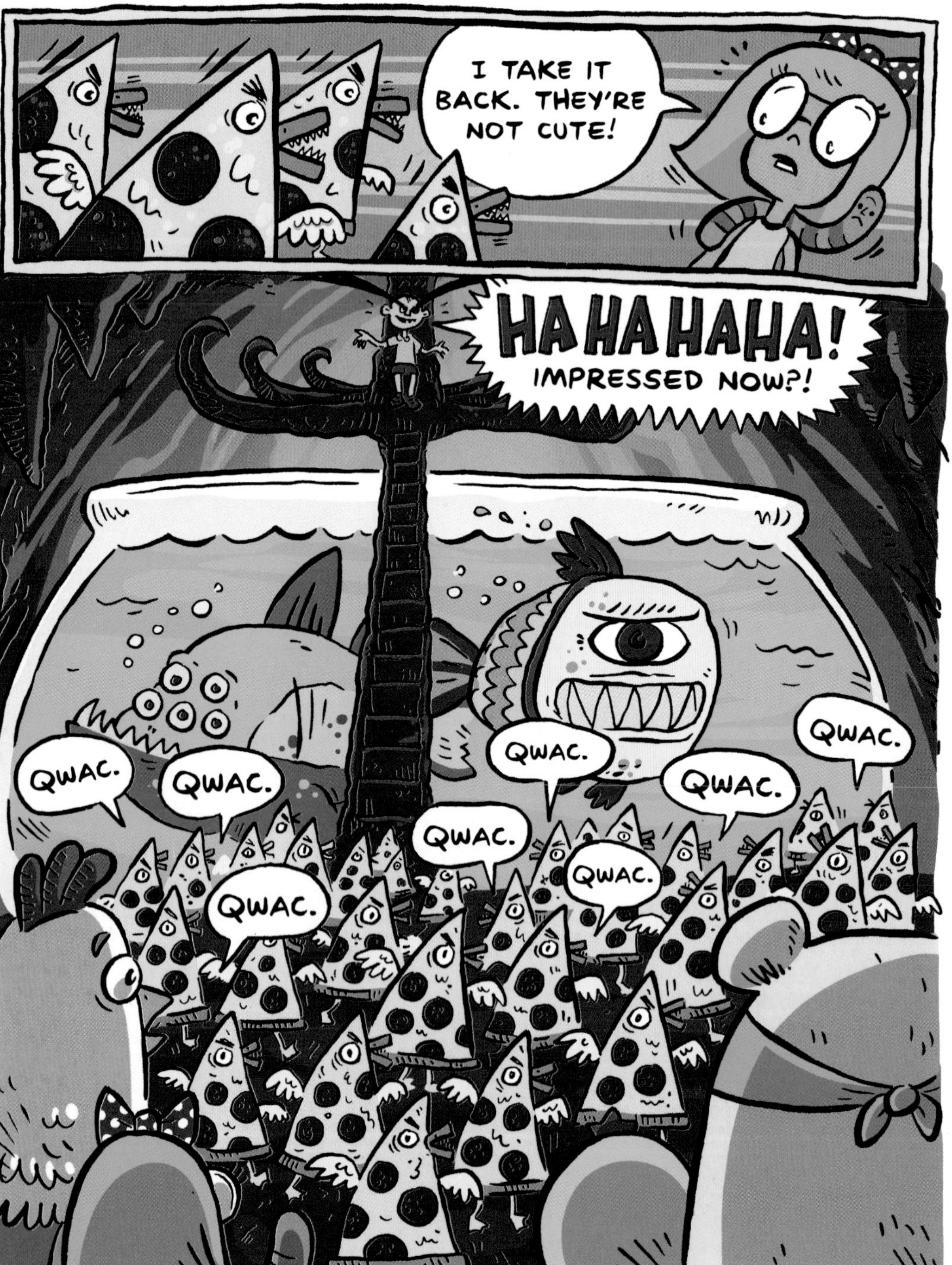
I TAKE IT BACK. THEY'RE NOT CUTE!
HAHAHAHA!
IMPRESSED NOW?!
QWAC.
QWAC.
QWAC.
QWAC.
QWAC.
QWAC.
QWAC.
QWAC.

Chapter 9

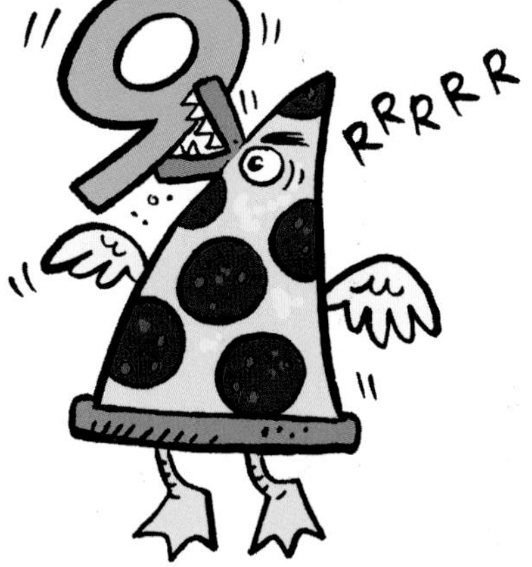

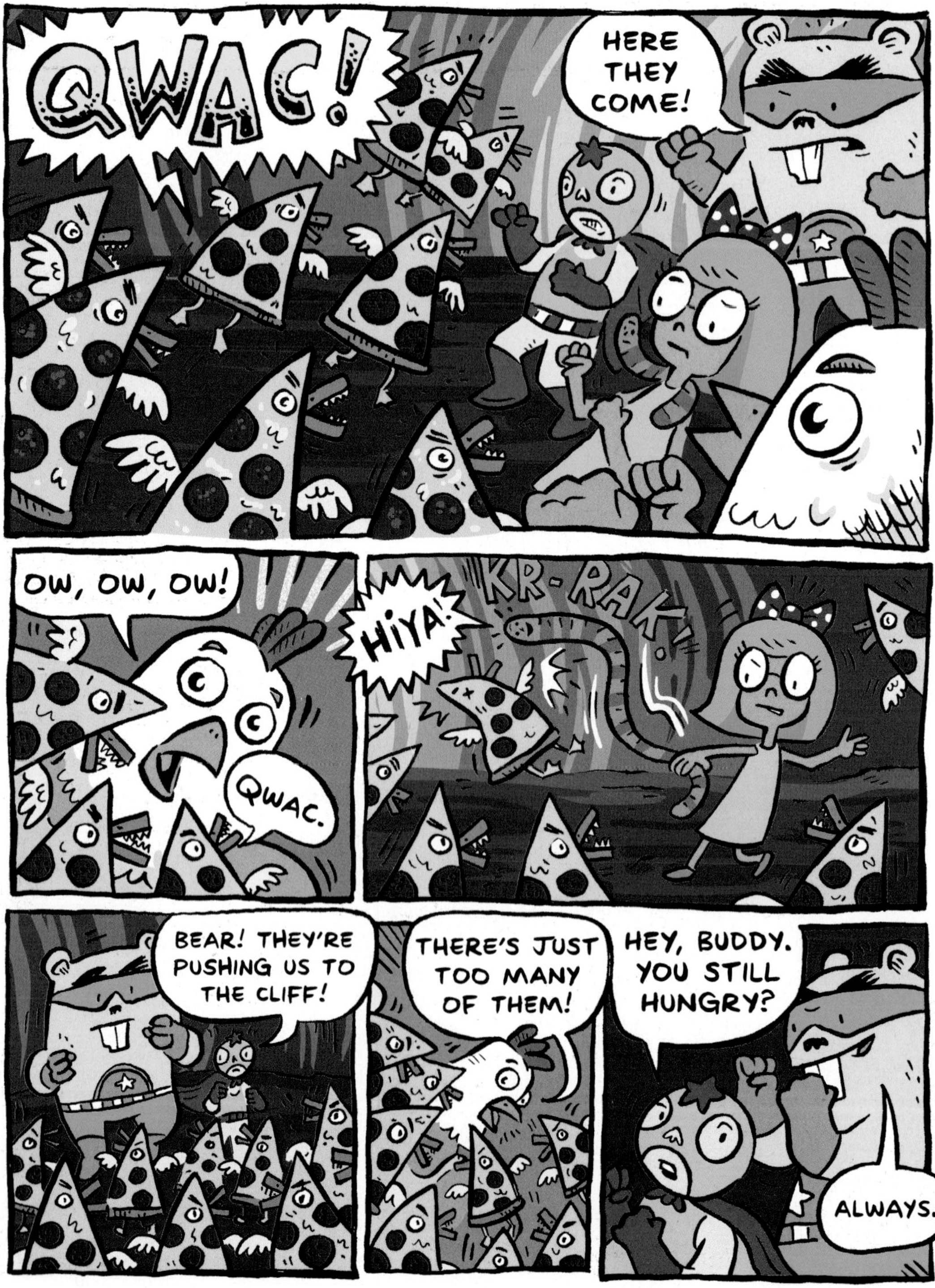
QWAC!
HERE THEY COME!
OW, OW, OW!
QWAC.
HIYA!
KR-RAK!
BEAR! THEY'RE PUSHING US TO THE CLIFF!
THERE'S JUST TOO MANY OF THEM!
HEY, BUDDY. YOU STILL HUNGRY?
ALWAYS.

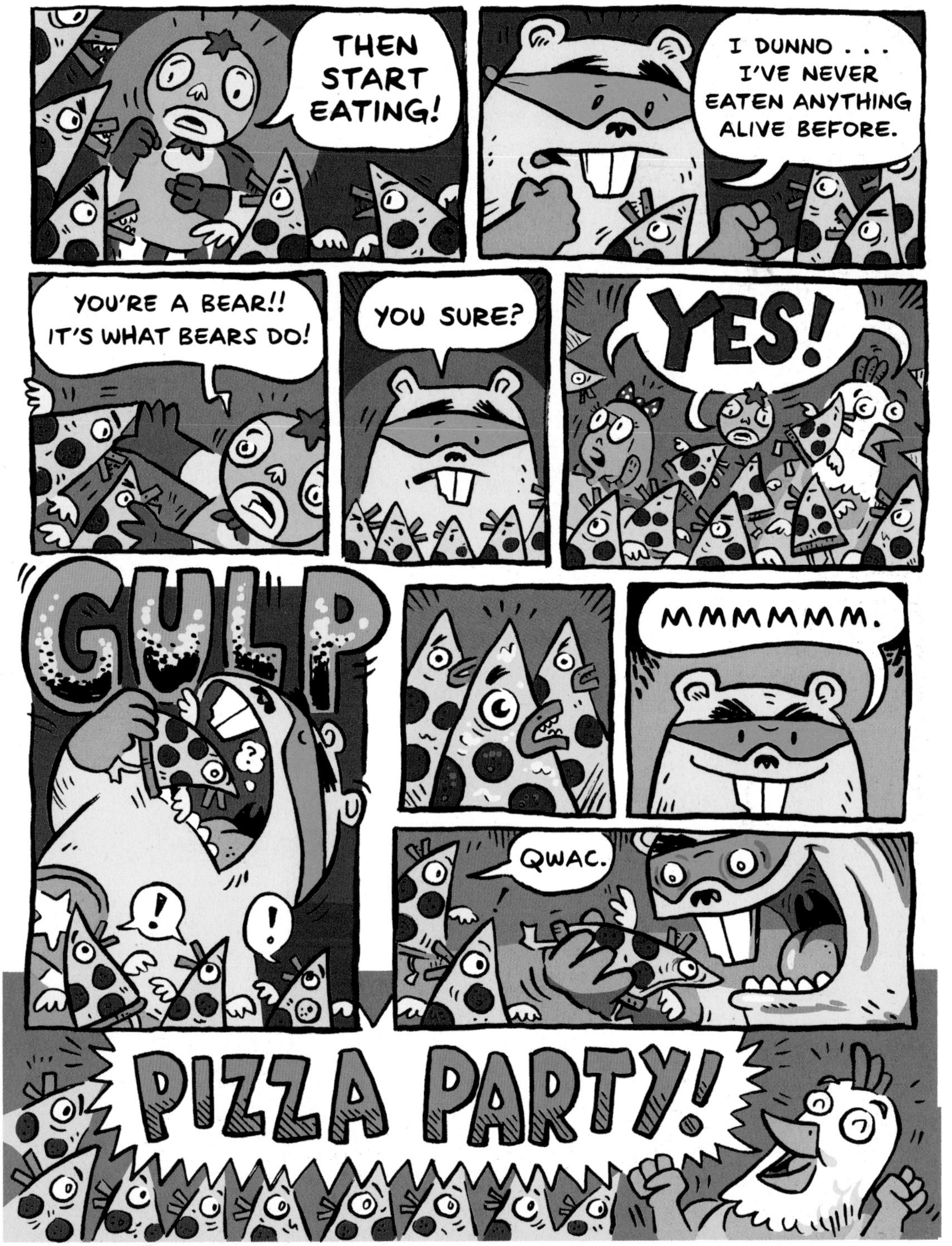
THEN START EATING!
I DUNNO . . . I'VE NEVER EATEN ANYTHING ALIVE BEFORE.
YOU'RE A BEAR!! IT'S WHAT BEARS DO!
YOU SURE?
YES!
GULP
!
!
MMMMMM.
QWAC.
PIZZA PARTY!

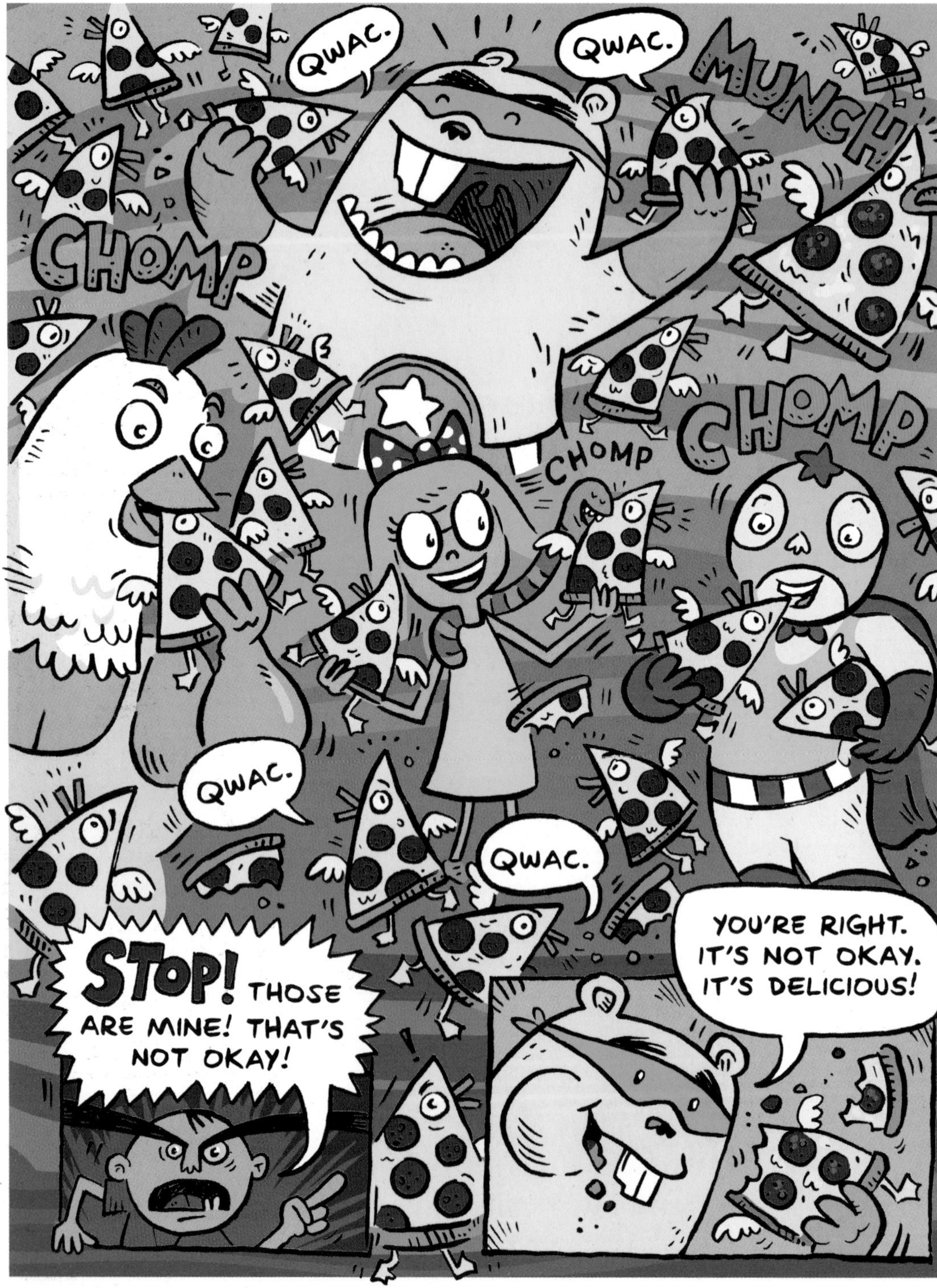
QWAC.
QWAC.
MUNCH
CHOMP
CHOMP
CHOMP
QWAC.
QWAC.
STOP! THOSE ARE MINE! THAT'S NOT OKAY!
YOU'RE RIGHT. IT'S NOT OKAY. IT'S DELICIOUS!

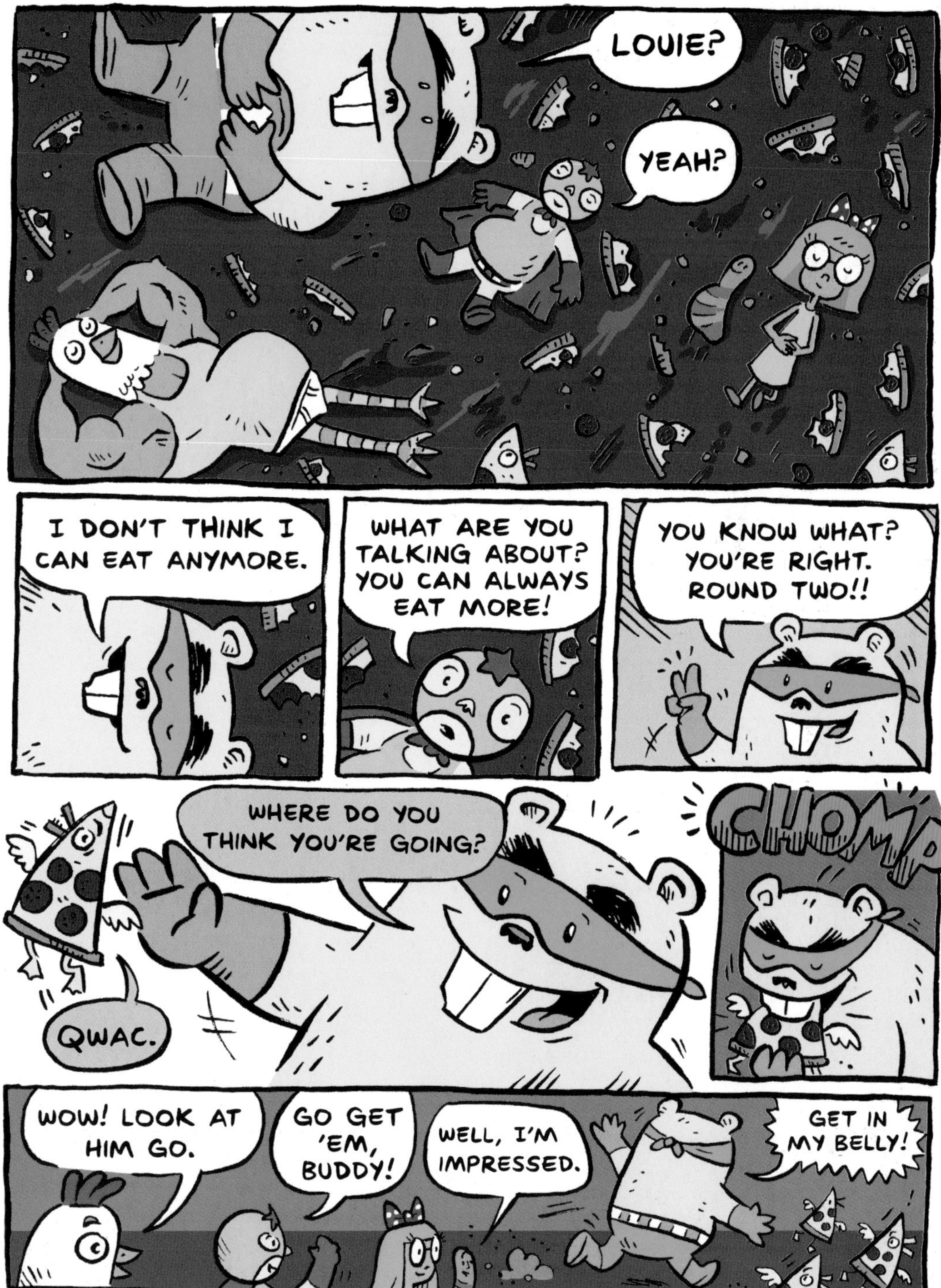
LOUIE?
YEAH?
I DON'T THINK I CAN EAT ANYMORE.
WHAT ARE YOU TALKING ABOUT? YOU CAN ALWAYS EAT MORE!
YOU KNOW WHAT? YOU'RE RIGHT. ROUND TWO!!
WHERE DO YOU THINK YOU'RE GOING?
QWAC.
CHOMP
WOW! LOOK AT HIM GO.
GO GET 'EM, BUDDY!
WELL, I'M IMPRESSED.
GET IN MY BELLY!

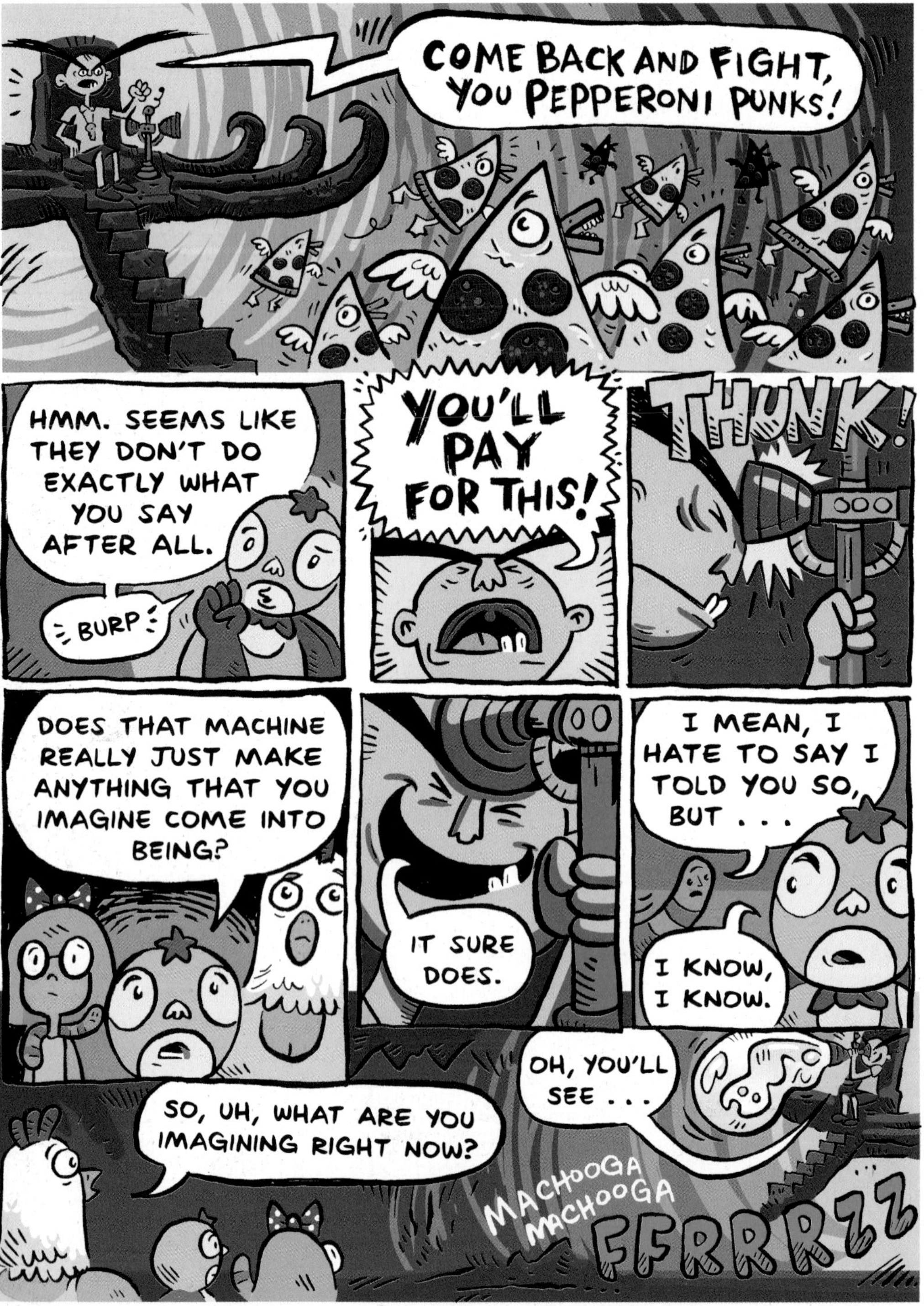
COME BACK AND FIGHT, YOU PEPPERONI PUNKS!
HMM. SEEMS LIKE THEY DON'T DO EXACTLY WHAT YOU SAY AFTER ALL.
BURP
YOU'LL PAY FOR THIS!
THUNK!
DOES THAT MACHINE REALLY JUST MAKE ANYTHING THAT YOU IMAGINE COME INTO BEING?
IT SURE DOES.
I MEAN, I HATE TO SAY I TOLD YOU SO, BUT . . .
I KNOW, I KNOW.
SO, UH, WHAT ARE YOU IMAGINING RIGHT NOW?
OH, YOU'LL SEE . . .
MACHOOGA MACHOOGA
FFRRRZZ

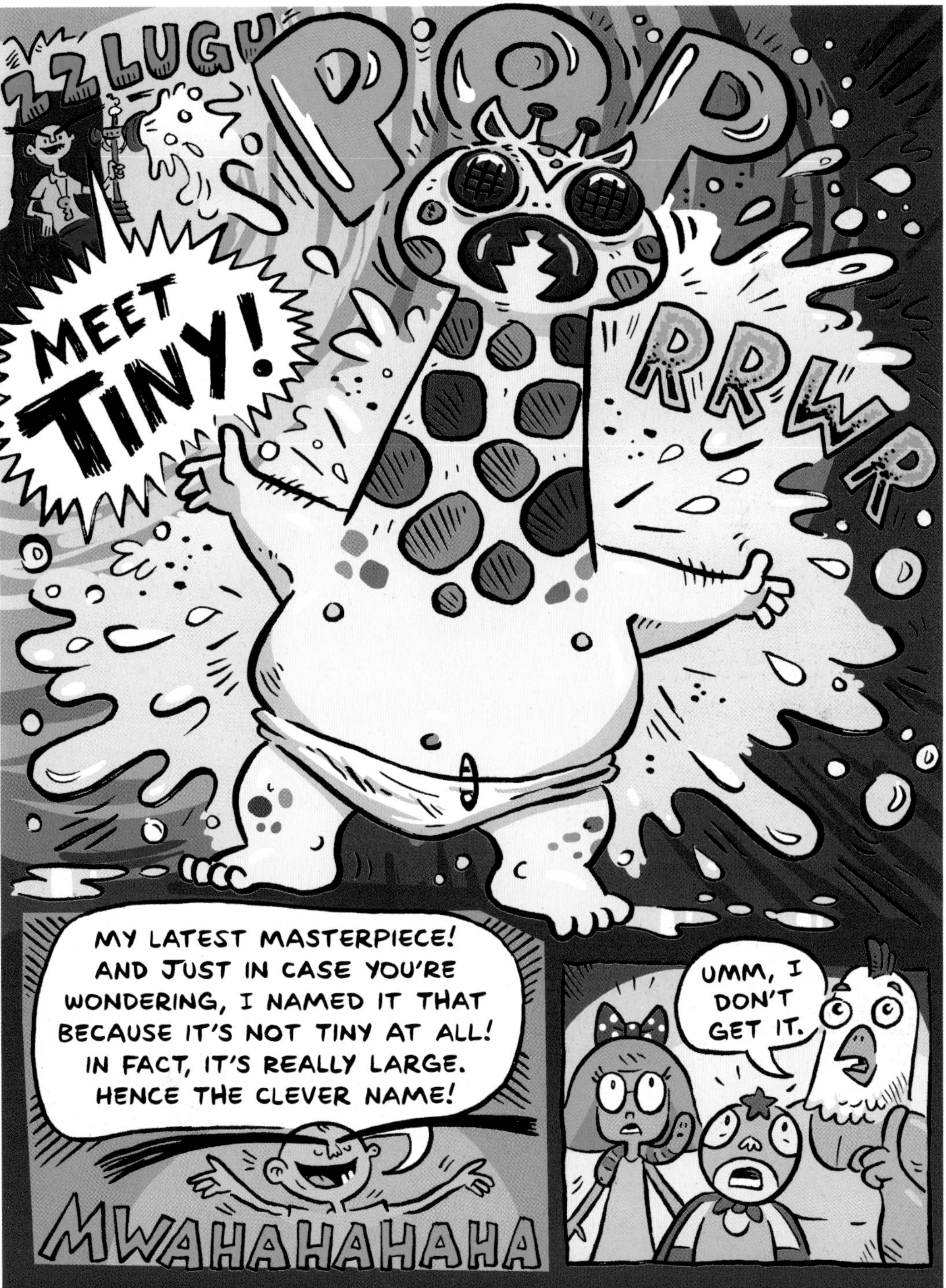
ZZLUGH
POP
MEET TINY!
RRWR
MY LATEST MASTERPIECE! AND JUST IN CASE YOU'RE WONDERING, I NAMED IT THAT BECAUSE IT'S NOT TINY AT ALL! IN FACT, IT'S REALLY LARGE. HENCE THE CLEVER NAME!
MWAHAHAHAHA
UMM, I DON'T GET IT.

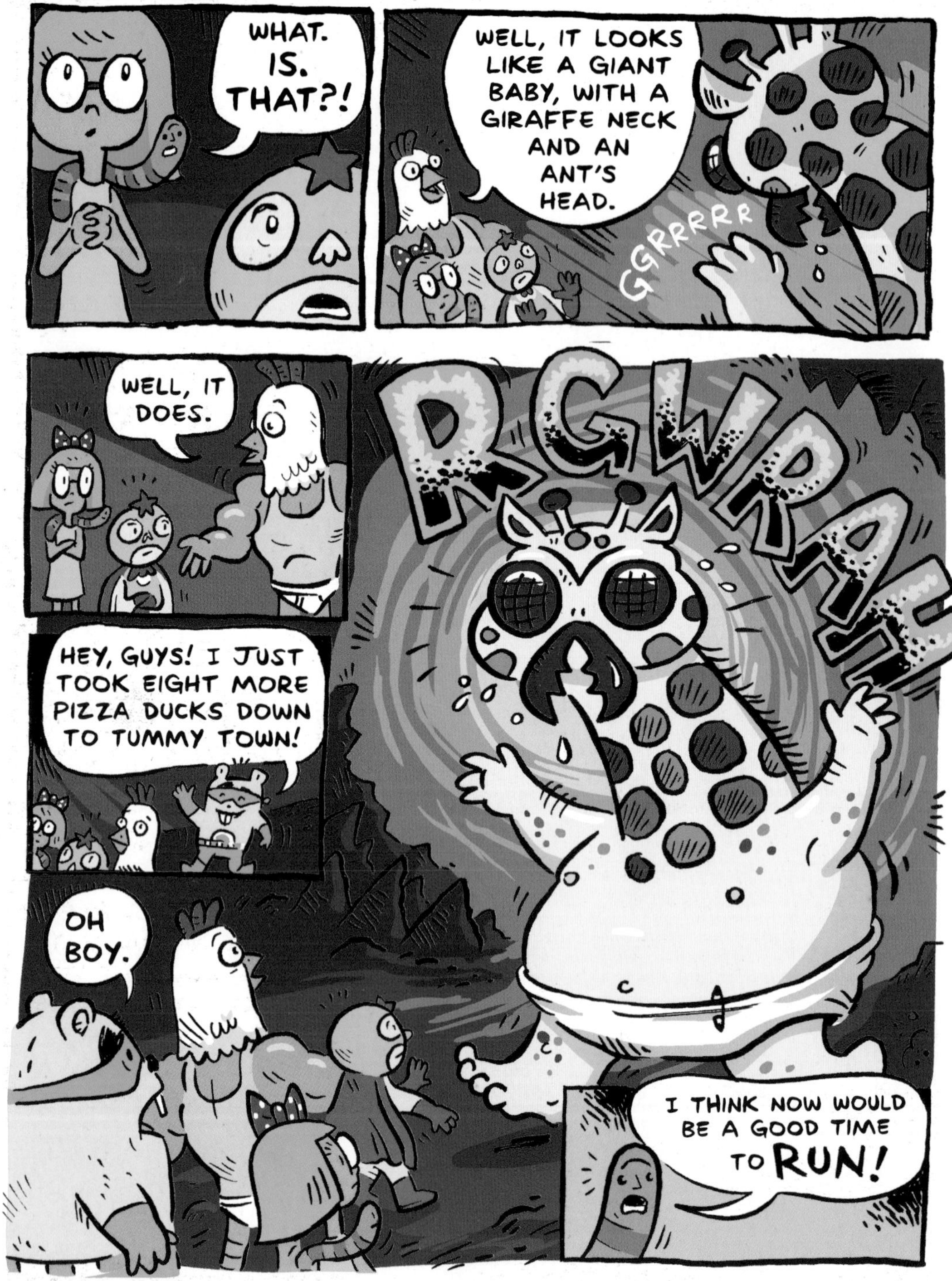
WHAT. IS. THAT?!
WELL, IT LOOKS LIKE A GIANT BABY, WITH A GIRAFFE NECK AND AN ANT'S HEAD.
GGRRRRR
WELL, IT DOES.
RGWRAAU
HEY, GUYS! I JUST TOOK EIGHT MORE PIZZA DUCKS DOWN TO TUMMY TOWN!
OH BOY.
I THINK NOW WOULD BE A GOOD TIME TO RUN!

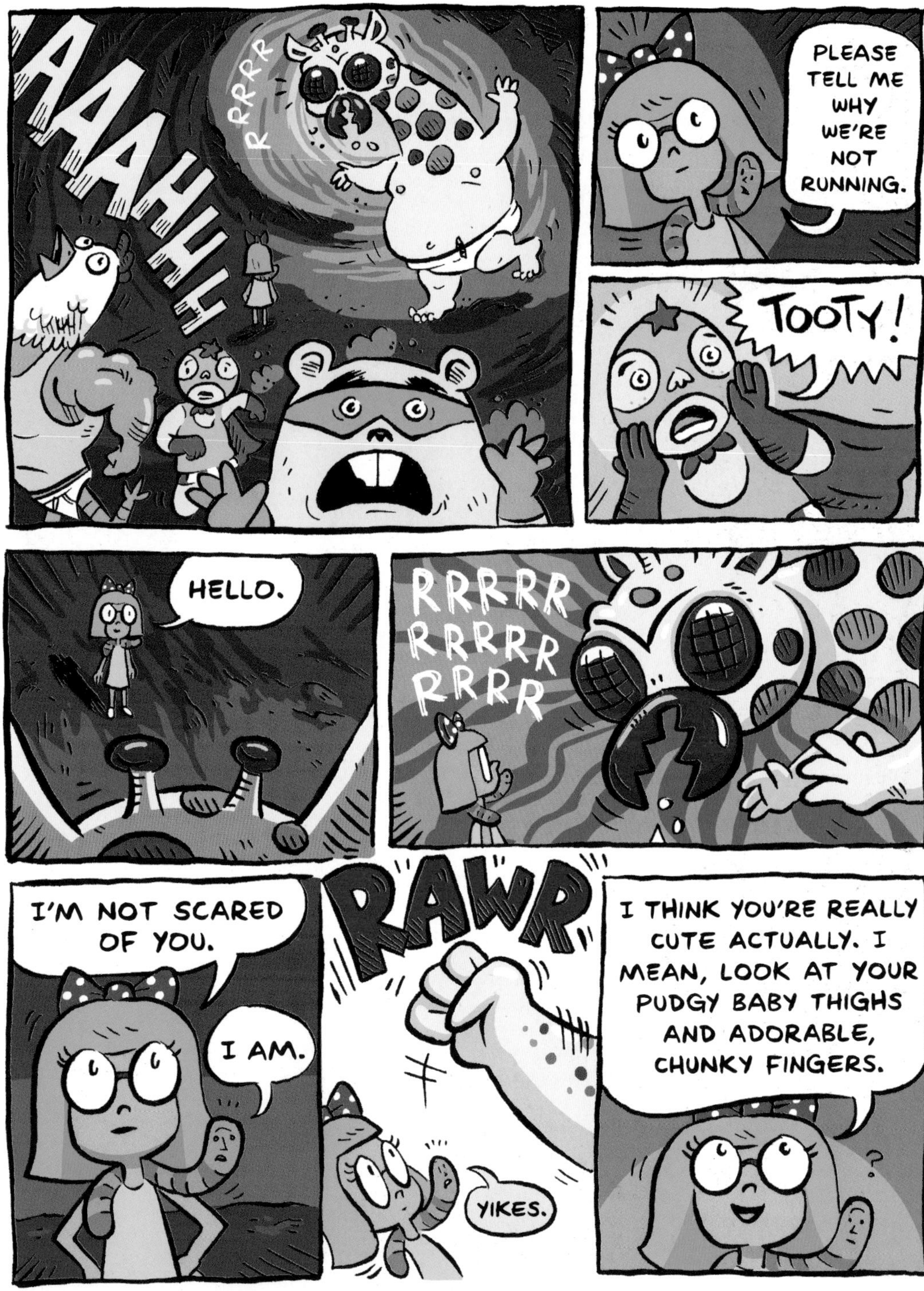
AAAHHHH
RRRRR
PLEASE TELL ME WHY WE'RE NOT RUNNING.
TOOTY!
HELLO.
RRRRR RRRRR RRRR
I'M NOT SCARED OF YOU.
I AM.
RAWR
YIKES.
I THINK YOU'RE REALLY CUTE ACTUALLY. I MEAN, LOOK AT YOUR PUDGY BABY THIGHS AND ADORABLE, CHUNKY FINGERS.
?

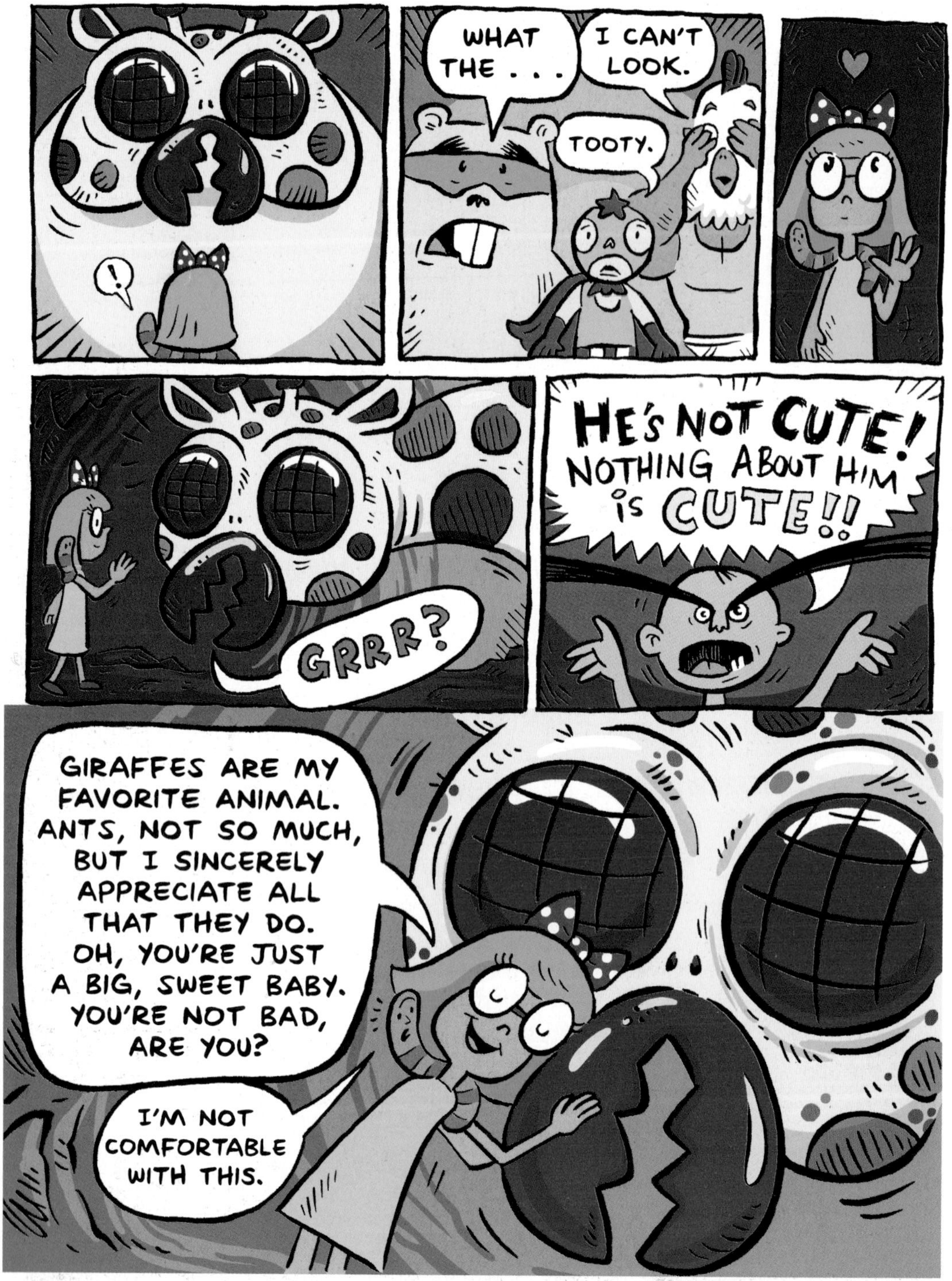
!
WHAT THE . . .
I CAN'T LOOK.
TOOTY.
GRRR?
HE'S NOT CUTE! NOTHING ABOUT HIM IS CUTE!!
GIRAFFES ARE MY FAVORITE ANIMAL. ANTS, NOT SO MUCH, BUT I SINCERELY APPRECIATE ALL THAT THEY DO. OH, YOU'RE JUST A BIG, SWEET BABY. YOU'RE NOT BAD, ARE YOU?
I'M NOT COMFORTABLE WITH THIS.

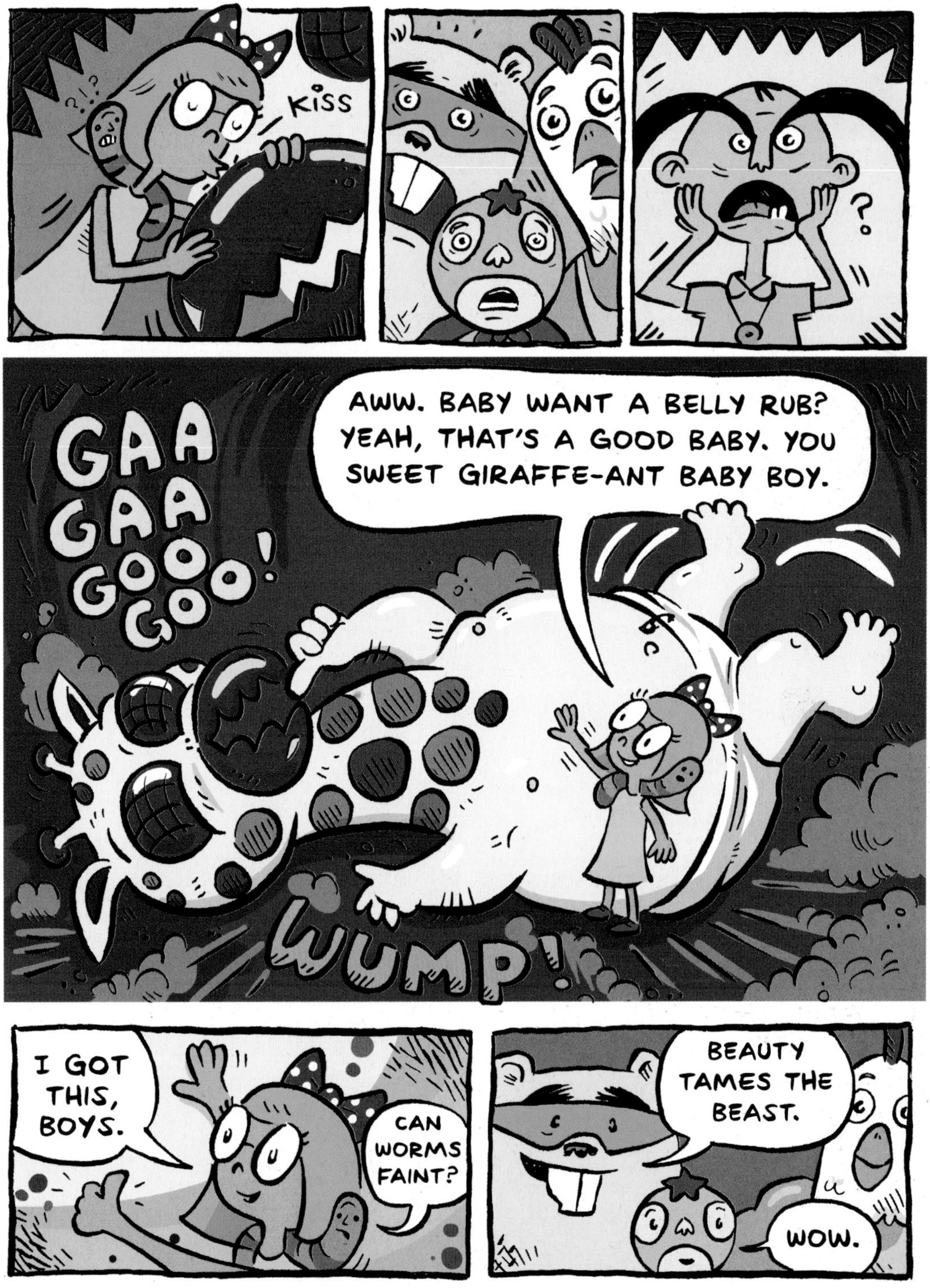
KISS
?!?
?
AWW. BABY WANT A BELLY RUB? YEAH, THAT'S A GOOD BABY. YOU SWEET GIRAFFE-ANT BABY BOY.
GAA GAA GOO GOO!
WUMP!
I GOT THIS, BOYS.
CAN WORMS FAINT?
BEAUTY TAMES THE BEAST.
WOW.

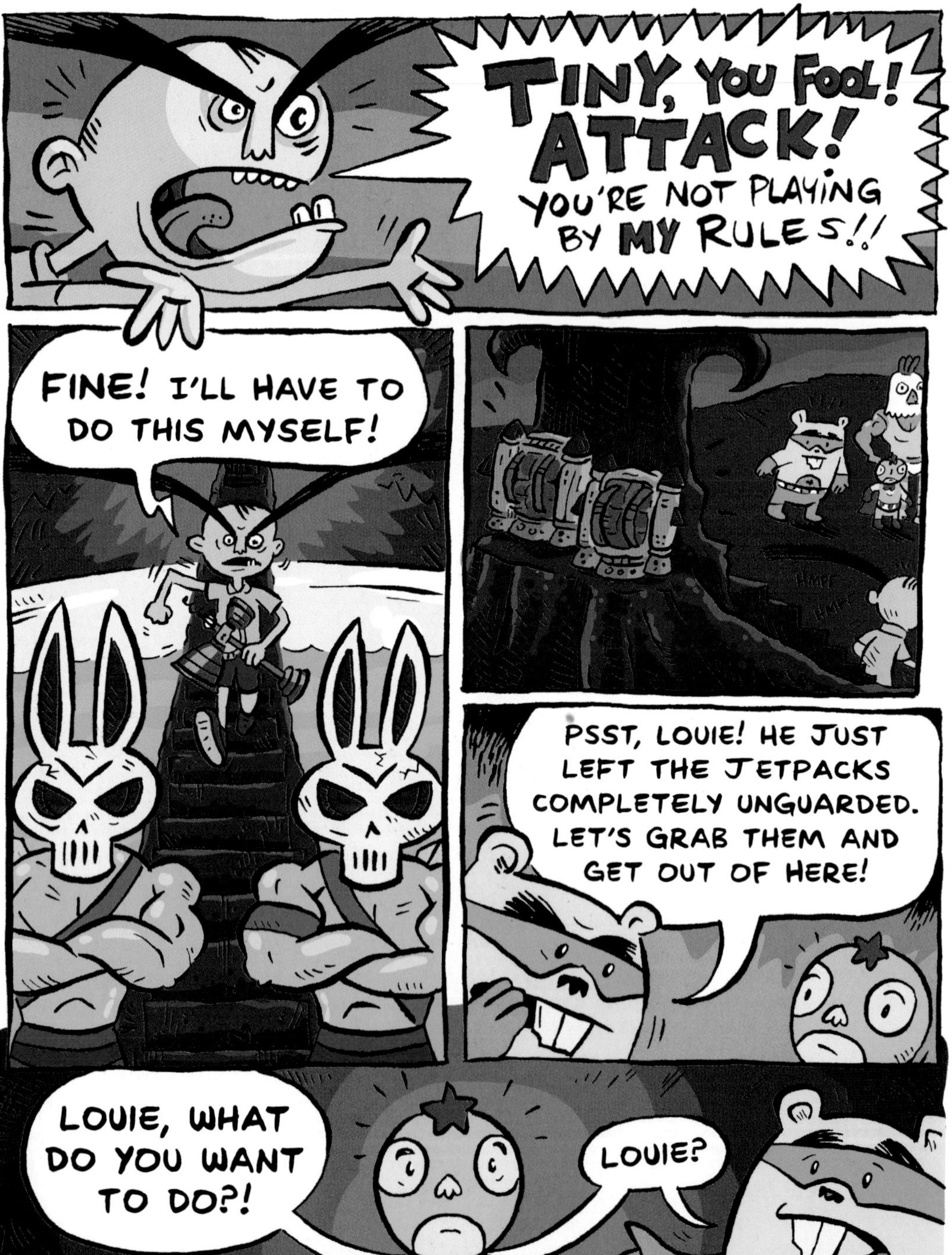
TINY, YOU FOOL! ATTACK!
YOU'RE NOT PLAYING BY MY RULES!!
FINE! I'LL HAVE TO DO THIS MYSELF!
PSST, LOUIE! HE JUST LEFT THE JETPACKS COMPLETELY UNGUARDED. LET'S GRAB THEM AND GET OUT OF HERE!
LOUIE, WHAT DO YOU WANT TO DO?!
LOUIE?

CHAPTER 10

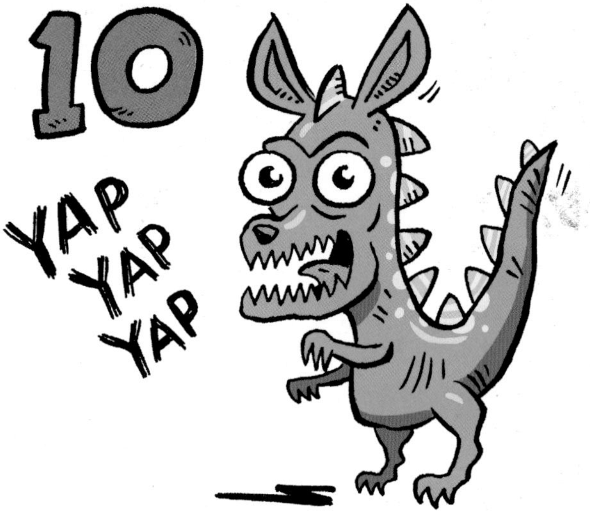

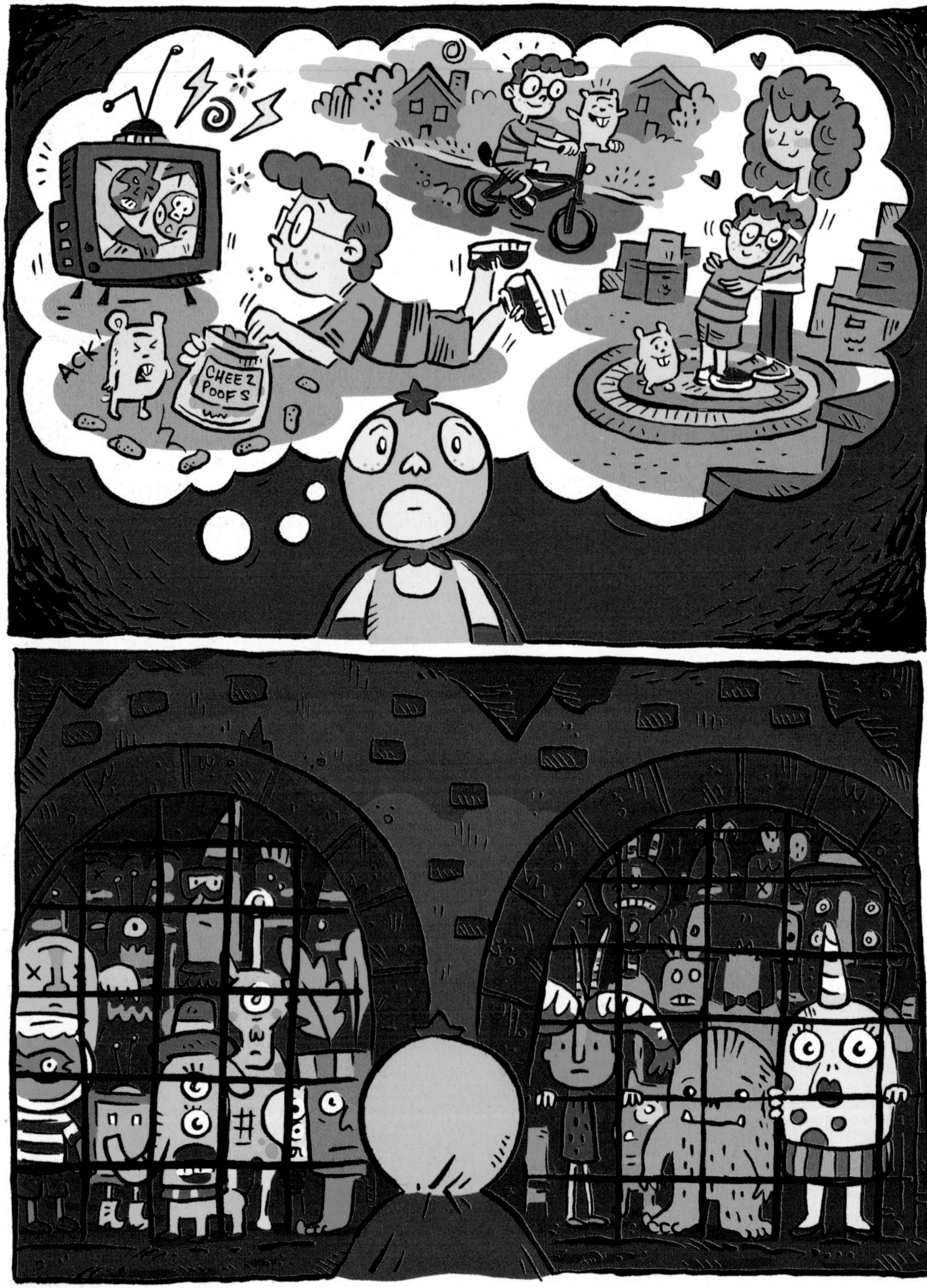
ACK!
CHEEZ POOFS

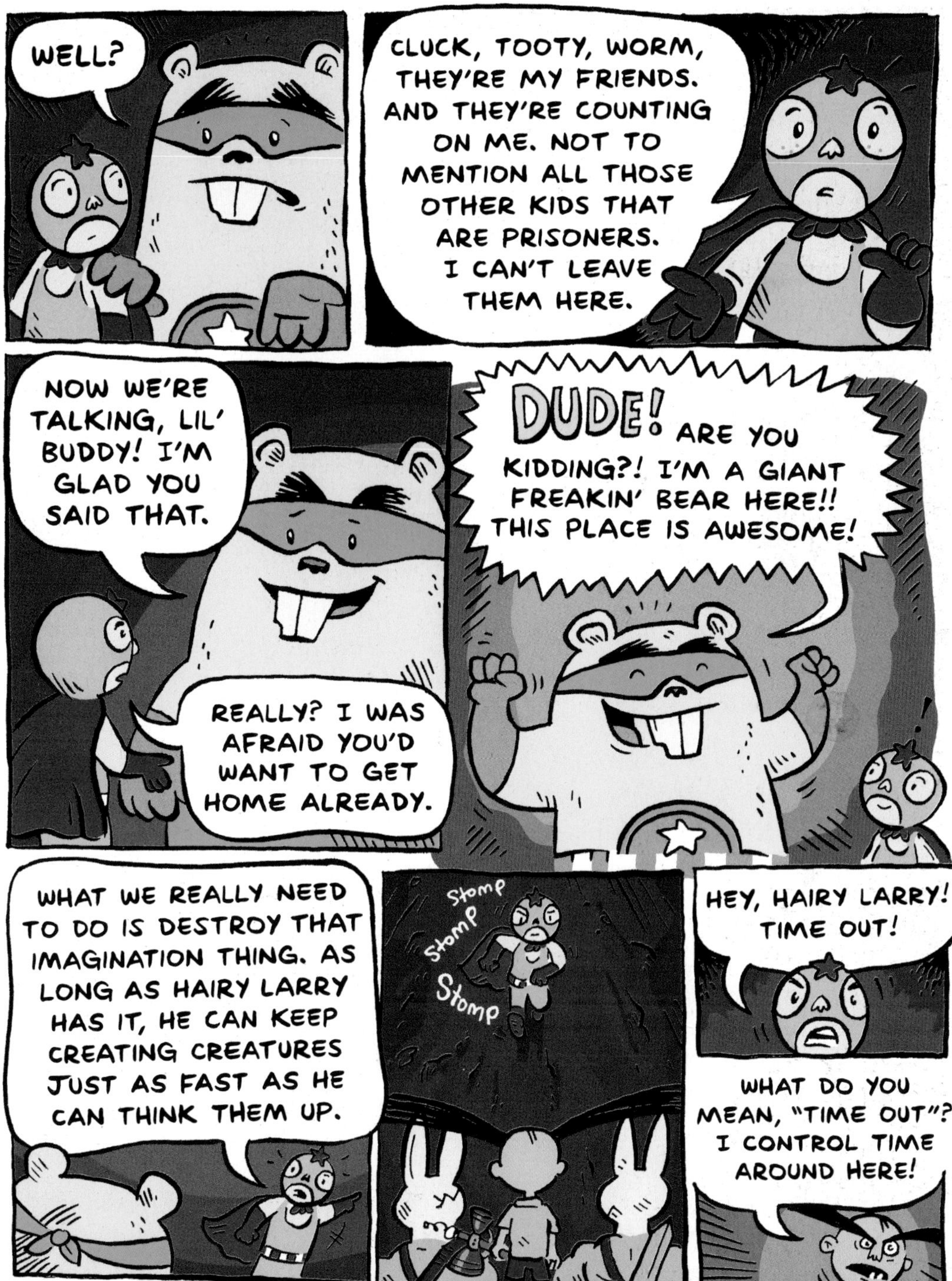
WELL?
CLUCK, TOOTY, WORM, THEY'RE MY FRIENDS. AND THEY'RE COUNTING ON ME. NOT TO MENTION ALL THOSE OTHER KIDS THAT ARE PRISONERS. I CAN'T LEAVE THEM HERE.
NOW WE'RE TALKING, LIL' BUDDY! I'M GLAD YOU SAID THAT.
REALLY? I WAS AFRAID YOU'D WANT TO GET HOME ALREADY.
DUDE! ARE YOU KIDDING?! I'M A GIANT FREAKIN' BEAR HERE!! THIS PLACE IS AWESOME!
WHAT WE REALLY NEED TO DO IS DESTROY THAT IMAGINATION THING. AS LONG AS HAIRY LARRY HAS IT, HE CAN KEEP CREATING CREATURES JUST AS FAST AS HE CAN THINK THEM UP.
Stomp
Stomp
Stomp
HEY, HAIRY LARRY! TIME OUT!
WHAT DO YOU MEAN, "TIME OUT"? I CONTROL TIME AROUND HERE!

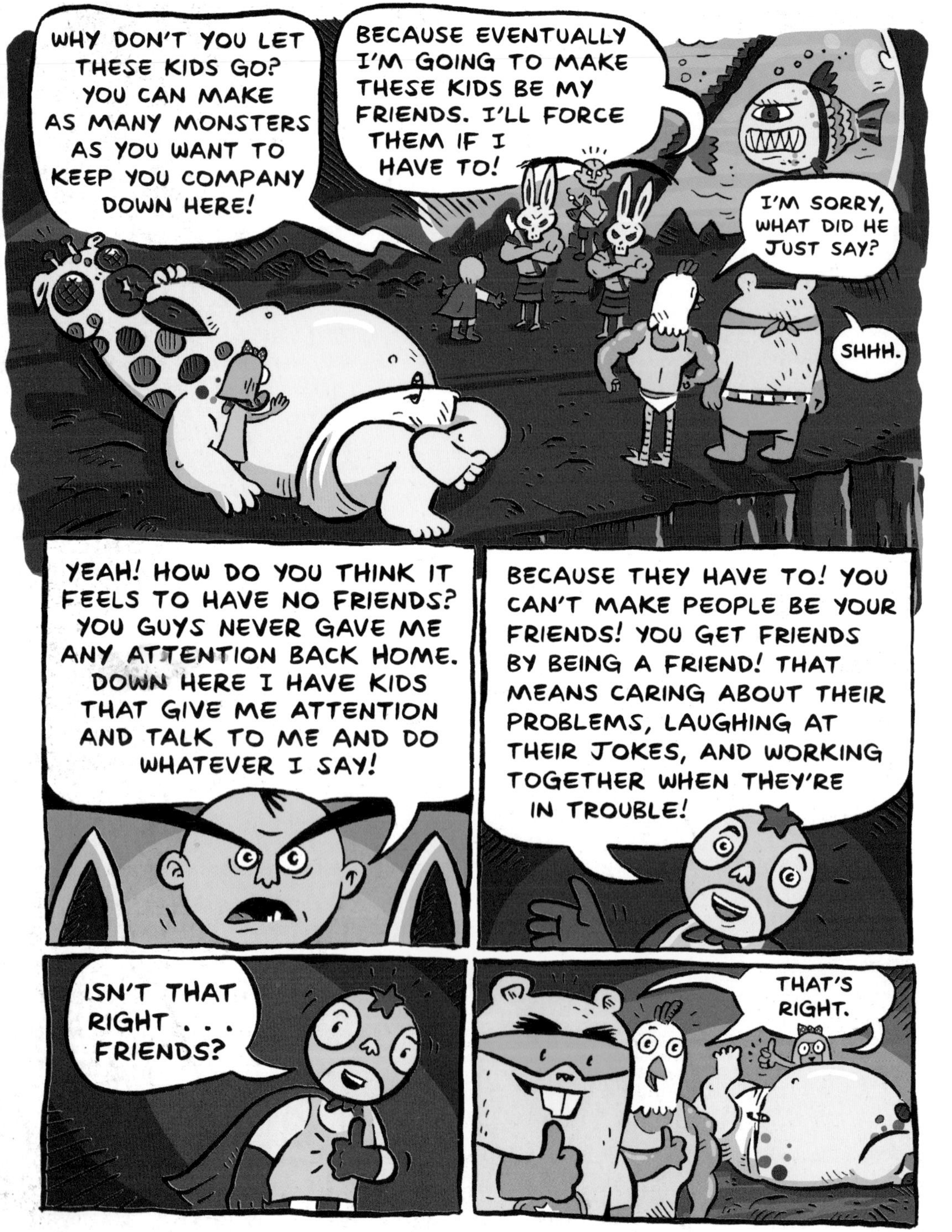
WHY DON'T YOU LET THESE KIDS GO? YOU CAN MAKE AS MANY MONSTERS AS YOU WANT TO KEEP YOU COMPANY DOWN HERE!
BECAUSE EVENTUALLY I'M GOING TO MAKE THESE KIDS BE MY FRIENDS. I'LL FORCE THEM IF I HAVE TO!
I'M SORRY, WHAT DID HE JUST SAY?
SHHH.
YEAH! HOW DO YOU THINK IT FEELS TO HAVE NO FRIENDS? YOU GUYS NEVER GAVE ME ANY ATTENTION BACK HOME. DOWN HERE I HAVE KIDS THAT GIVE ME ATTENTION AND TALK TO ME AND DO WHATEVER I SAY!
BECAUSE THEY HAVE TO! YOU CAN'T MAKE PEOPLE BE YOUR FRIENDS! YOU GET FRIENDS BY BEING A FRIEND! THAT MEANS CARING ABOUT THEIR PROBLEMS, LAUGHING AT THEIR JOKES, AND WORKING TOGETHER WHEN THEY'RE IN TROUBLE!
ISN'T THAT RIGHT . . . FRIENDS?
THAT'S RIGHT.

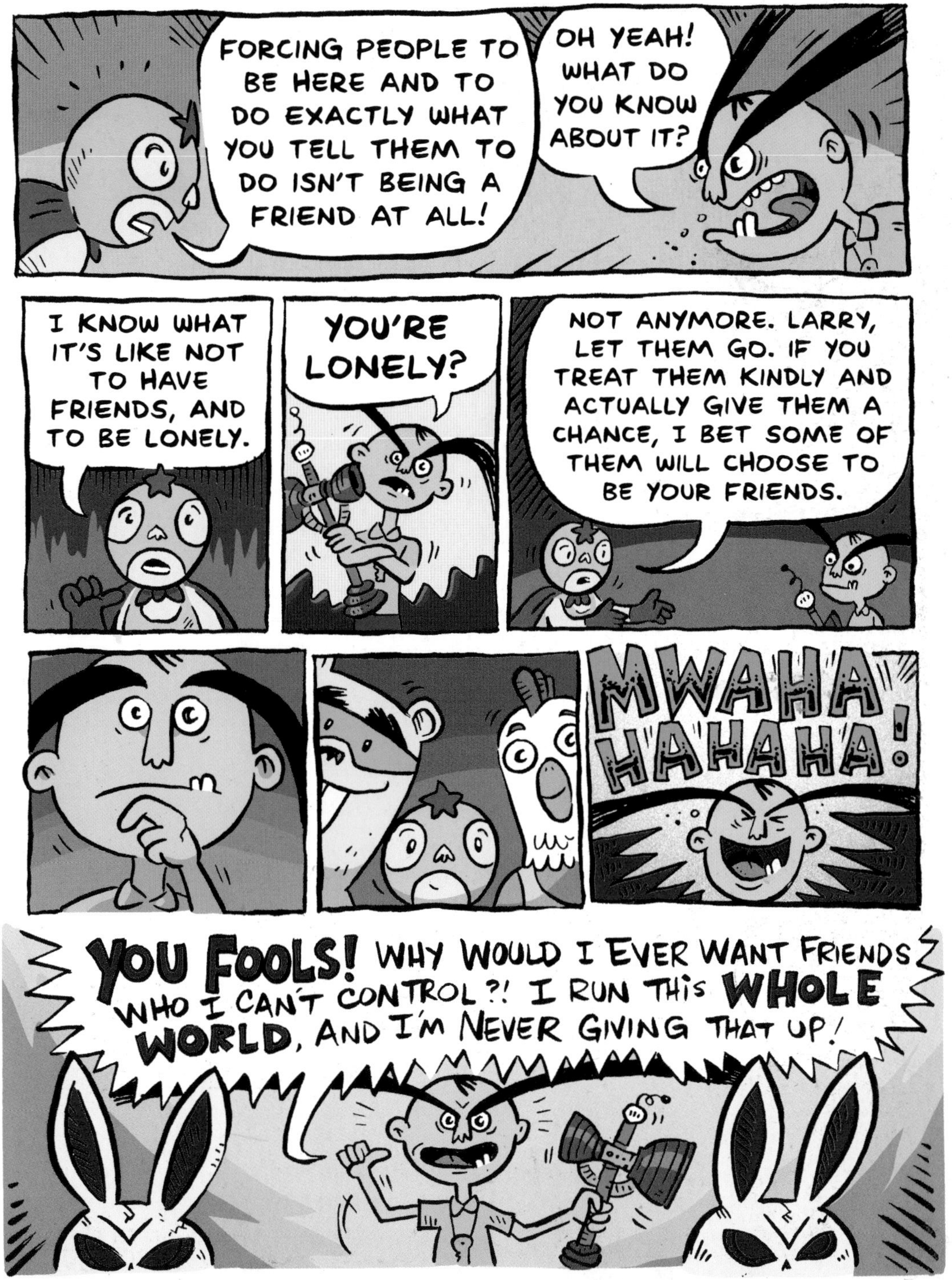
FORCING PEOPLE TO BE HERE AND TO DO EXACTLY WHAT YOU TELL THEM TO DO ISN'T BEING A FRIEND AT ALL!
OH YEAH! WHAT DO YOU KNOW ABOUT IT?
I KNOW WHAT IT'S LIKE NOT TO HAVE FRIENDS, AND TO BE LONELY.
YOU'RE LONELY?
NOT ANYMORE. LARRY, LET THEM GO. IF YOU TREAT THEM KINDLY AND ACTUALLY GIVE THEM A CHANCE, I BET SOME OF THEM WILL CHOOSE TO BE YOUR FRIENDS.
MWAHA HAHAHA!
YOU FOOLS! WHY WOULD I EVER WANT FRIENDS WHO I CAN'T CONTROL?! I RUN THIS WHOLE WORLD, AND I'M NEVER GIVING THAT UP!

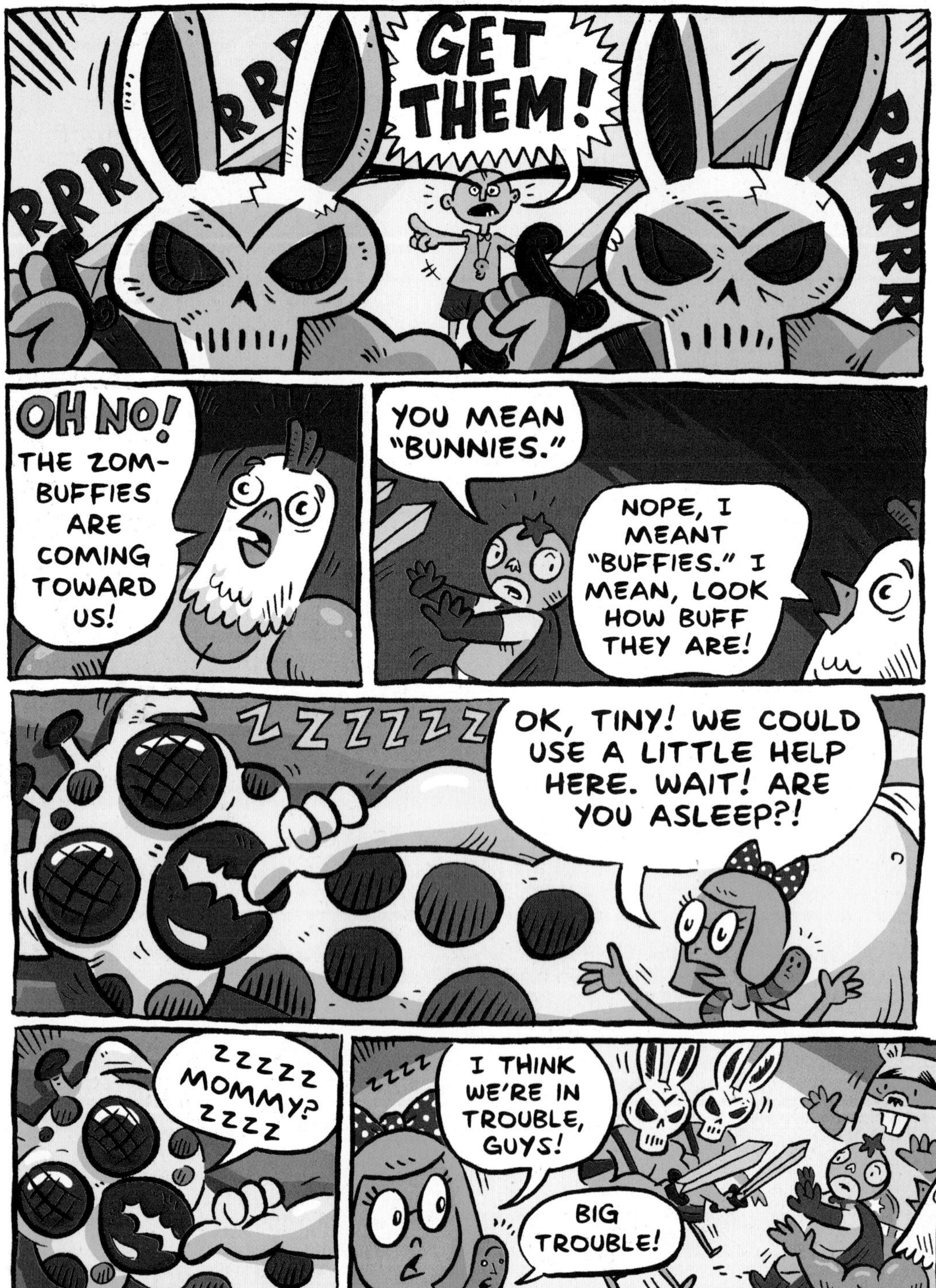
RRR
RRRR
GET THEM!
PRRRRR
OH NO! THE ZOM-BUFFIES ARE COMING TOWARD US!
YOU MEAN "BUNNIES."
NOPE, I MEANT "BUFFIES." I MEAN, LOOK HOW BUFF THEY ARE!
ZZZZZZ
OK, TINY! WE COULD USE A LITTLE HELP HERE. WAIT! ARE YOU ASLEEP?!
ZZZZZ MOMMY? ZZZZ
ZZZZ
I THINK WE'RE IN TROUBLE, GUYS!
BIG TROUBLE!

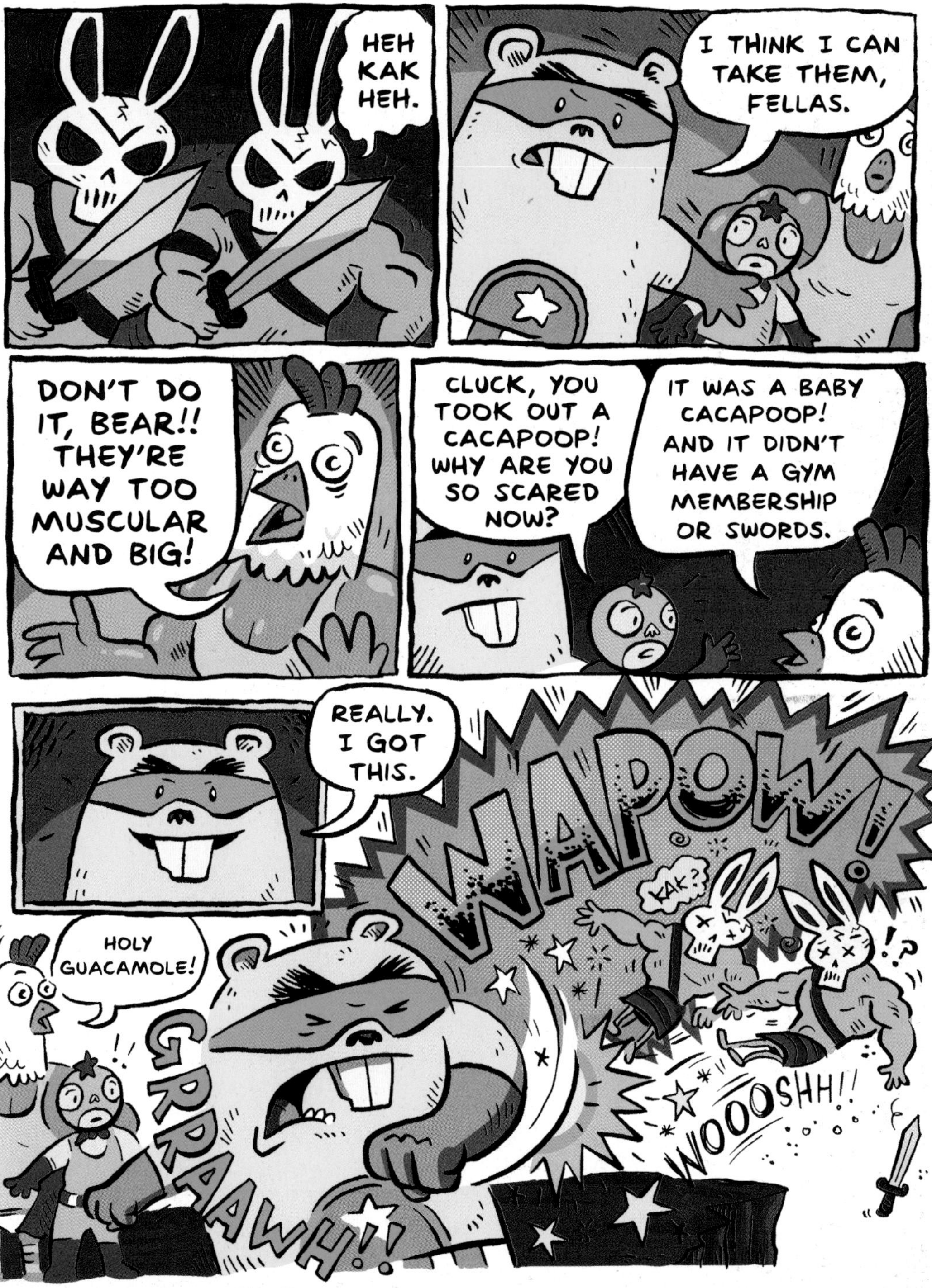
HEH KAK HEH.
I THINK I CAN TAKE THEM, FELLAS.
DON'T DO IT, BEAR!! THEY'RE WAY TOO MUSCULAR AND BIG!
CLUCK, YOU TOOK OUT A CACAPOOP! WHY ARE YOU SO SCARED NOW?
IT WAS A BABY CACAPOOP! AND IT DIDN'T HAVE A GYM MEMBERSHIP OR SWORDS.
REALLY. I GOT THIS.
WAPOW!
KAK?
!?
HOLY GUACAMOLE!
!!
GRRAAWH!!
WOOOSHH!!

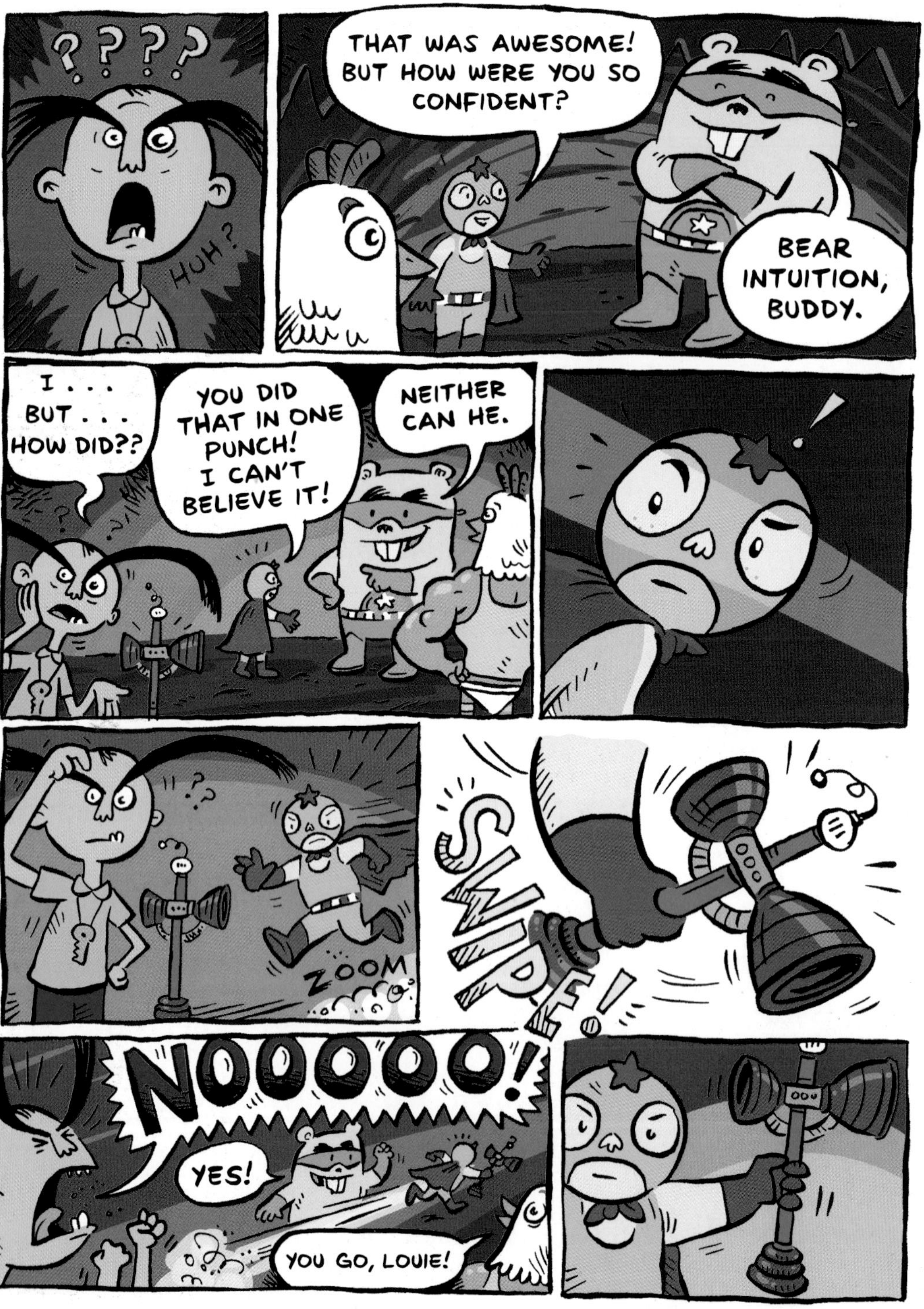
????
HUH?
THAT WAS AWESOME! BUT HOW WERE YOU SO CONFIDENT?
BEAR INTUITION, BUDDY.
I . . . BUT . . . HOW DID??
YOU DID THAT IN ONE PUNCH! I CAN'T BELIEVE IT!
NEITHER CAN HE.
!
ZOOM
SWIPE!
NOOOOO!
YES!
YOU GO, LOUIE!

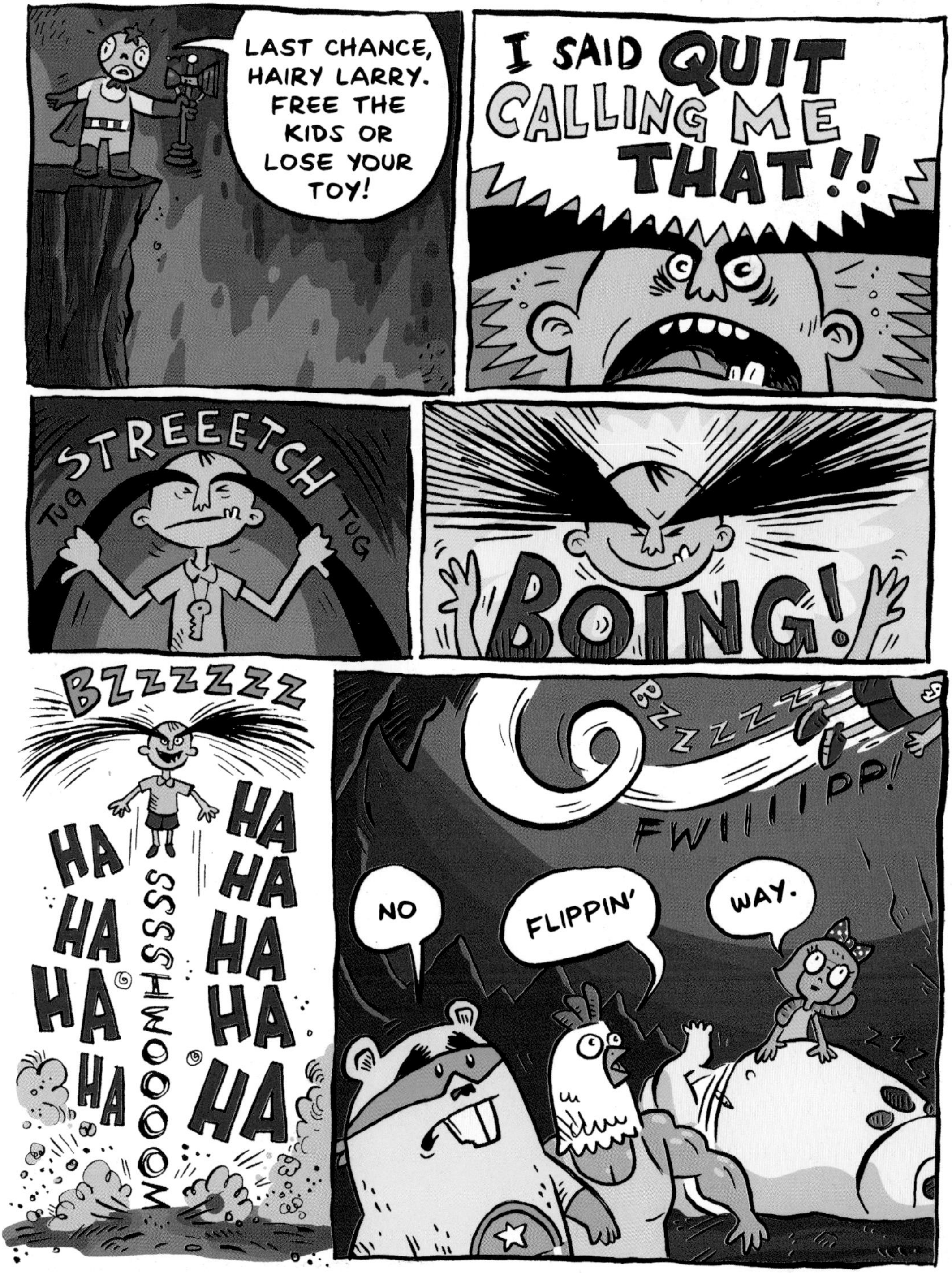
LAST CHANCE, HAIRY LARRY. FREE THE KIDS OR LOSE YOUR TOY!
I SAID QUIT CALLING ME THAT!!
TUG
STREEETCH
TUG
BOING!
BZZZZZZZ
HA
HA
HA
HA
WOOOOWHSSSS
HA
HA
HA
HA
HA
HA
BZZZZZZ
FWIIIIPP!
NO
FLIPPIN'
WAY.

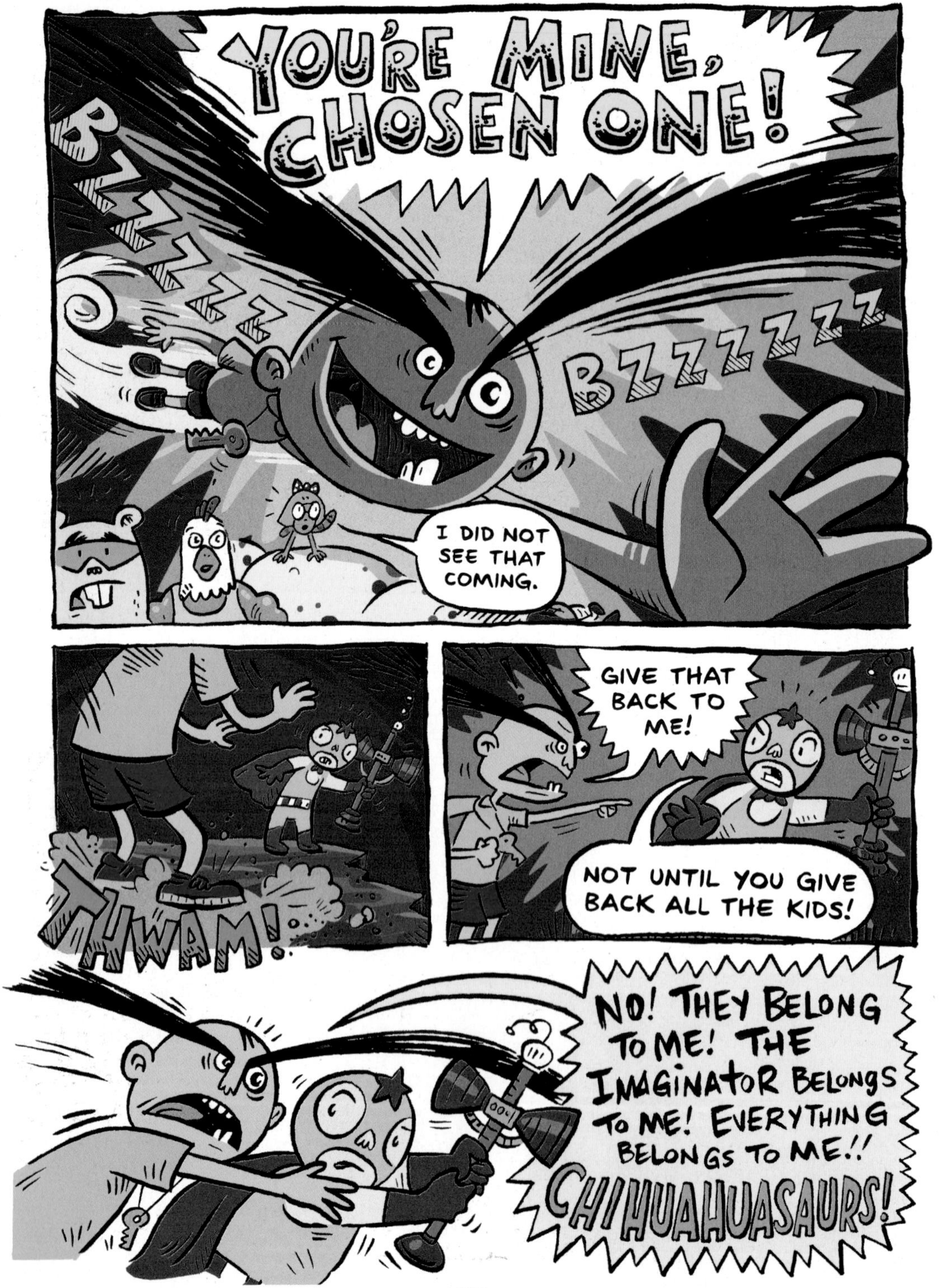
YOU'RE MINE, CHOSEN ONE!
BZZZZZZ
BZZZZZZZ
I DID NOT SEE THAT COMING.
THWAM!
GIVE THAT BACK TO ME!
NOT UNTIL YOU GIVE BACK ALL THE KIDS!
NO! THEY BELONG TO ME! THE IMAGINATOR BELONGS TO ME! EVERYTHING BELONGS TO ME!!
CHIHUAHUASAURS!

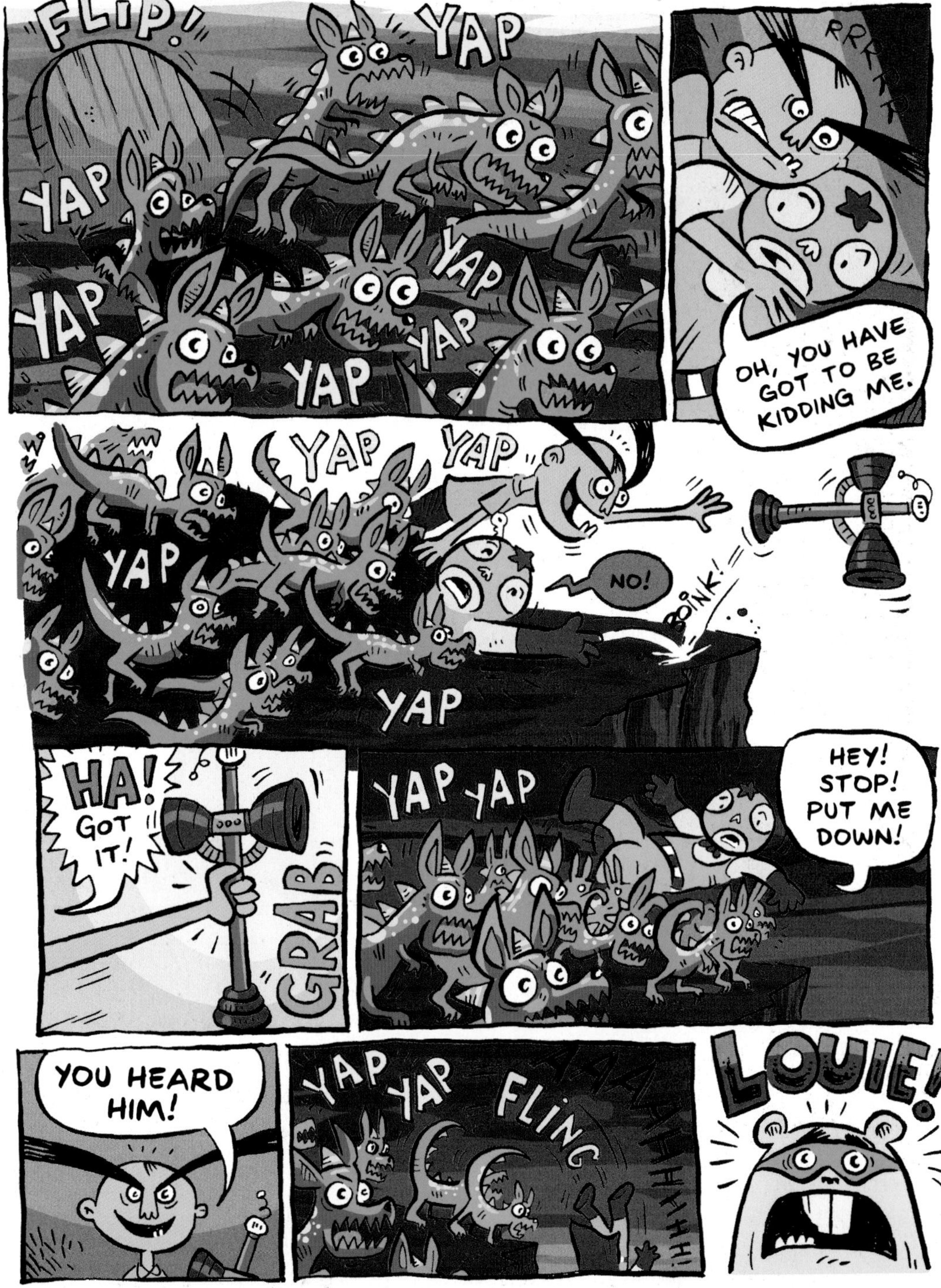
FLIP!
YAP
YAP
YAP
YAP
YAP
YAP
YAP
RRRRRR
OH, YOU HAVE GOT TO BE KIDDING ME.
YAP
YAP
YAP
NO!
BOINK!
YAP
HA! GOT IT!
GRAB
YAP YAP
HEY! STOP! PUT ME DOWN!
YOU HEARD HIM!
YAP YAP
FLING
AAAAHHHHHH!
LOUIE!

CHAPTER 11

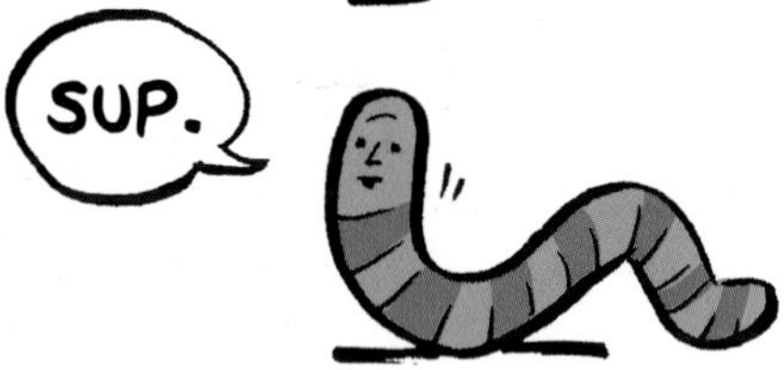
SUP.

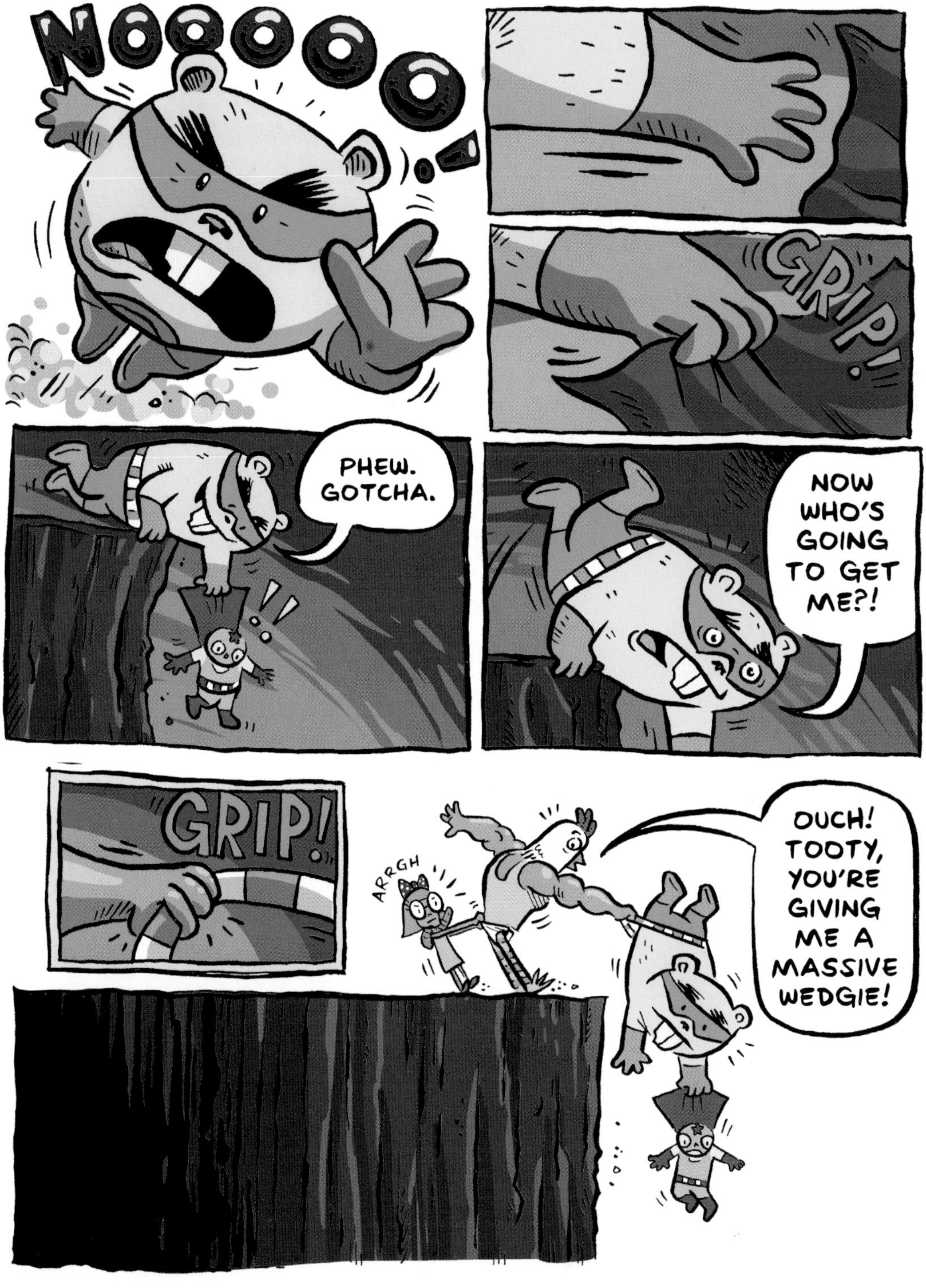
NOOOOO!
GRIP!
PHEW. GOTCHA.
!!
NOW WHO'S GOING TO GET ME?!
GRIP!
ARRGH
OUCH! TOOTY, YOU'RE GIVING ME A MASSIVE WEDGIE!

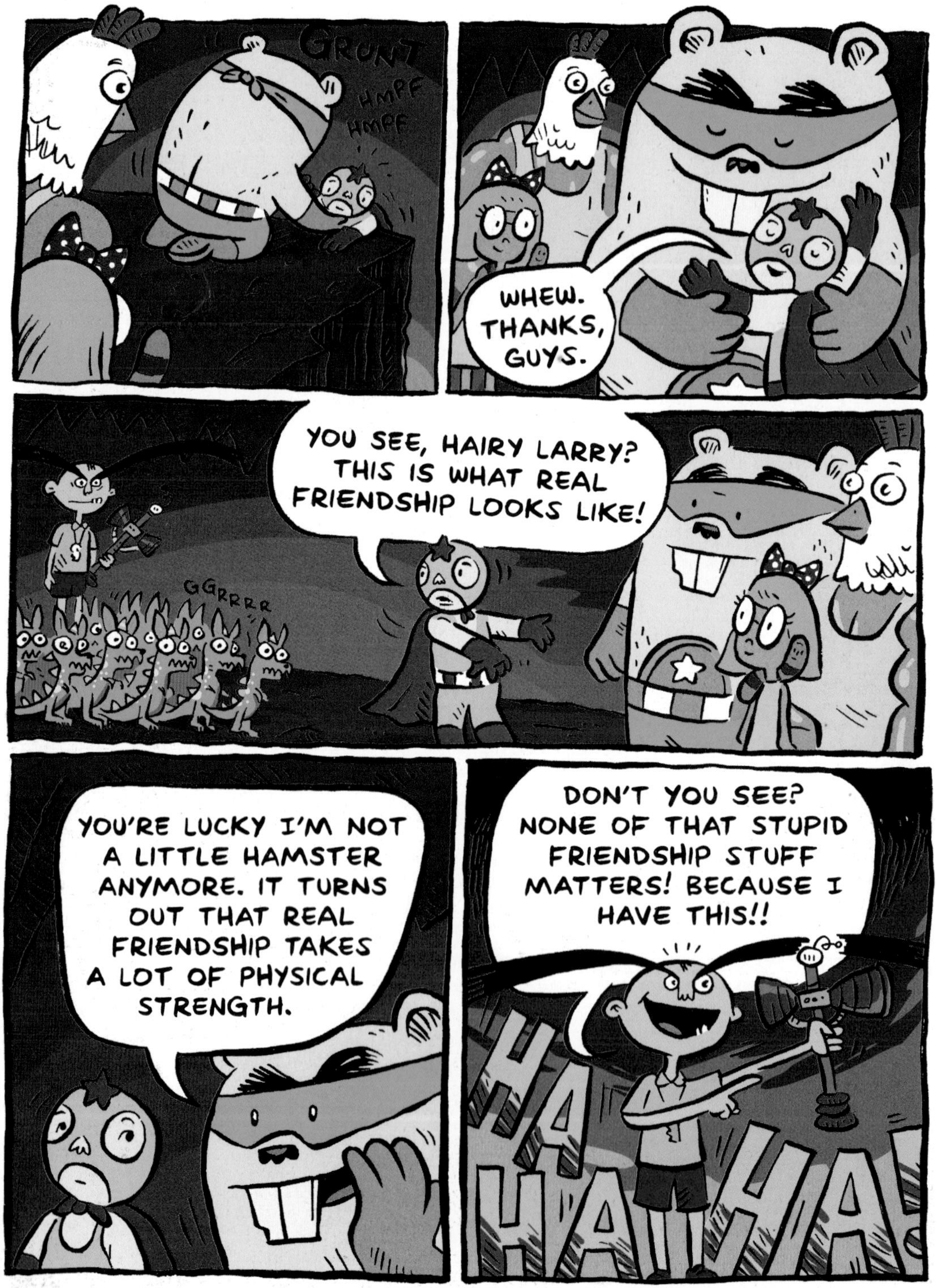
GRUNT
HMPF HMPF
WHEW. THANKS, GUYS.
YOU SEE, HAIRY LARRY? THIS IS WHAT REAL FRIENDSHIP LOOKS LIKE!
GGRRRRR
YOU'RE LUCKY I'M NOT A LITTLE HAMSTER ANYMORE. IT TURNS OUT THAT REAL FRIENDSHIP TAKES A LOT OF PHYSICAL STRENGTH.
DON'T YOU SEE? NONE OF THAT STUPID FRIENDSHIP STUFF MATTERS! BECAUSE I HAVE THIS!!
HA HA HA HA!

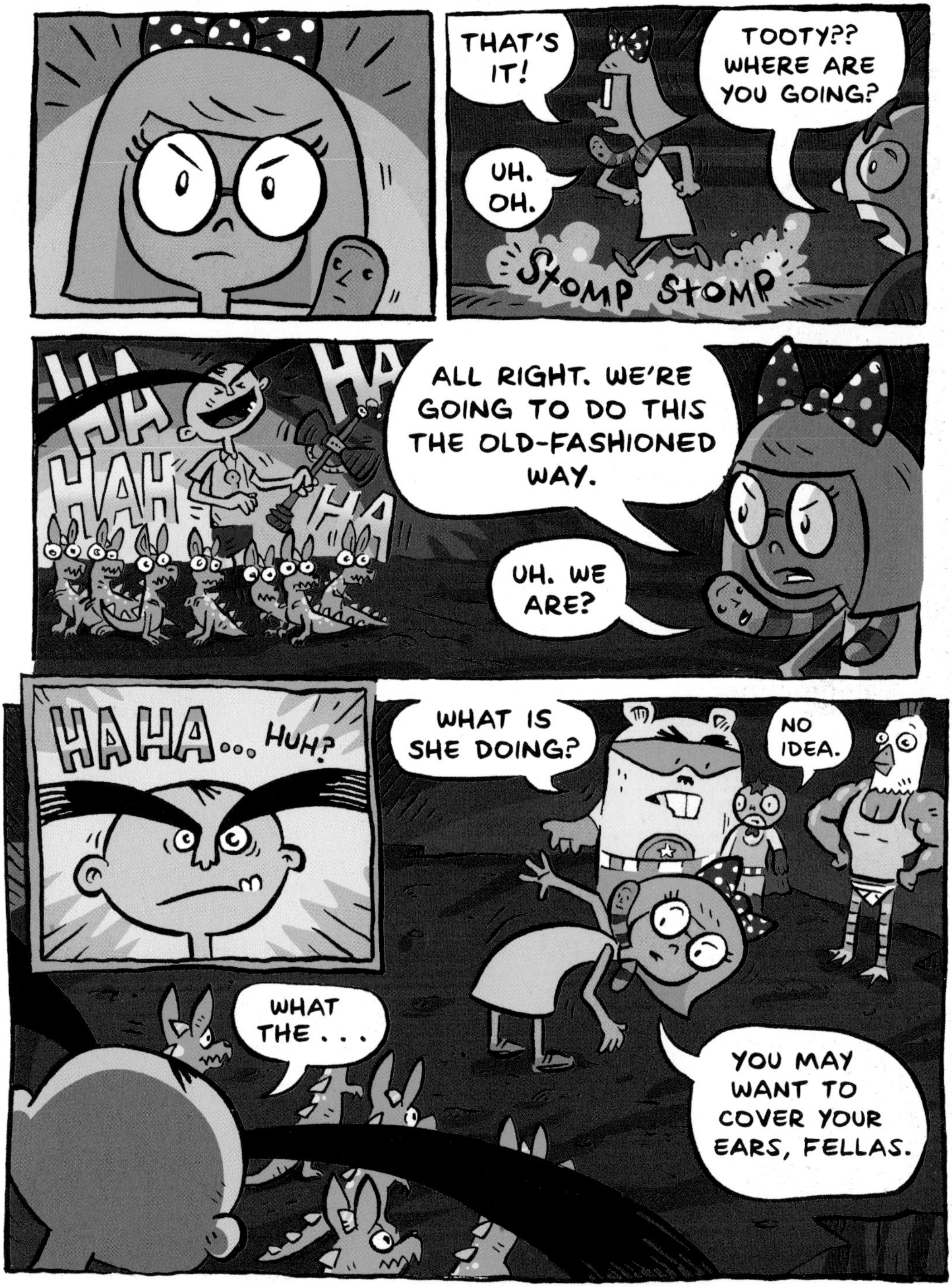
THAT'S IT!
TOOTY?? WHERE ARE YOU GOING?
UH. OH.
STOMP STOMP
HA HA HAH HA HA
ALL RIGHT. WE'RE GOING TO DO THIS THE OLD-FASHIONED WAY.
UH. WE ARE?
HAHA... HUH?
WHAT IS SHE DOING?
NO IDEA.
WHAT THE . . .
YOU MAY WANT TO COVER YOUR EARS, FELLAS.

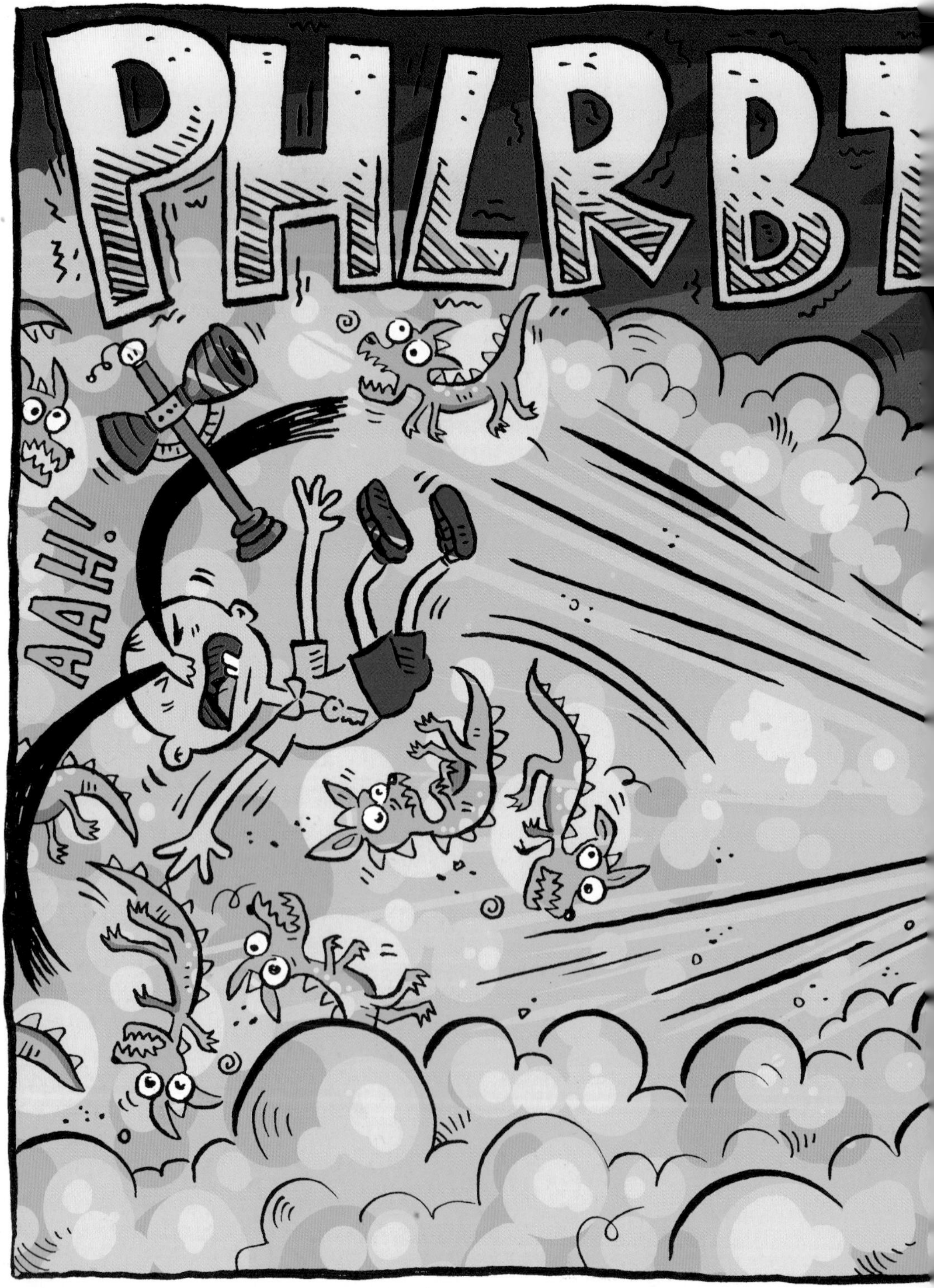
PHLRBT
AAAH!

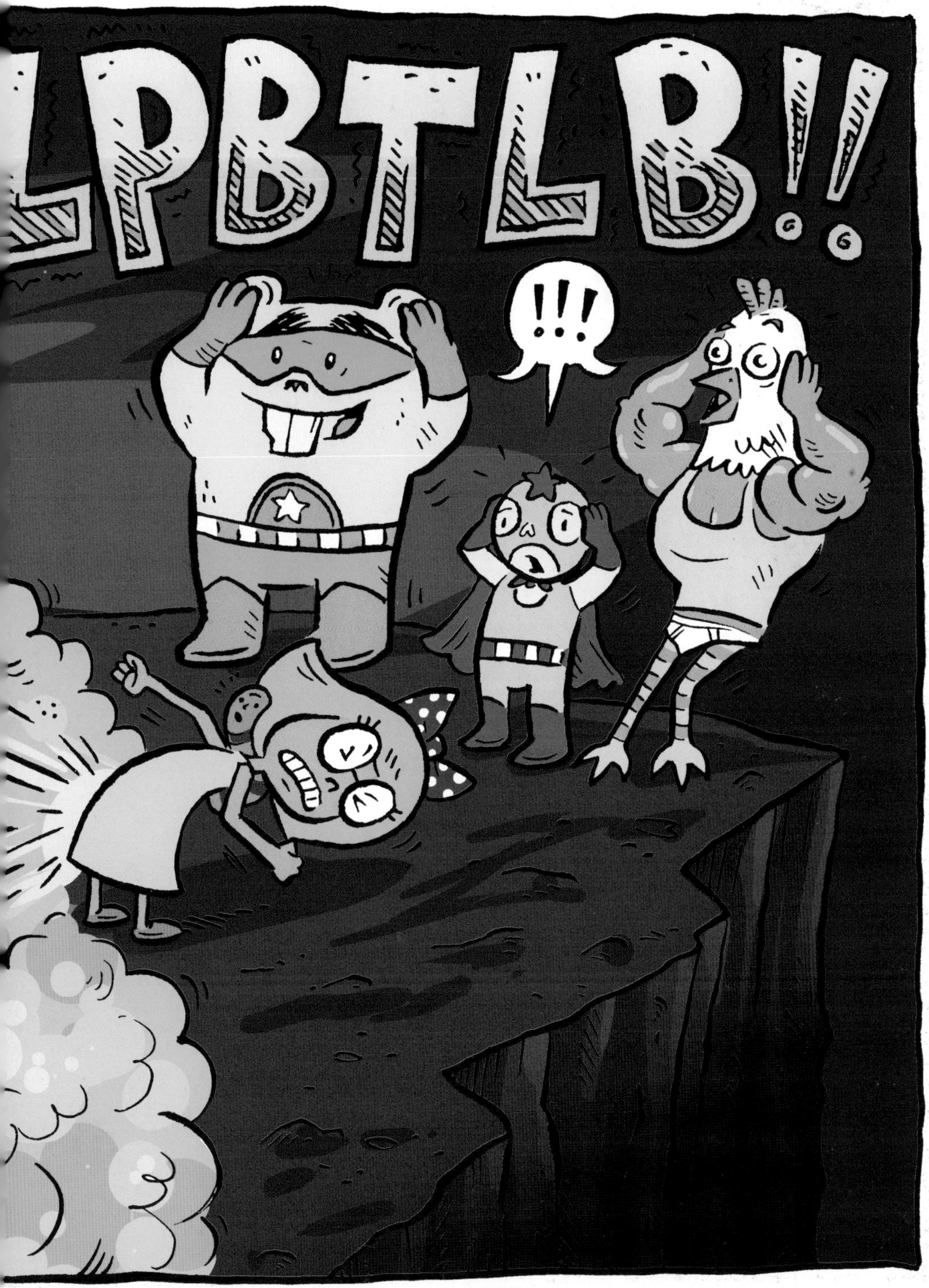

LPBTLB!!
!!!

BONK!

ZING

FWOOOSHH

KAPOWSKI

NO, NO, NO!

WZZZ

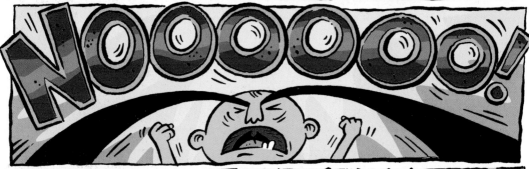

NOOOOOO!

YAAAAYYY!

I DIDN'T KNOW YOU COULD DO THAT!!

I MEAN, MY NAME IS TOOTY, THAT WASN'T A TIP-OFF?

YOUR NAME SHOULD BE ATOMIC BUTT BLASTER! THAT WOULD BE MUCH MORE ACCURATE.

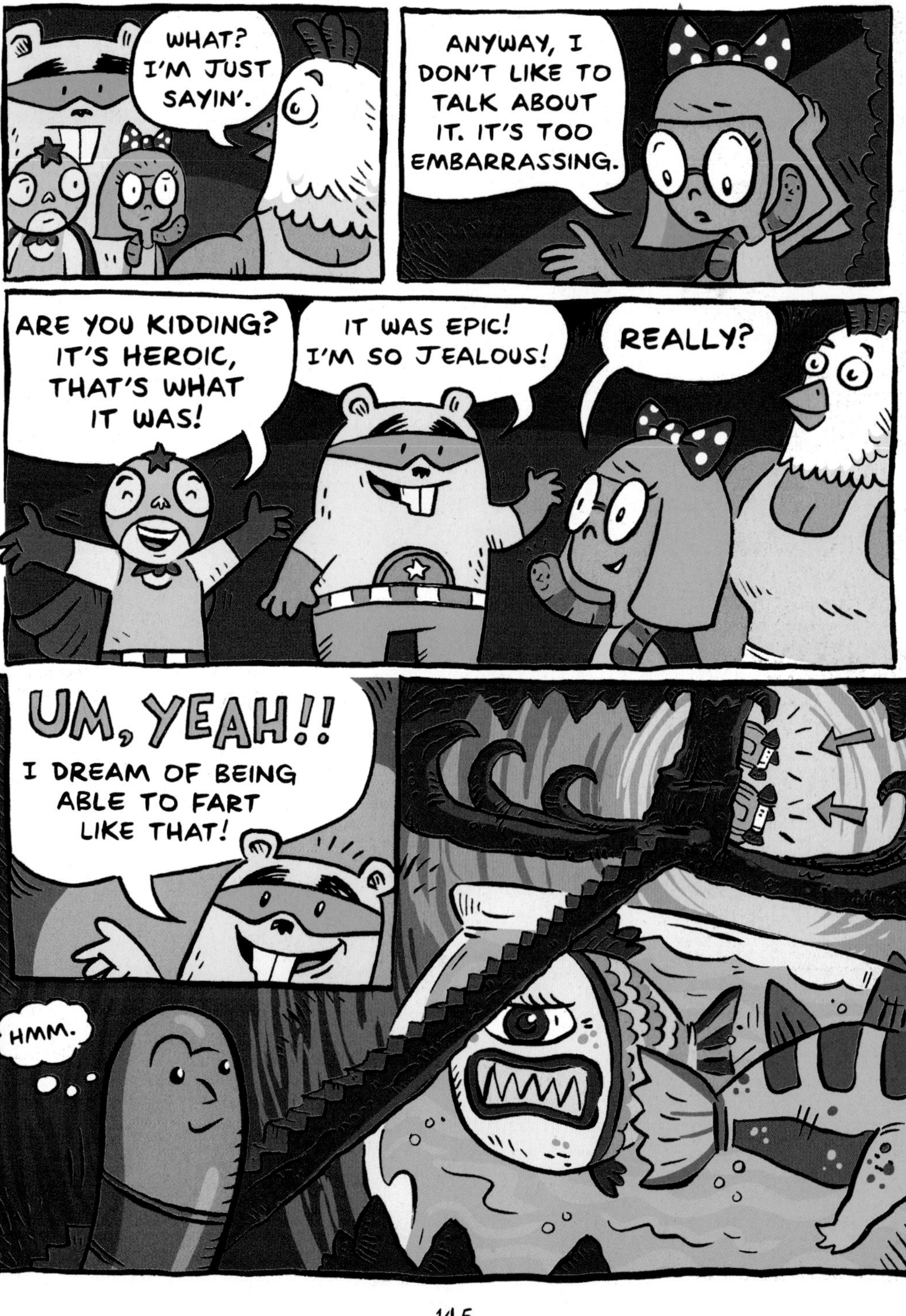
WHAT? I'M JUST SAYIN'.
ANYWAY, I DON'T LIKE TO TALK ABOUT IT. IT'S TOO EMBARRASSING.
ARE YOU KIDDING? IT'S HEROIC, THAT'S WHAT IT WAS!
IT WAS EPIC! I'M SO JEALOUS!
REALLY?
UM, YEAH!! I DREAM OF BEING ABLE TO FART LIKE THAT!
HMM.

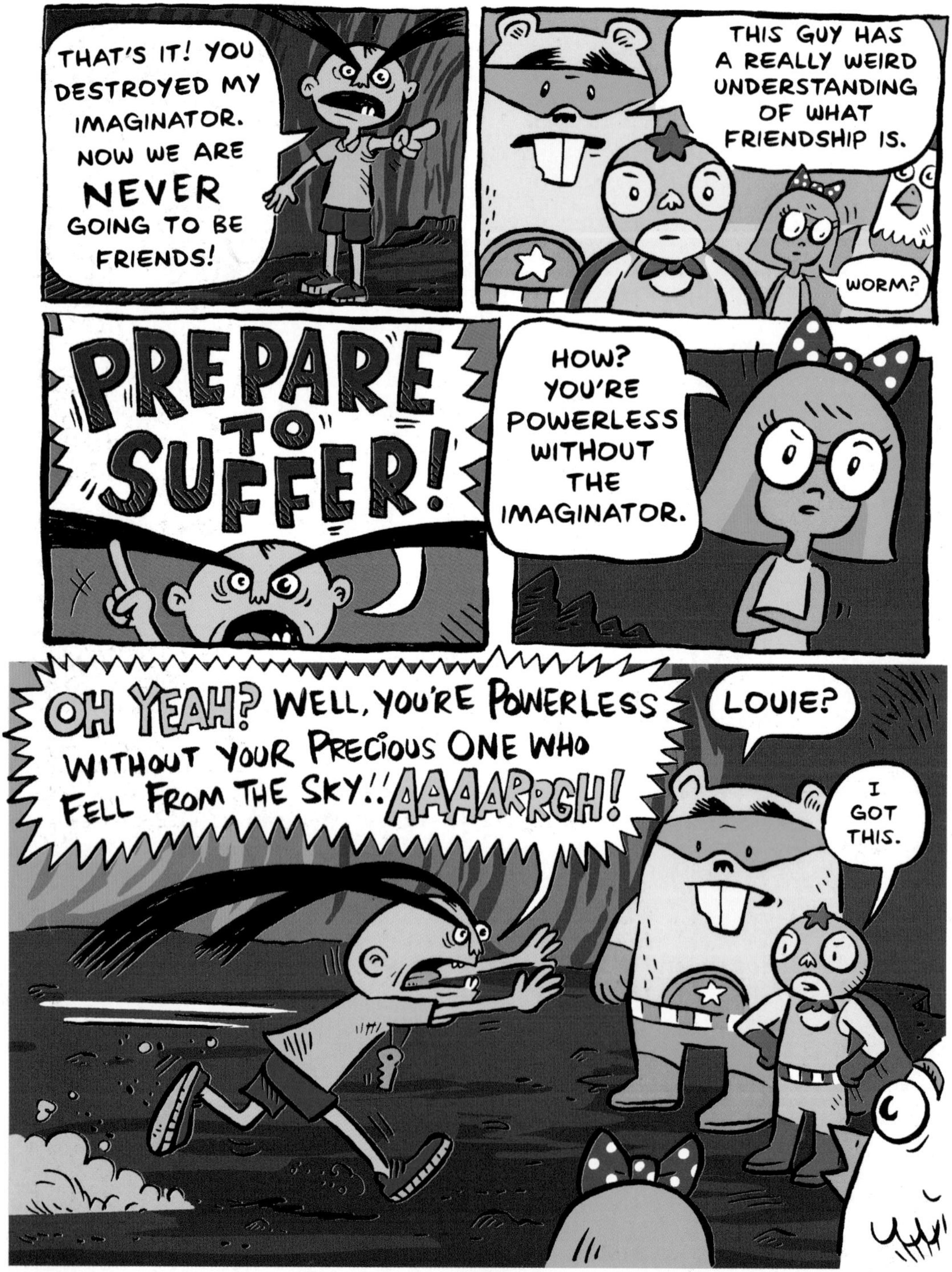
THAT'S IT! YOU DESTROYED MY IMAGINATOR. NOW WE ARE NEVER GOING TO BE FRIENDS!
THIS GUY HAS A REALLY WEIRD UNDERSTANDING OF WHAT FRIENDSHIP IS.
WORM?
PREPARE TO SUFFER!
HOW? YOU'RE POWERLESS WITHOUT THE IMAGINATOR.
OH YEAH? WELL, YOU'RE POWERLESS WITHOUT YOUR PRECIOUS ONE WHO FELL FROM THE SKY!! AAAARRGH!
LOUIE?
I GOT THIS.

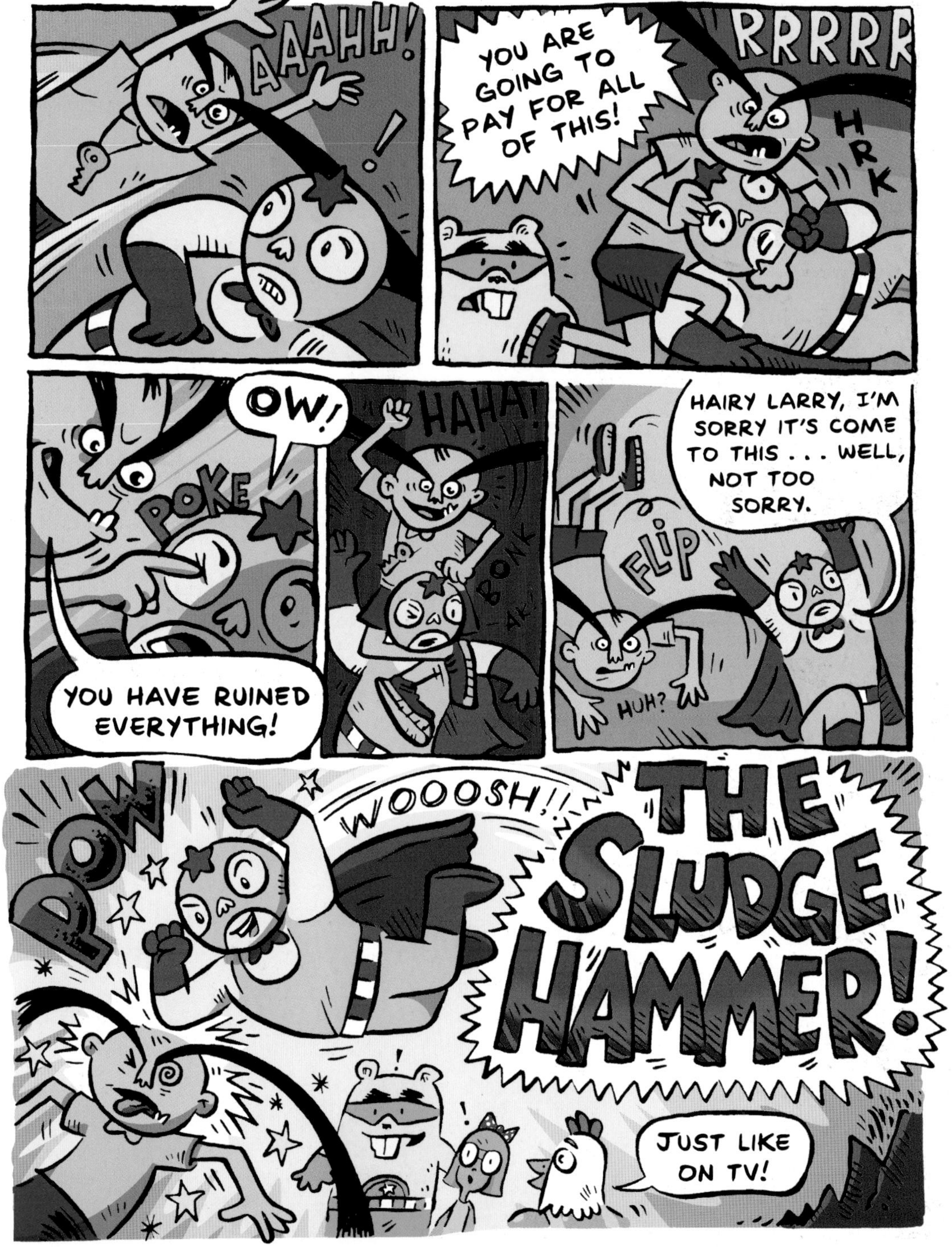
AAAHH!
!
YOU ARE GOING TO PAY FOR ALL OF THIS!
RRRRR
HRK
OW!
POKE
YOU HAVE RUINED EVERYTHING!
HAHA!
BONK
AK
HAIRY LARRY, I'M SORRY IT'S COME TO THIS . . . WELL, NOT TOO SORRY.
FLIP
HUH?
POW
WOOOSH!!
THE SLUDGE HAMMER!
!
!
JUST LIKE ON TV!

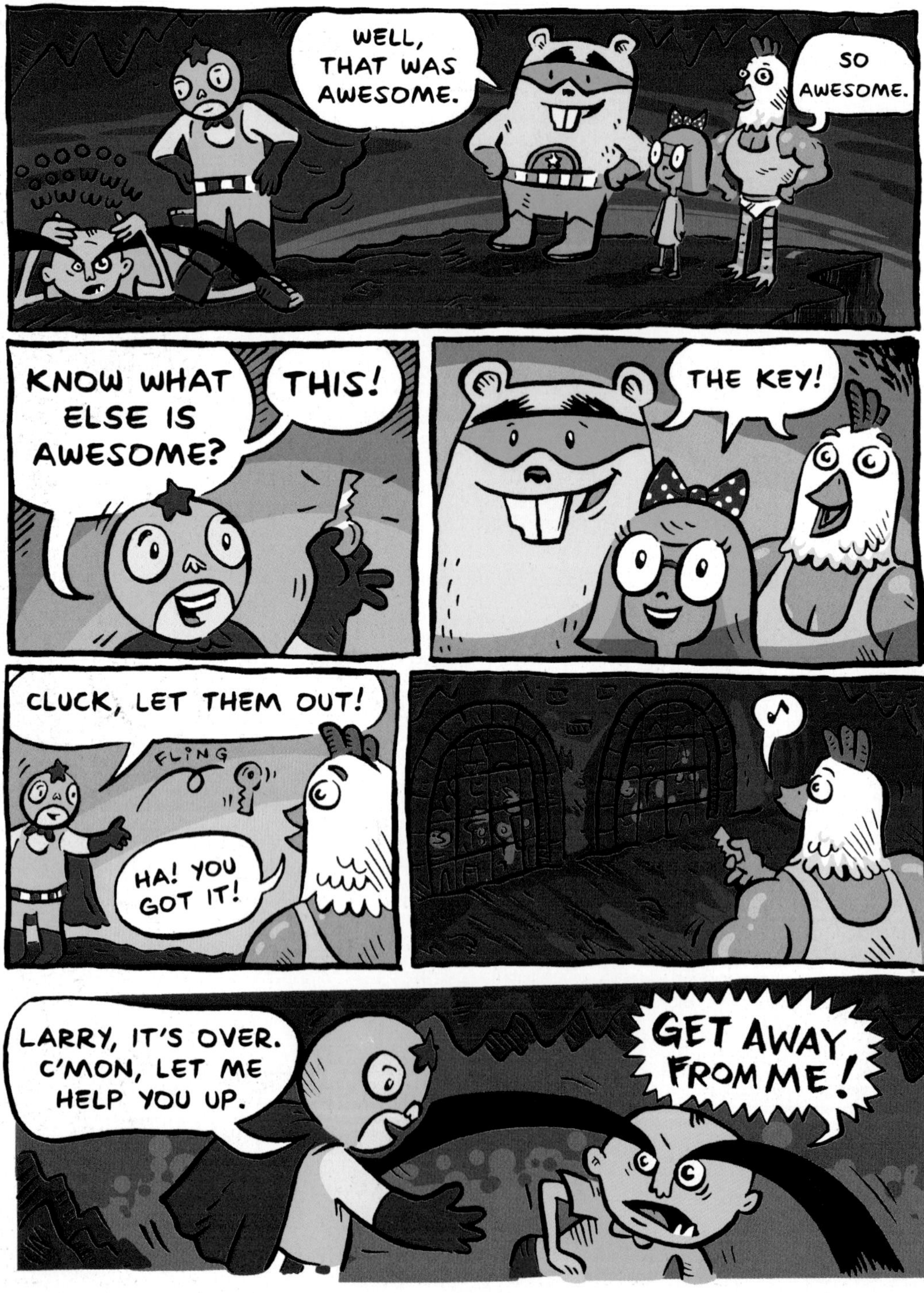
OOOOOO OOOWWW WWWWW
WELL, THAT WAS AWESOME.
SO AWESOME.
KNOW WHAT ELSE IS AWESOME?
THIS!
THE KEY!
CLUCK, LET THEM OUT!
FLING
HA! YOU GOT IT!
LARRY, IT'S OVER. C'MON, LET ME HELP YOU UP.
GET AWAY FROM ME!

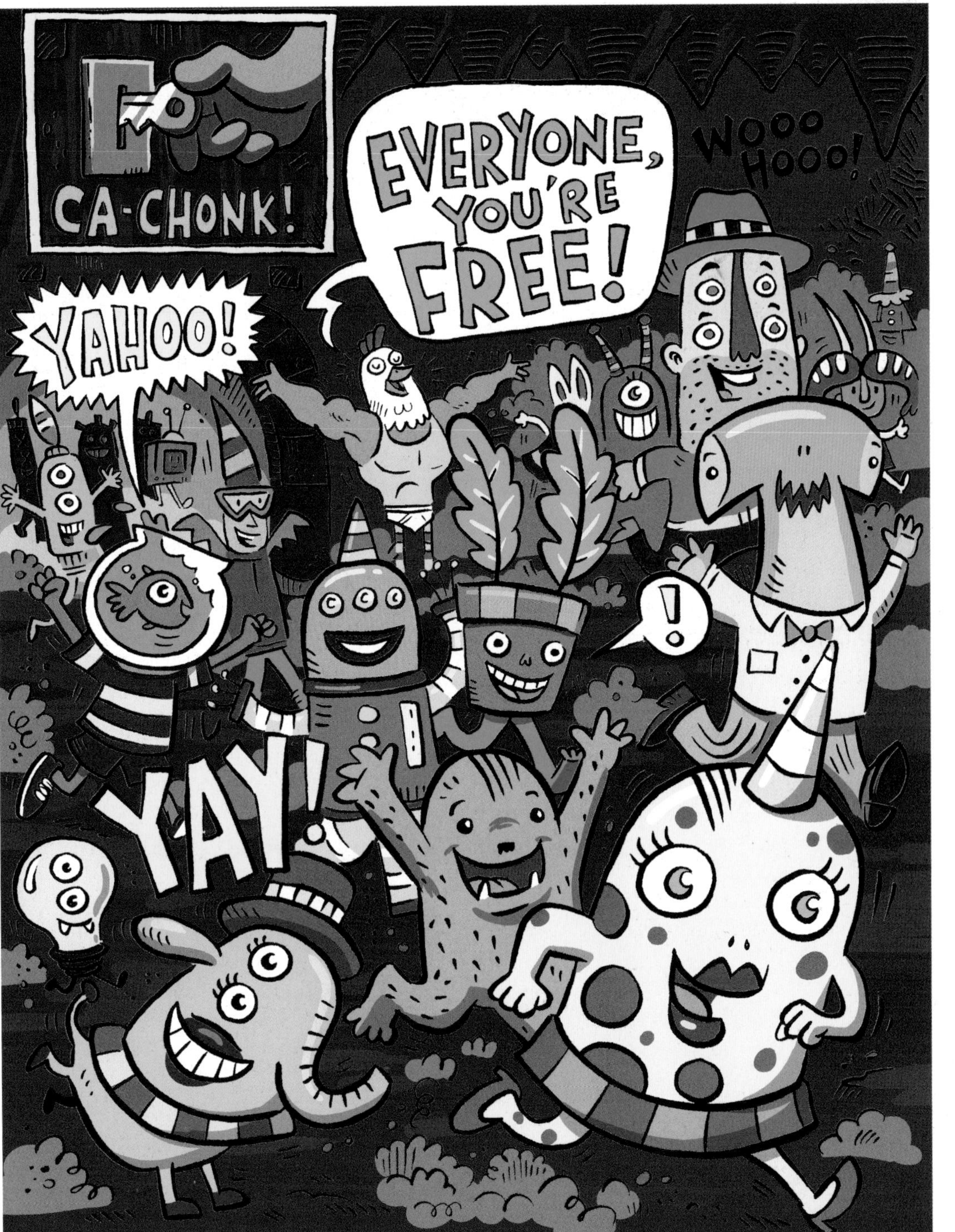
CA-CHONK!
EVERYONE, YOU'RE FREE!
WOOO HOOO!
YAHOO!
!
YAY!

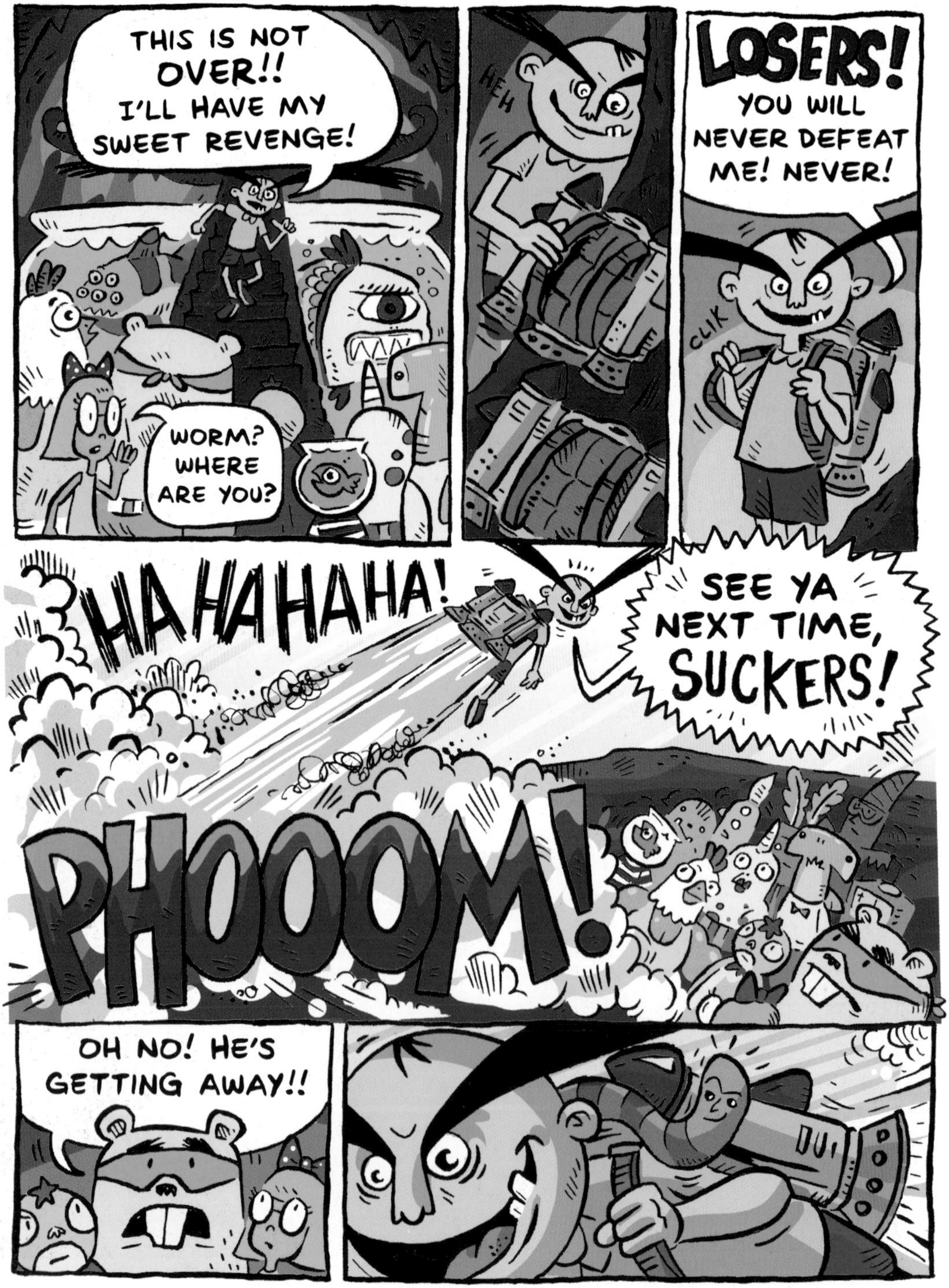
THIS IS NOT OVER!! I'LL HAVE MY SWEET REVENGE!
WORM? WHERE ARE YOU?
HEH
LOSERS! YOU WILL NEVER DEFEAT ME! NEVER!
CLIK
HAHAHAHA!
SEE YA NEXT TIME, SUCKERS!
PHOOOM!
OH NO! HE'S GETTING AWAY!!

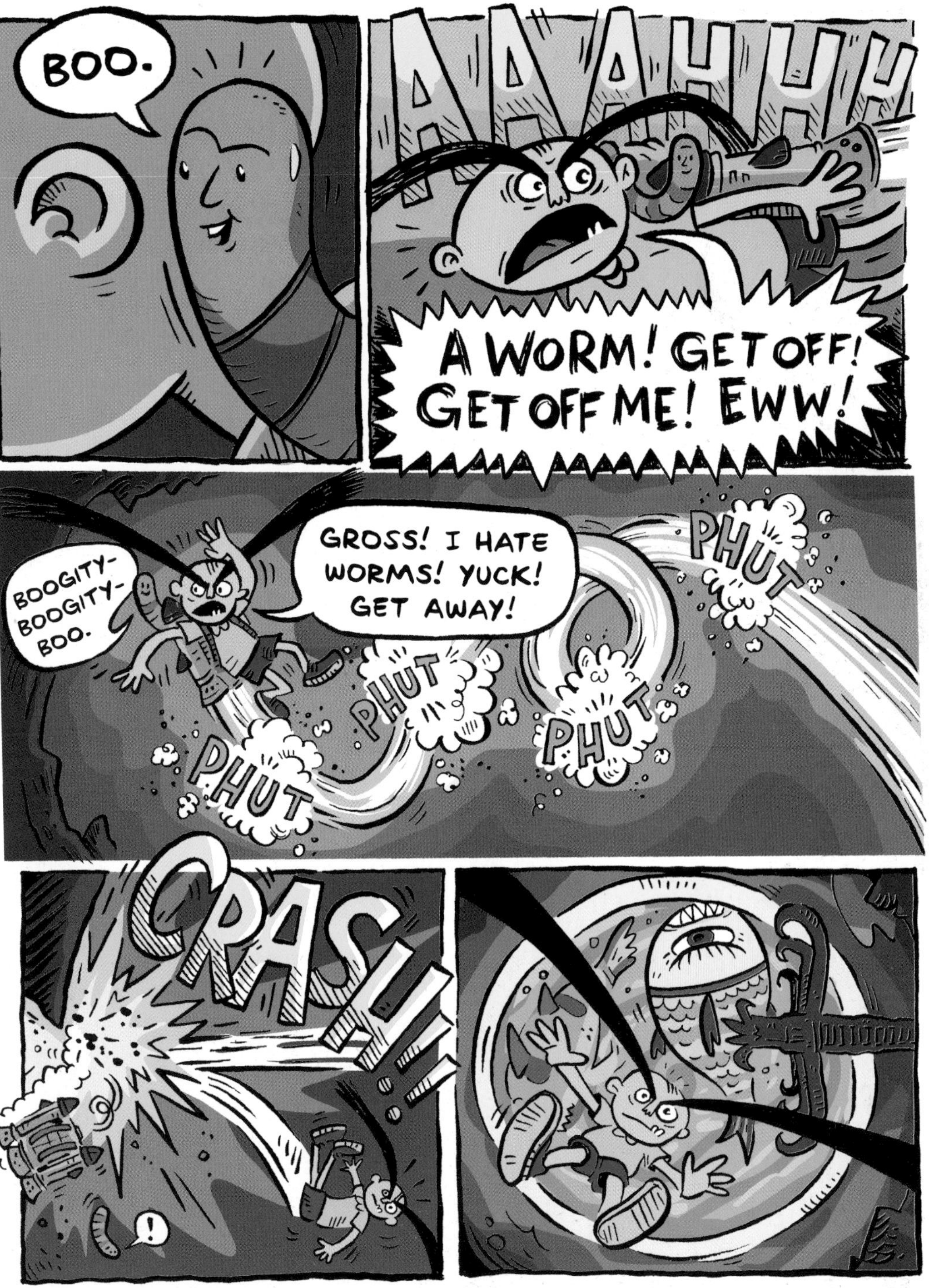
BOO.
AAAHHHH
A WORM! GET OFF! GET OFF ME! EWW!
BOOGITY-BOOGITY-BOO.
GROSS! I HATE WORMS! YUCK! GET AWAY!
PHUT
PHUT
PHUT
PHUT
CRASH!!!
!

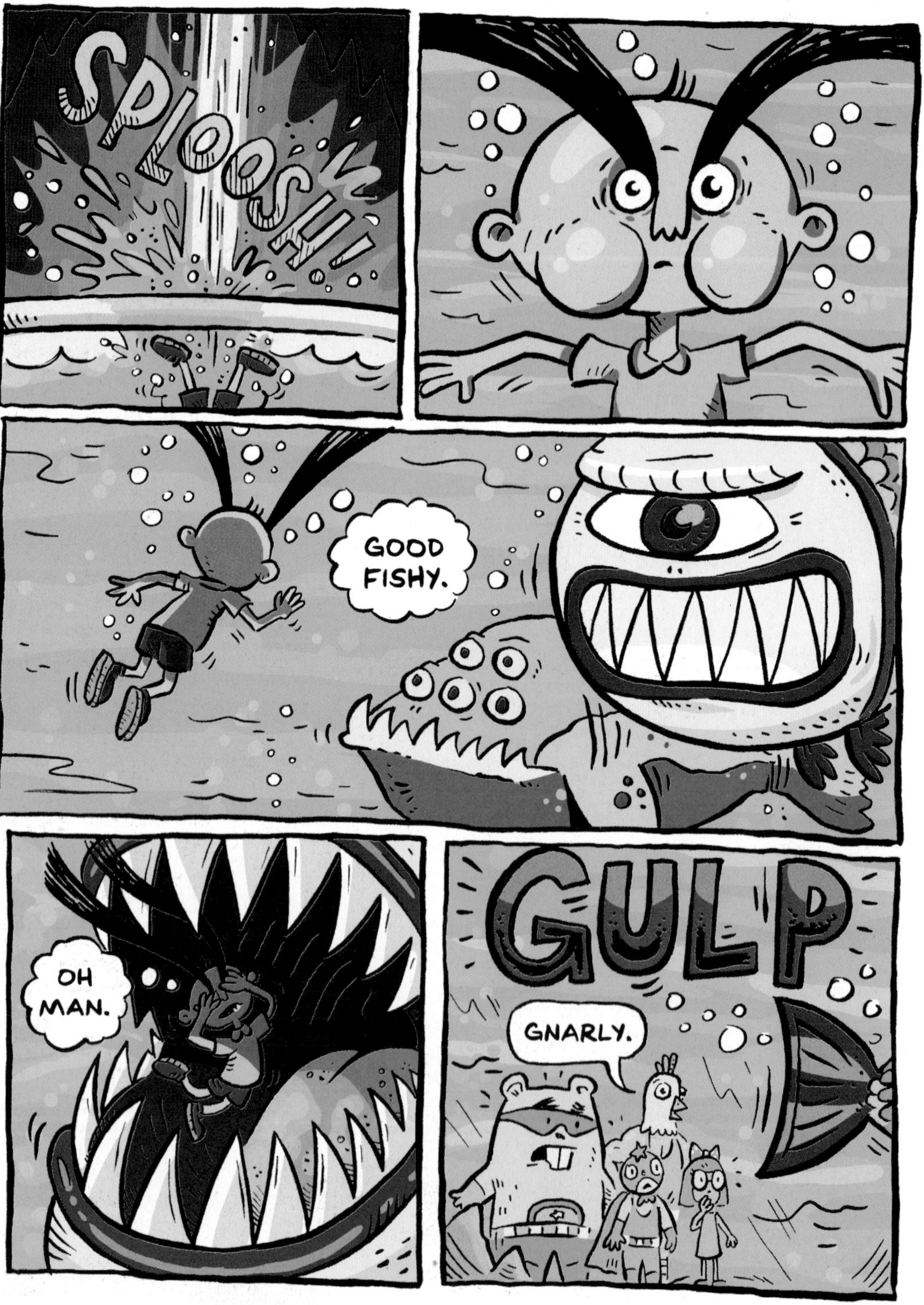
SPLOOSH!!
GOOD FISHY.
OH MAN.
GULP
GNARLY.

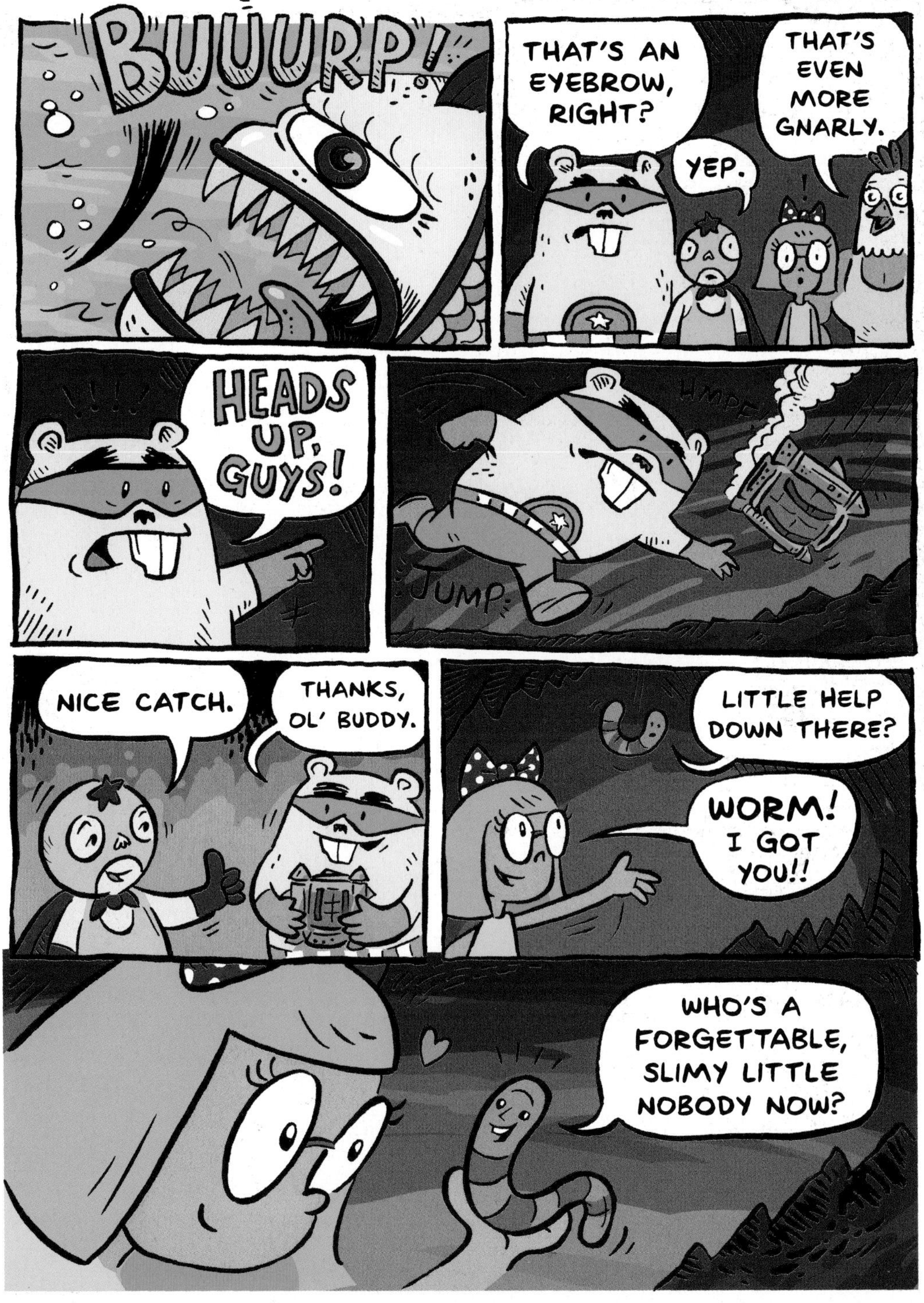
BUUURP!
THAT'S AN EYEBROW, RIGHT?
YEP.
THAT'S EVEN MORE GNARLY.
HEADS UP, GUYS!
JUMP
NICE CATCH.
THANKS, OL' BUDDY.
LITTLE HELP DOWN THERE?
WORM! I GOT YOU!!
WHO'S A FORGETTABLE, SLIMY LITTLE NOBODY NOW?

Chapter 12

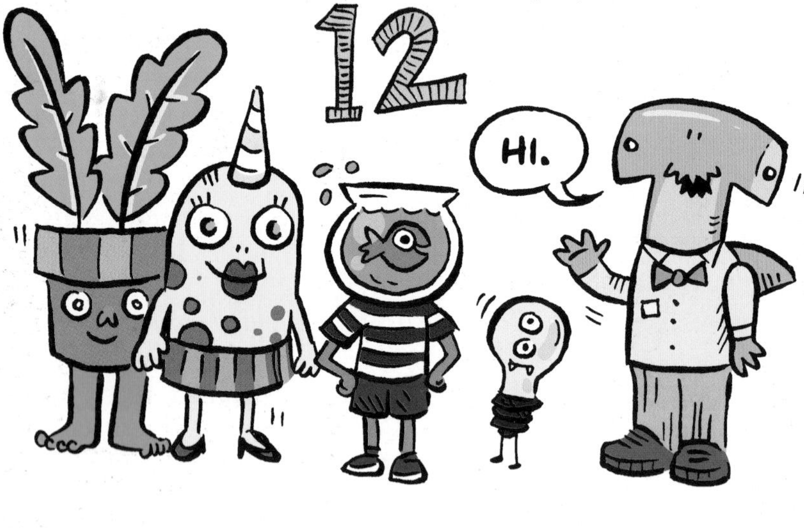

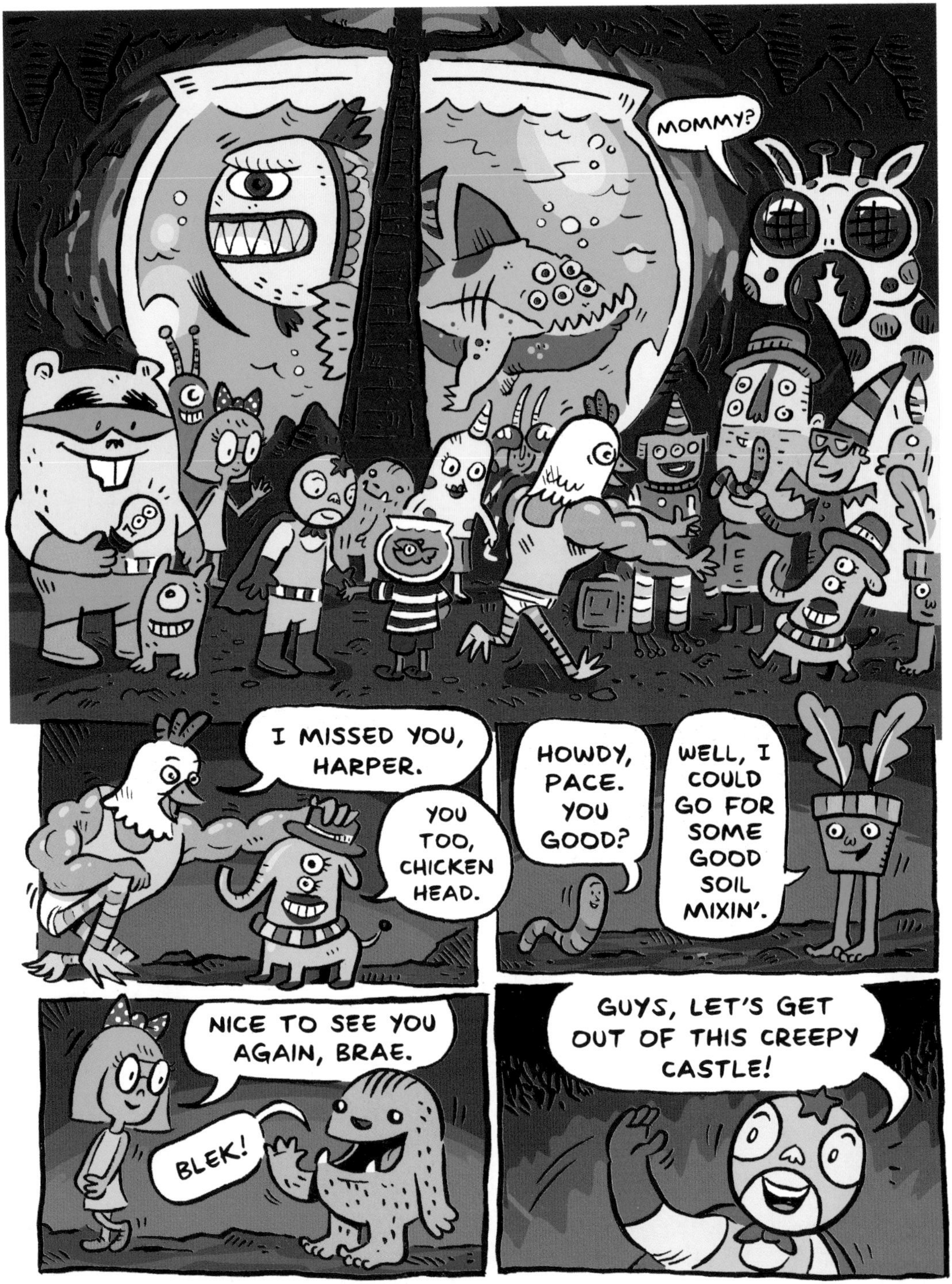
MOMMY?
I MISSED YOU, HARPER.
YOU TOO, CHICKEN HEAD.
HOWDY, PACE. YOU GOOD?
WELL, I COULD GO FOR SOME GOOD SOIL MIXIN'.
NICE TO SEE YOU AGAIN, BRAE.
BLEK!
GUYS, LET'S GET OUT OF THIS CREEPY CASTLE!

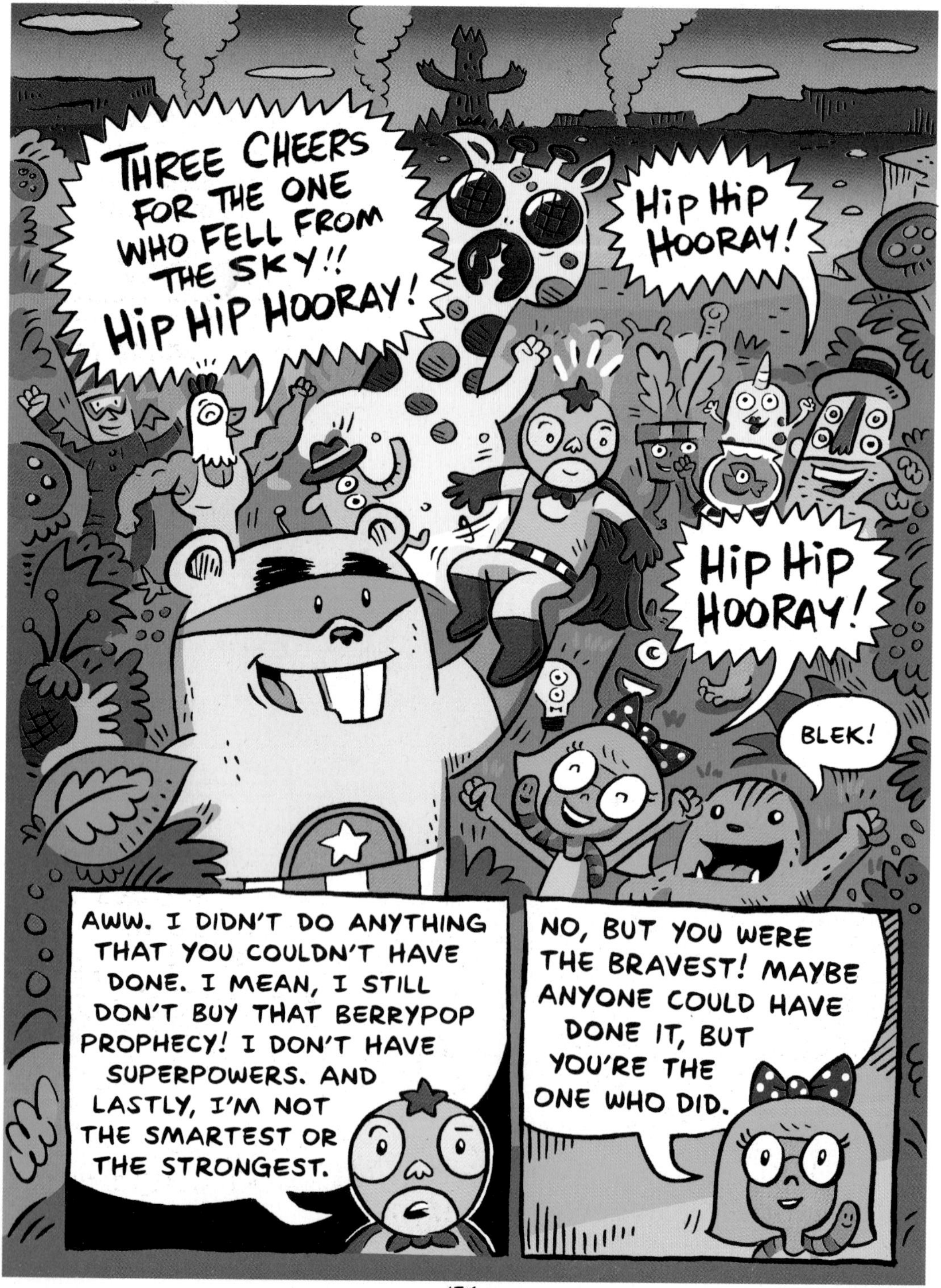
THREE CHEERS FOR THE ONE WHO FELL FROM THE SKY!! HIP HIP HOORAY!
HIP HIP HOORAY!
HIP HIP HOORAY!
BLEK!
AWW. I DIDN'T DO ANYTHING THAT YOU COULDN'T HAVE DONE. I MEAN, I STILL DON'T BUY THAT BERRYPOP PROPHECY! I DON'T HAVE SUPERPOWERS. AND LASTLY, I'M NOT THE SMARTEST OR THE STRONGEST.
NO, BUT YOU WERE THE BRAVEST! MAYBE ANYONE COULD HAVE DONE IT, BUT YOU'RE THE ONE WHO DID.

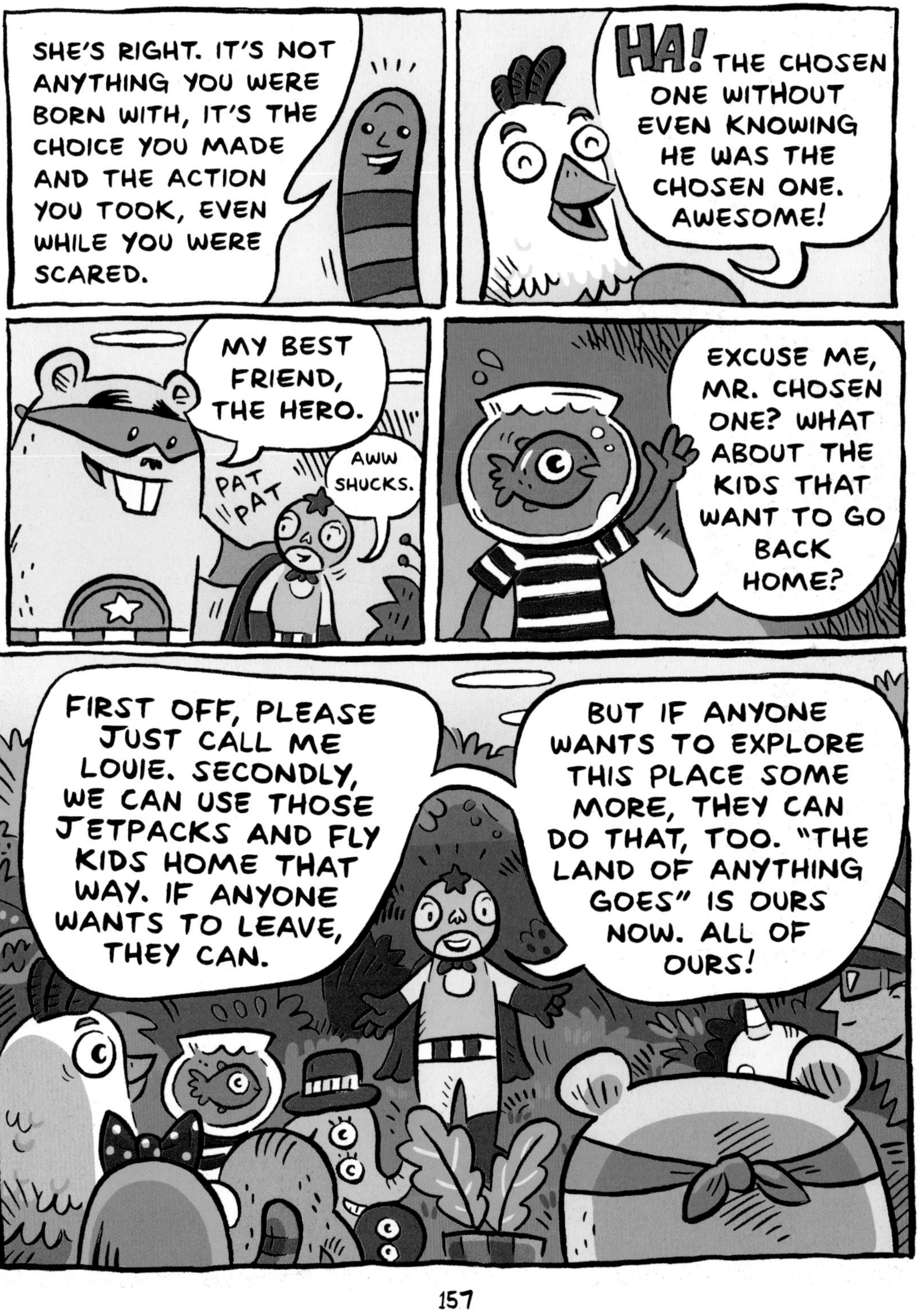
SHE'S RIGHT. IT'S NOT ANYTHING YOU WERE BORN WITH, IT'S THE CHOICE YOU MADE AND THE ACTION YOU TOOK, EVEN WHILE YOU WERE SCARED.
HA! THE CHOSEN ONE WITHOUT EVEN KNOWING HE WAS THE CHOSEN ONE. AWESOME!
MY BEST FRIEND, THE HERO.
PAT PAT
AWW SHUCKS.
EXCUSE ME, MR. CHOSEN ONE? WHAT ABOUT THE KIDS THAT WANT TO GO BACK HOME?
FIRST OFF, PLEASE JUST CALL ME LOUIE. SECONDLY, WE CAN USE THOSE JETPACKS AND FLY KIDS HOME THAT WAY. IF ANYONE WANTS TO LEAVE, THEY CAN.
BUT IF ANYONE WANTS TO EXPLORE THIS PLACE SOME MORE, THEY CAN DO THAT, TOO. "THE LAND OF ANYTHING GOES" IS OURS NOW. ALL OF OURS!

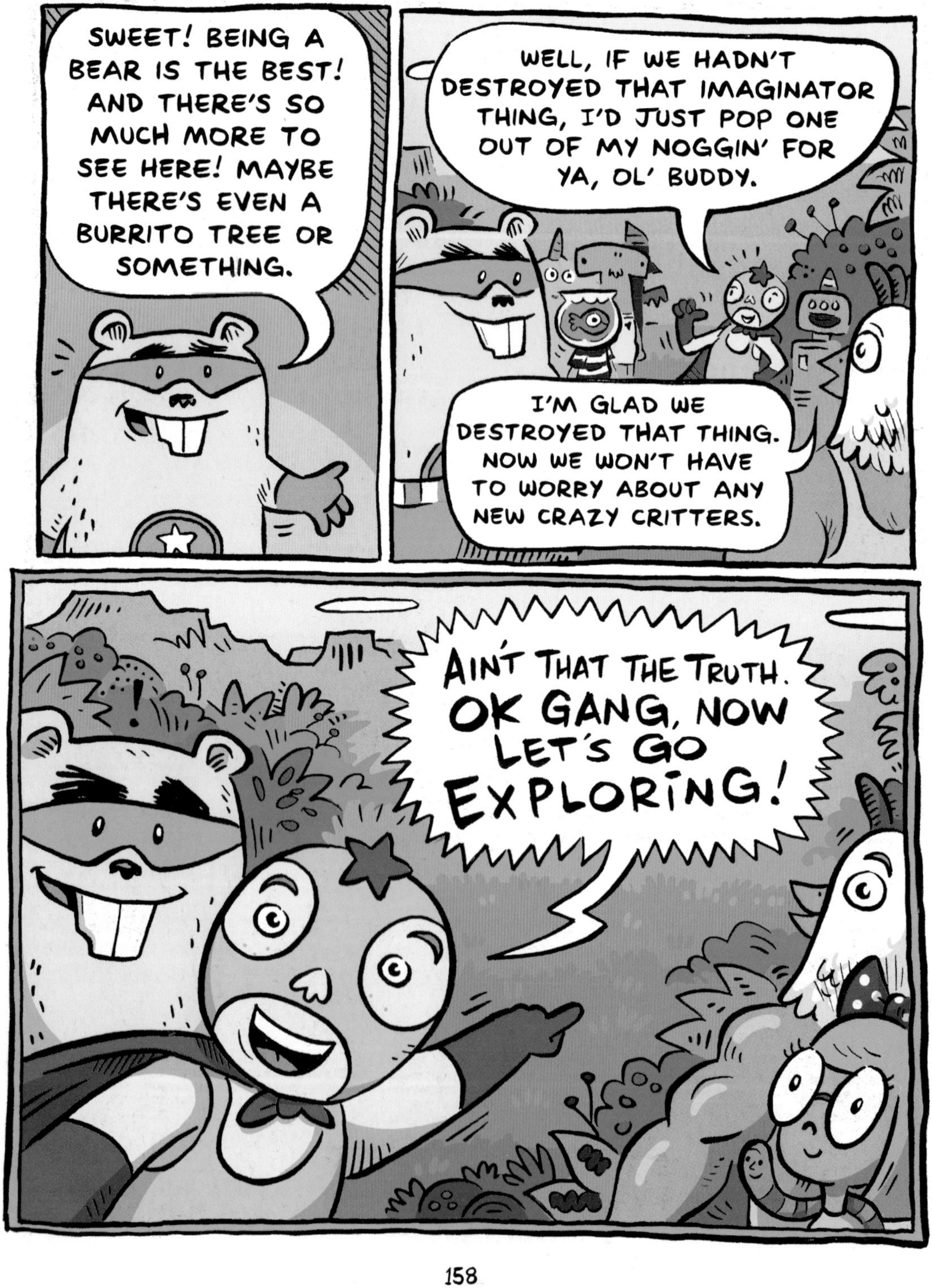
SWEET! BEING A BEAR IS THE BEST! AND THERE'S SO MUCH MORE TO SEE HERE! MAYBE THERE'S EVEN A BURRITO TREE OR SOMETHING.
WELL, IF WE HADN'T DESTROYED THAT IMAGINATOR THING, I'D JUST POP ONE OUT OF MY NOGGIN' FOR YA, OL' BUDDY.
I'M GLAD WE DESTROYED THAT THING. NOW WE WON'T HAVE TO WORRY ABOUT ANY NEW CRAZY CRITTERS.
AIN'T THAT THE TRUTH. OK GANG, NOW LET'S GO EXPLORING!

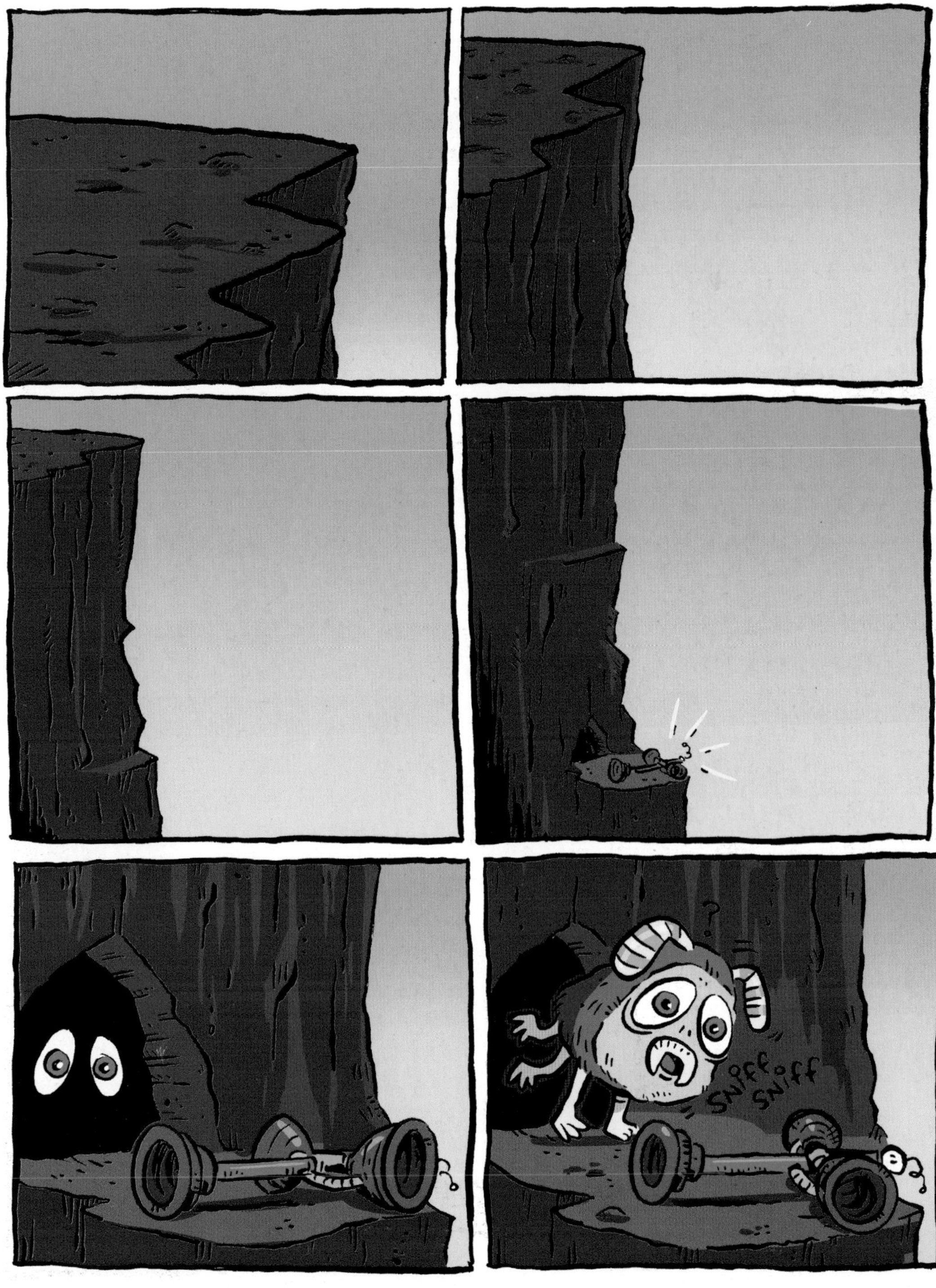
?
SNiff SNiff

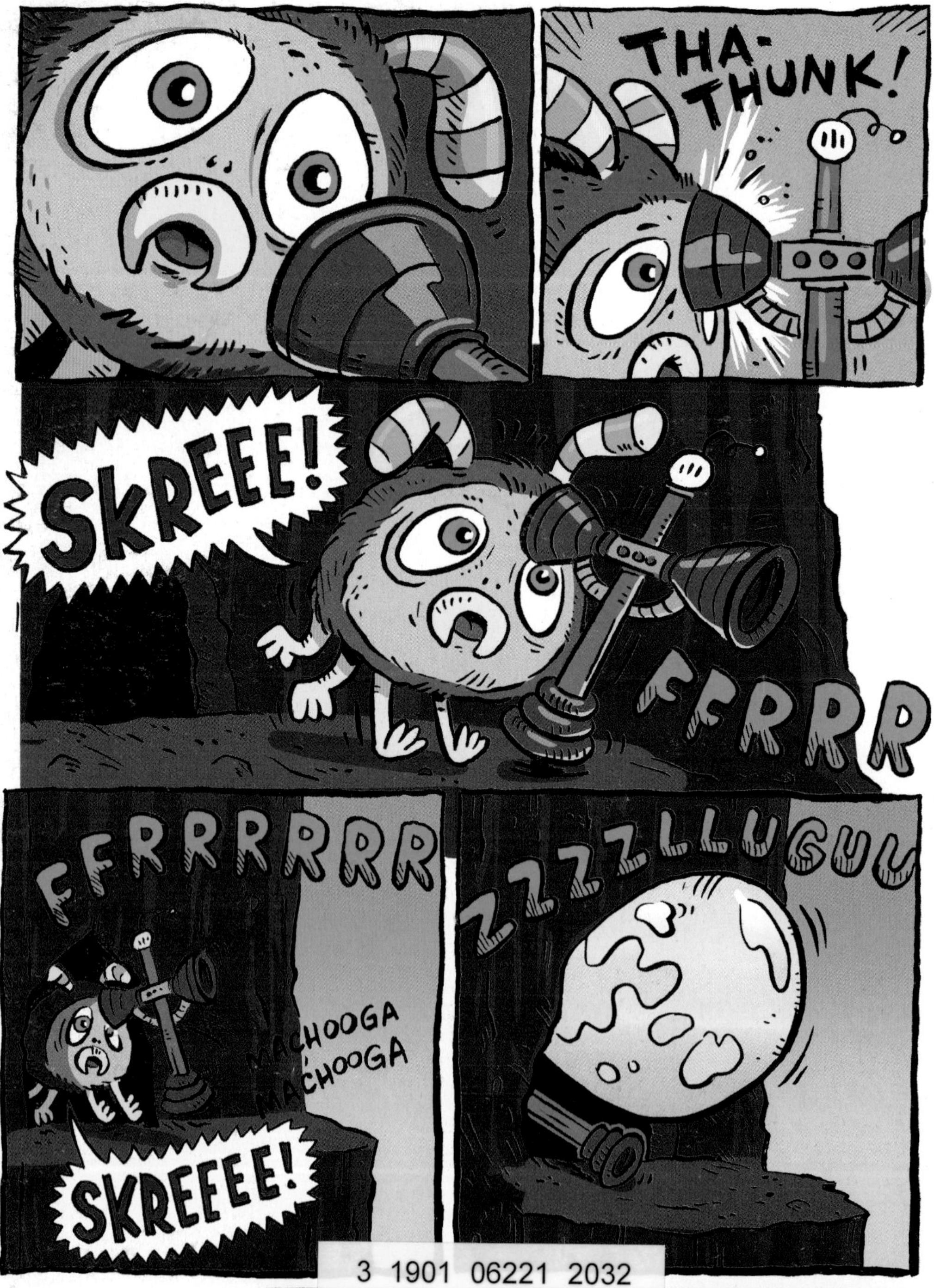
THA-
THUNK!
SKREEE!
FFRRR
FFRRRRRR
MACHOOGA
MACHOOGA
SKREEEE!
ZZZZLLUGUU

NOWHERE NEAR . . . THE END!